DARKNESS CALLS

MARJORIE M. LIU

ACE BOOKS, NEW YORK

THE BERKLEY PUBLISHING GROUP
Published by the Penguin Group
Penguin Group (USA) Inc.
375 Hudson Street, New York, New York 10014, USA

Penguin Group (Canada), 90 Eglinton Avenue East, Suite 700, Toronto, Ontario M4P 2Y3, Canada
(a division of Pearson Penguin Canada Inc.)
Penguin Books Ltd., 80 Strand, London WC2R 0RL, England
Penguin Group Ireland, 25 St. Stephen's Green, Dublin 2, Ireland (a division of Penguin Books Ltd.)
Penguin Group (Australia), 250 Camberwell Road, Camberwell, Victoria 3124, Australia
(a division of Pearson Australia Group Pty. Ltd.)
Penguin Books India Pvt. Ltd., 11 Community Centre, Panchsheel Park, New Delhi—110 017, India
Penguin Group (NZ), 67 Apollo Drive, Rosedale, North Shore 0632, New Zealand
(a division of Pearson New Zealand Ltd.)
Penguin Books (South Africa) (Pty.) Ltd., 24 Sturdee Avenue, Rosebank, Johannesburg 2196,
South Africa

Penguin Books Ltd., Registered Offices: 80 Strand, London WC2R 0RL, England

This is a work of fiction. Names, characters, places, and incidents either are the product of the author's imagination or are used fictitiously, and any resemblance to actual persons, living or dead, business establishments, events, or locales is entirely coincidental. The publisher does not have any control over and does not assume any responsibility for author or third-party websites or their content.

DARKNESS CALLS

An Ace Book / published by arrangement with the author

PRINTING HISTORY
Ace mass-market edition / July 2009

Copyright © 2009 by Marjorie M. Liu.
Cover art by Craig White.
Cover design by Judith Lagerman.
Interior text design by Laura K. Corless.

ISBN: 978-0-441-01730-0

ACE
Ace Books are published by The Berkley Publishing Group,
a division of Penguin Group (USA) Inc.,
375 Hudson Street, New York, New York 10014.
ACE and the "A" design are trademarks of Penguin Group (USA) Inc.

PRINTED IN THE UNITED STATES OF AMERICA

10 9 8 7 6 5 4

For the nomads, the rootless, and the free . . .

ACKNOWLEDGMENTS

Every book I write is a journey, and I'd like to thank the following people who have traveled this novel's path alongside me:

My wonderful editor, Kate Seaver—and my equally fantastic agent, Lucienne Diver. All the good people at Berkley who have made this series possible, especially Leslie Gelbman and Susan Allison. My copy editors, Bob and Sara Schwager. My friends and family, who still giggle at this job I have—and my lovely readers, who support me in countless kind ways.

I'd like to thank Adam Minter, as well, for being a wealth of information about St. Ignatius Cathedral in Shanghai, China—and for always taking the time to answer my questions.

To learn more about the Hunter Kiss series, please visit my website at www.marjoriemliu.com.

Though my soul may set in darkness,
it will rise in perfect light;
I have loved the stars too fondly
to be fearful of the night.

—SARAH WILLIAMS,
  "THE OLD ASTRONOMER TO HIS PUPIL"

CHAPTER 1

ZOMBIES had a bad habit of shooting me in the head. Most of them knew better, but there was always that one who wanted to get lucky.

It was a wet Monday morning. Almost dawn. Broken streetlights and glass in the road; and the hulking shadows of abandoned warehouses towering above me. Dead city, dead hour. Seattle was a dark place, even with the sun. Some days felt like living in the aftermath of a nuclear winter; as though a mushroom cloud had blown over and never left.

Quiet, too. Nothing to hear except harsh breathing, a soft whine; my cowboy boots scuffing concrete and the sharpening of claws; and the rumble of the freight trains at the rail yard across from the docks, mingling with the growls vibrating softly in my ears: baby symphonies of thunder. Good music. Made me feel safe.

I rubbed wet hair out of my eyes. "Zee. Hold him tighter."

Him. Archie Limbaud. Scrawny man, sinewy as a garter snake, saddled with a crown of short brown hair plastered to his soaked skin and flecked with enormous flakes of dandruff. He was a fortysomething man who smelled like the private bathroom of a teenage boy: unwashed and vaguely fecal.

He was also a zombie. Not the brain-eating, shambling kind, either. Not a corpse. Just a man, possessed by a demon—who was using his body like a puppet. Practically the same as being dead, if you asked me.

I did not want to touch him. He sprawled on the edge of an empty parking lot, crammed against the bottom of a chain-link fence, the contents of his wallet scattered on the ground in front of me. More condoms than cash, along with one credit card, and an expired driver's license. Minutes ago, there had been a gun—a .40-caliber pistol, pointed at my head—but that was gone now. Eaten.

I hated guns. I hated zombies. Put those together with what I knew about the possessed man at my feet, and I didn't know whether to cry, scream, or kick the fuck out of his testes.

I eased off my gloves, shoved them in my back pocket, and extended my palm. A sharp little hand passed me a switchblade. Pretty thing, with a mother-of-pearl handle and silver accents. Razor edge, still wet with blood. Engraved with the initials A.L. I waved it in front of Archie's ruddy face, and his dark aura fluttered wildly around the crown of his head.

"Some night," I said quietly. "I found the body."

Archie said nothing. Part of that might have been the aluminum baseball bat pressed down on his throat. Stolen from the Seattle Mariners, if I had to guess. I could see the stadium walls of Safeco Field from where I crouched, and Zee and the others were going through a baseball phase. Babe Ruth was in; Bill Russell was out. Which pained me. At least my boys were still obsessed with Bon Jovi. I couldn't have handled that much change.

Zee, Raw, and Aaz were down on the ground, pinning Archie to the pavement. Little demons, little hounds. Rain sizzled, trickling down bony backs the color of soot smeared with silver, skin shimmering with a muscular fluidity that resembled water more than flesh. Razor-sharp spines of hair flexed against chiseled skulls while silver veins pulsed with slow beats that, if I had pressed my ear close, would have sounded like the steady thrums of bass guitars.

Red eyes glinted. I used the switchblade to tap Aaz on the back of the head, and his hair cut through the steel as if it were butter. Raw caught the bits of blade before they hit the pavement and stuffed them in his mouth, chewing loudly.

"Ease up on the windpipe," I said to Aaz. "I don't want the host harmed."

Aaz blew a kiss at the zombie and removed the baseball bat from his soft, bruised throat. Archie started coughing, fighting to move his legs. No luck. Raw was sitting on his ankles, and Zee had his wrists pinned to the pavement. Not quite crushing bone, but close. My boys were strong.

"Please," Archie whispered hoarsely. "I want to convert."

"Liar," rasped Zee, before I had a chance to tell the zombie to go fuck himself. The little demon leaned close to lick the air above Archie's brow. "Cutter lies, Maxine. He still hungers."

"He murders," I said, gripping the remains of the switchblade in my fist as a young face flashed through my mind, bloody and sliced, long brown limbs naked, splayed. Torn doll. Torn in places I did not want to remember. "She was just a kid."

"She was a prostitute," Archie said. "She was already prey."

Dek and Mal, coiled heavy on my shoulders, peered from beneath my hair and hissed at the zombie. Unlike the others, they were built like snakes, with two vestigial limbs good only for clutching my ears. Heads shaped like hyenas. Sharp smiles. Fire in their breath. Archie stared at them, and trembled.

I reached through his thunderous aura to place my hand on his clammy brow. He shied away, but the boys held tight, and in that last moment before I touched him, his eyes rolled back, staring at the delicate armor surrounding the entire ring finger of my right hand: a slender sheath of quicksilver, replete with a delicate joint at the knuckle, which allowed my finger to bend. Fit like a skin. Sometimes I forgot it was there.

"Prey," I murmured. "And what does that make you?"

"One of a million," he whispered, shaking; staring at me with hate in his eyes. "You can't kill us all. When the prison walls fail—"

"You'll be rat meat to the rest of the demons," I interrupted, still thinking of the girl I had found in an alley only blocks from here, summoned to her still-warm body by Zee and the others, who had roused me from bed to hunt her killer. "Your kind will be slaughtered, just like the humans. You're nothing to the others. Even your Queen has said so."

"Hunter—" Archie began, but I didn't let him finish. I knew everything he was going to say. I had heard it thousands of times since my mother's murder, and thousands of times before that, as well.

I was going to die. I was never going to reach old age. The world was going to end.

All of which was true. But, whatever. His voice hurt my head. His sour scent, hot and prickly, made me want to vomit. I was tired, and cold all the way through to my soul, and there was a girl who had lost her life tonight for no good reason. She had suffered a bad death—and only because the parasite possessing this man had wanted to feed on her pain. I did not even know her name. No ID, no nothing. Lost forever.

Not the only one, either. The world was a big place. Too many predators: human, zombie, or otherwise. And just one of me. Nomad, born and bred, who had settled in this city longer than any other. Abandoning all others, so I could have some semblance of a normal life.

Right. Normal.

I ground my palm even harder against Archie's brow, and exhaled a soft hiss of words: sibilant and ancient, a focused tongue that made my skin tingle, and my hand burn. Archie's breath rattled, and he strained upward as his aura swelled, trying to escape me.

No such luck. The demon was young. Easy to exorcise. I drew it out, watching the passage of its wraithlike body churn through the human's open mouth like poisoned smoke. Archie went limp. Raw and Aaz released his legs, while Dek and Mal slithered off my shoulders, winding down my arms to be near my hands. Their tiny claws pricked my skin like kneading cats, and their soft, high-pitched hum of Bon Jovi's "Social Disease" filled the air.

When the last trail of the parasite's writhing body was free of the human man, I held it in my hand with that soft, shrieking darkness spilling through my fingers, and felt a cold bite in my skin, like a glove of frozen nettles. Zee stepped over Archie's still body, and the others extended their razor-tipped claws.

I gave them the demon. I did not watch them eat it.

I knelt by Archie and checked his pulse. Strong, steady. His eyelids fluttered, but he stayed unconscious, and I backed away quickly, rubbing my sweaty palms on my jeans. I had no way of knowing what this man had been like before being possessed, though I guessed he hadn't been the happy type. Stable, mentally robust people did not get possessed by demons. Too much work. No cracks to exploit.

But this man, Archie Limbaud, would wake up a murderer—and never know it. Demons left no memories in human minds. Just chaos, ruined lives. Friends and family who would never look at you the same way.

"Maxine," Zee rasped, rubbing his mouth with the back of his sharp hand. "Sun coming."

I knew. I could feel the sun, somewhere beyond the black skies and rain, slowly creeping up on the cloud-hidden horizon. I had minutes at most.

"Pay phone," I said to Zee, and he snapped his claws at Raw and Aaz, who were prowling the edges of the dark lot, slipping in and out of shadows. Both of them loped close, graceful as wolves, and whispered in Zee's ears. Zee cocked his head, listening; and after a moment, pointed.

I said nothing. Just walked away from Archie. I did not rush. I did not look back. I held the handle of the switchblade and slid it into my hair. Listened to metal crunch as Mal chewed and swallowed. I could have left it. Evidence.

But I wanted the man to have a second chance. I wanted him to wake up, confused and amnesiac, but without the burden of murder. No one deserved that—even though there was a small part of me that felt like his hands were dirty. Dirty as mine. I could not stop rubbing my palms against my wet jeans. Felt as though Archie Limbaud's stink was all over me.

Early morning continued to be quiet, the drizzling mist softening the streets and rough, broken edges, and I drank in the cold air, savoring the chill of wet hair curled against my flushed cheeks. The boys moved through the shadows, invisible except for brief glimpses of their red eyes. I kept wiping my hands and thinking about the dead girl. And my mother. She had warned me before she died. She had warned me it would be like this. Always, victims. Victims, everywhere. And me, never fast enough. Always playing catch-up.

I found a pay phone two blocks away. Battered relic, covered in graffiti. I dialed 911 and left a brief message with the operator—teenager dead, murdered, several blocks south of Safeco Field—and hung up. Wiped off my prints, then remembered I could have worn my gloves. I was still rattled, not thinking straight. I wanted to go back to the dead girl and wait with her body—as if that would make a difference. Ease, somehow, the pain and loneliness of her murder.

Instead, I kept walking, taking a westerly route away from the rail yards, toward Chinatown. I saw no one but caught glimpses of headlights crossing distant intersections. The rumble of the trains seemed louder. The air tasted sharper, and suddenly electric, as though a city full of alarms had just gone off and I was feeling the pulse of thousands of eyes opening at once. In my ear, Dek and Mal began humming more Bon Jovi. "Have a Nice Day."

"You, too," I said hoarsely, reaching into my hair to scratch their necks. "See you tonight."

I stopped in the shadows, well off the street, and the rest of the boys slipped free of the darkness to gather close, hugging my legs, running their cheeks against my knees. The boys liked to be tucked in. I slid my knuckles against their warm jaws and savored the rumble of purrs. Their skin steamed in the rain.

Zee peered up at me and tugged on my hand until I knelt before him. Very carefully, he cradled my face between his claws, searching my eyes with a sad compassion that made my throat burn.

"Maxine," he rasped gently. "Sweet Maxine. Be your heart at ease."

We had seconds, nothing more. I kissed my fingers and pressed them against his bony brow. I thought of my mother again and caught myself in heartache. She had said good night to the boys like this, for all the years they were hers. I could not stop thinking of her tonight.

"Dream," I whispered. "Sleep tigh—"

I never finished. I got shot in the head.

Just like that. Right temple. Not much sound. The impact shuddered through my entire body, every sensation magnified with excruciating clarity as the bullet drilled into my skull—the inexorable pressure of a small round object, crushing my life. I could feel it. I could *feel* it. My brain was going to explode like a watermelon. I had no time to be afraid.

But in that moment—that split second between life and death, the sun touched the horizon somewhere beyond the clouds—

—and the boys disappeared into my skin.

The bullet ricocheted, the impact spinning me like a rag doll. I fell on my hands and knees, and stayed there, stunned and frozen. I could still feel the punch of the shot—the sensation so visceral I would not have been surprised to reach up and find the bullet grinding a path into my skull.

I touched my head, just to be sure. Found hair and unbroken skin. No blood. My entire right arm trembled, and a dull, throbbing ache spread from my sinuses to my temple, all the way through to the base of my skull. My heart pounded so hard I could barely breathe. All I could see was pavement and my hands.

My transformed hands. My skin had been pale and smooth only moments before, but tattoos now covered every inch: obsidian roping shadows, scales and silver muscle shining with subtle veins of organic metal. My fingernails shimmered like black pearls, hard enough to dig a hole through solid rock. Red eyes stared from the backs of my wrists. Raw and Aaz. I closed my eyes, trying to steady my breathing, and felt five corresponding tugs against my skin. Demons, inhabiting my flesh. Minds and hearts and dreams, bound to my life until I died.

My friends, my family. My dangerous boys.

Somewhere distant I heard police sirens wailing. My 911 call, coming this way. I had to get up. I tried, and fell. Gritted my teeth and dug my nails into the concrete. Tried again.

This time I managed to stand. I started walking, stumbling, but did not go down. My head pounded. I bent over once, still moving—afraid to stop—gagging uncontrollably. Felt like my stomach was going to peel right up through my throat, but instead of making my head hurt worse, the pain eased.

I touched my right temple with a trembling hand, savoring the smooth, unbroken skin. Momentarily in awe that I still lived.

I had been shot before. Frequently. All over. Never felt a thing. Bullets bounced off me during the day. A nuclear bomb could hit me in daylight, and I would survive—without a scratch. Might be a different story at night, when the boys peeled off my body, but I never underestimated their ability to keep me alive.

But no one—no one—had ever had the foresight—or the balls—to try killing me in that moment between night and day, caught in transition between mortal and immortal.

Near-perfect timing. Any earlier, and the boys would have killed the shooter before the bullet could be fired. Any later, and I would have been invulnerable. Which was exactly the case. Saved by a fraction of a second.

Too damn close. I scanned the shadows but saw nothing except for warehouses and dark windows, and the glitter of downtown Seattle to the north, all the lights of the city frozen like the unwavering pose of fireflies. Nothing unordinary. No shooter, waving a flag. But I felt watched. Someone, somewhere, out there in the darkness. Long range, or else the boys would have felt their presence well before the attack.

Zombie, I thought. Had to be. No one else who knew what I was would try to hurt me.

"You almost died," I said out loud, needing to hear the words, to hear myself—as though I required some proof of life. Maxine Kiss. Almost taken out, just like my mother— with a bullet through the brain.

A zombie had killed her. But that was different.

It had been her time to die.

CHAPTER 2

I T took me thirty minutes to return to the Coop. The walk did me good. By the time I reached the rear door of the homeless shelter's kitchen, I had stopped shaking, stopped suffering those gulps of weakness in my knees and hands. But I still felt the bullet, pushing into my head. Nor could I dismiss my absolute certainty that whoever had shot me knew exactly where I lived. Which meant they probably knew who I cared about.

Nightfall could not come soon enough.

The sky had lightened, revealing a canvas of clouds. Still gloomy out. Raining harder. I remained bone-dry. Even when asleep, the boys had a knack for consuming things, and all the water that had been dragging down my clothes and hair was no exception—absorbed within minutes of dawn, and now within seconds of hitting me. I only hoped no one thought too hard about how I managed to stay dry when everyone else coming inside looked as though they had been dunked in a pickle barrel.

That was the problem with secrets. There was always

something to trip you up. Especially if you stayed too long in one place.

The Coop took up an entire block; a jumble of warehouses that had been renovated and linked together to form a center for the homeless that provided temporary shelter, meals, and a host of other services. Corporate and private donations funded some of it, but not enough to name rooms after anyone or hand out gold stars. Almost all the bills were paid for by one man, Grant Cooperon—and he preferred it that way. There was no such thing as a price on autonomy.

Seagulls hovered, screaming. The loading dock was crammed with vans, white and unmarked. The shelter had a system of sending out vehicles in the middle of the night, scouring local bakeries and grocery stores for day-old food that might otherwise be thrown out. Doughnuts and bread were a popular castoff, though I passed several giant crates of oranges being wheeled in through the back. One of the new volunteers, a young woman with blond dreadlocks sticking out of her striped hemp cap, staggered in front of me under the weight of several gallons of milk, piled high in her arms.

I snagged two of them—nodded brusquely at her startled yelp of thanks—and kept walking. My leather gloves were back on, hiding my hands, and my long-sleeved navy turtleneck hid the rest of my upper body. I had a limited wardrobe. With some exceptions, I never let anyone see my tattoos. Raised too many questions, too many possible problems. The boys, after all, disappeared from my skin at sunset—and never slept in the same place twice.

I could feel them all over me—beneath my hair, between my toes—in unmentionable places. My face was the only area the boys did not regularly protect, their one concession to my vanity, although a small trace of a tattooed body curled from my hairline, just below my ear against my jaw: a wink of dark scales, a silver glimmer of Dek's tail. Just large enough to cover my only scar.

The kitchen was hopping. Crazy clocks shaped like cats covered butter yellow walls, and a dozen calendars were tacked up, surrounding a white erase board where the day's jobs were written—and that someone kept decorating with pictures of flowers. Grease sizzled, overwhelming the air with the scents of bacon and eggs, and a radio crackled; some deep voice dispensing the weather report in a vaguely ironic tone: rain, rain, and more rain, with a break tonight— maybe—and a shot at viewing the moon. All around me, a mostly female crew of yuppies and hippies bumped hips—a clash of pearls and hemp, cashmere and fleece, loafers and Birkenstocks—creating an earthy, irreverent vibe that was, nonetheless, just slightly pretentious. Seattle had that way about it.

I hovered for a moment, soaking it all in—listening to laughter and shouts; the bang of pans, the squeal of rubber soles on the tile floor. Industrious noises, folks getting things done. I liked that. It was homey. Refreshingly normal. I had no sense of temperature during the day, but the sounds of good living made me warm on the inside in ways the sun never would—regardless of the weather.

This is what you're fighting for, I told myself. *All the lovely moments of the world.*

I placed the milk on the stainless-steel counter, next to some bags of frozen blueberries set out to defrost. There were muffins within reach, and I grabbed one and took a bite. Banana and walnut. Very nice. I was suddenly starving. I had a lot of bodies to feed. Based on the way my morning had already started, I might not have another chance to eat for a while. And I was not a good grouch when the blood sugar dipped. Hell, no.

"You're late," said a quiet voice, off to my right. No accusation, just a statement of fact.

"Five minutes," I replied, leaning against the counter. The tip of my scuffed cowboy boot nudged an equally dirty tennis shoe. "Sorry."

"S'okay. I knew you'd be here." Said in that same matter-of-fact tone. Said with trust. A rare compliment, startlingly unfamiliar to me, and one that made my heart do a funny little twist. My mother would not have approved.

The boy in front of me was young, no older than fifteen. Byron. No last name. Maybe not his real name. A mystery, in more ways than one. Thin as a rail, with black spiky hair that framed a pale, elfin face. Tough, sweet kid, in that quiet way people underestimated. No swagger, no charm—just a backbone made of pure intelligence. He had lived on the streets, been abused on the streets, and was finally adjusting to a roof over his head. Regular meals. Toilet paper. A lock on his door.

He had jeans on, and a loose, long-sleeved gray shirt that was fraying around his bony wrists. Over that he wore a stained white apron covered in red lips, like some giant woman slathered in lipstick had kissed the hell out of him. Byron hated the thing, as any self-respecting teenager would, but the rest of the kitchen staff loved seeing him in it, and the kid was surprisingly polite—or appropriately terrified—when it came to talking back to an army of women.

He held a folded newspaper, which he slid onto the counter. Nothing interesting about the headlines, except for one brief column that read: MONSTER OR HOAX? SIGHTED IN PARIS.

I leaned in, too sensitive to weird news to dismiss anything out of hand, but all the article said—with an air of utter disbelief—was that some woman claimed to have been bitten by a very hairy man with extremely long and pointy teeth—and that he had apologized profusely afterward, and run off sobbing. Not exactly what I would call a sign of demonic activity.

I raised an eyebrow. "I've told you not to talk to hairy strangers, right?"

"Define hairy," Byron said, but there was a rare faint smile on his face, and I almost smiled back.

"So, did you finish it?" I asked him, taking another bite out of the muffin. Trying not to think of the dead girl when I looked at his face. She had been his age. It could have been Byron dead in that alley, once upon a time. I was beginning to regret letting Archie Limbaud off the hook.

I had killed the demon responsible for the girl's death, but that did not feel like enough.

You never blame the hosts, whispered my mother's memory. *Not even for the weakness that let the demon in. We're all weak, baby. Just in different ways.*

Byron scowled. "The math, or Schopenhauer?"

I handed him a muffin of his own, forcing myself to breathe. "Both."

He picked at the paper wrapper with a chipped black fingernail. "I left the algebra problems on Grant's desk. I also read the pages you gave me."

"And?"

"And I'm not in college," he replied, though he sounded older, and more mature, than most of the university types he had begged money from not so long ago. "German philosophers make no sense."

"You're smart," I said, knowing I was pushing him; knowing, too, that he could take it. "Tell me what you read."

Byron rubbed his nose. "Stuff. Reality is an illusion. Desire, instinct, is a thing."

"Good." I crumpled my muffin wrapper and tossed it in the garbage. "Think about that, then write me a paragraph or two about whether you agree, and why. I want it by tomorrow."

He froze in midbite. "You gave me history homework yesterday. And more math."

I ruffled his hair. "So?"

Any other kid would have shot back some zinger, a roll of the eyes—a tremor of defiance, at the very least—but Byron was not like most teens. He studied me with a solemn thoughtfulness that made his young face age—boy to man, to wizened sage—but it was his eyes that made him appear profoundly old, as though years beyond reckoning were piled upon his soul.

It's time, I thought, caught in that gaze. *He's going to ask me why I try so hard with him.*

But Byron didn't. He finished taking a bite out of his muffin and nodded slowly.

"Tomorrow," he said, still chewing, and looked behind me, just for a moment. I glanced over my shoulder. Found the dreadlocked girl who had been carrying the milk deep in conversation with one of the older volunteers, a woman with tanned, sinewy legs, who wore shorts and clunky sandals every day—no matter the weather.

They were staring at me. The young woman flinched guiltily when she found me looking, but the other woman— Doreen, I think she was called—held my gaze, frowning.

"Let me guess," I said to Byron. "I did something."

"She thinks you're violent," replied the boy bluntly. "She told me so. Warned me to stay away from you."

I gritted my teeth and deliberately smiled at the middle-aged woman. "Obviously, you listened."

I had an ugly smile. Doreen finally looked down and turned around to busy herself with unpacking cereal boxes. Byron said, "She doesn't know anything. Except that you sleep with Grant. And that you scare her."

"She told you that, too?"

"No," he said softly. "You make a lot of people uneasy."

I gave him a sharp look. "Is that how you feel?"

"I feel safe," he replied, without hesitation; and finally there was some defiance in his voice, in the tilt of his chin and the glint that flickered in his eyes. Again, my heart twisted; and again, I thought of my mother. *Dangerous,* she would have said. *You put yourself, and others, in danger. Our kind were not born to make roots. Or friends. Or love.*

But I was not my mother. I was a sucker. An idiot. My free will was my reality—for better or worse.

"Good," I said, which was all I could manage; and then: "Stick close to the shelter for the next couple days, okay? If you decide to go running around, find me first. Find Grant. But don't go out by yourself. Got it?"

Byron frowned. "No. Why?"

Because someone shot me in the head this morning, and he might know you're a weakness of mine. But all I said was, "Perverts."

"Perverts," he said, giving me a piercing look. "Right."

I patted his shoulder—and then turned around to look at Doreen again. Her, and the rest of the kitchen. Watching faces. Letting the men and women watch me in turn, on the sly, from the corners of their eyes. For six months I had avoided answering personal questions—as had Grant—and so gossip and speculation had become my own mythology and mystery: the woman who lived with the man in charge, the quiet woman, the dangerous woman. Reinforced, here and there, by the occasional act of violence. Folks who came to the shelter occasionally misbehaved. I lent a hand when that happened. And though I had never stayed in one place long enough to earn a reputation, I had one now.

I was security. A good right hook. A thousand yard stare. A woman reduced to adjectives, all of them well placed and accurate—in that way only half-truths could be.

I took another look at Doreen's back and got hit with a wave of loneliness so profound I wanted to run—run back to the solitude I had left behind. Being alone was easier than this. I had no skills in dealing with running mouths and bad opinions. I had never imagined I would find myself in a situation where I would give a damn.

And I still didn't. I couldn't. I mustn't.

I looked for Byron and found him already on the other side of the kitchen in the serving line, spooning hash browns onto trays. Penned in by two old ladies, his head carefully down—though he made brief eye contact with the few women who held out their trays to him. None of the men, though. He avoided men, except for Grant.

The boys stirred against my skin; a rumble in their dreams, some uneasy discomfort that tugged suddenly, quite sharply, between my breasts. Pulling me forward, toward the serving line. Not to Byron, I sensed. Something else. I started walking, weaving around workstations and volunteers, and peered from the kitchen into the cafeteria. I couldn't catch sight of much. Mostly just the center of the dining area, in front of the double swinging doors.

Which was enough to see the man who walked in, moments later.

He was not a zombie. But he made my skin crawl—literally—and the boys, even in their dreams, went wild with fury, their agitation so violent their tattooed bodies felt like bubbles in my blood, breaking against the underside of my flesh. I rubbed my arms to calm them, but the boys kept fussing. They wanted to kill that man.

He was not entirely ordinary. Tall, reedy, with a long face that was deathly pale except for two red splotches high on his cheeks. His brow shone with sweat, though it was only forty degrees outside, and his posture was so straight he reminded me of a nail. He was also a priest. Black slacks, black shirt, that little white square of a collar peeking through his unzipped black Windbreaker.

It should not have made a difference, but it did. I had been very nearly murdered less than an hour before, and now a priest had shown up whom the boys wanted to kill. I did not like coincidences—even if this one failed to add up.

I tapped Byron on the shoulder. "Go get Grant for me, will you?"

He looked back at me, his eyes black as coal, and old, so old. "Because of that priest, right?"

He was good at surprising me. "Smart kid."

Byron did not blink. "I don't like him."

Smiling never came naturally to me, but my mouth tilted, just so. "Better than smart. Brilliant. Now go get Grant."

Byron ducked his head and nudged the volunteer beside him, handing her his spoon before he stepped out of the serving line. He hung his apron on a hook by the kitchen door and left. Fast, efficient. Good at not asking questions.

I looked again at the priest. He had moved deeper into the cafeteria and was turning in a slow circle, searching the crowd. Zombies watched him. Three, scattered amongst the humans. Auras stirring black and listless. Two men, one woman, wearing dull frayed coats and knit caps. Cold-weather clothes for a cold Seattle winter.

It amazed me, always, that humans could be so blind to

the dangers around them. No one looked twice at the zombies. Folks sat elbow to elbow with them, chatting, making nice.

But I knew. I stared. Only one of them met my gaze. Brief, haunted. Pale. His leg twitched under the table. I did not look away. I liked his fear. It tasted bloody and warm, and the boys were always hungry for a fat demon: a little possessor; zombie-maker, parasite. Burrowers, borrowers, drifting on the outskirts of human minds, searching for weakness, a hot harvest.

Demons made pain. Demons ate pain, which was nothing but another kind of energy: a dark emanation. Demons whispered inside the ears of the soul and turned grandmothers into murderers, awkward boys into rapists, men like Archie Limbaud into sadists. All of them, zombies. Human shells inhabited by creatures who thrived on patterns of suffering, ever-widening circles of despair.

I was good at killing the parasites. I had to be. No one else was around to do it. Hardly anyone knew they existed. I was the last of the Wardens, all that was left of a race of men and women created to stand against an army of demons, the very worst of which were caught behind the veil: a multidimensional prison, floating in time and space. Weakening, ready to fail.

When it did, the world would end. Ten thousand years of peace, about to get broken into a million little pieces.

But here, in this homeless shelter, a sanctuary for the devils. Because I had made a promise.

I left the kitchen through a side door that led directly into the cafeteria. The priest had his back turned. I listened to the soft roar of breakfast conversation as I walked toward him. Beneath the voices I heard strains from *South Pacific* playing softly over the intercom. One of the volunteers had been to New York City to see the revival at Lincoln Center, and it was his new obsession. I walked to the perky beat of Mitzi Gaynor washing men out of her hair, and found myself sympathizing. At least, with regard to the priest.

He turned as I approached. Closing the distance did
nothing to improve my feelings about him. He was taller
than me, almost skinnier—and the dark clothing, the pale
translucence of his damp face and brown, stringy hair, only
enhanced the skeletal qualities of his body. The red flush
in his upper cheeks looked as though he had jammed his
fingers in a pot of rouge, and rubbed and rubbed.

The priest tilted his head, a faint, tremulous smile touching his mouth. His eyes were bloodshot.

"Hello," he said, his accent Italian, his voice far calmer
than the twitch in his cheek, the flutter of his eyelid. His
looked at me as if we were already on a first-name basis,
and the familiarity of his regard made me uncomfortable;
even nauseous, as though his facial tics were a rocking
boat.

"Can I help you?" I asked, holding steady as Zee pulsed
in agitation between my breasts. Dek and Mal tugged beneath my scalp—like twin barbs twitching in a fish's
mouth—while Raw and Aaz burned against my hands,
simmering in soft rumbles that scorched me to the bone.
Something wrong. Something wicked.

The man did not immediately answer. He held my gaze,
unblinking, as though he was not a priest but some spiri-
tual scientist, dissecting my soul in strips, cutting and cutting with delicate, deadly precision. A fast analysis, cold,
and as with his voice it belied the sweat and unease, the
radiating uncertainty of his posture. *Just a mask,* I thought.
Or a symptom.

"I am looking for someone," said the priest, with a curious dead tone in his voice. "The man who owns this place."

I was not surprised. But I wanted to lie. I wanted to get
mean. Letting this priest near Grant would be a terrible
mistake. I should never have sent Byron to find him. I
could feel it in my gut, like a bad meal churning into bile.

Too late. I heard a distinctive clicking sound outside the
cafeteria. Faint, but growing in strength like a heartbeat.
Familiar as the hearts of the boys, pulsing hot against my
skin.

Grant pushed open the double doors, leaning heavily on his oak cane. It was like being in an old-time saloon—conversation quieted, chairs scraping as men and women turned, staring. I felt the power of that mass regard like a living weapon, and it made me as uneasy as any promise of death. I should have been used to it. Grant had that effect on people.

Demons, too. I glanced at the three zombies and found adoration in their eyes, a devotion I would have expected in parishioners praying to the cross. Even the flare of their auras quieted in Grant's presence, as though simply seeing him eased the darkness of their natures.

Unnatural. Unnerving. I killed demons. I killed them because I had been taught they were dangerous—and they were. I killed them without conscience because I believed they had none: irredeemable, less than a flea or a tick. I still believed that. Even after all this time, I could not reconcile the Archie Limbauds of the world with these creatures, who were exactly the same—but who had come here of their own free will, to become something different, something . . . better.

Grant complicated everything.

He was a tall man, with strong, broad shoulders that strained against a soft flannel shirt, faded to a pale green. He had recently gotten a haircut, but his brown hair was still wildly tousled, a fine contrast to the hard lines of his face and the crinkle of his eyes, the easy tilt of his smiling mouth.

The strap of his flute case hung across his chest, and I caught a hint of polished wood behind his shoulder; a new instrument, carved with his own two hands. Made a mournful, throaty music, which I would have liked hearing in the natural chapel of the forest outside the city, near the sea. Dawn music. Silver music, soft as the fog that built a wall from ocean wave to rock and leaf. Music that was part of his blood and bone, and in his eyes: primal, otherworldly, sharp like the gaze of a wolf.

Beautiful man. My man.

Grant saw me first. He always saw me first, no matter

where, no matter the crowd—and it was like hitting a raw nerve: being seen, being known. Truly known, without secrets. Too new to feel natural. I had spent my life as a shadow. I had believed I would die one, too. No one to remember me but the boys, and if I was lucky, a daughter.

The priest took a sharp breath when he saw Grant. It was loud, dramatic—I half expected to see the man swoon—but there was nothing weak about his face. His jaw was tight, lips thin and white, and his upper cheeks paled to a faint pink that resembled two healing welts against his skin.

All the warmth drained from Grant's eyes. I saw it happen, like watching death move in; as though the priest were a gun, an adder, a plug of slime. Nasty and vicious. I had never seen Grant look at anyone like that, and it was nothing I wanted to become a habit. He was a gentle man. A gentle, dangerous man.

The priest went very still. He and Grant stared at each other. Folks in the cafeteria, who had resumed their meals, started watching them again. Byron peered through the double doors, then disappeared. I moved closer to Grant and glanced back at the priest. Caught the edge of a cold, piercing smile.

"Father Cooperon," said the priest, with a touch of acid in his voice. *"Un pezzo che non ci si vede."*

Grant's gaze remained steady. "Not long enough, Antony."

The priest's smile faded, shadows gathering in his eyes. "Indeed."

I brushed up against Grant. "We should take this elsewhere."

His hand slid around my own, and I savored the heat of his body through my glove. I felt nothing on my skin while the boys slept—not even the whisper of the wind, or the rain, or sunlight—but Grant's warmth seeped through their tattoos. The boys liked him.

The priest's gaze fell upon our joined hands and stayed there. He looked unhappy. Maybe disgusted. Or jealous.

Not much of a difference between any of those emotions, in my experience.

Grant did not turn his back on the priest. He shifted sideways and gestured with his chin toward the doors. His knuckles were white around the cane. His hand tight against mine. I squeezed once, keeping my gaze on the priest as he glided past, his shoulders round and hunched. He smelled like yeast and hot beeswax.

Grant began to follow the priest. I held him back, stood on my toes, and in his ear whispered, "What the hell is going on?"

"Don't know," he muttered, tugging me close. "But that's the man who tried to convince the Church to kill me."

CHAPTER 3

W E walked to Grant's office. There was a crowd in the hall. Bulletin boards hung on the walls between framed posters: *Charade* mingled with temporary job openings, while Indiana Jones, in all his *Raiders of the Lost Ark* glory, rubbed shoulders with new announcements for night classes and cheap housing. I recognized some of the faces reading the crisp papers pinned to the board; mostly men, dressed in varying degrees of comfort and cleanliness— none of whom wore the shadow of a zombie.

The men moved aside for Grant as he limped past. I watched faces, searching for dislike, some edge of danger. I found nothing. Just respect, a distant wariness. Appreciation. Grant moved amongst them with easy confidence, murmuring words, touching shoulders. Sharing moments of grace, in passing—bringing light, a particular alertness, into the occasional pair of dull, tired eyes. A melody in his voice, which skimmed over my skin, making the boys tingle.

Former Father Cooperon. Working his magic.

I walked beside the priest. He did not seem to notice the

people around him, or the curious looks sent his way. His focus was entirely on Grant. And me. I listened to Zee and the others simmer in their dreams, heating my skin. Almost ten hours until sunset, and they were raring to go.

"And you are?" asked the priest, glancing at me.

"Annie," I lied, which was the name I had been using around the shelter for the past six months. I was a fan of the movie *Speed*, and the name sounded cheerful, nonthreatening. Nothing like me.

Only a few people knew my real name, though two of those were cops, and they had probably written it down in a computer, or some ugly file. Which was crap for me, even though I still clung to my old alias. Hard habit to break.

"Annie," echoed the priest, as though he did not entirely believe me. His cheek twitched. "You may call me Father Cribari."

Sounded cold. Made me think of circus clowns juggling knives and weeping painted tears. I almost said so. Maybe it showed on my face. I was a bad actress. I watched Father Cribari's mouth tilt, his eyes filling with a darkly amused condescension that seemed far too knowing. He wiped his sweaty brow with the back of his pale, skinny hand, and said, "Grant. Where did you find this girl?"

Grant's pace faltered, and he glanced over his shoulder, briefly meeting my gaze before looking at the priest. "You're not interested in her, Antony."

"Of course not," replied Father Cribari. "But *you* are."

His edge was unmistakable, as was the sly tone, the cold, implacable humor. A pissing contest. Between a former priest and the real deal. There was a joke in this somewhere. But nothing funny—not in the slightest—about the anger that filled Grant's eyes. Or the way his left hand twitched toward his flute.

Grant stopped walking, so abruptly we almost ran into him. Which made it easy when he leaned in, almost nose to nose with Father Cribari, and very quietly said, "You bring her into this, Antony—"

"—and you will finish what we started," interrupted the

priest, just as softly. "Yes, I know. But I did not come here for that."

"Just the messenger," Grant whispered, his voice holding a hint of a melody, so deadly a chill raced through my bones. *Careful,* I thought. *Careful of those lines you should not cross.*

But Grant reached out and took my hand, pulling me close as he started limping again down the hall. I leaned into him, and his arm slid around my waist. Father Cribari lingered behind us. I whispered, "And here I was thinking of running off with him."

A grim smile touched Grant's mouth. "You could try. But then I'd have to drag you back."

We reached Grant's office, located near the front of a long hall painted with flowers, bumblebees, and mermaids: courtesy of the children who attended the shelter's day-care center, located on the other side of the main wing, far from the adults who passed through the facility. I could hear the children laughing—high, sweet, uninhibited—and behind that, the nasal chime of cartoon voices, something more modern than what I was used to. *Tom and Jerry* was not much in fashion, anymore.

A scarecrow of an old woman stood by Grant's door. Wild white hair blazed from her head as if she wore the wig of Einstein, and a crooked potato-sack dress decorated with pink poodles covered her skinny frame. The old scars of track marks covered her upper arms, and she held a tin full of homemade brownies, which made me almost as wary as the priest standing at my side. I knew this old woman. She liked to use special ingredients in her baked goods. Highly illegal, occasionally leafy, ingredients.

"Mary," Grant said gently, but firmly. "I'm sorry, but I'll have to meet with you later."

The old woman hardly seemed to hear him. She stared at Father Cribari like he was a dirty itch, and took a step that somehow placed her between Grant and the priest—a move so smooth I hardly realized what she had done until she was up in the man's face, peering into his eyes with her upper lip peeled back over her teeth. Not quite a snarl. More like she was tasting the air.

"Used man," she whispered suddenly. "You made your soul a slut."

Father Cribari reared back as though slapped. Grant grabbed Mary's arm, but not before she smiled fiercely and laughed.

"Gabriel's Hounds will kill you," she said, and looked from me to the priest. "Hot damn."

Father Cribari made a choking sound. Grant pushed open his office door, gave me a look—and I shoved the priest through, out of Mary's sight. I heard words behind me, very soft, then Grant limped heavily into the office. He closed the door behind him. A faint flush stained his cheeks, but his eyes were calm.

"This is not an insane asylum," snapped Father Cribari, yanking on his sleeves. "There are places for women like—"

"There's no place for a person like Mary," Grant interrupted smoothly. "Not in this world."

Which was, quite literally, the truth.

Father Cribari looked as though he wanted to continue arguing the matter, but he yanked on his sleeve again and compressed his mouth into a thin, hard line that made his lips disappear, so that he resembled a snake.

Grant did not sit. His hip brushed the edge of the desk, and he leaned hard on his cane, knuckles still white. His office was small, and sparsely decorated. Little of his personality adorned the room. Just white walls and a desk. Two soft armchairs. One lamp. Notebooks and pens, as well as some wrinkled papers covered in algebraic equations. A thick FedEx envelope, ripped open and bulging.

And a framed picture of us, sprawled together on driftwood while the ocean roared behind our backs and the clouds split silver with sun. No other photograph of me existed, not as an adult. I was happy with that one.

I stood beside the office door, behind Father Cribari, and leaned against the wall, staring at the back of the priest's head. Arms folded over my chest, subtly rubbing my arms as Zee and the others rumbled like little earthquakes erupting all over my body.

"There's been an incident," said Father Cribari, without preamble. Still sounding calm, despite the twitch of his cheek and the sweat rolling down the back of his neck, just above the collar of his Windbreaker.

Grant said nothing. Neither did I. No need. Silence could break a man more easily than questions. And Father Cribari had not come here to simply stand in a room and sweat.

But it took him a while to say anything else. He was stone, pale as marble clothed in shadows, and the sweat could have been the aftermath of winter rain. Cold man. Standing near him, doing nothing, was difficult. I was used to action. Zombies. Demons. Exorcisms. I saw a problem, I fixed it. No waiting, unless it was for the right moment. And right moments were easy to find if you kept your options open. If you let yourself dwell in possibilities.

Father Cribari said, "Murders."

Just like that. A declaration. Murders. No explanation. Grant's jaw tightened. "Who were the victims?"

"Three nuns. Taken in quick succession. Tortured before their throats were slit."

Grant showed nothing on his face. He leaned back, gaze flicking to the air above Cribari's head. Studying the man's aura.

I could see auras, but only those that belonged to demons. I wished, though, that I could see what Grant did, though I doubted that was a responsibility I could have handled with even half his grace.

Grant had a syndrome, a brain disorder that had afflicted him from birth: synesthesia. Which meant that every sound he heard, every sigh and creak and chirp, translated itself into color. Grant could *see* sound.

He could see others things, too. Energy. Auras. Reflections of souls, bound in color, colors that had meanings, that formed a language only he could decipher. No person could hide from Grant. Masks meant nothing. To be seen by him meant being stripped down to the essence of some personal truth—no matter how damning, no matter how good. Not something most people would have been pleased to know about. Souls were supposed to be private. Souls— even the souls of demons—were supposed to be inviolate, unalterable by any human or creature.

But no other human or creature was like Grant. No one I had ever met had the ability to alter the very nature of a living being—with nothing but a song.

"You have investigators," replied Grant.

"Ah," said the priest, with a smile, "but the killer was a friend of yours."

I was looking at Grant when he said that. I was staring straight into his eyes, and so I saw the flinch, even though his body stayed still as death.

"I had a lot of friends in the Church," Grant replied, but I knew him too well, and a fist of dread pushed into my stomach. Unfamiliar sensation. Ugly. I had felt dread while my mother lived. I had felt dread after she died. Dread, when it was just me and the boys, up against the world. Trivial, though. My mother had been indestructible, larger than life—and I was merely hard to kill. Even my close call with the bullet was nothing, in the long run.

This was different. I suffered, in quick succession, anxiety and dismay—and it was not for me. It was for Grant. And that was worse. Worse than I could have imagined, all those years spent alone.

"Father Ross," said the priest. "He asked for you."

Grant finally looked down at his hand, still gripping the cane. "Where is he?"

"Shanghai." Father Cribari wiped his brow with the back of his sleeve. "We could not bring him to you. It may be difficult to move him for some time yet. He was sent as part of a special mission from the Vatican to explore relations with our brothers and sisters in China, but something happened while he was there. He . . . changed."

"He murdered," Grant said softly, still looking down. "But that's impossible. He was a good man. I know it."

I had wondered for some time what *good* looked like to Grant. What it meant to have a *kind* aura, or a *gentle* spirit. Grant said I had all of those things in me—which meant he was the best liar I knew—but I believed him when he said the same of others. If his Father Ross had been a good man when Grant knew him, then it was true.

Father Cribari took a step toward the door. I did not budge, not even when his back came close to brushing against my body. Zee writhed against my skin, lunging in his dreams toward the priest. I tried to ignore the sensation. Tried not to think about what it would look like if it were night and Zee were awake, lunging for real at that man's back. I guessed there would be a hole the size of a Frisbee where his spine should be. My boys were good like that.

"He asked for you because he said you would know what to do," said Father Cribari.

Grant's gaze snapped up. "If I remember correctly, we had a similar discussion ten years ago. About all the things I could do. You suggested I would be better off dead."

"But you are not, are you?" The priest sidled backward again, and this time did touch me. My arms were still folded over my chest. I felt the hard muscles of his back through my clothing. He was built like a whip. The scents of yeast and beeswax were strong, and even though I had never thought about the hairs in my nose, I could suddenly feel every one of them, tingling.

Father Cribari did not move away. He stared over his shoulder into my eyes. No words, just silence. I gave him the same treatment. No sweat off my back. I could stand like that forever. Or at least until the sun went down.

Grant said, "You want me to go to Shanghai; is that it?"

Father Cribari did not move or look at him. Just held my gaze. "Yes. We can arrange a visa through one of our local contacts in Seattle's Chinese embassy, but you will have to fly a commercial airline and enter the country as a tourist. We do not want to bring attention to this situation. It must be handled in secret."

"Secret," I said, before Grant could reply. "For a man with secrets, you sure spilled your guts in front of me."

"And why wouldn't I?" said Father Cribari, with a smile—though there was a trace of unease in the lines of his mouth. "Dark Mother."

I blinked, and the priest backed away, his eyes glittering. Skin slick with sweat.

Grant whispered, "Get out of here."

Father Cribari pulled a white business card from his pocket and laid it on the desk. "I'll need your answer within the hour."

He turned to the door, and this time I stepped aside. There were reasons not to. I had no idea what *Dark Mother* meant, but the man obviously knew something about me— and the boys hated his guts—which was more than enough to judge and convict.

But it was not the right moment. Not a good opportunity for truth.

Father Cribari moved past me without a glance, opened the door, and walked out—though he paused, just slightly, in the hall. Looking around with a wariness that made me think he was afraid of meeting one particular old woman. I hoped Mary found him and stuffed some of her brownies down his throat.

He left the door open. I listened to his footsteps fade, then reached out and closed the door. I locked it, but did not turn to face Grant. I stared at the brass knob, thinking hard. All my secrets were shit.

"Maxine," Grant said.

I tasted blood. "Who was he?"

"A long arm." The desk creaked, and I glanced over my shoulder, watching as Grant eased himself onto the hard surface with a sigh. He laid his cane beside him and started kneading his bad leg. "He would have been an Inquisitor in another life."

"He still is. That man wants you dead."

"He already tried that. He thinks I work for the devil."

"Well," I said with a faint smile. "Mostly they work for you."

Grant also smiled, but it was wry and tired. "I have to go. Doesn't matter who asked."

"Ross," I said quietly. "He was a good friend?"

"My best," Grant replied, but with little happiness. "He was the only one I told, the man I confessed to, about my . . . ability."

That surprised me. I could recall, with perfect clarity, the first night I had met Grant, when he had told me about a fragment of his life, how he had been driven from the Church. A friend had betrayed him. A friend he had confided to—who had feared what Grant could do instead of embracing it.

"Grant," I began, but he shook his head.

"I have to go," he said. "Never mind the past. Father Ross was not a man capable of murder, let alone torture. If he did commit such acts . . ."

Grant did not finish, but there was no need. When a good man went bad, without warning or explanation, there were few reasons why such a thing could happen. Possession was one of them. Demons. Zombies. The kind of creature now asking for Grant. Maybe.

I sat on top of the desk beside him. "You know this is a trap."

"Antony wasn't lying about Father Ross, but his aura *was* dark. Not demon dark, but almost as bad. Full of conflict. Unease. It was worse around you. You scared him."

I scared a lot of people, but hearing that I made Father Cribari squirrelly did not tickle me as much as it should have. "What does *Dark Mother* mean?"

"I'm not certain. But he knows too much." Grant flashed me a hard look. "Did I lead him to you, Maxine?"

"No," I said, and meant it. "I need to have another conversation with him."

He smiled, without humor. "Leave some pieces for me."

"Spoilsport." I drummed my fingers against his hip, feeling the boys toss gently in their dreams; like a soft wind, rushing through my skin. "China. Shanghai. No matter what Cribari said about your friend, it feels like he's going to a lot of trouble to drag you away from here."

"Believe it's just a coincidence?"

"That depends on what you think he really wants with you. And how much he knows about the two of us." Strangers, prying into our secrets. Strangers, knowing our secrets. I hated it.

"We'll figure it out," I finally said, holding out my pinky. A ghost of a smile touched Grant's mouth, and he snagged me with his own little finger. We shook with all the solemnity of five-year-olds, then wrestled back and forth for a moment.

"You're my Wonder Woman," he said softly. "My Amazon."

"Pied Piper," I whispered. "My best, favorite man."

He did not smile. "What happened this morning?"

Pain pulsed. I thought of the dead girl. Archie. "Same thing as always. I got there too late."

"You were hurt."

I rubbed my head. "Not worth mentioning."

Grant's frown deepened. "I was talking about your heart."

"I found the demon," I said, not wanting to discuss the bullet that had almost killed me. "I took care of it."

"Maxine," he said roughly, and his fingers grazed my brow, warm and gentle. He examined my head, parting the hair around my right temple, no doubt catching glimpses of the silver tattoos covering my scalp. I did not bother asking how he suddenly knew what had happened. Maybe my voice had told him. Maybe the bullet had punched more than my skull.

"You were shot," he said softly.

"You can tell that from my aura?"

"There's a dent around your head. Like your spirit is still suffering from the fear you felt." He peered into my eyes. "But I've never seen you afraid of a gun."

"It was close," I admitted, unable to lie. "I think I've put you in danger."

Grant's jaw tightened. "Did you see who did it?"

"No. Long range. Just before dawn. I'll put Zee and the others on the scent tonight." I nudged him in the ribs. "Business as usual."

"No, it's not." He pulled me closer, squeezing me so tight I almost ended up in his lap—which was suddenly not close enough. I twisted, straddling him, taking care not to put too much weight on his bad leg. Heat spread between us, soft and rich. I fiddled with his collar, hardly able to look past his throat, the hard line of his stubbly jaw. He smelled like cinnamon and sunlight, warm as summer stone, and my gloved hands looked very small against his tanned skin.

"I was fine before I met you," I whispered. "I was fine."

"I know," he said softly, and his lips brushed mine. "But you scare me sometimes."

I scared myself. I glanced over his shoulder at the bulging FedEx envelope and felt another pang of unease. "Are those the results?"

Grant hesitated and reached backward. "Arrived first thing this morning. I haven't . . . looked at it like I should."

"But you did look."

He gave me a wry glance. "I learned from you that prying into a mother's secrets is dangerous business."

"Oh, please," I said. "How bad can it be?"

Grant sighed, dumping the contents of the envelope across his desk. A bound manila file thumped out, along with a heavy gold necklace that slid a short distance across the battered wood surface. I was no expert on jewelry—I wore none, except for the finger armor, and that was not my choice. But the necklace in front of me was eye-catching. The metal gleamed like velvet infused with sunlight, warm and rich. Pure soft gold, the kind a person could bite down on and bend.

A pendant hung from the thick chain. A coil of lines, like a rose.

"My mother was my world," Grant said quietly, fingering the necklace. "You know she died while I was in high school, right? Cancer. Devastated my dad and me. But especially him. He didn't want to talk about her. And you know . . . you know how you never think to ask certain questions, you take everything for granted, then . . . then once that person is gone, all those things you never knew about her just keep coming at you, over and over?"

"Yes," I said. "I know."

He pushed the necklace aside and slid his fingers lightly over the folder. "I didn't do anything about it then. I don't think I ever would have, except . . ."

"What happened changed things," I finished for him, and he gave me a long, steady look that was both calm and pained.

"What happened," he agreed heavily, "when that . . . thing . . . called me that name."

Lightbringer, I thought, and imagined a tremor in the delicate armor surrounding my finger; as though a small heart fluttered, briefly. I clenched my hand in a rough fist, and heat passed through my tattooed skin.

I did not believe in the supernatural. The supernatural was fairy-tale. I dealt in reality; cold, hard facts. And one of those facts was this: More than demons walked the world. Other creatures existed, also capable of possessing human flesh.

Avatars. Manifestations of sentient energy in bodily form. Ancient beings who had done battle with the demons and built the prison veil to jail the demons—made my kind, the Wardens—and then abandoned this world for others, where the memory of battle did not cling so thick.

Not all of them had left, though. Some had stayed by choice. Others . . . not so much.

But one thing had been made clear: Avatars recognized something in Grant, something they had a name for, and it had scared one of them shitless. Or just shocked her so much it was practically the same thing. Made me feel like a pussycat in comparison. Insignificant. A mere pretender in the art of death.

I had killed that Avatar. I had destroyed her—and a part of myself—with only a touch. No choice in the matter. No way to question her about Grant. And the only other individual who knew the full truth of what my man was had disappeared like a ghost, gone now for three months.

My grandfather. Jack Meddle.

"So," I said. "The file."

"The investigator I hired was thorough."

"And?"

"And," he said, not looking at me, "my mother didn't exist before she married my dad. Not on paper, not anywhere. There's nothing, Maxine."

I hesitated. "She could have been from another country. Immigrated on the sly. Easy enough to do."

"Yes." Grant finally met my gaze. "But the investigator found old neighbors, some hospital records. According to what he uncovered, I had already been born. *Before* she was married. I was at least a year old."

Scandalous, that was not. But something in his tone made me careful. I sat in his lap, and he was tense as a blind man in a minefield, and I wanted to hold his hand, hold him tight. I waited, though, unmoving. Until he said, "I was told something different by my parents."

"Ah," I replied, and thought of all the lies my mother had told me. "So?"

"So nothing," he muttered tersely, reaching back to swipe the necklace off the desk, the chain flashing soft and golden as it draped over his wrist. "But a year is a long time, Maxine. The nine months before that even longer."

I finally understood. "Your real father might be a different man than the one who raised you."

He was so grim. "Wouldn't make a difference. It wouldn't."

But it would. Not in love, but in identity. Blood was serious business. It was good, knowing the roots of what flowed in your veins. Helped put your feet on the ground, when you had nothing, no one else to anchor your heart.

I did not know who my father was.

Grant held up the necklace and studied the gold links, the pendant sunk deep in his large palm. "I thought she was buried with this. But after my father died, it was found in his papers."

I studied the golden lines, knotted in a circle half as large as a compact disc and almost as flat, with a natural opening near the top where the chain looped through. No end, no beginning, just a tangled coil that became ever more intricate the deeper one looked; as though there were layers buried in layers, buried deeper still, despite the deceptively level shape of the disc. Made me dizzy. I had to look away, blinking hard. Grant's fingers closed around the pendant.

"First time I've seen it," I said, nauseous.

"I bring the necklace out about as often as you handle your mother's guns. Receiving those files made me want to hold it again."

I leaned in, pressing my brow against his warm, hard shoulder, trying to steady my upset stomach. "So, what now?"

"I don't know." Grant slid his fingers through my hair. "My dad . . . was normal. All business. Aggressive, ruthless. But not . . . not like me. I took after my mother. Except for . . ." He waved his hand—still holding the pendant—around his head. "If she could see what I saw, do what I did, she never let on. And I only told her . . . a little."

"You thought you were unique."

"But I'm not. Especially if what I do marks me with a name."

"Lightbringer," I whispered.

He held me closer and placed his mouth against my ear. "Not human."

I closed my eyes. "Old news, man. Join the club."

He set down his mother's necklace. "I need to find out what I am. I need more information. I've been running on instinct all this time because I thought that was all I had. I thought I was alone in what I do. But I'm going to slip one day. I'm going to do something I shouldn't. Push a mind too far. Make too big a change in some person's soul. Maybe it'll be an accident. Maybe not. But if there's someone who could teach me—"

Grant stopped, a tremor running through him. "It's in me, Maxine. The possibility of becoming what I hate. I don't . . . want to hurt people. I don't want to be the man who justifies hurting people. I don't want to be that man who believes in his own righteousness, without question."

I did not want that, either, though I had more faith in Grant than that. The boys liked him. That said a lot. If Grant did go sour, I had a feeling it would not be the end of the world. Not that I could tell him that. My own brand of callous realism was not something he particularly needed, not now. His urgency was painful—which pained me, too, because Grant was a good man. Driven, in that same spirit, never to do harm. But when you could influence, with nothing but the sound of your voice, the very integrity of a person's soul—

Well.

I reached between us, sliding my hand up his thigh. "How's your leg?"

He gave me a wry look. "Don't distract me. We still have a bullet to discuss."

"Bullet done gone and rebounded into a building," I replied, with more ease than I felt. "And it was an honest question, about your leg."

"Then it's honestly sore. Crushed bone never does heal right." He leaned in, brushing his lips over my cheek. "I need a heating pad, baby. A lawn chair on the North Rim of the Grand Canyon."

"It's probably snowing there, you know."

"With you in nothing but your tattoos."

"Because looking at demons on my breasts is such a turn-on."

"And no one," he breathed, kissing my ear, "no one for miles around."

I turned my head and kissed his mouth. Warmth slid through my heart, down to my toes. I felt catalyzed by his heat: turned over, mixed, becoming something new. His strong hands—already beneath my sweater—moved a fraction higher, his thumbs caressing me, just so; and my breath caught. I tilted back my head, arching into his touch. Aware, keenly, that feeling anything at all was due to the good graces of Zee and the others.

Bothered me, sometimes. I had never had privacy in my life. But a person could get used to anything. Almost.

I wanted him to forget. *I* wanted to forget. I wanted something better to remember than bullets and zombies and dead girls. I wanted to be free and warm, and human.

I brushed my lips over his cheek, and reached for the zipper of his jeans.

CHAPTER 4

I could not fly in an airplane; that much was clear. Not a commercial aircraft, and probably not even a private one. Airplanes were dangerous territory. Short flights, I suspected, would be all right—but long international travel, the kind that crossed date lines where the sun rose and set while you were in the air, might prove disastrous. The boys woke when the sun went down. Peeled straight off my body, hungry and ready for trouble. Simple as that. No matter where, or how inconvenient it might be.

Nor did I have time to arrange the proper documentation for a visit to China. A quick search on Google made that perfectly clear. I had a passport, but no visa. Grant's luck was better, if more dubious. Due to whatever influence Father Cribari had brought to bear on his contact in the local Chinese embassy, Grant would have his visa within hours as opposed to days. He was scheduled to fly to Shanghai late that morning. Which meant I had less than the wink of an eye to come up with a solution.

Luckily, I had one. If I could find him.

But first, that bullet. I needed some answers. Confirmation, if nothing else. Which led me on a circuitous path through the homeless shelter, searching for a zombie.

I found Rex in the basement. Years ago the warehouses that made up the Coop had been used in the manufacture of furniture. Most of the old equipment had been cleared away, but the lower levels—off-limits to everyone but a handful—still housed an array of mysterious and elaborate iron machines whose purpose, I was sure, could not be nearly as remarkable as what I preferred to imagine (which was that some genius inventor had made his home in this concrete tomb and assembled, in wild fits of mental operatic fury, his own collection of devices meant to change the world into an odder place than it already seemed to be).

The basement smelled like damp concrete and motor oil. My cowboy boots were loud on the floor, and Dick Van Dyke's voice echoed merrily through the shadows; the *Mary Poppins* sound track, Chim-Chim-Chereeing against steel pipes and iron gears. I followed the music to a room that was a good distance from the stairs, watching shadows move through the light that spread from the crack around the half-closed metal door.

I peered inside. First thing I saw was row after row of racks holding wooden flatbed containers filled with soil and careful rows of small green plants. Sunlamps hung haphazardly from chains and ropes strung from the ceiling. In the aisles, on the floor, were some very pretty rag rugs—homemade, I knew—and several cardboard crates piled high with brightly colored yarn and bolts of cloth.

I heard muttering beneath Dick Van Dyke's voice. Choice expletives. I pushed open the door a little more and saw a dark aura thundering above a bowed brown head covered in a red knit cap. Grizzled hands flexed, and a tool belt hung low around narrow hips.

The zombie was watching Mary, who seemed completely oblivious to his presence. She was singing along with the music, barefoot, standing on her toes as she carefully, and with a great deal of affection, watered her marijuana. She had pulled back her wild white hair, stuffing it into a bun, and her arms were bare. No trace of fat, just sinew and bone. Old track marks covered her pale skin. Grant had found Mary in an alley, years ago, almost dead from an overdose. Nursed her back to health. The old woman had never left. I wasn't certain she could.

"Jesus Christ," Rex muttered. "Holy fucking shit."

"Yes," I said, surveying the illegal growth. "Remarkable how this happens."

Rex turned, giving me a dirty look—though his aura betrayed his fear, flaring in all directions like rockets powered the shadows in his soul. He was the oldest of the zombies who had come to be converted by Grant—oldest, in that his parasite was old—and while I distrusted the idea that any demon could willingly desire a change in its nature, I was convinced of this zombie's devotion to Grant. For now, that was enough to let him live.

"I just found this new stash," Rex said, like he thought I would try to blame him. Make good, finally, on my longstanding threat to exorcise the shit out of him and feed his writhing body to the boys.

"Last week it was the south side of the basement," I replied mildly, watching Mary, who was now singing along with the always-melancholy melody of "Feed the Birds." "Any clues yet to where she's getting all the equipment?"

"Fuck," muttered the zombie. "Take your pick. Just one of her harvests could pay for an army of little helpers."

"No one else has been down here. I'm certain of it."

"Whatever." Rex rubbed his jaw, aura settling; assured, maybe, that he was not going to immediately meet his end. "If the police ever find out, Grant's ass will burn. All of us will."

"No one would blame Grant," I said, but I knew that was not the point. Grant loved Mary. He had saved her life. If she went to prison for selling drugs, it would hurt him in ways I did not want to contemplate. Problem was, Mary and marijuana were like conjoined twins: where one was, so was the other, no matter how impossible. The woman loved her weed.

Mary still ignored me. I thought about all the effort it had taken to get rid of her last harvest, and sighed. "Someone tried to shoot me this morning."

Rex laughed. "Lovely. Did it make you feel closer to your mother?"

I punched him. He staggered to one knee, clutching his face. I bent close and, in a loud, sickly-sweet voice, said, "Wow. Those migraines are really bothering you, huh?"

"Bitch," Rex murmured.

"Don't fuck with me," I whispered. "I want to know if a demon was responsible."

"I don't know," he snapped, staggering to his feet—one hand pressed to his face. "Doubtful. The smart ones all left town, and no one else would dream of trying that stunt. None of us could get away with—" Rex stopped, staring. "They got *away* with it?"

"They just think they did," I snapped, still peeved about his remark concerning my mother. "So if it wasn't one of you, then who?"

There was a gleam in his eye I did not like. "Nothing large has escaped the prison. Not recently. And anything powerful enough to break through those walls wouldn't use a bullet to kill you."

I'd already had a sense of that. I would have felt a crack in the prison veil if a demon larger than a parasite had come through. "And before my time? Something already here?"

"There were some breaks from the outer rings of the veil. But that was centuries ago. Again, a bullet would not be their style. Too human."

Demons did not lie. Even if the zombie had told an untruth, I would see it in the shadows of his aura, which remained steady, unflinching.

I thought of Cribari, though the idea of humans hunting me was more disturbing than a demon. "You ever heard about anyone in my bloodline being called *Dark Mother*?"

"No. But all you bitches do is breed and kill. That's plenty dark."

"Mouthy little parasite," I replied. "I bet you wouldn't like that body so much if it was missing its tongue."

His aura flared, though his expression remained flinty. "Try another one. You don't harm hosts. Not like that. And you won't kill me because that would mean breaking your word to Grant. You won't even exorcise me, because I would just find another body to inhabit. No-win situation, Hunter."

"We'll see," I said, looking past him at Mary, who had finally stopped watering her plants and now studied me with that piercing, farseeing gaze that was all kinds of crazy and sane and otherworldly; a mixed bag for a mixed-up mind. She took a step toward me and held out her hand.

On her palm, in ink, was an exact drawing of the pendant Grant had shown me only an hour before: his mother's necklace, etched in neat coils and knots, tumbling into eternity upon her pale skin. My vision blurred. I swallowed hard, gut churning like I was riding a roller coaster on a full stomach.

"Iron hearts make murder," I heard her say, though her voice sounded very far away. "Those who eat sin will be cast away and burned."

The boys rippled. A chill raced through my bones. I said, "Mary," and she shook her head, folding her hand into a fist that she pressed above her heart.

"We are lost in the Labyrinth," she whispered, closing her eyes. "We are lost."

⥥

DEMONS were not of earth, any more than a comet might be. Demons had journeyed to this world, as had the Avatars. As had humans, though I still questioned that particular revelation.

Either way, the method for reaching this planet had not involved space travel—though it had involved travel through space. A particular space.

The Labyrinth.

I still did not understand, not fully. I could not bring myself to imagine the possibilities. Other worlds, doorways into alternate realities. A maze of interdimensional highways bound together by a neutral zone—a crossroad between here and there—a place of possibilities that was a world unto itself. Or so I had been told. I had traveled through only a fragment: a prison, a place where souls were thrown to be forgotten. I had fallen into the Wasteland. Walked the dark side of the Labyrinth.

I had forgotten myself there. Forgotten everything. Buried alive. Nothing but a heartbeat in the endless dark.

According to Jack, I was the only person ever to escape the Wasteland. And though I knew, intellectually, that the Labyrinth was much more than that dark, endless hole, I could not help but associate one with the other. Because even if you fell into the good side of the Labyrinth, you might find yourself lost, forever. Wandering from your world to another, and another: a stranger, eternally in a strange land. Abandoned in the maze.

As Mary had been abandoned. Elsewhere, far from this world. Only she knew how or why it had happened, or where she was from, but it was enough that she was here. Grant called her an Alice who had fallen through the rabbit hole. Like fairy tales told, of men and women who discovered hidden hills, or magic stones; or fell asleep, only to find a hundred years had slipped by. Time passed differently in the Labyrinth. Everything did. And not everyone who stumbled through its doorways was human.

The demons had used the Labyrinth to slip from one world to another, again and again, harvesting human lives that had begun elsewhere. Following trails of flesh. Until, ten thousand years ago, they had come to earth—and this planet had become the last stand between the demons, Avatars, and humans. As it would be again, when the veil failed. We were all alien in our origins, our roots and blood soaked in worlds I could not dream existed.

I tried questioning Mary about the drawing on her hand

but gave up when she turned away, floating on her toes like an aged ballerina, and started singing *Mary Poppins*'s "A Spoonful of Sugar." I left Rex to handle her, and the marijuana. My mother was probably turning in her grave. A Hunter, working with a zombie, trusting a zombie to be left alone with a human. I was so far removed from everything I had been taught, I hardly knew myself anymore.

I had friends now. I had a man I loved. I no longer lived in my car or in hotels scattered across North and South America. I was making roots, day by day, and never mind my concerns that I was doing the wrong thing.

Because if I was here, in this city, no one else was *out there*. On the road. Traveling from city to city to save the day like some ball-busting, demon-hunting crime fighter (a one-girl *A-Team*, I liked to imagine). No matter if running around two continents like a chicken with its head cut off had been, in retrospect, the least productive way to save this world from the impending failure of the prison veil. Never mind that there was only one of me, and all I could do was scratch an itch on the toe of a giant. At least I had been doing *something*. I had saved some lives. Changed a few for the better. Small consolation for knowing that I was going to spend my entire life mostly alone. And die young, murdered. In front of my own child.

I had no illusions. No way out. I would have a daughter one day. Eventually, the boys would abandon me for her—as they had abandoned my mother. When that happened, I would die. Perhaps shot in the head, just like her.

Nor was going childless an option. My blood belonged to Zee and the boys. My body, their immortality—their only connection to this world. If I died, *they* would die. If I never had a child, they would die with me. The boys would never let that happen. They had survived for more millennia than even I could guess, and part of that existence had been upon the bodies of my ancestors—a line of women stretching so far in the past I could not dream their existence beyond my mother and grandmother: a steely-eyed woman murdered six years before my birth.

My only consolation was that the boys would remember me—in dreams, of women dead and buried and turned to dust. But that did not make the melancholy any less. That did not make me stop missing my mother. Even now, with Grant in my life.

Nor did it make my choices any less difficult. I still hunted demons, here in Seattle. Tried my best to save people. But it felt wrong not to be on the move. Like a sin. A crime. My mother's voice, always in my head, telling me I was doing something infinitely wicked by staying more than one night in any city. *Move, move now.* Or invite yet more pain.

Bad enough that I didn't know what to do about the prison veil. How to stop it from failing, how to save this world. I had no plan. No answers.

And I needed some. Fast. But not just about that.

I found Byron in the hall when I walked out of the basement stairwell. The door was kept locked from the outside. Mary did not have a key, but changing the locks once a month did little to deter her. Smart crazy woman.

The teen leaned against the wall, his eyes cold and dark, and his mouth tense. I had a feeling he had been waiting for a while.

"There's a pervert here to see you," he said.

"Well," I replied, after a moment. "Introduce me."

He led me down the winding corridors to the lobby of the homeless shelter, what had once been the corporate entrance of the furniture company. Old-time elegance was in the details: a mosaic in the expansive tile floors, dark wood trim, and stained glass in the windows alongside the oak door. A small office was visible through two archways divided from the lobby by staffed desks screwed into the floor. One desk was to check in folks who wanted to use the shelter—and the other was part of a help center where men and women could make appointments to meet with volunteers about jobs, housing, and educational opportunities.

The check-in line did not open until after three in the

afternoon, but there was a good crowd in front of the help desk. I saw one of the zombies from breakfast making an appointment. He did not notice me, but Archie Limbaud's face flashed before mine, as did his victim's. Little girl lost. I swallowed hard, tearing my gaze from the zombie. Wondering if he had ever forced his host to murder.

Byron did not need to point out the pervert. I saw him as soon as I entered the lobby. He sat on a wooden bench, alone, eating a hot dog and peanuts. Dressed in a tan suit and wrinkled blue dress shirt that strained over a round stomach. A loosened striped tie hung around his neck, silk, stained with ketchup. He was bald on top, and his glasses were dirty. So was his chin. He ate violently. Each bite looked strong enough to tear a steel pipe in half. Peanuts mashed around his mouth, which I saw clearly because he continued shoving food between his teeth before everything had been swallowed.

"So," I said to Byron, as we stood on the other side of the lobby. "I can't imagine you struck up a conversation of your own free will."

"I was around the office. I heard him talking. He wanted the woman in charge, so I volunteered to find her."

"You thought of me?"

He shrugged, scrutinizing the stranger with a cold, hard stare that belonged to a war-torn veteran, not a teenage boy. "I used to know men like him."

"Not anymore," I murmured grimly, and pushed past the boy to walk across the lobby.

Pervert or not, the man was gross—and not just because of the remnants of a hot dog greasing his lips. An indefinable *something* was wrong with him, and his pale, bulging body made me imagine cockroaches, millions of them, swarming under his straining skin. He studied my feet as I approached, then the rest of me, small blue eyes wrinkling into slits behind the dirty lenses of his wire-rim glasses.

"Ah," he said, around a mouthful of hot dog and peanuts. "My Lady."

His tone was surprisingly elegant. I tilted my head, searching his gaze. "Someone said you were looking for me?"

"Across eternity," he replied, wiping his mouth with his tie. "And eternity has become *now*. Lovely how that works, is it not?"

Zee rippled between my breasts, struggling in his dreams. I hesitated. "Who are you?"

"You may call me Mr. King. Mr. *Erl* King, if you will." The man heaved himself off the bench, bits of peanut falling to the floor. Ketchup still smudged the side of his mouth, and he held out one hand for me to shake. His palm looked greasy, sticky and red. He smelled like onion and nuts.

I did not take his proffered hand. His smile widened, though it was tight-lipped, without a hint of teeth. He let his hand linger between us for a moment longer, then dropped it into his pocket. I thought, *Gun*, but what he pulled out was a wax parcel, which he quickly unwrapped to reveal a small pizza pocket. It looked cold, but he clamped down his jaws upon the soft crust, and red sauce flowed around his mouth like blood.

Mr. King closed his eyes, sighing as he chewed. I stood, watching him. Waiting. Waiting for something to break. He was ready to break, though there was nothing brittle about him. Just a load of dynamite stuck in a dam. Fuse lit.

"Well," he said finally, around a mouthful of pizza. "This was most pleasant."

And like that, he turned on his heel and shuffled away, toward the front door—parts of his body wiggling in opposite directions, as though those insects I imagined still fought to be free. I stared, and followed.

Mr. King was already outside when I caught up. I did not touch his shoulder, but matched his pace so that we walked down the steps, side by side. I said, "You had a reason for coming here."

He glanced sideways at me and poked the last of the

pizza pocket into his mouth. Chewing did not stop him from speaking, which was a wet, red, and messy affair. "Merely to see how things stand, to remind myself that worlds may change, but some things stay the same. Like you."

Again, he wiped his mouth with his tie and stopped to look me square in the eyes. He was quite short and had to gaze up, teetering as he did on his toes. I did not move under his scrutiny, not even to blink—as though that would reveal some insufferable weakness. Instead, I studied him in turn, forcing myself to stay calm even as my heart began to race. Zee shuddered against my skin; all the boys did. Fighting to wake. Hate curling in their dreams.

Gross little man, I thought, suddenly. *Do not touch me.*

His tongue slipped over his lips, licking them. Hungry, piggish eyes blinked once, slow and drowsy. The scent of onions suddenly reminded me of blood, and it was too easy to imagine that the stains around his mouth had little to do with tomato sauce.

Mr. King pulled a piece of red licorice from his pants pocket and jammed it halfway into his mouth. Again, without another word he turned and walked away, accompanied by the sound of his teeth smashing candy.

I stood, watching him go. Then followed. This time from a distance. I let a Dumpster come between us, just for a moment, but when I rounded the corner, the man had disappeared. Gone clean away, on a street that was empty except for two parked cars in the distance, and a ramshackle line of chain-link fences so battered the next rainstorm might bring them down.

I checked the inside of the Dumpster, but Mr. King had not stashed himself inside. He was gone. Into thin air. Except for the scent of onions.

I stood very still, thinking about that, and after a minute got some young company. Both of us stayed quiet, until finally I lied. "He didn't seem to want anything."

Byron replied, "Men like him always want something. Some just take longer to get around to it. Depending on how much they think they'll have to pay." He glanced at me with red-rimmed eyes. "Or how hard they sense you'll fight not to give them what they want."

"Byron," I said.

"But sometimes," he continued, whispering. "Sometimes a fight is what turns them on."

CHAPTER 5

I lived above the homeless shelter with Grant. His loft was accessible via a private outer door and one long staircase—steep for a man who could hardly walk without a cane. He said it was good exercise. Whatever.

The door stood open at the top of the stairs. Golden sunlight raced through immense windows, chasing the floors with heat. I entered the apartment and felt washed in warmth, steeped in light like dry tea leaves dropped in miracle water. Expanding, growing, shedding flavors—becoming more, and more, myself. Bookshelves lined the walls, crowding paintings and hanging masks, while a grand piano held court in the corner, along with guitars and a table heavy with half-made flutes. My own belongings were there: my mother's trunk, her leather jacket, hanging on the arm of the couch.

I loved this place. Made me feel safe, in ways I had forgotten since my mother's death. I was an impossible woman to hurt. A hard woman to kill. But that did not mean I had ever felt safe: safe in the heart, safe in spirit. Not for a long time.

Flute music floated from the spare bedroom, swelling high and sweet. *Peer Gynt,* I thought. My mother had taken me, years ago, to see James Galway perform—and while I could not say that Grant was the man's equal in technique, the soft power in each of his notes carried so true and pure it was as if every breath pulled me close, easing the sores in my soul.

And yet, I was immune to his power. Zee and the boys were, as well. I had found no one else who could resist him. Demons could possess, overpower—but not affect the human soul, or consciousness. Those were simply buried. Grant had no such boundaries. He could rearrange the colors of the spirit to make something new.

Which he did, regularly, in bits and pieces. Healing broken hearts, mending mental fissures. Small and profound acts that sent people away better, more capable, more hopeful.

My mother, my grandmother—every woman in my bloodline—would have killed him for the things he could do. For what he could make demons—and humans—do. His potential was dangerous. His potential terrified.

But no worse than mine.

Mary was with Grant. Sitting on the edge of the bed with her eyes closed and spine straight—ankles crossed demurely. Her hands rested in her lap. I could not see her palm. Grant sat opposite her, near the door, his golden Muramatsu flute pressed to his lips. He nodded when he saw me, and a moment later the melody faded. Mary did not stir, and I had to look close to make certain she breathed.

Grant slid his flute into the case slung across his back; like sheathing a sword, which he did with reverence and appropriate seriousness. I grabbed his hand and pulled him from the chair. He was pale, with faint shadows under his eyes. I had seen that sick weariness on his face more often than not. He told me that using his gift did not tire him, but I had a feeling he had been hedging the truth.

He took his cane and limped from the room. Mary

remained unmoving, as though in a trance. I closed the door behind us.

"She show you her hand?" I asked.

Grant rubbed the back of his neck. "I went looking for you in the basement. She could hardly contain herself."

"Had she seen your mother's necklace before?"

"No." A grim smile touched his mouth. "Funny how that works."

Hilarious. I was in stitches. "She give you any explanation?"

"She mentioned the Labyrinth." Grant limped toward the bedroom, and I saw through the open door a small carry-on suitcase on the bed. I followed him, watching how his knuckles turned white around the cane, and listened to the hard pound of wood against wood, which was louder than usual. "She started sobbing. I brought her up here to see if I could calm her down enough to talk. So far, nothing."

Grant stood in front of the bed, gazing down at the suitcase as if it were a live snake. I said, "You can still change your mind."

"I need to do this," he replied heavily.

"Not just for Ross."

He glanced at me. "I left the Church in a bad way. Forced out. I wasn't ready. I believed in my calling. Like being married to someone you love with all your heart, then waking up one morning to find them looking at you like you're filth, the most disgusting thing that ever crawled. Destroyed me. Then I got better. But seeing Cribari again, hearing about Ross . . ."

I stripped off my gloves. Took his hand. "You still have issues, man."

"A few," he said wryly, and turned over my palm, staring at the glittering veins of organic metal that wound through the scales and flattened claws of my tattoos. Red eyes glittered from my palm, staring at Grant, and a faint purr of pleasure rumbled against my skin. Grant kissed my hand.

"I'm not sorry they kicked you out," I said quietly, heart aching for him. "But I'm selfish."

He smiled, and squeezed my hand with that gentle strength, which always made my eyes burn at the most unexpected moments. Like now.

Grant said, "I'm worried about leaving you, Maxine. I've got a bad feeling."

"Told you, I'm coming along."

"You haven't said how."

"I think you know.

He gave me a long, steady look. "And you're sure?"

"Grant," I said quietly. "I've never had answers. I just do what has to be done. Same as you."

"Same as me," he murmured, and then: "You need me. You need someone to watch your back."

"Trust me, I'm covered."

"Ha," he said. "You're afraid. Ever since this morning, you've been afraid."

"No."

Grant's fingers tightened. "Bad liar."

I shoved his hand away. "Don't look at me."

He grabbed me again, but this time it was a fistful of my hair. It did not hurt, but the way he did it, the intensity of his gaze, shocked me into stillness.

"I love you," he said, dragging me so tight against him I could hardly breathe. "You're an easy woman to love, Maxine, but you're a hard one to be around. Because of this. Because the world hurts you, and I can't stop it. Because I know . . . I know we won't have fifty years. Maybe not even twenty, or ten, or one." Grant leaned in, and I felt swallowed by the pain in his eyes; a mirror to mine, that I had never voiced, never dared say out loud.

"You're going to leave me," he whispered. "By choice, or by death. And maybe . . . maybe you'll leave someone behind. Someone we'll make together. But you'll still be gone, and you don't know . . . you don't *understand*—"

I placed my hand over his mouth before he could say

another word. I understood. I knew. I had been the one left behind.

I said, "We have time."

Grant closed his eyes. "I want time. But I want something more, Maxine. I want to protect you. I want you to let me help you. Because I'm not going to let you die. When the boys leave you—when they abandon you for your daughter—I'm not going to give up. I'm not going to say good-bye. Not like that. You're not going to be like the others in your family. I want you to die an old woman, with me. In our bed. In my arms. Your heart's going to give out, Maxine, but it'll be when you're ready. And not because a demon put a bullet in your brain."

I stared, stricken. No idea I cried until I blinked, and tears rolled down my cheeks. I started to wipe them away, but Grant kissed my face, and his thumb brushed my skin, and my heart pounded so hard I could not breathe.

"Maxine," he murmured, in my ear. "Don't cry."

Don't die. Not before me, I replied silently; and sniffed hard, rubbing my nose. "You go. I'll be there. We'll take care of this together."

He hesitated. "You thought it was a trap."

"Still do. So go, or don't—but not because you're worried about me. Otherwise, you'll always wonder. You'll regret. And regrets . . . can turn to resentment." I forced a smile, trying to be light. "You talk about wanting me all old and wrinkly, but let's try to get there without you wishing you'd done things different."

Grant shook his head. His cheeks were flushed, the skin around his throat mottled. Eyes bloodshot. He swept my hair from my face, his palm lingering over my temple, where I had been shot. Whether he touched me there on purpose, or by accident, I could not tell—but the heat of his hand was a comfort.

"Stubborn," he said. "If something happens?"

"I'm hard to kill," I replied dryly. "You're just flesh and bone. Frankly, I'm more worried about you."

"I feel obligated to remind you that I am a grown man, and not without some ability to take care of myself."

"You're very capable."

A bemused smile touched his mouth. "Say it like you mean it."

"I mean it," I said. "Any of those priests even sniff at you wrong, you fuck them over until they see Jesus."

Grant laughed quietly. "Yes, ma'am."

Behind us, the bedroom door creaked open. Mary walked out, but her eyes were still closed. She moved upon her toes like a dancer, and the poodles of her shapeless dress swirled around her pale, hairy, sinewy legs. She never opened her eyes, but I thought she must be looking at us through her lashes, because she took an unerring path directly toward us, and stopped only an arm's length away.

She reached out. Grant took her hand. I hesitated, and then did the same, gingerly. Trying to be gentle. I was not good at healing. I had no gift for setting things right. Just tearing apart. Hunting for the good kill.

She made a low, grunting noise, and her voice slurred from her chest, deep and slow as fat molasses.

"Grant," she murmured. "You're going to die."

I froze. "Mary."

But the old woman said nothing else. We stared at her, and I felt sick to my stomach, sick to death. Proclamations of doom were nothing new, but there was something in the way Mary voiced the words that felt worse than a promise, as though there was truth in her insanity, a taste of some fate that had already come to pass—only, I had not yet realized it.

"Well," Grant muttered. "I feel good about this trip."

⊰⊱

I drove him to the airport. SeaTac smelled like gas, stale air, and despair—all poured into a concrete bunker. Not much different from prison.

I stayed long enough to see him through security. Cribari

had already left on a different flight. I was glad Grant wouldn't have to sit next to the creep, but that was cold comfort.

It was raining again when I left the airport. Low clouds, gray as old socks. I kept the window down. Tina Turner burned through the radio. I jacked up the volume as she wailed about not needing another hero. *Mad Max,* I thought. Loner, man with no mission but survival. Still managing to be a cop and do-gooder, even in the apocalypse. My mother had made me watch those movies. She said he was a good role model. I honestly could not disagree.

I did not drive back to the Coop. I needed to think, but we had left Mary in the apartment, and I had nowhere else to go. The Mustang was as much my home as any other: shelter, mobility, music—better than four walls, any day. And yet, for one moment I felt as lonely as I had in years; homesick, for something I could not name. In some ways, it had been easier without people in my life. I had gotten used to it after my mother's death. I'd had no expectations. I had forgotten the difference.

I thought of Grant sitting alone in the airport, traveling to help a man who had betrayed him—and squeezed the steering wheel until Raw and Aaz seemed ready to pop from my knuckles. I had to strip off my gloves. The leather felt too tight, as though I were suffocating through my hands.

Tattoos glittered in the dull morning light. I flexed my fingers, and suffered the rubbing heat of the iron armor covering my ring finger. The metal had chameleon qualities; earlier, before dawn, its surface had been bright as a mirror; silver, sharp, and keen. Now, though, it had faded dark and soft as my skin, and was etched with scales and roses, resembling the boys, or the lines of a labyrinth. The armor seemed to draw in light, blending with my tattoos until it was difficult to see where one began and the other left off. I could almost pretend the armor did not exist, so sweetly did it rest around my finger—like a cocoon, seeping through the boys as though the metal had settled roots made of silk and fire into my bones.

Sometimes, like now, I wondered if the armor *was* my finger, if it had evolved so without me realizing it, and that perhaps I was becoming some archaic medieval cyborg. I had used everything short of a chain saw to remove the damn thing, and nothing had worked. I had been told it would come off only at my death—and I believed it now. Yet another legacy. Another mystery. An object that fulfilled the desires of its bearer, but with a price.

The armor had once been much smaller, little more than a ring.

It had stopped raining. The streets were slick. I drove into downtown Seattle and ended up at Pike Place Market. It was not entirely a conscious choice. I was attracted to areas where the prison veil was thin, and the market—caught between land and sea—was thinnest of them all. Things got loose on a regular basis, though only from the first level of the veil, which housed the rats and cockroaches of the demonic race—those zombie-makers, which had crawled to the top of the food chain in the absence of their stronger brothers and sisters. When the prison failed, when their powerful brethren locked in the outer rings were let loose, those parasite bastards were going to suffer as much as humans. Not that I felt sorry for them.

I parked the Mustang on the north side of Pike Place Market and took a long walk. Just one of the crowd. I searched for dark auras, but found nothing on the crowded cobblestone street except humans dressed for a Northwest winter: fleece, jeans, those damn ugly sandals and wool socks, with umbrellas and hoods and baseballs caps to ward off the intermittent rain. Expressions grim and tired as the storm clouds hovering overhead. No one looked happy. But then, this was Seattle. Putting on a dour face was practically part of the wardrobe.

Mr. King filled my mind. I remembered his voice, wet and smacking with half-chewed food, and Byron was suddenly in my thoughts, as well.

They always want something. Some just take longer to get around to it.

I had been shot at, and nearly killed. Grant was heading for what most certainly felt like a trap, and the priest who had invited him had called me a singularly unique name. And then, that piggish little man. Coming to pay a call. To see how things stood.

All of those disparate pieces belonged together—I could feel it in my gut—but it was like having a box full of fingers, and not knowing which part of the hand I should attach them to.

I was on the south side of the market, near the big pig statue whose name I had forgotten—except for the fact that Zee and the others always wanted to eat the damn thing. Tourists all around me; and some locals. Everyone minding their own business. Cars, shops, chatter. I watched it all and suddenly felt like the only normal person in a surrealist landscape; as though the world were wavering into something peculiar and alien, while I stayed the same: outsider, unchanging, caught in time. Little more than a constant stranger.

Near me stood a tall bald man wearing dark sunglasses, an earring, and a white MSU sweatshirt. He held a little boy in one arm, a camera in the other, and when he saw me glancing in his direction, he pointed at the giant pig that other parents had plopped their crying children upon. "Would you mind?"

Zee rumbled ominously on my skin. I almost said no—wondering what, exactly, this man would say if he knew about all the demons sleeping on my body—but the kid in his arms looked at me with big blue eyes, and I was a sucker. I took the camera, and snapped some shots for them. It was another surreal moment, gazing through a lens at those smiling faces; baby bouncing and his father making little bunny ears with his fingers.

I wondered how long they would live when the prison veil failed.

I passed back the camera, waving good-bye as the man's

son continued to ride the pig, patting its head with a chubby hand and laughing delightedly. *There must be a way to stop it. You have to. It can't be hopeless.*

Some way, somehow. I had spent my life with a very narrow focus. See a demon. Kill a demon. Nothing subtle about it. Not much strategy involved. Zee and the others did all the heavy lifting.

That could not last. The stakes were higher now. I had to be smarter, faster. If I was not careful, the world was going to end while I slept in a warm bed with a warm man and pretended I was a normal girl with demons living on her skin. My mother would have been ashamed. Her daughter, the wolf, turning into a house cat.

It's not just comfort that keeps you tame, I told myself. *You fear the alternatives. You fear what you will become if you do as you must. You are afraid of the darkness that sleeps so lightly in your heart. More afraid of yourself, than the end of the world.*

True enough. But I was not simply afraid of the possibilities.

I was terrified.

I found a Starbucks on my way back to the car and bought some hot chocolate. Sat for a moment on a wet bench between wood barrels full of decorative ferns and ignored the drizzle floating down in a silver mist. The boys soaked up the water seeping through the bottoms of my jeans and sweater, and I had never minded a little rain on my face. Felt good and clean. Rain was something that never changed. Rain was part of the world, beyond human, beyond me. There was another kind of immortality in it, an agelessness that would last longer than even the boys— who were dependent solely on my bloodline for their longevity.

One day the enemy would get lucky, whether in my lifetime or the next. I wondered if my mother had suffered any close calls. I could ask the boys, but Zee and the others did not talk much about their previous hosts. Memories pained them.

I could sympathize. I was thinking about my mother when I saw a familiar MSU sweatshirt at the corner of my vision. Took a moment to register.

A moment too long. Shadows gathered. I was surrounded. Hands lifted me, and I fought, screaming, listening to the roar of a car engine. The boys thundered against my skin.

Too late. I was always too late.

CHAPTER 6

ONE night while staying in a cheap motel in Lubbock, Texas, I saw a news report on what to do if you ever got stuffed inside the trunk of a car.

People were all fired up at the time. Some big case in a town thirty miles south had started it. Four vehicles found inside a lake, girls trapped within every one of them. According to the papers, the teens had still been alive when the waters started coming in.

The security expert interviewed for the report was a pudgy white man with silver hair, a flat nose, and jowls that trembled every time he used a vowel. *Break out the taillights,* he rumbled. *Find the release lever. Better yet, be vigilant. Don't get caught. Fight like hell.*

Fine advice. Problem was, people froze. Got taken off balance. Behaved in unanticipated ways. Something I should have remembered.

Maybe if I had, I would not have been thinking of those murdered girls—four years later—and feeling ridiculously, impossibly irritated. Mostly at myself. Rocking and rolling in a small dark space with my arms and legs bound in crushing knots, a strip of duct tape over my mouth.

I was not in the trunk of a car. I was inside a box. A box that had once been a coffin, but with all the bells and whistles stripped off. Just plain wood. No silk. No other body but mine. I was hot, and the air was bad. My nose felt stuffy.

The coffin was sliding around the back of a windowless white van that I glimpsed just before being passed inside like a loaf of bread. I was a strong girl—stronger than most men—but I lost my chance to fight in the first two seconds of the attack. My fault. I had forgotten my own rule: *Expect the unexpected.* Worse, the men were professionals, and I had not dealt with many of those. Calm, fast, with an exact knowledge of what I was. No guns, no knives, no attempts to hit me over the head. No sedation. Just brute force, and nothing else.

I thought about that as I lay in the coffin. I thought about those four girls in Texas and how it had been the end of their world—the same end others faced every day, and that yet more would endure, in different and varied ways once the veil came down. I remembered the zombie who killed those girls, and the look on his face as I exorcised the demon living in his soul. I had made him a man again.

He was arrested twenty-four hours later, and after a speedy trial, given the death penalty for four murders he barely remembered committing. Quickest execution in Texas history. Up until the day he died, he claimed he was innocent. That someone had framed him.

I understood how he felt.

❊

I stayed in the coffin for a long time. Felt the day trickle down as though the movement of the sun were in my blood.

Near sunset, the van stopped moving. I heard no voices, but somewhere a door slid open. The coffin jiggled, then slammed up and down, tilting at wild angles until it felt as though I were pitching around inside a clothes dryer. I somersaulted, hovered, bounced. My stomach crawled up my throat.

I should have suffered a head wound getting so knocked around, but the boys swarmed over my face at the first skip and hop. Felt like being pushed under hot water; all five of them, stretching over my cheeks and forehead, eyes and lips. Ready for anything. Pissed off. Hungry for sunset.

The coffin finally dropped. Hit the floor so hard my teeth rattled, and the wood panels cracked. The lid had been nailed shut—as if my kidnappers could not be bothered to pay the five fucking dollars for a lock—and I listened as a crowbar was used to pry me out of the box.

I found myself in a pitch-black room. My vision was excellent in darkness. I saw men ranged around me. At least four, wearing street clothes and night-vision goggles. They smelled like cigarettes and sweat, but if any were surprised that tattoos now covered my face, no one showed it. The men were professionally unexcitable.

The coffin was upended, again—and that white MSU sweatshirt ghosted in front of me as I thudded against the floor. I smelled damp concrete. A basement scent, like I was in an old, rusty house that needed a good dose of Raid and a toxic-mold examination.

Someone began stripping off my gloves. I balled my hands into a fist, trying to stop him, and a moment later felt a knife sawing through the leather. I craned my neck, trying to see, and found the man in the MSU sweatshirt straddling me, switchblade in one hand, remains of my gloves in the other. He no longer looked like a goofy father. More like a soldier. Stone-faced, compact. The kind who shaved his head on purpose because he thought it made him a badass. He was the only one in that pitch-dark room not wearing night-vision goggles. Just his sunglasses. He seemed to see me fine.

MSU finished cutting away my gloves and barked a short, sharp word. The other men moved silently toward the single door, set beneath low, gurgling pipes—like someone was upstairs, using the water. I saw no light when they opened the door, not even a sliver. Just more darkness. No sounds but the water, and their shoes, and rough breathing.

MSU waited for the others to leave before he pushed back his sunglasses and flipped a switch in the wall. Bright lights slammed, blinding me. My eyes watered. MSU moved sideways, out of sight, and after a brief silence I heard several distinctive clicks. A camera. He was taking pictures.

The man said, "Yes, she's wearing the ring. I'm sending you the photos now."

I lay on my stomach, arms bound behind me. My right hand was in plain sight. I rolled over on my back, hiding the finger armor. The man sighed. I tried looking at him, but again he stepped away, nothing but a glimpse, a ghost.

Raw and Aaz began heating up my hands. Within seconds the wrists of my sweater singed. So did the duct tape. I smelled the faint, acrid taint of burning plastic, and gave an experimental tug. Something ripped.

"Yes," said MSU, behind me. "I've made the preparations. And thank you, again. This has been an honor."

I turned my head. Finally got a good look at the man. Nothing about him had changed. His sunglasses were on again. He closed his cell phone and shoved it into his pocket. Caught me staring, and did the same for one long moment—like he was judging me. Some Anubis with his scale, and feather, determining the lightness of my heart.

And then he stopped looking, and stripped off his sweatshirt. He wore nothing underneath except for a shoulder holster and gun. One tattoo covered his chest.

A labyrinth. Grant had been feeding my newfound fascination on the subject with as many books as he could find. The tattoo on the man's chest resembled photographs I had seen of the labyrinth at Chartres Cathedral in France: four quadrants, eleven circuits, with a rosette design at the center that resembled the four arms of the cross. Sometimes called the Road of Jerusalem, the Chartres labyrinth had meant to serve as a substitute for the actual pilgrimage, walked as part of a quest, a journey to God and enlightenment.

Somehow, I had a feeling his tattoo had a different meaning. When the man turned to toss aside his sweatshirt, I saw another design on his back: a large black cross. Maybe it was the curve of his spine, or the roll of his shoulder blades, but the icon had a sinuous, crooked quality to it that made my vision blur, and my heart give up an odd pained flutter.

The man pulled the gun from the holster. A .44 Magnum, *Dirty Harry*–style. I did not feel particularly lucky. True sunset was several minutes away, but the man placed the gun against my brow, and clicked off the safety. Sweat rolled down his chest, but his hand was steady. He was going to get it right. His timing was going to be perfect.

So was mine. I tested my bonds, and the duct tape fell apart, little more than wilted silver petals hanging from my hot wrists.

The man had no time to react. I rolled over and the gun went off, bullet skimming the side of my head as I planted my bound feet in his gut, and kicked out. He fell, cracking his skull against the side of the coffin. Not dead. Not even unconscious. But it stunned him for a precious moment while I dug my nails into the duct tape around my ankles and ripped it away.

I was free before he began to move, and pinned his throat with my hand, pressing him into the concrete floor with crushing strength—pinching the nerves of his wrist until he released the gun. I grabbed the weapon and slammed it hard into the concrete floor. Bits of it flew apart. I tossed the rest into the corner.

I ripped off the duct tape covering my mouth. Then did the same to the man's sunglasses. I wanted to see his face. I wanted to memorize it before the boys woke up and had their way.

But I got a shock.

His eyes were not human.

No whites. Just a black, inky darkness that covered his

corneas. Not contacts. Flesh and blood, full of dark life. He blinked rapidly, like a lizard, and a thin protective lid—bright as a mirror—briefly encapsulated his eyeball. I saw my tattooed reflection, distorted; then the lid rolled down, revealing once again those impossible, enormous, obsidian eyes.

"Fuck," I whispered.

He gave me a look filled with terrible scorn. I hardly noticed. Those eyes. *Jesus Christ.* Those eyes were not remotely human. Demon, maybe, but there was no taint, no dark aura. He was something else.

But man enough to fool you, I told myself. *Man enough to answer to someone else.*

Cell phone. I searched his pockets, trying to ignore his cold, reptilian gaze. Skin crawling, and not just because of the boys.

"So," I muttered, wincing as I shoved my fingers deep into his front pocket. "Who wants me dead?"

He gurgled. I was pressing down on his throat too hard, but I didn't relax. I managed to hook my fingers around his cell phone and dragged it from his pocket, thumbing immediately for his most recent calls. More water gurgled through the pipes above my head; I heard a child crying. Maybe the kid from Pike Place Market.

I found a number and hit the call button. Heard ringing, a click.

"Greetings, Franco," said a smooth male voice. "Is it done?"

Fuck no, and fuck you, I almost said, and hung up. Powered off the phone for good measure. And then smashed it into the floor, following up with my fist. Concrete cracked. So did the SIM card and the rest of the phone's components.

I did not recognize the voice on the other end of the line, but even so, I knew who was responsible for sending the man beneath me. I could take a hint. Tattoos of crosses were not exactly subtle.

"Cribari," I said slowly. "You were sent by Antony Cribari."

The man, Franco, flinched—which was confirmation enough. *Cribari.* Cribari had been responsible for having me shot at—this morning. Two good attempts to kill me. Two attempts that should never have happened. No priest, no human, should have known I existed—let alone my weakness.

Nor did the priest's involvement explain the inhuman eyes. Not in the slightest.

I shook Franco. "Why?"

Franco's mouth tightened, and his body writhed upward, trying to buck me off. I held on, grabbing his ear, and yanked his head toward mine. He grunted in pain, red-faced, sweating.

"This world is no longer yours," he hissed, silver lids briefly encapsulating his eyes. "I won't let you take my soul."

"Keep it," I snarled. "Tell me what I want to know."

He grimaced, slamming his fist into my gut. I did not budge. He wrapped his fingers around my throat, but strangling me was about as effective as tying a California redwood into knots. He tried everything to make me let go, but I was patient. It was going to be sunset soon. I had all the time in the world.

"Why?" I asked him again, when he slumped against the floor, panting. "What *are* you?"

Franco's gaze remained righteously defiant, feverishly bright. He looked at me like I was the biggest piece of shit-sin he had ever seen, and that if I did not burn straight out after dying, then at the very least I was going to be highly and hellishly uncomfortable for the rest of eternity.

He spat on me. My skin hissed. Acid in his saliva. I slapped his face so hard his lip bloodied. Behind us the door creaked open. Dim silver light poured through the room. I glanced over my shoulder, staring at the silhouettes of men, who grunted with surprise.

Franco choked out an unintelligible word, and the men rushed me. I was already low to the ground, and rammed my fist into the kneecap of the first man who came at me. Momentum did most of the work, but I also had brute strength on my side. I heard a snap, his leg bent backward, and the scream that filled the room as he went down was more animal than man.

Franco scrabbled backward. I hooked the front pocket of his jeans and used my full body weight to slam my knee into his groin. Bone crunched, and he arched upward, breath rattling in his throat.

Hands snatched at my hair. Someone kicked me in the face, striking my tattooed cheek. I felt no pain from the impact, but flew sideways, crunching into the coffin. Another boot tried to stomp on my throat. I grabbed that meaty ankle, and my attacker staggered, cursing.

I felt something hard beneath the leg of his jeans. A sheath, a knife. I yanked out the weapon and released the man. He danced away from me, eyes wary. All the men, staring, casting shadows in the dull light from the open door.

I barely saw them. I stood, swaying. All I could think of was Cribari. Alone with Grant.

Something in me broke. Inside my heart, beneath my ribs, a dark force fluttered. Familiar and cold, stirring into wakefulness; an alien entity separate from me, independent of the boys.

I had no name for it. I did not know what it was. I did not know where it had come from. But when it stirred, bad things always happened. Inside me. Around me.

No, I thought. *No, don't.*

You need us, whispered a sibilant voice, and the men in front of me suddenly seemed small in the shadows; like mice, eyes glittering. Made me smile. Hard, fierce, like there were daggers on my tongue, or death, and I fought myself. I fought so hard. Smiles did not belong here. No such thing as laughter in violence.

But I felt it. I drowned. All it took was a moment, but something rushed through me, and I knew the feeling—

like the bloom of panic, or rage. Only, this was darkness. Darkness, swelling into euphoria, stretching within my chest like a long body rising from sleep.

Hunter, whispered a sibilant, coiled voice. *We are one.*

I shuddered, unable to control myself. It was almost sunset, and I pushed up my sleeve, revealing tattoos that glimmered in the air with strikes of silver light; scales, claws, red, glinting eyes shining like chips of rubies; and though the boys were not yet smoke, they were close, so close that when they surged upon my skin, I saw them ripple; and I knew the men saw, too. I slid a knife over my arm, sharpening the blade. Feeding steel to the boys. Sparks lit the dim air. The men flinched, and choking hunger bubbled up my throat, making my heart break open like the cloud of a burning storm.

"Tell me," I whispered. "Tell me why Cribari wants me dead."

The men said nothing at first—perhaps they did not even hear me. They were too busy staring at my arm, horrified, making the sign of the cross.

Franco stirred, though, coughing. I looked down and found his cheek pressed against the tile. Saliva ran from the corner of his mouth, but his inhuman eyes were open. Gazing at the finger armor on my right hand.

"You are an abomination," he whispered, and the gloom of the basement was suddenly the dead of night, hollow and stale. "Dark Mother. Dark Lady of the Labyrinth. We are sworn against your promise."

I held up my right hand. "And this?"

"A relic that does not belong to you," he breathed, then snapped off a sharp word that sent the men moving. Guns flashed in the dull light. I felt sunset pushing—pushing close—

One of the men fired too early, the roar deafening, so much like a crash of thunder the floor trembled. The bullet bounced off my chest.

And that terrible hunger snapped.

I could not stop it. I bared my teeth, a wet rictus of a

smile that tasted of blood, and that filled me with an exhilarated terror that was rapturous and horrifying, as though it were someone else smiling, stretching beneath my skin, stretching so much I imagined seams tearing around my joints—me, rag doll. My vision blurred. I went blind. But the men—the men began to scream—and my ears worked just fine.

My entire world became those screams. The sound of them tasted like wine on my tongue, cut with the nuance of each man's voice, which broke in rising discordant rhythms that my body swallowed and swayed to, as though riding the strums of a macabre guitar. All my horror could not compensate for the delight of the creature inside me, but I fought—I fought myself as though my life depended on it—because I was going to die from those screams. Something of me was going to die when those screams *stopped*.

Please, I begged. *Please.*

The boys rumbled over my skin. My right hand burned. Light filled my vision. I could suddenly see again, but not the men. Just the finger armor: glowing, as though infused with moonlight and pearls, piercing the shadow writhing slow and easy around my heart. The light made me think of my mother—*take care, baby, take care*—and just like that, as though her memory was an antidote, the slow-coiled presence rising beneath my skin receded. Darkness, gone—but the absence felt like teeth had been pulled from my soul, leaving tender holes. My knees trembled. Chills wracked me. Going into shock.

I held my ground. Planted my feet and pretended I was stone. No more smiles. No more. I had always wondered what it would feel like to be possessed—and now, again, I had a taste.

I hated it. I hated that I could so easily be lost. Lost to nothing but myself, with no understanding, not a goddamn clue as to why, or what was inside me. My hand curled into a fist, and the light in the ring died. I finally saw the men.

They were still alive. Mostly. And I was touching them.

I had no recollection of approaching the men. No memory of laying a hand on them. Only, I stood before a pile of limbs, piles of parts still attached to bodies, and my hands were buried elbow deep into the tangled flesh. I stared, horrified. The men had collapsed together so tightly, so knotted, that for a moment it seemed as though the air had dismembered them where they stood and that they had merely dropped to the floor, as one.

But they were separate: hands twitching, heads nodding spastically. Full-bodied, strong men—still alive—but their faces were frozen in expressions of pure agony and horror, jaws open in silent screams.

I staggered, yanking free my hands. I still clutched the dagger, but the blade was turned inward, pressed flat against my forearm. No blood on the steel. I had not stabbed anyone. Just turned them into gibbering idiots with nothing but a touch.

I was going to be sick. I clutched my stomach, then my right hand—so tightly it felt like I was trying to pull free of something—maybe free of myself. The finger armor was warm through my tattoos, which were stirring, stirring. Sunset, swallowing me. Seconds, at most.

"Why?" I whispered to the men, who no longer seemed conscious of anything, save breathing, and who certainly, at this point, were beyond blame, or the ability to answer any inane question my brain vainly fixed on.

"Because you are you," said an aged, deep voice, directly behind me. "And because you bear a key to the Labyrinth."

I began to turn, but strong hands grabbed my shoulders, pulling me against a warm chest that smelled like leather and books; or the men who worked the ranches out in Montana: old cowboys, hard with dust and sunlight.

"Dear girl," whispered Jack Meddle, my grandfather. "You are in a great deal of trouble."

And then he pulled me out of the world, into the abyss.

CHAPTER 7

I remembered, in the darkness, what it felt like to be lost. I had tried to forget. I had fought to keep my dreams clean of the Wasteland, the endless night of the Labyrinth oubliette. And though I knew—*I knew*—this was not the same, something else in me died when Jack dragged me into the abyss. Consumed by the void, stripped of sight and sound and touch. Hovering like a long heartbeat, reduced to a thud of muscle and blood. Fighting not to scream.

Until the moment broke. I returned to the world, slipping from the dark into silver shadows, and found my body, and breath, and swallowed my voice before my pride broke, as well.

I fell. My knees hit snow-patched grass, packed hard and wet, crunching beneath me like a soft mash of bone. It was full night, with a hook of a moon in the sky. Hours ahead of schedule.

Sun down, sun gone. The boys woke up.

It hurt. My skin burned. My heart shimmered into fire. Like being swallowed naked down a throat full of barbs and acid. My gloves were lost, and all I could see as I bowed my head were my hands as tattoos dissolved into black smoke, sparking with glints of red lightning—flaying me from my toenails to the roots of my hair. I could not breathe. I could not make a sound.

The boys ripped free. No beginning, no end. Just a weight that gathered on my shoulders, a sliding heat from sinuous bodies unfolding as though they were petals dripping with lava. Claws scraped. Whispers pattered. In small pieces, the pain eased.

Hard not to shake. I remembered the first time the boys awakened from my body—the night after my mother's murder, the night after my first inheritance—and it was always that night, again and again.

"Maxine," whispered Zee. "Sweet Maxine."

My mouth was too dry for words. Cold pinched through my thin sweater. I had not dressed for snow, had not anticipated such a quick fall into night, somewhere else, where the temperature felt like true winter. Snow stung my palms, and a stiff breeze yanked against me like a chain of ice. Had the sun been up, I would have felt nothing of the cold, but my skin was vulnerable now. I was human again. Until dawn.

"Maxine," said Zee again, breath stirring hot against my cheek. I looked up. Met a solemn gaze, red as rubies buried in tumbled steel, steel that was skin the color of soot smeared with silver and veins of mercury.

Raw and Aaz appeared: twins, little hunters. Steam drifted from the rakish spines of their wild hair, razor-sharp as the rest of their skin. Less than a minute upon waking, and they had already been busy. Metal flashed between Aaz's claws. He held up a brace of knives. Small daggers sheathed in a custom shoulder holster. My mother's weapons of choice, stored in her oak trunk back in Seattle. I was stupid not to have worn them earlier, but carrying those blades against my body felt like trespassing, sometimes. Or like I was too much of a kid again. Not grown-up enough to handle the sharp stuff.

Raw slid around his brother, holding another of her

belongings: a battered leather jacket and her gloves, the soft black leather laced with steel.

Seeing her things made the tight knot in my heart unwind, just a little. I needed my mother right now. I needed to feel her around me. I planted quick kisses on Raw and Aaz, while Zee pushed close for a hug. Dek and Mal hummed a Bon Jovi classic: "I'll Be There for You."

"My boys," I whispered. "You wonderful boys."

Zee looked past me, dragging his claws through the snow. "Meddling Man."

I looked over my shoulder, but did not see Jack. There were no lights, except for the grace of the moon. I saw the bones of a broken, slumping Ferris wheel, and a battered merry-go-round that had been stripped of horses, leaving nothing but cracked mirrors and chipped wood. Collapsed tents had been abandoned in the dirt, and an iron cage stood with the door propped open. Nearby, torn apart, was half a crate with a clown's face painted on the side, grinning from ear to ear. Felt like I was inside the corpse of a circus.

"Find him," I said to the boys, throat aching. "Now."

Zee snapped his claws. Raw and Aaz disappeared into the shadows, while Dek and Mal poked free of my hair, testing the air with their tongues. I scratched their heads, grateful for the warmth of their bodies, and began stumbling through the snow, shrugging on the shoulder holster and my mother's coat. Zee loped ahead of me.

Near the decaying remains of a battered wagon—wheels missing, wood siding ripped away and pocked with bullet holes—I heard the sounds of someone vomiting. I broke into a run.

I found Jack on his knees in the snow. Suffered a rush to my head, a roar of blood in my ears. I skidded to his side, breathless. Raw and Aaz were already there, peering at Jack from beneath the wagon. Somewhere, somehow, they had found time to reach into another part of the world for a bag of popcorn and two Yankee baseball caps, which they wore at identical slants upon their heads. Punks.

"Old Wolf," I whispered, sliding behind the man. I wrapped my arms around his chest and drew him back against me, trying to share my warmth; to hold him; to assure myself he was alive. Alive, and still with me.

My hand grazed the side of his face, and lingered. "You're burning up."

He tried to bat me away, and slumped forward again in the snow to retch.

"It's nothing," he said hoarsely, seconds later. "I'm not . . . made . . . for cutting space. In fact, I'm so ill equipped for this method of transportation I find it easier to pretend it doesn't exist at all."

"Yes, well," I muttered, snapping my fingers at Zee, who gave Raw and Aaz a dirty look before disappearing into the shadows. "I had no idea you were capable of . . . whatever that was. Though if you did have to make yourself sick, you should have transported us to your apartment."

"*That* would have been a supremely poor idea." Jack slumped sideways into the snow, and I fell with him, still trying to protect his body from the cold air. He grabbed my hand and held it over his chest. I buried my face, briefly, against his shoulder. Savoring the hard, quick thump of his stolen human heart.

"I'm a wanted man, my dear," said my grandfather quietly. "And so, I'm afraid, are you and Grant."

❧

ZEE brought back a tent. Given the sleeping bags and thong underwear I found when I poked my head inside, I had a feeling it had recently been in use. I looked back over my shoulder, staring at the little demon. He shrugged.

"Left them a car," he rasped.

"How magnanimous of you," Jack murmured, crawling into the tent, which was only several degrees warmer than outside. He fell on his side with a sigh and flicked away the thong underwear with both idle curiosity and distaste. "And how good to leave us this slingshot with which to hunt for our dinner."

"Yes," I said dryly. "I'll go now and take down a deer with it."

Jack rolled over on his back. I lay on top of the other sleeping bag, a headache pricking the base of my neck, spreading upward into my scalp. Dek and Mal wound through my hair and began pressing their tiny claws against my head. Little masseuses. One of my ancestors had studied briefly with a master of acupuncture. Three hundred years later, the boys still remembered some things.

Raw and Aaz tumbled into my lap, already sucking on their claws. Purrs rumbled, and I smelled popcorn on their breath. Babies. I rubbed their hot, round tummies. Zee crouched by the tent entrance, gazing into the cold night, and the moon glinted against the silver scales of his blunt little nose.

I openly studied Jack. The old man must have been in his eighties, but he seemed younger. Lean and strong, with silver hair and a strong, rugged face. Handsome as a classic movie star. Respected archaeologist and adventurer, a man of dignity and secrets. Not-quite-human secrets.

He was dressed in khakis and a battered navy overcoat, beneath which I spied a pale blue denim shirt that matched the color of his eyes. A stained cloth messenger bag that looked as old as the Russian Revolution slung over his chest.

"How did you find me?" I asked quietly. "Why now?"

Jack's eyes glittered, even in the darkness of the tent, human eyes, with an inhuman soul, in residence. "I found you easily, my dear. I felt you. I felt . . . it. And so I came."

It. Inside me. I closed my eyes, bowing my head as Dek kneaded a particularly tender knot. "I needed you before that. Months ago. But you disappeared, without a word. Not even the boys could track you. I was . . . worried."

Frantic. Terrified. For the first time since my mother's death, I had family—an impossible, miraculous discovery—and then Jack had gone away. My mother had been murdered. I could not discount the possibility that the same had happened to my grandfather.

And now that he was sitting in front of me, I still could not relax.

Jack said, "I had business. Matters that needed my attention, not the least of which was cleaning up the mess Ahsen created during the brief time she was free."

"I could have helped you."

The old man hesitated, glancing down at Zee, who watched him, as well, red eyes glowing faintly. "Yes. But it was something I wanted to do alone."

I forced myself to breathe, and the air around my mouth puffed white. I suddenly noticed the cold again. I was freezing. Zee reached up and brushed his knuckles across my brow, gazing deep into my eyes. "Hard dreams, Maxine."

"Strange days," I told him, and gently squeezed his little hand. "Need you to do something for me, if you can. Find Grant, wherever he is. If he's on the plane, you must take care."

Zee nodded, scratching his bony spine. "Words?"

"Warn him about Cribari. Tell him to stay away."

"Sharp man," he said, glancing at the others, who all looked at him with red, glittering eyes. "Dead man."

"Not dead yet," I warned him. "First Grant. Find him."

"Done," Zee whispered, and disappeared into the shadows. My heart went with him. I could not predict what would happen once Cribari realized I was still alive—but whatever he had planned could not be good.

Jack tried to sit up. "Grant. He's on a plane?"

"Going to China. A trap."

"You let him go?"

"I had a plan," I replied roughly. "Tracker."

Even saying his name was difficult. *Tracker.* A man betrayed by my ancestor five thousand years ago, and now slave to the demon Oturu—a demon who had pledged himself to my bloodline in perpetuity. Both had disappeared months ago, vanishing as surely as Jack—but Tracker had the ability to slip through space. Just like the boys.

Only, he could take me with him.

I needed that. And Oturu had been drawn to my need,

once before. I had hoped he would come to me again, bringing Tracker with him.

But now I had Jack, for better or worse. The tent was very small. The old man had only to reach out to touch me, and I let him. His fingers brushed back my hair, sliding warm and dry against my skin. He stared at the scar below my ear.

"A poor plan," he whispered.

My cheeks warmed. I pushed away his hand. "Who's hunting you?"

"One of my own kind." Jack cradled his hand, his gaze far too compassionate for comfort. "We share the same pursuer, my dear."

Same hunter. Avatar.

Franco. His eyes.

Pieces fell into place. New possibilities. I had thought, at first, that Franco might be a traveler from the Labyrinth. Demons had come to earth from other worlds, after all; as had Mary, and God only knew what else.

But Franco had perfect American English, with a slight Southern twang. If I had heard him on the phone, I would have guessed he was a normal professional, someone who liked to go to football games and drink beer with his buddies at the bar. If I could forget his eyes, I would say he was human, unequivocally.

Franco is from earth, I told myself. *From earth and human.*

Human. Until he had been physically altered.

I had seen it done before. Men and women, transformed so profoundly it was impossible to tell that they had ever been human. It was an ability of the Avatars. Mind over matter. Mind over DNA.

Ahsen, I thought, recalling the Avatar: her stolen face, her voice. I had killed her. She had turned humans into monsters, stripped them down to bubbling skins of sinew and bone, tearing away noses and ears and eyes—until nothing was left except gaping holes filled with teeth.

First of the grafters, she had named herself. *First of the spinners and connivers. First to master the Divine Organic.*

Genetic manipulation, I called it. Accomplished with nothing but thought.

"Shit," I muttered to myself. "Goddamn it."

You killed one of their own. You thought none of them would notice?

Jack raised his brow. I tapped the corner of my eye. "One of the men who kidnapped me had been . . . altered. Here. His saliva, too."

"Ah." Jack was silent a moment, lost in thought. "What else did you learn?"

"That my kidnapper is working in association with the Catholic Church—and that I was taken there to die," I told him simply. "He knew about a weakness I hadn't considered. That moment between the transition."

Might as well have spoken pure lightning. Jack's mask slipped, and something ancient and terrifyingly deadly moved through his gaze. I began to shake—with cold, I told myself—and reached without thinking into my hair, grabbing the razor ruff of Dek's neck. Clutching the warm little demon for comfort. Mal growled.

And then the moment faded, and Jack became nothing but an old man again, pale and too thin. Run ragged. Starving. Chilled to the bone and lost in winter. I realized suddenly that a profound toll had been taken on his body. He was gaunt beneath his clothing. I glimpsed his collarbone beneath the open neck of his denim shirt, and it was sharp and pronounced.

"Old Wolf," I whispered.

But he said nothing. Just remained grim and quiet; and dangerously thoughtful. Zee slid from the shadows. I knew as soon as I saw him that it had not gone well.

"Sun still shines," he rasped. "No go on Grant's side."

"And Cribari?" I asked, still shaken, almost breathless. "Can you get to him?"

Zee snarled, punching his fist through the floor of the

tent, creating a hole as deep as his elbow into the frozen ground. "Tried. Out of reach. Still got sun."

Raw and Aaz snuggled deeper into my lap, though their eyes slivered open and they pushed back the brims of their hats to watch their brother fume. Against my throat, Dek and Mal purred Bon Jovi's "Wanted Dead or Alive." I scratched their heads and looked at Jack. "Tell me what's going on."

"I was careless," he said, with a straightforwardness that surprised me; as wily, and full of riddles, as he had been in the past. "I did not forget that Ahsen had allies on this world, but I underestimated her ability to free some of them."

"But she did."

"Months ago. It must have been one of the first things she did upon gaining her freedom."

"I thought Ahsen was the only one of your kind who had been imprisoned in the veil."

"She was," he said, after a brief hesitation. "But there are other prisons on earth."

I stared. "How many?"

Jack looked away from me, rubbing his jaw. The shadow beneath his stubble suddenly looked too much like a bruise. "A handful. That's why I left. I had a sense that one of the seals had broken. I've spent the past several months strengthening the others."

"Is it Avatars or demons who are trapped on earth?"

"Both," said the old man, still refusing to meet my gaze. "This world was never meant to be a penal colony, my dear. Regardless of what you might think."

I hadn't been thinking much except *Holy Shit*, but imagining this planet as one big prison for nonhumans elevated that to *Holy Fucking Shit*. I glanced down at Zee and the others. Raw and Aaz were staring at Jack, idly picking their noses and eating the large, steaming black lumps sliding down the tips of their claws. Baseball hats still askew. Zee, on the other hand, was very still. Intent, quiet, thoughtful. Dangerous.

I said to the little demon, "Did you know?"

Zee shrugged. "No harm crossed paths. No matter."

Which was a definite *yes*. The problem with the boys was that if they didn't want to tell you something, they simply wouldn't. If they didn't think there was a problem in their Hunter's life, they wouldn't cause one. And if a Hunter didn't know the right question to ask—the answer would simply never exist. Riddles were their game. Patience had to be mine.

"Just one . . . seal?" I said to Jack, unsure what that meant, though I had an idea. "One Avatar loose?"

Jack stared at his very human hands. "One is enough. Especially this one. He was Ahsen's protégé. Another master of the Divine Organic, though he fancied himself an artist more than a realist of the flesh. He made . . . creatures . . . that should not have been."

"What kinds of creatures?"

"Creatures with an instinct to kill," he replied shortly, glancing at Zee. "You know of them. The Gorgon and harpies. All manner of vampire. Werewolves. Banshees. More, and more than I can count, or remember. Think of the dark lives of legend, my dear, and you can most certainly lay the blame at this one's feet."

My brain hurt. "I thought—"

"—that myths are not real?" interrupted the old man gently. "Sweet girl. If it can be imagined, then there is always the possibility of reality. We are *made* of possibilities."

Whatever. I had no time to confront the incredulity I felt at the idea of *vampires* running loose on this world. Jesus Christ. I had enough problems. I leaned forward, close to grabbing Jack's wrist. My fingers hovered just above his skin. "If Ahsen freed him, then he's been loose for months. You can't tell me he's only just started to cause trouble."

"He's been laying the groundwork. Establishing himself."

Establishing himself with members of the Catholic

Church, for starters. Fuck knew what else. "So why target you? Why any of us?"

"I imprisoned him. A long time ago. It was . . . unpleasant. He probably thinks I could do the same again, and I've tried these months to capture him." Jack hunched over himself. "But I had help the first time."

"You imprisoned Ahsen, too. And others?"

The old man remained silent, studying me. I tried not to be bothered. He had done this before: stolen moments simply to stare at me like I was rare, and curious. But it felt odd, just as being near him remained strange to me; too new for comfort. I had never called him *Grandfather*, not to his face. I did not think I could do it now, not even under duress, no matter how strongly I felt our connection in my heart. The word did not come naturally. Nor did his presence, near mine.

"Old Wolf," I finally managed. "Why are you staring?"

"Because you are so much like my Jeannie," he replied gently. "I look at you, and I see her staring back."

Not even hearing my grandmother's name could make me smile; or help me feel less vulnerable than I did at that moment. "Does this Avatar want revenge on me for killing Ahsen?"

"Perhaps." Jack still watched me carefully. "Though I suspect he is more interested in the ring you wear."

I held up my hand. The finger armor hugged my skin, riding every groove of my knuckle and nail, as though it was little more than metallic paint. I remembered the glow of it in the basement and shivered as other memories flowed, deep and hard, into my mind. "You called it a key to the Labyrinth."

"A key to many things. But then, I think you've had a taste of that," Jack replied, very gently.

I looked away from him, down at Raw and Aaz, who reached simultaneously into the shadows and pulled out a teddy bear; brand-new, store tag still attached. Dek slithered from my neck and attached his mouth to one furry ear, tugging the bear up my body, toward my hair. I turned

my head, ignoring the sounds of teeth grinding as two demons ate bear legs, while two more chomped down on ears
and plastic eyes. Stuffing drifted into my lap like snow.

"He has to kill me to take it off my hand," I said. "Why
not do the dirty work himself? Why manipulate humans?"

"Because that is his way." Jack's voice was elegant and
quiet in the confines of the tent. "It is his habit and game."

"I murdered one of your kind. That might be reason
enough to avoid me."

"*If* he knows, which he might not. No Warden was ever
made who could kill an Avatar." The old man touched my
hand, carefully. "It would be best if no one ever discovered
that you had."

I did not like the sound of that. "And Grant? Why him?"

Zee pushed under my arm, hugging me. Jack hesitated.
"Because he is just as dangerous to my kind as you. More
so, my dear. More so by far."

Lightbringer. Ahsen's voice crept into my thoughts.
Lightbringer.

I closed my eyes, balling my hands into fists. "Jack—"

"We have to move," interrupted the old man, with a
delicate edge to his voice that said quite clearly that he did
not want to answer questions about Grant.

But soon, I thought, heart clawing up my throat as I
watched him stumble out of the stolen tent. *Damn soon.*

CHAPTER 8

THERE was a road. Moonlit, buried in the forest surrounding the dead circus. Curved like a malformed spine, out of sight, out of mind, and I stared at the snow-riddled track and thought of fairy tales breathing the winter air. Vampires and elves. Werewolves. Dragons, maybe, exhaling dreams of fire.

Demons who walked as men, and spirits who did the same.

"Where are we?" I asked, as we walked away from the circus corpse.

"Eastern Europe. As far as I could take us. There should be a village nearby." Jack stumbled in the snow, and I grabbed his arm, hooking it through mine. "No one comes here anymore. Bad things happened, and the Romani clans put a curse around the borders of this place. To set foot on this land means death."

I glanced over my shoulder, and found Aaz and Raw trailing behind, red eyes blinking lazily in the shadows. "What kinds of bad things?"

"Genocide." Jack kicked something out of the snow. I

looked down. Saw what I thought was a polished white stick, until the contours of its shape began to burn in my mind. Bone. I was looking at bone. Part of a leg or arm. Too small to belong to an adult.

Spots of light danced in my vision. I forced myself to breathe. Zee pressed his nose to the bone and hissed.

I almost asked when these people had been murdered, but I was afraid of the answer. Six years, ten years, twenty—made no difference whether I had been born, or inherited the boys. People had died in a part of the world very far from me, and I could not have saved them, even had I wanted. People were dying at this very moment that I could not save—and not just from demons. From humans. All of us, wicked in the bones.

I looked back one more time, just before the forest curved and swallowed the circus graveyard. "You act like that curse means something."

Jack gave me a sharp look. "Because they believed, and you must respect the power of belief. Because humans are not always so . . . mundane. Tricks can happen, my dear, quirks of birth. Those who were given gifts long ago still pass them on to their descendents, in blood. Best not to underestimate that."

"Like the man who kidnapped me," I said slowly, thinking of that little boy in Franco's arms—wondering if that was his real child. "He'll pass on those physical changes?"

"He might have," Jack replied. "But I believe you took care of that."

And then some. I almost placed a hand over my heart, as if that would help me listen to the secrets buried deep inside me. Instead, I shoved my fist into my pocket, stubborn and frightened. "He seemed willing. Grateful for the opportunity to kill me."

"Perhaps he thought he was answering the call of his god."

"A false god, if an Avatar had anything to do with it."

"What are gods?" Jack threw back his head as he trudged through the snow, and the moon made his hair glow; and bitterness touched his mouth. "I was a god once. As others have been. You know the stories. Deities, discovering beautiful maids and filling their bellies with children gifted with power. Or men blessed by gods with only a single touch, granted abilities that make them legends." He finally looked at me, and the bitterness was replaced with grief. "And in our temples where humans prayed and sacrificed, gods might be there, yes. But only for the right kinds of skins."

I did not let go of his arm, but his bones and muscle suddenly felt brittle; and my knees, my heart, could sympathize. I said, quietly, "You make it sound as though humans were cattle."

"You eat cattle. You don't play with them. Humans are closer to dolls. Dress them up, toss them about. Experiment with all the endless variations."

"You don't mean that."

"I did, once." Jack's gaze turned dead and cold, glinting hollow; then he turned his head, staring into the darkness of the forest. "We can be killed, my dear. My kind are not true immortals. But we *are* hard to murder, and so we have lived years past the size of death and dreaming. We have lived past sanity. And to creatures like us, who exist as little more than energy and thought, keeping sane was, long ago, a preoccupation you might not understand."

"I was in the Wasteland," I told him, feeling a different kind of cold. "I think I've got a clue."

Jack tried to pull away, but I held him close. *Slippery road,* I told myself. Snow up to our ankles. The cold bit through my cowboy boots. Zee ranged ahead, while Raw and Aaz continued to watch our backs. I heard owls hooting, and the rustle of branches as a soft breeze kicked more frigid air against our bodies. I shivered. Dek and Mal warmed my ears with their breath, but Jack's chest rattled, and I snapped my fingers at Zee.

The little demon paused, glancing over his shoulder— from me to the old man—then slipped sideways into the shadows, vanishing from sight.

Jack said, "We found humans. And we discovered that to be in their flesh kept us sane. That was enough, at first."

"You played games with their lives. You entertained yourselves."

"We juggled worlds," he whispered. "Until one day we found ourselves believing our own lies."

Zee reappeared with a small bundle in his arms. Two hot water bottles, two hats with earflaps dangling, and a pair of wool gloves for Jack. The old man slid the hot water bottle beneath his coat and held it, sighing. I tugged the hat over his head and helped him with his hands, which refused at first to uncurl from their fist shapes. I slid his mittens on, and jumped, startled, when his lips brushed my brow.

"Dear girl," he said softly. "You were right, all those months ago, when you compared us to the demons."

I could not look at him. Just shook my head, took his arm, and started walking again. "Do you still feel the same about humans?"

"No. Many of us changed our thoughts about them."

"Some who didn't?"

"Just as many," he said, breath white in the moonlight. "Particularly those who doubted their own ability to stay sane without their grafter games and connivances in the Divine Organic. The internal struggle was put aside during the war with the demons, and afterward, when many of my kind left this world to tend their wounds, the issue became moot. Those of us who stayed behind were inclined to guide the humans who had managed to survive the devastation. And help guard against breaks in the prison veil."

I lost the moon behind the trees. Zee disappeared into the forest, and Raw took his place, nose low to the ground, baseball cap tugged backward. Razor spikes of hair poked through the cloth, and the sharp spines of his back flexed. Dek and Mal purred a familiar tune; Richard Marx, for a change. "Children of the Night."

I peered into Jack's gaunt face, trying to see his eyes.

"Why are you telling me this now? I begged you for answers months ago, and all you gave me were riddles."

Jack hesitated but said nothing. Simply pulled me to a stop, staring ahead of us at the road, where Raw had suddenly disappeared. Aaz pushed close against my cold legs, growling softly. Dek and Mal quit singing.

I heard crunching. Not snow. Something harder, crusty, as though in the forest some massive jaw chewed bone. A primal, ugly sound, dry and heaving, like I was listening to someone vomit backward, down a deep throat into a stomach lined with lead. I could almost see it: a mouth like a wood chipper, hands shoving corpses into the tooth-riddled maw. I could see it. I knew it. I knew that sound, somewhere deep in my blood.

And it got louder. I heard movement, in the shadows of the forest. Lips smacked.

My lungs refused to work. Took all my strength to breathe around the massive thundering in my chest. If my heart beat much harder, it was going to break. I forced my knees to bend. My legs moved. I stepped in front of Jack. Reached inside my jacket to unsheathe a blade. Metal gleamed in the night, silver and smooth as silk.

Raw reappeared, baseball hat gone. He reached over his shoulder and yanked a spike from his spine, wielding it like a spear. Aaz did the same, and the wet sounds of tearing flesh briefly drowned out the ghostly echoes of mastication emanating from the forest.

"Old Wolf," I whispered. "Can you take us out of here?"

"Not both of us," he said, staring at the trees. "He's tracking me faster now. Resurrecting his creations."

"How—" I began to ask, but Jack grabbed my arm and spun me around so that my face was buried in his chest. I felt, more than saw, his hand dip into the messenger bag hanging against his hip—but there was no mistaking the sawed-off shotgun he suddenly held.

"Find Grant," he said urgently. "Keep moving. Stay away from familiar places."

"Jack—"

"He wants Grant." The old man pushed me away, bending to peer into my eyes. "He wants to hurt me, he wants to kill you, but Grant . . . Grant he wants *alive*. You remember that."

"Where do you think I'm going?" I snapped. "I can't leave you."

He grabbed my right hand, holding it between us. Finger armor, glinting. Behind me, in the woods, I heard a wail so loud and pained I clapped my other hand over my left ear.

Zee, deep in woods, snarled a long, melodic word. Raw and Aaz flicked away into the shadows, and from those trees more sounds of movement: crackling, crunching, snuffling like an entire army was trying to breathe through one collective nose. Then, thrashing. Screams, broken like a thousand rusty hinges.

Jack gazed over my head into the forest, blue eyes glittering within the ghostly wash of his face. For a moment I could see my mother in him. She had held her gun the same way, one-handed, across her chest like a shield.

"Oh, a merry chase I'll lead," he murmured, and squeezed my right hand even more tightly.

I tried to pull away, frightened for him. "What are you doing?"

Jack remained impossibly grim. "I wasn't allowed to protect my Jeannie. Or our Jolene. Never even knew she was mine until it was too late."

"Jack," I whispered, beginning to understand. "Jack, no."

"He knows my weakness is you," he breathed. "Just as he knows your weakness is Grant."

Tears burned my eyes. I grappled with the old man. "What *is* Grant? What is a Lightbringer?"

Behind me I heard a crash louder than the others, mixed with the snarls of the boys. Jack did not look. He would not let me turn. Grief ravaged his face, so raw it burned through my heart, into my bones.

"The Lightbringers were first," he said hoarsely, and pressed his lips against the finger armor.

I felt a sucking sensation on my skin, a liquid heat that squirmed around my finger. Jack pushed me. I fell backward and did not stop.

I entered the abyss.

※

MOMENTS, minutes, hours, days. Time had no meaning in the abyss. Time was fluid, relative, a matter of perception. And I perceived nothing as I hung in the darkness, screaming for my grandfather.

And then the bubble broke, and I was spat free into a clear night sky with the ground far away beneath me. I plummeted, and glimpsed an explosion of lights: a city, glittering with neon diamonds, more numerous than the stars. The boys clung to my body, but I hardly noticed. Nothing mattered but the sensation of hurtling toward the ground, accelerating past the speed of gravity.

The world disappeared a second time—winked in and out—and I suddenly found myself on solid concrete. I was still screaming. My gut wrenched. I fell on my hands and knees, shaking.

It took me a long time to move. Every time I did, I had the very strong feeling I might faint. So I stayed still. I focused on breathing. On not having a heart attack. And when I was finally convinced that the ground would not open and swallow me up, I pushed myself to my knees, joints aching like I had aged forty years in forty seconds.

Concrete walls surrounded me. I was in a narrow alley that twisted like a crooked hair, and it was as lived-in as any old shoe. Battered doors lined the walls, framed by buckets and locked bicycles, and small wooden tables covered in newspapers. I saw windows cut in the stone, protected by iron bars, and cheap lights flickered shadows from within. I listened to pots bang, and smelled grease and rotting garbage, which were only slightly stronger than the scents of ammonia. Above me, clotheslines strung across the alley were covered in sheets and underwear. Even farther beyond that, a craggy maze of tall apartment buildings filled the night sky so completely I could see only a sliver of a cloud.

The air was cool and damp. I peered at the newspapers and saw Chinese characters. No date that I could read, but if I was in Asia, the sun should have been up. Which meant I had moved forward or backward in time—either of which was a possibility, given the finger armor's peculiarities. And I *did* blame the armor for my sudden shift in locale—though it had never occurred to me to use it in this way.

Jack, I thought, terrified for him. *Goddamn it.*

Raw winked through the shadows and pressed his mouth close to Zee—whispering a stream of quiet, unintelligible words.

Zee glanced at me. "Big man's already here."

So we were in Shanghai, in the future. Terror for Jack shifted, splitting hairs. "Is he with Cribari?"

"Just talking. Sharp man hasn't hurt him."

Cribari is working with an Avatar. The Avatar wants Grant. Alive.

But why the pretense? Why drag Grant across the world, only to talk to him? Grant was just as vulnerable in Seattle.

"What about Jack?" I asked Zee. "Can you still help him?"

"Cut blood from Big Tooth," replied the little demon, carefully. "But got you now, your need."

Which meant they had done what they could, and would do no more. Not with me here, exposed. Heading into something dangerous.

I tried to stand and could not. I realized I still held one of my mother's knives in my left hand. Gripping the blade so tightly that if my gloves had not been laced with steel, I would have cut my fingers to the bone.

I could not let go. My fingers would not unbend. Zee grabbed my hand, and the knife, and stared up at me with solemn red eyes.

"Faith," he whispered, and took the blade from me, very

gently. He reached inside my jacket and slid the weapon into its sheath.

Just have a little faith, my mother once said. *Game isn't over until you're dead.*

I exhaled slowly. Zee rubbed his cheek against my arm, while Dek and Mal hummed sweetly in my ear. Bon Jovi. "I'll Be There for You."

Zee helped me stand, clutching my hand and placing it on his warm, spiny shoulder. I rubbed my face, trembling. Raw and Aaz prowled, melting into shadows, reappearing almost instantaneously within nearby patches of darkness, behind me, above, in the nooks between walls and round clay eaves. I heard sniffing, crunching metal and stone. I hoped a stray cat or dog did not cross their paths.

"Grant," I said, struggling not to think of Jack, alone in the snow, with only a shotgun. Never mind he was an Avatar, an immortal. His human body was frail, old. And he had been afraid.

"Follow," Zee replied. I took another deep breath and stumbled after him into the streets of Shanghai.

I was in no state to appreciate the change of scenery, though a small part of me did and put it away for another time. I had been a nomad for the first twenty-six years of my life, with no brick-and-mortar home beyond a farmhouse in Texas that I visited only a handful of times—the last being the night of my mother's murder.

Instead, my mother had been home. Zee and the boys were home. Sometimes I had considered our car to be home. But that was it. I was born into the traveling life, forced to endure it, taught to love it—and until I met Grant, I never thought I would leave it. Never did the possibility occur.

Even so, I had never traveled past the ocean. I had journeyed only as far as a car could take me, from Canada to South America, and all those places between. My mother had been born in Asia, and had traveled through Europe for the first half of her life—before coming to America, by ship.

I could have done the same, in reverse. I knew that. Maybe

I should have. But my comfort zone, as incongruous as it might be, was a powerful thing.

I had no idea of the time, but there were people out in the street: impossibly skinny young women dolled up in tights and high-heeled boots, with perfect hair and stylish bags bouncing from their slender shoulders; and men with spiky hair drifting over their eyes and the collars of their jackets turned up. I saw old people ambling, and baby strollers, and children kicking balls on busy sidewalks while parents sat on benches and watched them play. Bicycles everywhere, and scooters, and cars; and the air tasted cold with a taint of exhaust every time a bus rolled past me down the street. It was night, but it might as well have been day. Restaurants rolled with people, and I looked through glass windows and saw tables packed with small dishes of food, and faces laughing.

And though it was China, it was still the same. Humanity and its comforts did not vary, nor did its sins and dreams.

I stood out. I saw other foreigners, but not many. No way to blend in, but no one seemed to care. I was just another body on the street, and I relaxed after a couple minutes. No real choice, and I had my hands full watching for the boys in shadows, tracking glints of red eyes and the roil of spiny shoulders from bushes and between the numerous nooks and crannies of battered old buildings. Dek and Mal clung snug and warm against my neck, receding into the shadows of my hair. Purring and singing, with their little tongues occasionally tickling my ears as they scented the air.

I glimpsed Zee watching me from a quiet side street and veered right, following him. The pop music playing from the stereo of a clothing shop at the corner instantly faded, and I felt swallowed and cocooned by a darkness walled in by tiled apartment buildings, parked cars, and some palm trees planted in random intervals against low concrete walls. I knew we were perfectly alone when Raw sneaked out from behind a squat blue van and pressed a soft, warm bun into my hand.

I bit in. Tasted hot and salty and soft, with a center full of turnip and roast pork. I ate fast, stomach roaring with an aching hollow hunger. I needed calories—and the comfort of food in my mouth. I had starved once. I had starved to death a thousand times over in the Wasteland, but the boys had kept me alive, in their own way. Ever since, it had been difficult for me to tolerate the feeling of hunger.

Raw passed me another bun as I walked, then a small plastic container filled with steaming dumplings. I never stopped moving. Just ate with my fingers, burning my tongue and the roof of my mouth. I did not ask where the food had come from, nor did I care. With the boys, it was better not to know sometimes.

Zee hopped up on the edge of a car roof. "Big man still safe. No sign of trouble."

I nodded, holding up the plastic container. Dek poked out his head and took a deep bite out of it, then another, until my trash was gone. Mal licked my fingers. "Are we close?"

"Minutes."

We left the side street, and I found myself walking through another fragment of Shanghai: light-filled, car-filled, a city that obliterated the sky. I saw a glittering oasis off to my left, an island intersection where the road was framed on one side by an enormous half sphere lit up like a neon blue ornament; and from there, two skyscrapers, slanted roofs made of white light and glass. Giant advertisements coated another set of sparkling towers, but that could have described any of the sleek buildings crowding the intersection. Taillights bled red. A wide pedestrian bridge spanned the road, and it was packed with moving bodies.

Five minutes later, I found the place.

It was a cathedral. An incongruous sight amidst such modern excess, but it held its own in an area that was dark and still, almost as though it sat within a bubble, just slightly beyond the rest of the city. Red brick, twin spires; a small and humble church. The longer I stared, the more I felt that I was gazing upon the physical manifestation of silence. A place where moments remained caught in time.

There was a high wall and a closed iron gate with a guardhouse just on the inside. I did not feel inclined to ask for permission to enter. I stayed away from the main entrance and walked around to the left of the cathedral, which was bordered by a landscaped garden that felt like a small park. Apartments also surrounded the church, and a side street that was pleasantly dark. Zee and Raw perched on top of the brick wall. I looked up at them, and they held down their tiny hands. Aaz gave me a boost. Within moments, I was over the wall.

Two men sat inside the guardhouse, eased back in their chairs, heads tilted at an angle. Talking or sleeping, I could not tell—but they were not looking toward the cathedral's double doors. I got in easily, and silently, and in moments was tucked within a recess on the side of a massive aisle. It was quite dark, and the air smelled like stone, cold from the earth. On my left was a delicate wooden altar, and in front of me a slender pillar and low, carved balustrade. Beyond the recess, past the aisle, massive drum columns framed my view of long benches and shadowed arches. I heard voices echoing. One of them belonged to Cribari.

And then, Grant.

Relief made me weak. All my fear, bottled up so tight, and it all rushed over me in one hard moment. I had been trying not to think too hard. Cribari, ordering my death. Cribari, orchestrating Grant's journey. Separating us. Trapping him. To what end I wasn't sure, but I knew it couldn't be good. Not if an Avatar was involved.

A memory touched me: Ahsen, before her death. Seeing Grant. Hearing his music. Suffering the touch of his power.

She had been horrified. Terrified.

She had been the first to call him *Lightbringer*.

Connections, I thought. Cribari. Grant. Me. Another Avatar in the mix. Pieces of the puzzle.

The boys coalesced from the shadows, scattering like

wolves and leaving deep scratches in the aged mosaic floor. Dek and Mal grasped my ears with tiny claws and poked their heads from my hair. I scratched their necks. Raw and Aaz disappeared, but I glimpsed the wink of red eyes from the shadows across the cathedral aisle. Little scouts. Grant's voice echoed faintly, and I began to peer around the column.

Zee tugged me back. I knelt beside him, and he pressed his sharp mouth against my ear.

"Maxine," he rasped softly. "We must take the sharp man."

"Cribari? Because he's responsible for trying to kill me?"

Dek growled. Zee whispered, "That, and older. Older still. He is the eyes of the old dark hand, and the debt must be paid. Blood for blood, on our old mother's grave."

Old mother was Zee's name for the Hunters who had come before. Blood for blood was a call of revenge, and the mention of a debt meant there would be no argument about it. I would not be able to stop them from taking what was theirs.

"When did you know him?" I whispered to Zee. "Did he try to hurt Mom?"

He shook his head, pressing the tips of his claws into the stone floors. "Not him, but one just like. Same heart. Gotta pay the debt. Gotta bleed."

I had no time to prod him for a better explanation. I placed a gentle hand on Zee's warm shoulder. "Business first, then do what you must. But not before Grant is safe."

"Big man first," he agreed, and searched my face with a gravity and concern that touched me to the quick. "Walk light in shadows, sweet Maxine. Walk with wings."

He had never said such a thing to me, but he placed his sharp hand over his heart as he spoke, and I bent close to kiss his brow.

"My little boy," I whispered. "My best friend."

"Until the end," he agreed softly, and faded into the shadows.

I still heard voices. I peered around the edge of the recess and was momentarily distracted by architecture: vaulted ceilings with carved spines that filled my vision like the frozen bones of bat wings; and columns that rose like bound silver trees made of stone. I imagined heartbeats inside the walls, as though the ghosts of prayers still lingered, and while the air felt as if it would collapse with shadows, I imagined strength, as well—quiet, solid, and enduring.

You should be like this, I told myself. *Be this.*

Instead of feeling as though the core of me was a butterfly, flitting from one flesh-eating flower to the next. No direction, no clue. Just hopping into the mouth of danger, because that was what butterflies did.

I did not want to be that stupid. No one in this world could afford for me to be so dumb.

The front of the cathedral felt very far away, but I saw three men standing beneath a few scattered lights, and one of them leaned on a cane. I debated my entrance—whether I should make myself known at all—but I heard Cribari use a sharp tone, and I gave up. I left the shadows and walked down the side aisle of the cathedral. The heels of my cowboy boots clicked like tiny gunshots. I felt watched, and tilted my head just enough to see movement on the balcony far above and behind, at the back of the church.

Ahead of me, the men turned. I was too far, and it was too dark, for me to be seen properly—but I glimpsed Grant's small smile. The sounds of my footsteps, he had told me, looked like licorice spitting sparks of quicksilver, and I thought of that as I walked, and put a bounce in my step as Dek and Mal bled close against me. They were coiled over my shoulders, but growing ever lighter—using the shadows beneath my hair to fade, and hide their mass from sight. Interdimensional trickery; like a bottomless bag they could rest within, emerging only when needed. Their tongues rasped against my ear.

I was grateful for their soft touch. Father Cribari looked like he wanted to eat some kittens when he finally saw me.

Sharp man, echoed Zee's voice in my head, and it was true. The priest suddenly reminded me of a new nail: functional, capable of causing damage, but not much good without someone to use him.

I wondered when I would meet the one holding the hammer.

Father Cribari started walking down the aisle as soon as he recognized my face, and was practically running by the time he reached me. *Surprise, surprise,* I thought. *You son of a bitch.*

Sweat glistened on his brow, and his cheeks were pink. His gaze roved down my body, pricking my skin—and I felt a wave of distaste ride over me like a hard fever.

"How unexpected," he murmured, a trace of actual confusion and unease flickering through his eyes, before being swallowed up by that frigid mask. I realized suddenly that he had not been in communication with anyone related to my kidnapping. He did not know they had failed; or, if he suspected, he had not expected me to be here. Not so soon, if at all. Which meant this really was a shock.

"Oh," I said. "It's only going to get better."

CHAPTER 9

FATHER Cribari's eyes narrowed, his skin slick enough to grease a pan. *Dark Mother,* I thought, and wanted to hear him say those words again, as though it might loosen something inside me. I wished Jack were here, too.

Grant reached us. His bad leg slowed him down, and he was breathing a little harder than normal. Still dressed in the same clothes I had last seen him in. He looked rumpled, unshaven, though his eyes were bright and sharp. His flute case hung from the strap around his chest. He had brought the gold Muramatsu, and I caught the gleam of it, just over his shoulder. Like a sword, or a single golden arrow waiting in its quiver. Relief swept through me, something close to giddiness. As though I stood in the storm of a small miracle.

"Darling," he said. "What *ever* are you doing here?"

"I decided to take a walk," I replied, loving the fierce, hot light in his eyes, "and ended up in China. What a remarkable coincidence."

Father Cribari looked ill. I heard feet shuffling, a faint cough, and the third man who had been present near the pulpit appeared from behind Grant. Another priest, dressed in black slacks and simple shirt. I noticed his hands first because they were clutched so tightly across his soft stomach. He had round cheeks, deep brown skin, and black curly hair cropped close to his skull. Large drowning eyes stared into mine.

He recognized me. I was sure of it. And then he glanced down, sideways—to Grant, Cribari, anything but me.

"She cannot be here," he said urgently. "She was not approved by our government liaison. If he returns . . ."

"Access to the cathedral is regulated by the Chinese government," Grant rumbled. "We had to have special permission for tonight. Our chaperone went outside to wait."

Father Cribari wiped the back of his hand across his brow, his fingers trembling slightly. "You must have jumped the fence to escape his notice. Or found some other . . . unnatural means of entrance."

The other priest gave him a stern look, but Cribari did not seem to care or notice. He was trying to act like a different man in this place, outwardly confident, less sickly in his appearance. Like a cat with one paw in the cream— and another on the corpse of a warm mouse.

But Grant had been right. I made him nervous. I scared him. Especially now.

Pretend, I told myself. *Pretend you don't know he had anything to do with hurting you.*

Grant stepped in and took my hand. His grip was strong, warm. "Come on. I want to show you something."

The other priest flinched. "No."

Father Cribari touched his shoulder. "It is allowed, Brother Lawrence."

He said the words like his tongue was gilded with steel. Father Lawrence gave him a hard look, but kept his mouth shut. Barely. He made a small gurgling sound as Grant led me back down the aisle—but not toward the pulpit. Instead, he walked with me toward the rear of the cathedral and the large wooden doors. His cane and my cowboy boots struck the floor in a quick, easy rhythm.

But as soon as his back was turned from the other two men, his face changed; calm levity draining into a stone-cold mask.

"The murders didn't happened here," he whispered to me. "And they won't let me see Father Ross. They insisted on this tour—a tour at *midnight*—and won't talk about anything but Gothic architecture."

"They're playing you," I said softly. "And you're playing along. Why?"

"Instinct," he said. "And because they're both hiding something big. Might be the same thing; could be different. I can see that Father Lawrence is a good man, but it's also clear he knows what Antony is doing. I don't understand that connection. Or why he recognized you, too."

"I'm a popular girl," I muttered, noticing for the first time how Grant refused to call Father Cribari by his proper title. It was always Antony. A small act of defiance. Refusing to give the man respect.

"You okay?" I asked him.

"Better now," he told me, but his voice was slightly hoarse, and for a moment all he did was stare at me. I could not look away. It was good to see Grant's face. So damn good.

"You made it," he said.

"Of course," I replied, though I suffered, for one moment, the memories of what had led me here, and what I knew.

Grant's gaze flickered to the crown of my head. "Maxine."

"Cribari tried to have me killed," I breathed. "Twice. I think he's getting his orders from an Avatar. All of this has been contrived. I just don't know why. I don't even understand why they haven't tried to kidnap you yet. They've had all the time in the world."

Grant froze. I caught him before he could turn around—squeezing his hand so hard he winced. I forced him to keep moving, but he stumbled, and the sounds of his cane hitting the stone floor sounded like gunshots.

"Don't let on you know," I told him urgently. "We'll find your friend—if he's really here—and then we get the hell out."

"First job is to get out of this cathedral," he whispered hoarsely, his fingers tight around mine. "Dear God. I'm going to kick Antony's rear end."

We passed through the massive open doorway into a still, cool night. Ahead of us, the iron gateway, and the guardhouse was there. The men were standing outside now, conferring quietly. Men who could make my life very difficult, in ways that had nothing to do with the supernatural.

I hated the intensity of their watchfulness. I hated my sudden sense of helplessness. I was supposed to be one of the most powerful people in the world, but I felt like a charlatan with a tin sword compared to human laws and bureaucracy—and the enormity of everything else I was responsible for. I was meant to save the world. I had been born to save lives. I could barely save myself.

"I miss zombies," I muttered under my breath. "I miss the goddamn demons. What the hell happened to me?"

"Your world got bigger," Grant murmured, and in a much louder, surprisingly inane voice said, "The Jesuits built this place. Nineteen-ten, I think, but the order's had a presence here since 1608. The land was given to them by a high-ranking Ming Dynasty official, who converted to Catholicism."

"Really," I said stiffly. "Do tell."

He continued leading me toward the gate as though I belonged there, and that this was part of some grand tour. Every step wrought a deeper transformation; arrogance rolled off him, entitlement, privilege; until a completely different man limped at my side, the kind who fit the stereotype of the filthy rich and handsome: an intolerable bore.

"The cathedral," he continued unashamedly, when we were almost at the gate, "was used to store grain during the Cultural Revolution. The nuns were kept under house arrest. See that building across the street? That's where they lived. Now it's a steak restaurant."

"Fascinating," I replied, but I would have said the same if he told me he liked to dress up as a chipmunk and juggle acorns. I hadn't heard a word he said. Father Cribari and Father Lawrence were behind us, and my focus was split between them and the men standing still by the guardhouse door, dressed conservatively in plain black slacks and short-sleeved dress shirts. Their eyes were cold, assessing. Especially when they looked at me.

I tried to put on my best face. I had never spent much time in front of a mirror, so I didn't know what that was, but I looked the men straight in the eye and tried not to appear guilty. Just confident. A girl on tour with her guy. Nothing worth spending time on—not at this hour, not at their pay grade.

"This," said one of the men, in faintly accented English, "was not part of the agreement."

Surprise and a hint of outrage filled Grant's face. "Mr. Shu, I know that Father Cribari and Father Lawrence arranged this tour at the last minute, but I was absolutely certain they told you my wife was coming along, as well."

Father Lawrence made a small choking sound. I got a cheap thrill. Mr. Shu narrowed his eyes and glanced at his companion—who looked me up and down with all the emotion of a rock. I had the distinct impression he was adding up all the parts of me—appearance, manner, the way I clutched Grant's hand—and coming up with a narrative that did not satisfy him in the slightest.

"I did not see you go in," said the man, and there was a wary tenseness to his voice that belonged to any man forced to do his job at an ungodly hour: tired, and a bit exasperated. I liked him. I wanted to give him an easy way out.

"I was running late," I replied, wondering if a person could look young and innocent simply by trying—suspecting I had about as much luck of accomplishing that as a crocodile would have of turning vegetarian.

The other official plucked a toothpick out of his pocket and jammed it in his mouth. "Passport."

"Ah," I replied. "I believe I left that at the hotel."

Or an apartment more than six thousand miles away. Since it was night here, then it was daylight in Seattle. None of the boys would be able to flash home to retrieve my passport. I saw Zee, Raw, and Aaz hunched around the gargoyles decorating the cathedral. Watching us, red eyes glowing softly. The irony of the situation was going to kill me faster than any well-timed bullet.

"I'm sorry," I added, and meant it. "I didn't mean to cause trouble. I just wanted to be with him." I patted Grant's upper arm when I said that, then replaced my hand with my cheek. Grant reached back to touch my hair, his fingers light and warm.

Both men stared. Grant put one hand on the gate. "Father Lawrence. Handle this. We're late for an appointment."

An appointment at midnight. Father Lawrence seemed ready to melt into the ground. Father Cribari folded his arms over his chest, but that was all. He showed nothing on his face.

Grant pushed me backward, through the open gate. No one stopped us, but I heard some rather sharp tones behind me, a mixture of Chinese and English. Limping fast, Grant led me away, and we walked left along the wall toward a quiet street.

"That wasn't so bad," I said, trying not to sound so breathless.

Grant gave me a sideways look. "Those men were members of the secret police. They had the authority to arrest us. Take us in for questioning, at the very least. Religious tolerance is growing, but the government is mindful of people who come here trying to politicize the situation."

"So you play like some rich boy showing off to his girl, and pretend you've done nothing wrong? Nice."

"I learned from my father," Grant said. "Same thing you learned from your mother, I suppose. Power is transient. Power can flow from one person to another. The most powerful person in a room isn't the wealthiest or the one with the most connections. It's the person who *believes* the strongest, the one who has the most confidence. And, sometimes, it's the person who can make everyone else feel like *less* of themselves."

"My mother wasn't big on emotional politics," I replied, as somewhere behind us the iron gate clanged. "She just had . . . a quality."

"Like you."

"I wasn't bluffing anyone back there."

"Sure you were. You were a beautiful woman without a clue. That was a better act than mine, any day."

He was teasing, but his words hit closer to home than I would have liked. Still, I smiled, trying to act like I got the joke—but my face felt like plastic and rubber.

Grant searched my eyes, humor fading—sliding into compassion, concern. His arm slid around my waist. He bent to kiss me, very gently, but I held the sides of his face and pushed closer, hungry for him. Afraid, suddenly, that I would never have another chance to taste him.

I heard voices, dimly. Grant stopped kissing me and pressed his bristled cheek to mine—our breathing ragged, his palm sweaty against the back of my neck. Dek and Mal rolled over his hand, holding him to me.

"Later," he murmured in my ear, fingers tightening as two sets of purrs got louder in my ears. "We'll be okay, Maxine. We're going to be fine."

And then he turned, just slightly. Father Cribari stood close, watching us—rather like a voyeur, I thought. Which made my stomach turn over.

"You think you are going someplace?" he asked Grant.

Grant smiled coldly. "I believe there was a man who requested my presence. Unless you lied and brought me here for another reason."

Father Lawrence frowned, bits of him jiggling as he bounced up and down on his toes. He very briefly glanced at me—a strangely significant look, as though he wanted to say something private—but then the odd light in his eyes died, and he became bumbling and soft, murmuring, "Father Ross is not ready. He was—"

"He's not talking," interrupted Father Cribari smoothly. "I doubt he can, anymore."

Something deadly passed through Grant's eyes. "What did you do to him, Antony?"

"Nothing."

"You said it was 'nothing' ten years ago, when you tried to convince the others to execute me. Or lock me up. What was it you said? There are cellars in the Vatican that run all the way to Hell?"

"You imagine things," Cribari replied. "They only run *halfway*."

Father Lawrence made a small sound of distress. "Please, the two of you, this is unnecessary. Not one of us would ever hurt another—"

"The various offices in the Vatican operate independently of each other," Grant said, none too gently. "You know this, Father Lawrence. There is bureaucracy, and there is, occasionally, bungling of that bureaucracy, but for the most part there are no conspiracies, and all too few secrets—because no one in a bureaucracy can *keep* a secret. But there are exceptions. Aren't there, Antony?"

The priest's gaze slipped from Grant to me. "If you like."

Grant edged sideways, so that he partially blocked me from Cribari's sight. "Take us to Father Ross."

But the man still held my gaze and would not let go. "I am confirmed in my beliefs of you, Grant Cooperon. Even more so now, with the company you keep."

"Yes," I said, smiling dangerously. "That's something you and I should discuss."

Father Cribari paled, but he did not back away, or visibly flinch. Grant squeezed my hand. "No games, Antony. You brought me here for a reason. Let's finish it."

Father Lawrence gripped his hands even tighter, uneasiness in his eyes—whether from the tension surrounding him or something he knew, I could not tell. But Cribari gestured at the brick building we had been walking toward. "See for yourself."

Famous last words, I thought, searching the shadows—and not just for the boys. We needed to go, run fast, but I knew Grant too well. This might be a trap, but if there was a possibility that his old friend was somewhere near, he would never rest easy knowing he had abandoned the man. He had to see for himself what was fact or fiction. Dek and Mal, little more than shadows beneath my hair, began humming Bon Jovi's "Bad Medicine" inside my ears.

We entered a quiet building that was a maze of narrow halls: long, plain, and poorly lit. The ceilings were so low I felt the urge to stoop. Even Grant hunched over, leaning harder on his cane. Worse, I saw no one else. I *heard* no one else. Even the sounds of our passage were muted, swallowed, each click and scuff dulled into death. A claustrophobic atmosphere, oppressive; like a cage of white straitjackets. Made my skin crawl.

We rode an elevator to the sixth floor. Each of us took a corner. I stood across from Cribari. He watched me, his gaze hooded and dark, and Grant watched him. Father Lawrence stared at the floor, his shoulders round and hunched. I considered the benefits of breathing.

The little priest led us to the end of the hall and removed a single key from his pocket. He hesitated, looking to Cribari for confirmation, then unlocked the door.

Grant started to enter. I was faster, and slipped in first. The room was small and lit by only one lamp that gave off a weak yellow light. I saw a narrow window draped in a thin pale curtain. The ceiling felt very low, and the air was cold and smelled like plaster.

There was the bed, and a man who lay in it. Father Ross.

I wasn't sure what I had been expecting. A zombie would have made sense, or no man at all—just guns pointed at us, or tranquilizers, or whatever Cribari had in mind, eventually, to subdue our sorry asses. But there was a man, and all it took was one look at Grant's face to see that it was the right man.

Father Ross had red hair. Freckles dashed across his nose. He might have looked like a nice, wholesome individual, once upon a time—but his cheeks were gaunt, and his body was so bony he seemed little better than a corpse. Bones jutted through the sheet that had been pulled up to his neck, and atop the sheet, black leather straps pressed down, restraining his hollow frame from shoulder to ankle.

His eyes were closed. He looked asleep. Grant stood very still, staring at him.

"Luke," he murmured.

"He disappeared for several days, and when he returned . . . when he returned, he was quite different," Father Lawrence said, hovering by the door. "He is very sick. He must have been, of course, to do . . . what he did. But there have been . . . other changes in him."

"What did you do with the bodies of the nuns?" I asked, feeling rather uneasy about the priest's careful choice of words. Remembering Franco and the changes that had been done to him.

"We made arrangements," Father Cribari answered, and Father Lawrence, standing just behind him, shot the priest a look so full of venom I wondered if it was my imagination.

I raised my brow. "Making arrangements for the dead, especially when you don't want anyone to *know* about the dead, is quite a feat. Not entirely a legal one, I imagine."

"You judge us?" Cribari said softly. "You, of all people? What would *you* sacrifice in order to preserve what you consider dear? What *wouldn't* you give?"

I would sacrifice everything, I told him silently. But that was between me and myself, and me and the people I loved.

Grant said, "Father Ross's brain has been damaged. And his body."

Father Lawrence frowned. "He was hit during the initial struggle, but not on the head."

Grant looked at Cribari. "You know what I can do."

"You don't deny it?"

"I never did." He reached for his flute. "Both of you, out."

"I think not," said Cribari.

"I won't work in your presence."

The priest bared his teeth in a terrible smile. "You seem to be under the impression that you have a choice."

"And he would be right," I muttered. "But first things first."

I grabbed his arm, and shoved him hard against the wall. He was strong. He resisted. But I was tougher than most men. I had to be, in order to bear the weight of the boys on my body—my boys who weighed the same, whether tattoo or flesh. Like Superman, surpassing earth's weak gravity. Fly, man, fly.

Father Lawrence was already in the hall, staring. Not in astonishment; but something else in his eyes that made me uneasy. I slammed the door in his face and added a kick for good measure. No lock, but I waited a moment, and the small priest did not try to come back in.

"You," I said to Cribari softly, "have been a very bad man."

"Take your hands off me," he whispered.

"I don't think so." I leaned in, close enough to kiss, and he shied away from me like my breath was going to burn his face off. "You were surprised to see me. You thought I was going to be dead. Poor little Franco."

Father Cribari began trembling. "He was a chosen warrior. As we all are. He knew the sacrifices."

A strong hand caught at my waist and held tight. I looked over my shoulder and found Grant staring at the priest with terrible fury.

"How could you?" he whispered. "How could you orchestrate this . . . violation . . . against Father Ross?"

Violation. I gave Grant a sharp look, but his focus was entirely on the priest. Cribari stared back with the same intensity, and not a hint of remorse in his pale face. "He was an opportunity. I knew you would come for him."

Grant narrowed his eyes. "Why me? Because of what I can do? You *had* me, ten years ago. You could have had me in Seattle. None of this was necessary."

Cribari made no reply. His back curled tight against the wall. His eyes burned with feverish light, and his dry, cracked lips moved in silent prayer—which stopped when our gazes met.

"He was told," I said quietly, instinct guiding my words. "He believes he was given a decree from a higher power."

"Gabriel," Cribari breathed. "The archangel who will blow the final trumpet on the Day of Judgment came to me, in flesh, as the spirit of truth, and passed to me his knowledge. He told me how to stop you both; you demons, you children of the Nephilim."

Comparing us to the half-breed offspring of humans and angels made an odd sort of sense, but I shook my head. "You knew about me before that. You *knew*."

Any fear that had been in his face faded into defiance. "We have always known. We have watched, and waited. Dark Mother. Dark Queen. From your blood will pour the armies of the Last Battle, and the night will descend in your eyes. Your heart will murder this world."

Your heart. I could not laugh it off. I could not pretend his words did not affect me. But the cruelty in his voice made me sick. I could see history in that moment, a glimpse of zealots and Inquisitors, men who struck fire to women, preaching brimstone to witches; suicide bombers and word twisters; ages upon ages of men wearing violence as religion, born again in his eyes. Then and now were all the same. The circle never ended.

"Enough," I said. "You're done."

"No," Cribari whispered. "You and I. We are *not* done, no matter what may come. You are an abomination." His gaze flicked past me to Grant. "Both of you, against the natural order. Our Lord will take you. *I* will take you, as charged. You will be destroyed."

Anger uncoiled in Grant's eyes. "You won't touch her."

"I will not stop." Cribari jerked forward, cheeks reddening, long pale fingers digging into the wall behind him like claws. "It ends here, before she breeds like the rest of those bitch queens and passes on the filth of her blood. All these centuries spent watching her lineage, leaving our marks so that our warnings would not be forgotten—"

Cribari kept talking, but I no longer heard him. Grant was quivering, his face so stony, so furious—utterly white with rage—that a great wash of heat flowed over me, and it was fear: stinking, bowel-loosening fear. I looked back, and saw Zee and the others peering out from under the bed.

Grant's flute was in its case, but his hand grabbed mine, squeezing like a sunlit vise, and I heard a rising rumble in his chest, felt power rolling off his skin, and when he opened his mouth, it was like hearing the sob of a mountain in winter, low and gray and aching with age.

Cribari's mouth snapped shut, and he swayed against the wall, clutching at his collar. He raked his nails across his throat, opening and closing his mouth like a dying fish—squeezing shut his eyes as though in terrible pain. He tried to speak, but all I heard was a hiss, and he clapped his hands over his ears. Grant showed nothing—no mercy, no compassion—just cold detachment, determination. He never paused to take a breath. His voice shed its humanity, undulating like the back of a dragon, and the air rippled with it, moving against me as though a great wind was being born, or a mighty fist clenched.

The priest screamed. Blood trickled from his ears. I felt, more than saw, Zee and the others creeping free from the shadows, staring, and I tugged hard on Grant's hand, calling his name. He did not look at me. In his eyes—in his eyes—I imagined a faint glow.

Lightbringer.

"Grant!" I shouted, and punched him in the face.

His voice finally broke, and the silence created a physical vacuum that made my ears pop and sucked all the air out of my lungs. He staggered, and fell to his knees. I went down with him, still holding his hand, trying to keep him from hitting the floor too hard. He was a big man, and I got dragged down.

"Oh, God," Grant breathed, chest heaving. He started to cough, then gag. He pressed his brow into the floor, hands balled into fists. A flush covered his skin, rising from his throat into his face. I wrapped my arm around his shoulder, holding him to me. Pressing my cheek to his. He coughed again, and blood spattered the floor.

I stared, horrified. Grant grabbed my hand. "What have I done?"

I tore my gaze from the blood to look at Cribari. The priest lay very still. I pressed my shaking hand to his throat and felt a pulse.

"He's alive," I said, and Grant exhaled sharply, closing his eyes. Murmuring a breathless, fervent prayer.

Zee and the others shimmered out from under the bed. My little wolves, hunched down, staring hungrily at the unconscious priest before moving on to Grant. Zee pushed close, placing one hand on the man's knee, while Dek and Mal slithered free of my hair, their tails coiled around my neck. Aaz watched us all, red eyes large.

I looked at Father Ross again. His chest rose and fell against the leather restraints, but that was his only sign of life. His face was slack, pale and waxen. Zee leaned over to smell the man, and his lips pulled back, revealing long shining teeth and a glistening black tongue. "Blood-runner. Blood soaked. Been meddled with, this one. Altered."

Bad, bad, bad. I could not imagine what had been altered inside the priest, though I thought of Franco and knew the possibilities were endless. Zee rattled off a stream of words to the others. Raw and Aaz went very still, while Dek and Mal growled, smoke puffing from their nostrils. All of them studied Father Ross.

"What?" I asked, sharing a troubled glance with Grant.

"Know that scent," Zee said, as Aaz quietly snarled. "Skinner scent."

"Do you have the Avatar's name?"

"Too many names," whispered the little demon, a trace of hate in his red gaze. "Too many skins he wears."

I heard footsteps pounding down the hall outside the room. Zee breathed, "Maxine. Trouble."

"How much trouble?" I asked him, as Raw and Aaz leaned against the door, digging their toes into the floor. Zee tilted his head, as though listening—and barked out one sharp word. The little demons fell away from the door, scrabbling for the shadows under the bed. Dek and Mal disappeared into my hair. Zee winked away last, shooting me an inexplicable look over his shoulder, just before he dove into the thin line of shadow beneath the door. Like watching a wolf get swallowed by a black thread. I blinked hard, trying to clear my eyes as Grant's music pulsed unabated in my head.

But the door swung open. And I had to blink again.

Father Lawrence stood before me. His breathing was ragged, his brown cheeks flushed. He was holding a gun.

"Hunter Kiss," he said. "You have to run now."

CHAPTER 10

I had no manners, not even with priests. I said, "What the
fuck?"

"The fuck is *this*," replied Father Lawrence, rather mildly,
as he pointed the gun at the ceiling. "You need to stand the
hell up and get your pert little ass out of this building."

I stared. Grant staggered to his feet, using his cane and
a chair to push himself up. He wiped blood from his mouth
and gave the short, round priest a careful once-over that
was distinctly wary. "Frank. It's been ten years, but you
didn't used to have a potty mouth."

"And you're a grown man who still uses the word *potty*.
Now move it."

I did not move. Father Lawrence was a great deal more
off-putting than zombies and men with reptile eyes. The
bumbling little priest was still soft-spoken, but that was the
only similarity between that man—and the one who now
stood before me. His transformation was utterly inexplicable. Even his posture was different. I looked at Grant, but
he was staring at Father Ross. Still unconscious. Relaxed
against his restraints.

"I can help him," said Grant, but there was a paleness to his face that was frightening, and when he suddenly coughed into his hand, he looked at his palm and closed it into a fist. Hiding it from me.

"No." Father Lawrence stepped over Cribari without giving him a glance. "You have to leave him. He's changed now. He's not the man you knew."

"Yes, he is. I can see it." Grant settled his gaze on Father Lawrence. "What are you doing here? What is this?"

"Insanity," said the priest, tapping the gun against his own chest. "And a series of events that, honestly, I don't understand your involvement in. *She*, on the other hand, makes perfect sense."

"That's great," I muttered, finally standing. "Lovely. Care to explain?"

Father Lawrence gave me a long, steady look. "Right now there are ten men trapped on the first floor of this building, some of whom are attempting to access a broken elevator. The rest are no doubt trying to batter down the locked and barricaded stairwell door. Eventually, they will manage to open it. And when they do, it would be best if you were long gone. Unless you feel like murdering men who are simply following orders."

"Men who want to kill me."

"Men who are supposed to capture *him*." Father Lawrence pointed at Grant. "And distract you. Throwing away their lives if they have to, which they will if they come near you with the weapons they're carrying."

"You know too much about me," I said.

"I know enough to be terrified," Father Lawrence replied. "Just as I know enough to feel certain that I shouldn't be."

He looked at Grant. "You really won't leave without trying to help him?"

Determination flooded his face. "No."

"Shit," said Father Lawrence. He pointed the gun at Father Ross's chest and pulled the trigger.

It was a small room. Big blast. Close range. Blood should

have been everywhere, spraying from a chest cavity the size of my head.

None of that happened. The bullet slammed into Father Ross's chest with as much disruption as a finger slicing through water. No blood. No wound. But the priest's eyes fluttered open, and he sucked a deep breath into his lungs, shoulders straining against the restraints. Pale as death.

Dek trilled a warning in my ear. Grant lurched toward Father Ross and I stepped in front of him, blocking his path. Our movements caught the priest's attention, though— and suddenly I felt like a mouse frozen in front of a snake. Desperate not to be seen.

Too late. He turned his head to look at us, without emotion, or recognition for Grant. His eyes were human, a liquid green, pale as sea foam. And for one moment, just one, I thought it would be all right.

But he changed. I saw it happen, a split-second strike that was human, and something more: primal, cold, as though a piece of the man's soul had been hacked away and replaced with the heart of some pure animal hunger, thoughtless and without remorse.

He lunged toward us, body rigid and straining. His jaw cracked open. The inside of his mouth was black as a cave. I saw rows and rows of teeth, impossible numbers of them, like a piranha—and I froze, staring, everything inside me shriveling into a hard, hot knot that made me sick at heart. The nameless *thing* inside the skin of the priest terrified me more than any demon, more even than the promise of the failing prison veil.

Demons had codes of honor, ruthless though they might be. This creature had nothing but the kill. I could taste it.

Resurrecting his creations, Jack had said. Setting them loose. Like this was some goddamn playground for murder. No telling how many humans the Avatar had modified— like Father Ross, or Franco, or that unseen thing in the woods that had stalked Jack and me.

Well, fuck that.

"You want to know why we didn't have to worry about

burial arrangements for the nuns?" Father Lawrence said quietly, as Father Ross fumed against his restraints. "Because there were no bodies left."

"I can reach him," Grant said urgently, staring at his former friend. "I can bring him back. I can *see*—"

"No," Father Lawrence said, and shot the priest again, this time in the head.

No clean wound this time. The bullet exploded through Father Ross's brow, and took most of his brain with it. Blood dripped down the wall. Flashed me back to my mother, but that didn't slow me down as I slammed into Grant, shielding his body. He fought to get past me—but not to the dead priest. He was staring at Father Lawrence, and there was rage in his eyes. Grief.

Father Lawrence stood back, meeting that terrible gaze, and the only sign of his remorse, or fear, was his trembling hands. His left fingers encircled his right wrist, holding himself and the gun steady. He pointed the weapon at the floor. If he had pointed it anywhere else, I think I might have killed him.

"Hate me," he said quietly, staring at Grant. "But there's more at stake than saving a murderer who *volunteered* to have . . . that . . . done to him."

"He wouldn't have," whispered Grant. "Not Luke."

Compassion moved through the priest's gaze. "I don't know why you were forced to leave the Church, but it's been ten years. After you were gone, Father Cribari groomed Father Ross. Brought him into our fold—"

"Your fold," Grant interrupted hoarsely. "What—"

"Later." Father Lawrence backed away toward the door, kicking Cribari in the head as he stepped over him.

The priest did not stir. Breathing, but still unconscious. Maybe in a coma. A girl could hope. I wondered why Father Lawrence did not shoot him, too, since he was so gun-happy—but I kept my mouth shut. Whether or not Cribari continued to function after what Grant had done to him was also a moot point. He was already a dead man. Zee had first dibs.

I tugged on Grant's arm. When he did not move, I kissed his shoulder and pressed my cheek against his chest. He made a choked sound, deep in his throat. I closed my eyes, aching for him. But not sorry to see Father Ross dead.

"Come on," I whispered.

"I could have saved him," he breathed, eyes red-rimmed with furious grief. "Maxine, I could see Luke in there, beneath those instincts. He was in so much pain."

I slid my gloved hand under his chin, and forced him to look at me. Said nothing. Just let him read my aura, my heart, my eyes. I thought, *I love you, I am here, I am with you,* and tried to send those feelings into whatever light surrounded me. Messages shining in a bottle.

Somewhere distant, a crash. Father Lawrence swore quietly. "Now or never."

Grant closed his eyes. His large warm hand slid up my jaw, his thumb caressing the corner of my mouth. He bent close and pressed his mouth to my cheek, kissing me softly. He was trembling, and smelled like sweat and sickness. It frightened me to feel that weakness in him. As though something vital had drained away.

"Hunter Kiss," said Father Lawrence urgently, standing in the hall.

Grant took my hand and white-knuckled his cane with the other. He led me silently from Father Ross's corpse, and over Cribari's unconscious body. We joined Father Lawrence, and neither of us looked back.

He led us down the hall. Earlier, in the cathedral, I would have said the priest walked like a muffin, his gait rolling and easy, soft. His walk was still the same, but I was looking at him with different eyes, and what had rolled was now graceful, and what was soft I could not call careful.

We entered the stairwell. I heard crashing sounds beneath us. Metal screeching. Father Lawrence began climbing stairs. Grant did the same, but there was a sluggishness to his movements that was unlike him, even with his dependence on a cane. He coughed again, but I grabbed his wrist before he could hide his hand. Blood spotted his palm. Not as much, but enough.

Neither of us said a word. Grant twisted his hand out of mine but squeezed my fingers before pulling away.

Father Lawrence tapped the railing impatiently. Grant started climbing again, faster now, pushing himself harder. I trailed behind, watching Zee pace me in the shadows, while Raw and Aaz scrabbled in perfect silence over our heads, clinging to walls and the underside of the stairs. The priest never noticed, but Grant glanced in their direction: jaw tight, gaze hollow.

Think of Father Ross like Old Yeller, I told myself, trying to feel some compassion for the dead man. Best friend to a sweet kid. Put down because of rabies. Tragic, a real tearjerker.

Cry me a river. I felt stone cold when I thought about the man. Unable to overcome my terror of someone else like him, set loose. In a schoolyard, maybe, or a hospital, or any city, in any part of the world.

So you go to the source. You kill the maker of the disease.

"What do you know about this . . . Gabriel . . . that Cribari has been taking his orders from?" I asked Father Lawrence, seeking out his small round frame in the darkened stairwell.

"Never met him," replied the priest sharply, though there was a moment of hesitation. "Don't want to. Seems to me that anyone who encounters that . . . thing . . . comes back changed. Whether they wanted to be or not."

"Does Cribari have a way of contacting him?"

"No." Father Lawrence paused on the landing, waiting for us to catch up. Sweat glimmered on his brow, and he was slightly out of breath, as was Grant. "It's not as though we're living on top of each other. People come and go. Cribari comes and goes. It's been like that for years, but three months ago everything changed. *He* changed. Up here." The priest tapped his head with a short, fat finger.

"He started saying an angel had come to him. That it was time to . . . to change the mission of our order."

"Your order," Grant said heavily, leaning hard on his cane. "The kind of order that condones the murder of sick priests in cold blood?"

Father Lawrence hesitated—no anger in his eyes, nothing but remorse. "Our mission is very old. We do what must be done. Even if it goes against . . . practices of forgiveness."

Grant shook his head. "You'll have to do better than that."

Father Lawrence's jaw tightened, and he held his gun out for me to hold. Grant took it from him instead, but my distaste for the weapon must have shown. It was too visceral. The priest gave me an odd look but said nothing. He rolled back his sleeve.

A tattoo covered the underside of his upper forearm, a dance of lines that swam briefly in my vision—because I lost my mind when I saw them. I knew those lines. I knew that symbol.

I wore it as a scar beneath my ear, against my jaw. Hidden by my hair.

"We have no name," he said quietly. "Just this."

Grant went very still when he saw the tattoo. I leaned into him, fighting for my voice. "What does it mean?"

Father Lawrence's eyes glittered. "Many things. Death, mostly. But death can be rebirth, or death can be destruction. Depends on how you look at it."

"Where did it come from?"

Father Lawrence rolled down his sleeve. "I don't know. But we watch for it."

I had more questions, but he took back the gun from Grant and, without another word, opened the landing door and gestured for us to follow. I did not want to, but Dek and Mal were purring, and Grant touched my elbow, very gently. Below us, shouts. The distant pound of boots on stairs. Our mysterious pursuers had finally broken through.

The hall looked the same as all the others: narrow, long, crowded with doors. Father Lawrence led us to the first door on the right, closest to the stairs, and opened it. Inside was a room like the one we had left, except the mattress was bare and a thick layer of dust covered the floor and furniture. Dust bunnies the size of real bunnies leapt away from my boots.

"After World War II and the Cultural Revolution, the Jesuits who came back to China were a bit paranoid," Father Lawrence said quickly, locking the door behind us. Quite a few locks were in the door—three dead bolts, two chains, and a thick bar that slid into the floor. The hinges had been reinforced, too. "So they took precautions when they had a chance to build this place. Safety measures that never made it onto the blueprints."

He opened the closet. Grant said, "You're kidding."

"Oh, please," Father Lawrence replied. "You were the historian. Don't tell me you're surprised."

Grant looked on as the priest lifted a panel out of the floor. "Secret doors and passageways? Of course not. I was talking about the size of that thing. You'll never fit."

"I'll have you know my fat gut is a highly malleable part of my anatomy," replied the priest. "You bet your ass I can make it fit through this hole."

He stood back, pointing at the open square in front of him, black with darkness. "Ladies first."

I sat on the edge, dangling my legs inside. Little hands grabbed my ankles with reassuring strength, and I lowered myself. There was no drop. My feet touched the floor immediately. The air smelled musty and cold. I had a feeling that not many people had ever used this secret room.

Red eyes blinked at me. I reached up, along with Raw and Aaz, to help Grant. It was a tight squeeze. His chest and shoulders got stuck, and he had to wiggle and exhale all his breath—with the rest of us pulling—before he got through. He hit the floor on his good leg, hopping slightly against our arms to keep his balance. The little demons scattered out of sight as Father Lawrence lowered the cane and flute case inside.

But he did not join us.

"I lied," said the priest. "I'm fat as a pig. Something our Brothers did not take into account when they made this escape hatch."

He held down a piece of paper, some money, and the gun. "There's an address written there. Go to the French Quarter. It's near here. Travel the main road, Henshan Lu, until you see a bar called Lucky John's. Ask for Killy. She'll help you."

Grant took the paper and gun. "What about you?"

"Those men know me. I'll be fine."

He was lying. I stepped directly beneath the hole, staring into his eyes. "Why are you helping us?"

Father Lawrence hesitated, and a faint but genuine smile lifted the corner of his mouth. Sad and wry, and tinged with fear. "Because I believe in you, Hunter. I believe you are good, and that your promise is good. I believe you can save us, even as you can destroy us. But I have faith in your heart. I have faith."

"Why?" I breathed. "How do you know so much about me?"

He leaned back, picking up the floor panel. "Not every mystery becomes forgotten. Not the demons. Not the Wardens. And not you, Hunter."

Father Lawrence slid the panel back into place. Just before he closed it for good, he said softly, "I'm sorry about Father Ross."

And then we were left in darkness.

⊰⊱

THE room was small. Against the wall, boxes filled with old rusty cans and jugs of water. Folded blankets that mice had gotten into. I found stairs behind us, wide enough for only one person, and steep. Grant could not see the steps, but my eyesight was fine.

I asked him to feed the gun to Aaz. I told him I was afraid of it firing by accident. Which I was. But that was only part of the truth. Grant knew, though. He understood, and did as I asked, without comment.

We moved slowly, carefully, down the stairs. I held his free hand. Zee guided his cane. No sounds permeated the walls. All I heard was the scuffing echo of our footsteps, and the rasp of our breath. Dek and Mal sang the melody to Elton John's "Someone Saved My Life Tonight."

"What colors do they make?" I asked, after a while. "When they sing?"

"A black rainbow," Grant replied, his fingers tightening. "Curving streaks of scales shaded with the deepest purple, and obsidian flickering with shooting stars. I see night when they sing. I see the Aurora Borealis, but without color, as though their voices come from a place too ancient to have known anything but darkness."

"And yet, you trust them."

"There's nothing wrong with an absence of light. It's just another way of being. A different kind of energy." He glanced in my direction, and I realized he could see me through the light created by the sound of my voice, and movement. "Conflict defines that energy, and we judge its worth on whether the action, and outcome, helps or harms."

"Cribari thinks I'm the Antichrist."

Grant grunted, and his fingers tightened again, almost painfully. "He can go to Hell."

I hesitated. "I'm sorry about your friend."

"No, you're not," he said. "But I understand why."

"You really think you could have reached him?"

"I know it. No one is broken forever, Maxine."

I had less faith in the matter. But *less* was not the same as *none at all*.

Took us almost thirty minutes to reach the bottom of the stairs. Grant was exhausted at the end of it. He had been fading since his encounter with Cribari and Father Ross. I let him rest on the lower steps until Zee and I found the exit, a metal door that opened into a claustrophobic alley much like the one I'd found myself in, after falling into Shanghai.

Cold air outside. Quiet night. No sounds of pursuit, or gunshots, or round little priests being dragged away. Grant pulled the address from his pocket and showed it to Zee. "Can you find this?"

The little demon studied the letters and numbers. Raw and Aaz peered over his shoulder, and the three of them quietly conferred in the melodic quiet language they shared only with one another.

"Done," Zee rasped. "But not so close. Take wheels."

Shanghai was not a city that slept. We left the alley and found ourselves on a crowded street bustling with steaming food stalls and small groups of young people standing around, talking, listening to headphones. Wagons filled with apples and oranges were parked on the corner, alongside women who stood near hot oil drums that had been converted into ovens. Baked sweet potatoes and roasted corn were displayed on top. We stepped around tablecloths on the sidewalk, covered in hairclips and fuzzy hats, packaged underwear, chopsticks, bowls, and other useful odds and ends.

The locals gave us some looks but nothing serious. Dek and Mal receded deeper into the shadows beneath my hair.

"I've been in this city before," Grant said. "Only for a day or two, years ago with my father when he came here on business. It was different then. Quieter. There was more farmland around the outskirts."

"You know this French Quarter we're going to?"

"No." Grant smiled briefly, painfully. "I sat in an office all day listening to him argue through a translator, which looked just as ugly as it sounded. I was sixteen."

"Guess I was six then. Probably sitting in a car, listening to Johnny Cash on the radio."

"I would have preferred that."

"Maybe." I glanced at him. "But never being able to settle down got old, too."

We reached a larger road, and after less than a minute

of walking, managed to hail a cab. Grant knew some words of Mandarin, and the driver was familiar with Henshan Lu. We got going in the right direction, and the boys rode along in the shadows between our feet, occasionally crunching on M&M'S packets and small bags of nails.

It was a short drive. We careened down streets that got progressively quieter, and darker, until we came to a district where the road was lined with immense trees and gray walls that were tall and cracked with green things growing from the stone; and narrow iron doors. The entire neighborhood gave the impression of being a fortress. I glimpsed, on the other side of the walls, clay-shingled rooftops and large windows.

Henshan Lu was not as elegant, or as residential. Neon sparkled. Restaurants beckoned. Bars everywhere. Until, finally, I saw a large blinking sign surrounded in white lights and yellow stripes, and in red letters the name: LUCKY JOHN's. Two slender Chinese girls stood outside the door, dressed identically in high-heeled black boots, dark hose, and denim miniskirts. Puffy white coats with fur hoods covered the rest of them, and they stepped lightly from foot to foot as we left the cab and approached. Cold, maybe. The bite in the air was getting worse.

Both of them smiled, but it was tired, fake, as though their smiles were part of the paycheck. Grant did not smile back. He said, *"Ni hao. Killy zai bu zai?"*

Smiles faded, and the girls stopped seeing through us and really looked at our faces. One of them muttered a short word, and her companion pointed at the door.

"Bar," she said, in faintly accented English. "Expecting you."

We went inside, traveling from a dark night into a darker interior that was decorated like a country-kitsch antique store for alcoholics. Vintage signs advertising liquor and loose women covered every inch of the walls, along with the occasional saddle, cowboy hat, and more than a handful of mounted antlers upon which small whiskey bottles had been hung, like Christmas ornaments. Yet more bottles—this time vodka—dangled from the ceiling in a massive chandelier, each of those slender necks stuffed with a tiny lightbulb. Smoke clung to the air. So did the mournful voice of Alison Krauss, playing on the radio.

The place was half-full. No zombies. Just tired drunks slumped in their seats, most of them white men with their ties loosened and hands clutching drinks. No one sat alone. Each had a companion, all lovely young Chinese girls who looked sober as stone but far more cheerful. All of them, smiling. Leaning in. Solicitous. Ignored.

All the men were staring at the bar. I stared, too. A woman sat on top, long legs crossed, dressed in a skirt so short I could see the edge of her ruffled pink panties. She wore a pink gingham shirt tied at the waist, and her cleavage sparkled. Red cowboy boots covered her feet.

She was Chinese, but something else, too. Short black hair framed a striking face dotted with freckles, and she wore a pink headband with little metal coils attached—alien antennae—the kind that had hearts stuck on the bouncing ends. A microphone was in her hands. She was singing along with Alison Krauss and doing a magnificently bad job of staying on tune. Not that anyone seemed to care.

"Wow," Grant said. "You should see what I'm seeing."

"Don't get any ideas," I replied. "I'm seeing plenty."

No one else was behind the bar serving drinks, and we shook our heads when one of the waitresses pointed to an empty table. I stood, half turned, keeping an eye on the front door. Zee peered at me from the shadows of the coatrack, and vanished. Raw and Aaz sat just behind a decorative pickle barrel, drinking beer and scratching their stomachs. Baseball caps on again. Red Sox, this time.

Grant touched my elbow. I looked at the bar again. The woman was still singing, but her gaze was locked on us. A faint furrow gathered between her eyes, and she tilted her head, ever so slightly, to the right of us. I saw a dark hall and glanced at Grant.

"Father Lawrence has interesting friends," I said.

"Father Lawrence is not the man he used to be," Grant

replied, and started limping toward the hall, away from the bar and that awful crooning voice pouring into the microphone. "Not that I'm complaining."

"You knew him well?" I heard dishes clinking ahead of us, and a door swung open, pushed by a waitress who held a tray full of pretzels.

"Not well enough," Grant muttered, and bypassed the kitchen. There was a door at the end of the hall, but also some bathrooms on our right. I grabbed his elbow. He nodded, started to enter the men's room—but I pulled him back at the last moment. Forced him to follow me into the ladies' room. I was afraid to let him out of my sight.

We were alone. My stall smelled dirty, and there was no toilet paper. When I finished and came out, Grant was already at the sink, staring at his reflection in the mirror. I joined him, studying my face.

I was twenty-six years old, but for a moment I could see myself at forty. A wrinkle was starting in my upper forehead. I looked tired and dirty, my black hair tangled, greasy with stress. Shadows gathered under my eyes.

My skin had never seen the sun. Only my face had color, but that was gone now, and my pallor was sick, exhausted. Grant looked like crap, too. Gaunt and pained, a trace of grief still in his eyes. Maybe a thread more of silver in his brown hair. We were aging overnight just from the trauma of living.

I looked at both of us, together. His broad shoulders filled the reflection while I stood just slightly behind him, my cheek pressed against his arm. Our gazes met in the mirror.

"Hey, pretty lady," Grant murmured. "Ready for the Grand Canyon yet?"

I tried to smile for him, but my mouth refused to cooperate. Grant turned, his strong arm sliding up my back, holding me close to a warm chest that smelled like cinnamon and the cedar of an old forest. I rubbed my cheek against his shirt, one hand clutching loose flannel, and listened to the rumble and pulse of his heart.

I noticed something hard beneath my cheek. Stood back, studying his neck, and saw a familiar gold chain glinting just outside the collar of his T-shirt. I reached up, fingering the soft, thick links. Grant's hand closed around my wrist, preventing me from pulling out the pendant.

"I thought it was important to bring her necklace with me," he said self-consciously.

I unzipped my jacket. Flashed him my mother's knives, holstered neatly against my ribs. Jewelry or weapons, there was no difference when it came to needing the comfort of something familiar against our bodies. I understood. I was the same.

"Like two peas in a pod," Grant murmured, and reached down to finger one of the blades. His knuckles brushed my breast, and lingered.

Behind us someone coughed. Grant flinched. I shut my jacket and turned. The woman from the bar was peering around the bathroom door, pink antennae bouncing. Her eyes were dark and serious, but her mouth quirked into a smile and in a pure Texan drawl she said, "I've got rooms for that. In fact, I've got a room just for the two of you."

"We were sent—" I began to say, and she cut me off with a shake of her head.

"Father Frank," she replied, smile fading. "I know. He warned me."

"Just what did he warn you about?" Grant asked cautiously.

"Oh," said the woman, a mysterious glint in her eyes. "Almost nothing."

She backed out of sight, but her soft drawl floated into the bathroom. "I'm Killy, by the way. Come on, now. Got a demon coming soon."

CHAPTER 11

KILLY led us through the door at the end of the hall and up a flight of narrow, creaking stairs. Her cowboy boots sounded sharp as mine, and we could have waked the dead with the racket we made climbing to the second floor. Pink panties flashed beneath her denim miniskirt. Dek and Mal angled for a better look. I slapped their heads, pushing them back into my hair. Grumbles rumbled against my ear, but they receded, warm and heavy, into the shadows of my scalp.

I managed to hold my tongue just long enough to make certain we were completely alone.

"What did you mean," I asked, "when you said that a demon was coming soon?"

Killy made a tuneless humming sound and looked past me at Grant, who was very carefully navigating the stairs with his cane. "You need a heating pad for that, honey?"

"I believe she asked you a question," he replied gravely, finally making it to the second floor, which was stacked with crates full of whiskey bottles and boxes of cigarettes.

She ignored him. "Someone took a sledgehammer to you, right?"

Grant stopped moving, and leaned hard on his cane; his gaze speculative and dangerous. "You're nice at heart, but don't push it."

Killy held up her hands. "Fine. But the offer still stands. You've only been able to walk for, what? A little over a year now? Bet you ache fierce."

"Demons," I said, stepping in front of Grant. Unsettled that she knew so much about him. Ill at ease about quite a few things.

Killy's lips thinned, and she walked backward to a nearby door, reaching for the handle. "It's a convenient word. Covers a lot of bases."

Inside was a bedroom. Nothing fancy. Just a mattress on the tile floor, with folded blankets stacked on top. One large window, hidden behind a partially drawn curtain. Low ceilings. Dirty white walls, holding in the strong scent of some acrid cleaning product that was not quite strong enough to hide an old odor of vomit.

Killy said, "Sometimes I let people sleep it off up here. Don't worry. I use bleach to clean up after them."

"I couldn't give a shit," I replied. "Who are you, and why do you know so much?"

She gave me a long, steady look, and it was her eyes, I realized then, that did the most to offset her appearance: large, heavy-lidded, and hazel. It was hard to hold that gaze, like I was exposing part of myself, and it occurred to me that I just might be. It was not such a hard concept to grasp, not after everything I knew about the world.

I could hear Jack's voice rumbling. *Tricks can happen, my dear, quirks of birth. Those who were given gifts long ago still pass them on to their descendents, in blood.*

A faint smile touched Killy's mouth, but it did not reach her eyes. Grant laid his hand on my shoulder, drawing me away from her—and I watched the woman's smile fade when she looked deep into his face. I saw the color drain ever so subtly from her cheeks, and her eyes narrowed, growing colder.

"I know what you do," she said softly. "Don't try it with me."

"Then stop," he replied, something deadly in his voice. "Stop looking."

A tremor raced through her, but she recovered instantly, shrugging, looking away from me. "Nothing to see, anyway. She's got a mind like a steel trap."

"And me?" Grant asked dangerously.

"You're on the Internet," Killy replied, and smiled coldly. "I did some research when Father Frank gave me your names."

She yanked off the headband and tossed it on the bed. "He said to hide you, so that's what I'm doing. Stay or not, but I'll do my best. I owe the man."

"And this . . . demon?"

"He's coming," she said, and shivered. "I can feel it. Someone is coming."

Killy turned abruptly and opened the door. I went after her, but she dodged my outstretched hand, and paused in the hall to look back at us. "Stay here. But if things get hairy, go out the window. There are stairs just beneath it."

She slammed the door in my face. I stood looking at it, then glanced over my shoulder at Grant.

"She has an interesting aura," he said, somewhat mildly. "It's . . . active."

I raised my brow. "How active?"

"It stretches from her. Surrounds people. I saw it happen in the bar, but it didn't make sense until she started talking to us. She can read minds. Some, anyway."

"Psychic," I muttered. "Damn."

Grant very carefully lowered himself upon the mattress. Dek and Mal poked free of my hair, and the rest of the boys pushed aside the curtains covering the window. Zee hopped to the floor on light feet, claws flexing. Raw and Aaz grabbed the curtains and swung down like little Tarzans.

All of them looked at me, waiting for an answer I did not have. I did not know what to do except keep moving. We had to keep moving. Someplace safer than here, which was too close to the church, Cribari, too much shit. Where and how, that was the problem. Where and how.

You know how. If I could make it work. If I could do it without ending up inside a brick wall, or in the wrong time.

I began to strip off my right glove and knelt by Grant. "Your leg?"

He winced, rubbing his calf. "Nothing to complain about."

"Tough man," I said. "I'll be sure to ignore the girly tears once they start."

He began to smile, glanced down at my hand, and froze. I looked, and did the same.

A needle-thin line of quicksilver stretched from my finger armor across the back of my hand—attached to an equally thin metallic band now encircling my wrist. I flexed my hand, and the metal moved fluidly with my skin, as though organic, embedded down to the bone.

I had been wearing my glove the entire time. Never suspected.

"Maxine," Grant said.

"My other plan for getting to China fell through," I whispered, finding it difficult to speak. "I used this to get here. It was an accident."

"It *grew*."

"That happens. You remember."

I remembered. I remembered the Wasteland, entombed in darkness, caught in the endless river that would have ended my life had the boys not kept me alive. I had found a corpse in that place. A body covered in armor, bearing a sword. A sword that had inexplicably transformed into a small ring upon my finger.

The corpse had been my ancestor. Another Hunter, thrown into the Wasteland. She had died there. The ring had been hers. Now it was mine. Before being transported to China, I had already used it several times—been flung back into time—and that was enough to make the ring grow over my entire finger. Not every use of the ring made a transformation happen, but once was enough.

And now, this.

I was suddenly beginning to think that the armor covering my ancestor's bones had not been there entirely by choice.

"This is a problem," Grant said, as though reading my mind.

I curled my hand into a fist. "We have bigger problems."

"Maxine," Zee rasped, tapping the tile floor with his claws. "Gotta go."

Below us, I heard screams.

⇥⇤

TROUBLE follows us, my mother once said.

"Stay with Grant," I said to Raw and Aaz. "Protect him."

"Maxine," Grant argued, struggling to stand from the mattress. I left him there, slamming the door behind me. Running down the stairs, taking them two at a time. I slowed down at the bottom, just before I entered the hall to the bar. I listened hard, heart pounding.

No more screams. Above me I heard a clicking sound. Grant, moving fast. Zee slipped from the shadows.

"Blood spilled," he said.

"How many bad guys?"

"Not the numbers," replied the little demon. "Just quality."

I gritted my teeth, reaching inside my jacket for a blade. Not that plain steel had ever helped much, but it made me feel better. The metal was cold against my fingers. I had forgotten my right glove upstairs.

I pushed open the door and entered the hall. Saw nothing. Heard nothing except a faint crunching sound that flashed me back to Jack and the forest and made my stomach hurt with fear. I swallowed it down, sweating, and crept forward. Zee kept pace, while Dek and Mal uncoiled, rising from my hair until I felt like Medusa with a heart full of stone.

The sounds of chewing got louder, maybe because everything else was so damn quiet. I reached the end of the hall and peered inside the bar.

I saw blood. Slick on the tables, spattering the walls in red splashes that looked like paint had been flung and heaved from cans and brushes. Bodies sprawled on the floor, crimson puddles expanding from wounds I could not see, and some that were plain: craters in heads, cracks in chests, as though sharp teeth and axes had been at work. Fast. So fast eyes were open, staring.

Crunch. Some jaw working hard. I turned, searching out that sound, heart beating so rapidly it was difficult to breathe.

A man sat at a table, his back turned to me. Short. Fat. Bulging from a wrinkled tan suit that fit so poorly I could see every excess roll in his round shoulders. He was eating from a bowl of pretzels. A dead woman slumped beside him. Half her head was missing, and the blood still trickled from her wound, pooling on the table. I watched the man dip his pretzels in her blood, then eat them.

Killy sat on his other side. She was still alive. Staring at him with absolute horror, so frozen and pale I wondered if her heart would give out, if her mind would make her faint simply to save her from dying out of fright. She looked ready to die.

The man paused in his chewing. "My Lady. So good of you to join us. And you, as well, Hound."

Zee snarled. Not at the man. He stared at the front door of the bar, and I discovered three slender bodies deep in the shadows, standing so still I had not noticed them. Even when I did, it was difficult to see much. All three stood close together, shoulders rounded, hunched tight as though sharing warmth. Tall. Pale. Clothed in simple black. Watching me.

I did not see them move. Not even a muscle. But in seconds they crossed that slick red floor.

All I saw were three gaping mouths, brimming with impossible rows of sharp teeth—piranhas and chain saws—so close to my face I could smell the blood on their breath, see giblets of flesh dangling from their gums. I raised my knife.

They never touched me. Zee slammed against them—and then Raw and Aaz were there, plowing so hard into the men, their small bodies lodged headfirst. The twins chewed their way through two of them, straight past spines and out the other side. The men continued to writhe, thrashing wildly. Staring at me—only at me—with their teeth flashing. Raw and Aaz ripped spikes out of their spines and plunged them through their necks.

Zee was more elegant. He waited for the last man to attack him—headfirst, hands pressed to his sides like a torpedo with teeth—and the little demon slammed his fist into the man's open mouth, breaking his jaw, catching him like a shark on a hook. Zee grinned, licking his lips, and opened his clawed hand inside the man's mouth.

I looked away. Seconds later I heard the solid thump of a body hitting the floor. That was all. None of the men had screamed. Not one had shown fear, even as they were mauled to death. Just that same cold, mindless hunger—rage, even.

My ears rang. I stared at the devastated bodies, but my mind refused to register faces. Instead, I heard Grant's voice in my head, telling me about Father Ross: how the real man had still been in there, trapped behind instinct.

Me or them, I thought, and turned away, drawing a deep breath into my lungs. Raw and Aaz flanked me, their skin absorbing the gore that covered them. I looked at the remaining man, still sitting at the table with his back turned. He had not moved once. Not once to look.

I walked toward him. I had no choice but to step in blood. The metallic scent was powerful. Zee kept pace, trailing his claws against the wet red floor. Dek and Mal growled.

I walked around the table, and looked into a sagging face and piggish eyes, half-obscured by the dirty lenses of his glasses. Killy's gaze ticked upward to glance at me, but the rest of her stayed perfectly still, and I did not look back. I stared at the man. I stared at him so long and hard my eyes began to burn.

"Mr. King," I managed to say. "What brings you here?"

"Oh," he said, stuffing some blood-covered pretzels in his mouth. "This and that. I wanted to stretch my legs."

Such a game he played. "Seems you managed that."

"Quite." He looked at Zee. "So here we are, Hound, again at the crossroads. Still bound to the blood of your Lady."

"Bound to kill you," rumbled the demon. "No more, skinner. No more cuts."

"You still think you can give me orders." Mr. King lifted his gaze and smiled at me, tight-lipped, the corners of his mouth stained red. "You should discipline them."

"They're perfect," I replied coldly. "Angels."

His smile tightened even more. "I have Jack, you know. I was pleased to discover him going by that name again. He's used it so often it must be his favorite. Old Jack. Jack in the Green. Jack the Giant Killer, Jack the Knave, Merlin Jack, Jack Rabbit, Jack Shit, *every man Jack of them.*"

He said the names faster and faster, his voice becoming rougher with each syllable he spilled, and bits of blood and pretzel sprayed from his mouth. It was terrifying to watch. I could feel his control slipping away, rushing, and behind him, behind him I saw movement, and it was Grant entering the bar, staring, seeing me first, then him, and the blood, the blood, and I flicked my fingers at Zee.

The demon attacked Mr. King. He hit the man in the chest, and Raw and Aaz joined him, raking his body with their claws. Flesh ripped. Jaws tore chunks from his bulging, suited body. I grabbed Killy by the arm and threw her away from the table. She fell on her ass in a puddle of blood, and scrambled backward toward the bar.

Mr. King laughed, and looked at her. "Don't go yet. Don't go, little girl. I got your scent in me now, and I like what I smell. Got some old-time magic in your blood."

He showed no pain. Not even a flinch. Just that tight-lipped smile. He reached around Zee, stroking his head, and the tips of his fingers sliced through the razor needles of the demon's hair and tumbled to the tabletop like fat, fleshy dice. Zee snarled as blood splashed against his face.

"Nerve endings," said Mr. King calmly, without a glance at his mutilated hand, "are the first thing any good grafter removes. Something Jack should have remembered. But then, he was always a bit . . . old-fashioned."

Saying Jack's name seemed to break his control again. Cold hate flickered through his eyes. I found myself taking a step closer, blade held loose in my hand. I heard the click of a cane, and Grant moved near, as well—staring at the man with such command and intensity he seemed more like a soldier in that moment; a warrior, as much a wolf as the boys. The bad leg, the cane—none of that mattered. He suddenly looked like a man who could kill an immortal, in his dark eyes, something primitive, more than human.

Mr. King turned his chair to look at him, and all that hate flickered into fear: primal, wild, like a buried instinct rearing.

Then it was gone, and he whispered, "Lightbringer. Imagine that, in the flesh."

Grant showed nothing, except a perfect mask of stone-cold menace. "You've hurt people I care about. You don't plan on stopping."

"So stop me," whispered Mr. King, as Zee jumped from his chest, slinking around to my side. "Or have you weakened yourself too much? Not strong enough to help even one friend?"

Grant snarled; guttural, formless words lashing from his mouth. Power whipped along my skin, and Mr. King threw back his head, choking.

Only for a moment, though. Grant's voice broke into a

cough, blood trickling from his mouth. He tried to take another deep breath and had to bend over, gasping like it was hard to breathe. Raw bounded close, peering up into his face with concern.

Mr. King shuddered. Veins had burst under his skin, lending him a mottled appearance. Saliva glistened at the corners of his lips. He stared at Grant with such hunger I could almost hear the cracking of bone between his teeth.

"So you *are* unbonded," he whispered. "Untaught."

"Shut up," I hissed.

He ignored me. "Lightbringer. Last of your kind, I think. But then, we will have to be certain, won't we? Before the Reapers break loose, we will have to tear this world to pieces to make sure you are alone." He held up his hand, where blood still leaked from the ends of his fingers. "Old Jack could tell you about the hunts if he was here. Chasing the skins of your kind across the Labyrinth. Stealing babies into shackles from their cribs."

I took a step, then another, and the world blurred until I found myself slamming into Mr. King, taking us both into the floor. He started laughing on the way down—and then stopped when I smashed my left palm into his forehead and began muttering words of exorcism. Zee and the others bounced from the shadows, landing on top of his arms and legs.

His mouth twisted. "Will you exorcise me? Will you drive me from this body? *Hunter.* It will be a shell. Nothing remains of the heart I stole."

I grabbed his face and felt behind my ribs a tickle, a flutter: darkness, rising. Pinpricks of hunger, slow-burning in my heart. I had killed an Avatar with such hunger. Ruined Franco and his men. If I let go, I would do the same to Mr. King. I needed to. I *had* to.

And if you hurt Grant?

Grant. He stood too close. I could touch him if I reached out. He would let me touch him, no matter what power raged inside me. If I were handling a nuclear bomb, he would take it from me. I tried to turn my head to look at him, to tell him to run, but my throat choked, and my right hand began to burn. Electricity raced up my arm. My vision shifted from eye to mind, until the room around me faded, and all I could feel was the spirit inside the body beneath mine. But it was wrong. I had exorcised demons, stripped the bastards from human souls—but this was different; there was no other soul left, nothing but a hollow shell. Whoever had owned the body before Mr. King was long gone. The skin beneath me had as much value as a good winter coat.

"You want me dead," I managed to whisper.

"I want you out of the way," he breathed, eyes glittering. "You were great once, Hunter. A treasure. But the Light-bringer is a better prize. As is the key you bear."

"This?" I held up my right hand, which still gripped my small blade. Quicksilver glinted along my ring finger and wrist. "You want this? You goddamn try to take it, you fuck."

And I slammed the knife into his forehead.

Bone cracked. Mr. King jerked, eyes widening, and when I wrenched the blade free, brain matter and blood seeped through the jagged hole. He still breathed, though—nostrils flaring as if scenting the air around me. Something wild and startled passed through his face.

"Your blood," he whispered weakly. "Jack. What have you—"

Zee reached out and snapped his neck before he could finish. Mr. King went limp. How that was a better killing blow than a stab wound to the head, I did not know—nor did I care. I felt the Avatar leave its body. In my gut, I felt it go. I could taste the damn thing: bitter, twisted, like sea-water mixed with sewage.

I leaned back, heart pounding. My right hand was sticky with blood, and warm, rough tongues licked my fingers and palm. Raw and Aaz rumbled with purrs. I felt cold. So cold. The knife slipped from my grip, and Zee caught it.

Strong hands gripped my shoulders, pulling me away from Mr. King. Grant knelt beside me, breath rasping like there was a razor caught in his throat.

"Maxine," he said hoarsely, pressing his lips to my brow. "Maxine, are you okay?"

"Dandy," I breathed, and leaned over and vomited.

CHAPTER 12

WHEN I was sixteen, a man in Mexico threatened to kill me. He put cold steel to my neck and asked my mother for money. I could still remember the acrid scent of his sweat, the nervous quiver in his voice. Not a bad man, just a coward looking for an easy way out. He let me go as soon as he saw the cash.

My mother never let go of anything.

She sliced open the major artery near his groin. His blood sprayed everywhere; in the dust and cobblestones, on my shoes. His screams were terrible. He begged us for help. He told us he had children.

My mother left him to die and forced me to do the same. I hated her for that. Not because she saved me, but because she had no mercy. She had turned me into a murderer simply by my own inaction, and it sickened my heart. I did not want to kill. Not even in self-defense. I did not want to be like her.

I told my mother that. I told her, and all she did was smile sadly, and brush back my hair, and dab at my bleeding throat with small, careful fingers.

Trouble follows us, she said. *No way to stop it, baby. You just deal with the hand, and play the cards, good and bad.*

Don't be afraid of mistakes. You'll make them.

Don't be afraid of yourself. Because you will be, sometimes.

Just have a little faith. Game isn't over until you're dead.

Took me years to figure out what that had to do with letting a mugger bleed to death. Sometimes I still wasn't certain. But the best I could figure, after all this time, was that she had known my self-righteousness would be worth shit after she died. That even if I didn't end up like her, I was going to be a close approximation. I would kill. I would be ruthless. It was inevitable, given our destiny, what we had been born to do.

And she was telling me, even then, in her own way, that it was all right. Trouble would follow me, but however I dealt with it, whoever I turned out to be . . . it was okay. *I* was okay.

Only, that was wrong. Nothing was okay.

And I never would be.

⚜

WE threw tablecloths and towels over the bodies. I covered Mr. King by myself, studying that lifeless face, pale in death, and empty.

Worse than the demons, I thought. Demons I understood. Demonic parasites inhabited bodies because they fed off the distinctive energy of pain. But this possession had been for nothing except pleasure. Just a skin to take a ride in. A long, hard murder: first, of the person; and then, the flesh.

My jeans were ruined, soaked in blood. I could feel it on my thighs. Killy had been wearing less, and was worse off after having scrambled across the floor. Both of us, red and stinking.

Zee brought me a new pair out of the shadows, denim stiff and dark. Tags still attached. He did so while the other

woman was upstairs, changing, washing. She had witnessed the boys in action—no way around it—but I did not
see any reason to continue pushing their existence in her
face.

Raw and Aaz prowled the bar, sniffing the floor and
dead bodies, taking long drags from the whiskey bottles
they carried. Dek and Mal were uncharacteristically silent—
as was Zee, though I saw him confer with the twins. Heads
bowed, making scratches in the floor. The spikes embedded in their spines flexed in agitation.

I stood naked in front of Grant from the waist down,
holding perfectly still while he sat in a chair and took a hot
rag to my legs. I would have done it myself, but he had insisted. Face pale, stifling coughs. He washed off my back-
side and thighs, cleaning away the bloodstains that had
come through my jeans. His hands were gentle. I ran my
fingers through his hair as he worked.

"You're sick," I told him. "You need to rest."

"I'm fine," he said roughly. "It's you I'm worried about."

"Easy to love, hard to be around," I whispered. "You
keep spitting up blood, and I'll start saying the same thing
about you."

Grant's fingers dug painfully into the backs of my
thighs. He closed his eyes, kissing the inside of my wrist,
and rested his head against my stomach. His breath warmed
my hip.

"Just the way I like it," he said quietly.

Tears burned my eyes. "Even after watching me stab a
man in the forehead? You've never seen me kill, Grant."

"You forget what I see." He gazed up at me, and there
was a compassion in his eyes that I had forgotten could
exist—forgiveness, unconditional and stern. "I know you,
Maxine. You can't make me run."

I lowered myself into his lap, kissing his mouth. I tasted
salt, tasted him, and he rocked me closer, his hands buried in
my hair, skimming over Dek and Mal, who purred softly.

"Love you," he breathed, pressing his lips against my ear.
"Don't you forget it."

Never, I thought, heart straining; my body too small for the river inside me; too small for what needed to be done.

Grant helped me dress. My hands stopped shaking by the time I buttoned up, but I knew if I sat down again, I would not get up, not for a long time.

"Doesn't make sense," I mumbled. "Jack told me that this Avatar would be cautious of us. You and I can kill his kind. Permanently."

Grant did not question the idea that he could murder. "So we lost an opportunity. He's gone now, in another body."

Bitterness flooded me. Pure, raw disappointment. I sucked down a deep breath, head pounding, adrenaline fading. "Maybe that was the point. Sometimes you have to risk your life to test a theory. He was testing *us.*"

"Was that all?" Grant said grimly, glancing around the bar. "Maxine, about Jack—"

"I'm ready," Killy said, appearing from the hall. She was dressed in black tights and fuzzy black boots, a long black sweater draped over her slender frame. An enormous black purse hung from her shoulder. Far cry from Hooker-Cowgirl-Barbie. She was pale, and did not glance once at the blood or bodies. Just kept her gaze straight, fixed on the front door and us.

We left fast. It was even darker outside with the lights in the bar sign turned off. The girls who had greeted us were gone. I had not checked the faces of the bodies left inside, but I hoped they were safe. Killy locked the doors and glanced up and down the street. She turned right. Grant and I followed.

She said, "Sorry, but I'm done. You're on your own."

"Where are you going?" I asked.

"Train station. I'll head north to Beijing, and from there I can disappear into Mongolia and Russia. Someone is going to find those dead people. I don't want to be in the country when that happens."

"I have questions," I said. "It won't take long."

"Already took long enough." Killy ran a shaking a hand

through her hair. "Goddamn it. Ask. But we keep moving. We can't stop for anything."

"Father Lawrence," I said. "Do you know anything about the order he's part of?"

She shook her head. "It's old; that's all. Got some quirks, a fascination with labyrinths. And you. I picked that up loud and clear lately, whenever I was around him. You're the reason it exists."

Grant struggled to keep up, his cane clicking loudly on the sidewalk. "For what purpose?"

"To watch the Hunter." She quickened her pace, and looked at me. "To watch you. I don't know much else, except there are demons involved. Not like . . . not like what we left in there. Something different." Killy shuddered, lurching to a stop as her hands flew up to her mouth. She stifled a quick, gagging cough. I stood back, watching with cold sympathy. I could still taste my own vomit.

"I didn't expect him," she whispered hoarsely, when her nausea had passed. "I knew something bad was coming, but I've dealt with bad. He was . . . something else."

Avatar. Grafter. Conniver. Jack's voice rumbled through my head, and my heart lurched painfully. Jack. He had Jack. My grandfather.

Could be a trick, I told myself. The old man might still be free. Somewhere, anywhere, lost in the world. I could not stomach the alternative.

"You need to be careful," I told her. "He's not really dead."

She gave me a sharp look. "I know. I felt him leave."

"Killy," Grant said gently, saying her name with a melody in his voice, a rumble that sent a powerful shiver through my bones. I frowned at him, concerned for his strength. Killy frowned at him, as well, but for a different reason, I suspected. She did not protest when he said her name again, though, this time with an even stronger twist.

I watched her eyes change. Sharp, but not so lost to fear. Tension drained from her shoulders. Her breathing eased. I envied that.

Until she punched Grant.

Or tried to. I saw it coming. Grabbed her wrist and used her momentum to swing her around and down to one knee. She spat on my boot.

"Calm down," I said.

She stopped struggling. "I told him not to spell me."

Grant appeared unmoved, but I knew him better than that. His knuckles were white around the cane. "I was try-ing to help. Make it easier."

"Don't want it easy." Killy gave him a baleful look, and I finally released her. She stood awkwardly, rubbing her wrist. "Don't want myself . . . changed from who I am. Not even a little. I've done the drug thing. Honey, you're the same easy fix."

Dek trilled a low warning in my ear. I turned. Raw was across the street, hugging an awning above a closed cloth-ing shop, while Aaz crouched in the bushes near the inter-section ahead of us. Zee hunched directly behind Killy, lost partially in the shadows of a parked car. Red eyes bright and cold. He gestured with his claws, holding up one of them.

Killy went still. Grant tilted his head, as though listening. Very slowly I said, "We're going to have company soon."

Soon, like now. The street had been quiet and empty—no traffic, no people out—but I heard a low rumble, the groan of old brakes, and a small car rolled around the in-tersection, headlights off. It was a cab, small and blue. It drove toward us, very slowly, and came to a loud and pain-ful stop beside us.

The window was rolled down. A zombie sat behind the wheel. Aura thundering. His human body was young and Chinese, sporting a Mohawk, earrings, and a pinky nail that was so long it curved under. The night was cool, but sweat covered his brow, rolling down the sides of his face. He looked at me like I was covered in live grenades, set to explode in three-two-one—but he gave Grant a once-over that was disturbingly intimate. Killy, he ignored.

"You need a ride," he said, in perfect English.

"Says who?" I asked.

The zombie flipped me the middle finger. "Rex."

"You switched bodies," Grant said disapprovingly. "What happened?"

"My Queen," replied the zombie sharply. Blocks away, up the street, headlights suddenly blazed. Car engines roared.

Killy said, "Oh, shit."

"A ride sounds great," Grant said, and opened the back door. He grabbed Killy's arm and shoved her inside. I made him go next. The zombie hit the accelerator before I was entirely inside, and Grant grabbed the back of my jeans, hauling me over his lap. The back door was still open. I managed to reach out and close it—at the same moment we got rammed in the bumper.

I slammed forward into the plastic barrier. Mal coiled over my forehead at the last second, cushioning me. We were hit again, and brakes squealed. I looked through the back window and watched the car veer off the road and crash through the display glass of a clothing shop. Dek and Mal cheered.

Another car accelerated toward us. Rex wiped sweat out of his eyes and muttered, "You have to kill that Avatar skinner. Do it fast. That's the message from my Queen."

"Old news," I replied, thinking of that lost opportunity—and then hit the side door as the zombie cut a sharp right into an intersection. Grant's cane almost took out my eye as he and Killy slid into me.

"No," said Rex, looking at me in the rearview mirror. His eyes were dark, full of fear. "You don't understand. You cannot let that skinner leave this world. You cannot let him kill you."

"Seems you'd want that."

Rex slammed his fist against the dashboard. "Fuck you. Fuck your bloodline. *Fuck us all.* If the skinner takes your life, Hunter, *the prison veil will come down.* The higher echelons of the demon army will go free, and my Queen and our caste will be enslaved, *again*. You think I went to so much trouble just to give you a fucking ride? This mind is strong. I'm going to be kicked out in less than a minute."

I stared, certain I had heard him wrong. "What the hell do you mean?"

Rex trembled, but clamped his mouth shut. Grant reached around the plastic barrier, and grabbed the zombie's stolen shoulder. "The Avatar must be working from a central location. Do you know where?"

Rex shook his head. "You can't let the skinner take you, either."

"Why does he want me?"

The zombie glanced back at him, aura thundering. "That's a story older than my kind, and I don't know it. But you have the stink of the Labyrinth in your blood, something *not* of this world, and that's something I never wanted to tell you."

Two cars veered into the road ahead of us, blocking both lanes. Rex swore, slamming on the brakes. Behind us, more tires squealed. Two black Audis veered into the sidewalks, and Zee crashed through the windshield, rolling like a tumbleweed. But the road was now empty.

"Reverse!" I shouted. "Put the car in reverse!"

Rex switched gears and accelerated backward. He was a lousy driver. We weaved across both lanes, nearly hitting one of the crashed cars. I glimpsed two little bodies tumbling out of the stalled Audis. Aaz held a child's baseball bat. Dek and Mal, deep in my hair, sang "Blaze of Glory."

Amen, I thought, and grabbed Grant's arm. Behind us, more headlights. Accelerating toward us. No room on the sidewalks to go around, and no side streets. Ahead, the cars that had blocked the road were also coming fast. We were boxed in.

Rex slammed his knuckles against his brow, still trying to steer the cab with his other hand. He was not watching the road. "I can't hold this body much longer."

Zee appeared between my feet and grabbed my right hand. I ignored Killy's gasp, and stared into his red-glowing eyes. Raw and Aaz slipped from the shadows, as well, clambering over Grant.

"Maxine," Zee rasped. "Time to go."

His claws squeezed. Rex shouted, and the world faded— into the abyss, swallowed down a throat of pure darkness. My right hand burned, and a terrible hunger filled my heart.

Make us safe, I thought.

Light burned the backs of my eyes. Light, inside the abyss.

I lost time. I lost myself. My innards tumbled into somersaults, and when I opened my eyes, I was somewhere else.

Alone.

I rolled over on my back. It was night. Tree branches waved gently above my head, and I saw starlight. I could hardly feel my body. Felt like I was floating inside my skin.

I heard a baby crying. Soft wails, filling the night. I began to sit up, and realized that Zee and the boys were hard on my skin—tattoos again.

That was not right. I had to be dreaming.

So, I treated it like a dream. I had no choice. I thought about Grant and home, and even Rex and Byron, but nothing happened. Trees surrounded me. The baby kept crying.

I walked. My feet did not touch the ground. As in a dream, I skimmed the earth, and pushed through the forest that grew around me tall and thick and far apart, with their leaves of autumn withered and faded. A softness filled me as I moved, a warmth that wrapped around my heart, dulling fear and love, and anger. I was a ghost, and only the baby's agonized wails had hooks—compelling me, sinking me.

I walked, and soon after, found the baby. Swaddled in soft cloth, resting in a pile of dried leaves. Small, pale, with chubby, strong limbs. Less than a year old, I thought.

She was not alone.

Zee was with her. All the boys were gathered close, muscles gliding beneath their skin, which was moonlit-clad, soft as liquid obsidian. They were peering at the infant, whose cries were agonizing, spirit-rending. Shocked me to see them. They did not appear to notice me.

There was a hole in the ground behind them. A woman lay inside, covered in small purple wildflowers and seashells—things that could not have been native to the forest where I stood—but that had been placed with such care around and across her body, I thought she must have loved them very much in life.

She looked like me, but all of us Hunters looked alike. Pale skin, black hair, fine features. She had been washed and dressed in clean white robes, but there was a ragged cut across her throat, so deep I wondered if she had almost lost her head.

Raw and Aaz kept glancing over their shoulders at the woman. Every time they did, low, grunting cries would escape their throats, and their claws would rake across their bellies, shedding sparks. Dek and Mal hung from their necks, making mewling sounds, but Zee had eyes only for the baby.

He picked her up, ever so carefully, and cradled her to his chest. His bristly hair was slicked back, close to his skull, and he closed his eyes, whispering soft words. The baby did not stop sobbing, and the boys began to sing: a high, soft song, without words, the melody simple and gentle. Their voices were eerie and choral, echoing as though the trees were the walls of a church, and the night sky a black glass roof of stars. My heart, which had begun to ache, quieted even as the baby quieted, and a hush fell, something deeper than silence, as the boys closed their mouths and bowed their heads: wolves, praying; demons, grieving.

Dek and Mal slid across Zee's body, and I watched as they used themselves to create a living harness that held the baby snug to the demon's barrel-shaped chest. Long, warm bodies, crisscrossed and safe. Zee clasped her to him, as well—and with his free hand helped Raw and Aaz push dirt over the woman in the grave.

Hunter. My ancestor. Somewhere lost in history, murdered well before her time. The boys would never have abandoned that woman before her child was able to feed herself.

I thought of the bullet that had been shot at my head. Franco and his gun. A cut to the throat was more intimate. The woman had known her attacker—or perhaps more than one person had held her down. Probably killed at sunset. The boys—especially Dek and Mal—would never have let anyone close enough for that killing blow.

He passed to me his knowledge, Cribari had said. *He told me how to stop you.*

Something moved in the forest, behind the boys. Zee and the others turned as one to stare, and my right hand burned when I saw the man who slipped free of the shadows. He was tall, slender as a swimmer, with a pale, chiseled face framed by long silver hair that drifted past his shoulders. His eyes were red and rimmed in amber. Ruby-encrusted caps of silver covered the tips of his pointed ears, and he wore a dark crimson tunic over loose black pants. His sinewy arms were bare, white as snow, and his nails were pure white and long as claws.

"So you lost your Lady," he said softly, with a smile. "How unfortunate. But then, I always wanted to be a father."

Zee snarled, hunching over the baby as Raw and Aaz crowded in front of him, dragging their claws through the dead leaves.

"Not yours," he rasped, eyes glittering. "Ours, not yours."

"Hound," whispered the man. "Beast. Demon. How will you care for a baby? You are nothing but slaves. She will *die* with you. And if she lives, she will be an *animal*." He held out his hand and snapped his fingers imperiously. "Give her to me. Now or later, you have no choice. The sun will rise in mere hours."

Zee held the baby even closer and turned his face up to the sky. Raw and Aaz did the same, closing their eyes. The

man watched them, frowning—with unease, I thought—
and hunger. Greed. Lust.

"Hound," he said again, more urgently. "Do not defy—"

He never finished. Zee and the boys vanished, taking
the baby with them. Taking me, as well. The last I saw of
the man—*Mr. King,* I named him—was the glitter of rubies in his ear, and the snarl that twisted his face into
something monstrous and grotesque.

Then we were elsewhere—on the rocky shore of a choppy
silver sea—and there was light in the east, and pink petals
of clouds, and the last stars of morning clinging to the purple sky behind me.

"Bright little heart," Zee whispered to the baby, rocking
her gently. "We be your old mothers now, bright and sweet.
Teach you fine."

Raw looked up at the sky, breath rattling. I felt a tinge
beneath my ear, deep inside my scar. An arrow of darkness
winked from the sky and dropped swiftly to earth, landing
on the tips of feet shaped like daggers, glittering and sharp.
A demon, or a creature so far beyond human, there was no
other name to give. A wide-brimmed hat covered much of
his face, and he had no arms—simply a cloak that moved
against the wind, and hair that snaked into the air as though
each tendril were a tentacle, and alive.

"We heard your call," Oturu whispered, and opened his
cloak. A man stepped free of the darkness within. His hair
was long and black, his cheeks sharp, his nose too large for
his face. He wore simple dark clothing, rough-hewn, as
though woven from a loom—and an iron collar glittered at
his throat.

Tracker. He stared at the baby.

"Ours," whispered Zee, holding the child tight. "But
hungry. Need to make her strong while the sun goes high.
Safe and strong."

Pain flickered through Tracker's eyes, but he crouched
and held out his hands. Zee hesitated, all the boys rumbling with unease.

"Zee," said Tracker quietly. "I remember how to care for a baby."

"We take her back tonight," Zee said possessively, and kissed the infant on her brow. She touched his sharp face with impossibly small hands, and smiled.

"Little Bright," he whispered again, and handed her to Tracker, who held the baby in his large hands and cradled her to his chest.

The sun crested the horizon. Zee and the boys vanished into smoke—shrouding the baby, sinking into her skin, glittering like stardust and becoming veins of silver and mercury—until her tattoos pressed so close together on her small body, she seemed carved from obsidian. She gripped Tracker's tunic with strong little fingers and sighed.

"Lady Hunter," Oturu murmured, and I realized the demon had moved—moved without my realizing it, so focused had I been on the baby and my boys.

I looked, and was startled to find him towering behind me, black cloak and hair flaring wildly in every direction. Nothing about him, past or present, was different; the brim of his hat still swept low, hiding his eyes. His pale jaw was sharp.

But he was looking straight at me, and a tendril of his hair shot out to touch my cheek, and the scar he had given me, tingling below my ear.

"Lady Hunter," he said again. "Go home."

My right hand burned. Light flashed in my eyes.

Moments later, I was gone.

CHAPTER 13

THE next time I opened my eyes, I found myself on my hands and knees. My ears were ringing, and my mouth tasted vile. The boys were asleep on my skin. I stared at my fingernails, black as oil—right hand dark with tattoos—glittering like mercury and quicksilver.

The armor had grown, again. The bracelet, which fit my wrist like a second skin, had expanded almost an inch up my arm. Metal gleamed, engraved with an intricate array of coiled lines, like scales, or roses, or the twists of a labyrinth. Blending in with my tattoos.

I was in Grant's apartment, on the floor of his living room. Rare sunlight bathed me in a glow. I peered blearily to my right. Grant was sprawled on his back, rubbing his face. I nudged him with my foot, and he gave me a slow, pained look that might have been his hangover face—if he ever decided to take up alcohol.

Killy lay several feet away, eyes closed. Breathing, but still. No sign of the Chinese man Rex had inhabited.

I fell down on my side and rolled over to stare at the ceiling. Grant grabbed my hand, but that was all. I almost asked him how long I had been gone, but it was clear I hadn't been missed. What I had passed through between leaving China and arriving here had been for me alone: a vision, a dream, a memory belonging to the boys.

Zee had said he knew that Avatar scent on Father Ross's body. Mr. King. Who, in another life, had conspired to murder one of my ancestors. Not to extinguish my bloodline—but to control it.

Made sense. Control a Hunter, and you controlled the boys. Must have seemed attractive at the time. Except he hadn't anticipated that Zee and the others would take matters into their own hands. Raise the child—with a little help.

But now he wanted me dead. Out of the way.

If the skinner kills you, Hunter, the prison veil will come down.

I shook my head, forcing myself to sit up. Rex had it wrong. His Queen was wrong. Up to her old tricks again. The only things he had said that I could be certain were true was that I had to kill the Avatar, next chance I got— and I could not let him have Grant.

Gold flashed. I looked at Grant again and saw that his mother's pendant had fallen just slightly out of his shirt. Most of the disc was obscured, but I could see enough of those curving lines to get hit with déjà vu.

I held up my right hand, checking out the newly expanded cuff that was molded to my wrist—metal flowing seamlessly into my tattooed skin.

Grant said, "You'll still look sexy when you're a cyborg."

"Thanks," I replied dryly, and pointed at the pendant. "Can I see that?"

He frowned, but pulled the necklace over his head and gave it to me. I held it next to my wrist. The engraved lines were strikingly similar. Too much so to be a coincidence.

"Huh," Grant said.

Killy twitched, eyelids fluttering. I returned the necklace to Grant, and he stared thoughtfully at the pendant before draping the gold chain over his head. "My mother looked human."

"So do I," I replied. "So do you. So did Mr. King, but we know what was on the inside."

"Never judge a book by its cover, right?"

"Don't judge your mother," I said. "Not before you know the facts."

"There are no facts." Grant sat up, reaching for his cane. "Just possibilities."

I grabbed his wrist, stopping him from standing. "You and I both know that you haven't stretched the limits of what you can do. I'm not even proposing you try. But a lot of powerful individuals think you're dangerous, and that means something. If your mother knew what you were capable of, and didn't tell you, there's a reason."

He pulled away from me. "Same reason your mother kept secrets from you?"

Secrets. Secrets about the darkness sleeping inside me, that threatened to possess and overpower me: a force, an entity, that had terrified my mother. And Jack. Others, as well. I did not know what frightened me more: that I was beginning to find a use for that power—or that I still didn't know what it was or where it had come from.

"Maybe," I replied, finding it suddenly difficult to speak. "My mother wanted to protect me. She wanted me to grow up as normal as possible, without that extra burden. We had enough problems."

"*I* was afraid," Grant said, his gaze burning into mine. "I was afraid of myself, and I bore it alone. I'm still afraid, but at least I have you. I just wish . . . if she could have . . . that it hadn't taken so long."

I grabbed his hand. "You know she loved you. You know that, right?"

Grant closed his other hand around the pendant, his thumb rubbing the engraved lines. Solemn, thoughtful. I waited, afraid of what he was going to say.

Until, very slowly, he leaned in and kissed me. His hand stroked my throat, his thumb sliding over my mouth, so gently I forgot to breathe.

"Thank you," he murmured.

Killy made another small noise. We pulled reluctantly apart, looking at her. She sat up, holding her head. Blood trickled from her nose.

I helped Grant stand, and he leaned hard on his cane, wincing as he put weight on his bad leg. I strode to the kitchen and grabbed a rag. Tossed it to Killy, who wiped awkwardly at her nose.

"Father Frank," she muttered, looking at the bloodstains. "Goddamn you."

"You know how to contact him?" I asked her.

"A landline number," she said, giving me a pained, angry look. "I doubt he's able to answer it at the moment."

"This wasn't his fault," Grant said reluctantly, with an added weariness that seemed born from the bone.

Killy tried to find her feet, ignoring my outstretched hand. "But he's part of it. He knew I wouldn't say no when he asked for my help."

I did not understand her relationship with the priest, but the hurt on her face went deep—deeper than mere acquaintance would explain. Her eyes were cut with betrayal. I felt sorry for her.

Something thumped in the guest bedroom. I reached inside my jacket for a knife—the same one I had used on Mr. King. I had not cleaned it well enough, but I held the steel in my right hand, and the boys began absorbing the blood. Killy looked at the tattoos and flinched. For once, I did not mind letting a stranger see them.

I walked across the living room to the closed door. Pushed it open.

A man sat on the edge of the bed. I knew his face, but there was no dark aura thundering over his head. Red cap askew, tool belt missing. Not Rex, not a zombie. Just a man, waking up for the first time in a long while.

Even without the aura, I would have seen the difference. His face was slack, his eyes dull and tired. Not just from years of possession but from something deeper, more profound: as though breathing took too much effort.

Grant came up behind me, staring. I said, "Did you ever wonder about his host?"

"I always wondered," he rumbled. "But I never found the right answer. To allow a possession is a terrible thing, but to commit murder against a creature simply trying to survive, and become something better, is equally unspeakable."

Once, not so long ago, I had suffered no such doubts. It was simple. You never let demons in. You cut them out when you found them. All those Archie Limbauds of the world had to die.

But I did not move when a shadow suddenly flickered into the room. I did not remove my other glove and raise my tattooed hands to the demon hovering behind the sitting man's head. I should have. I should not have hesitated. All I could see, though, were those tired eyes staring sightlessly through me, without question or concern about where he was, and why, and how—and I made a calculated decision. Strategy over morality.

Grant did nothing, either, but his indecision ripped through me, and I grabbed his hand, squeezing tight as the demonic parasite seeped into the man's body, leaving behind a trail of thunderclouds that hovered over his head. I watched the transformation. Sharp intelligence filled his eyes, and something I could describe only as *the will to live* carved new lines into his face.

Rex. I should have felt disgusted—I should have worried for his host—but I was so fucked up all I could manage was an odd, tired relief. Rex was a demon. He was a bastard, and I might kill him one day. But he was a better bastard than Mr. King. I needed every ally I could muster, even if this zombie was dedicated only to Grant.

But it was still too much. I turned around, pushed past Grant, and left the room.

Killy was at the front door of the apartment, fumbling through her purse. Counting the cash in her wallet, which was entirely in Chinese currency. I said, "We're in Seattle, in case you were wondering. Plenty of planes and buses."

"Overseas was convenient. I could get away with more." She tapped her forehead, almost absently. "Dress up, mix drinks, act a little cheap. Men with money never look too deep. Don't notice you picking their brains."

Who *would* pay attention? If I could live unnoticed with demons existing on my body, being a psychic should have been a breeze. "You can use my credit card to buy a ticket. Anywhere you like."

Killy gave me a sharp look. "Most of my money was tied up in that bar. I can't pay you back."

I had never stayed long enough in one place for anyone to return anything. "Not necessary. You shouldn't be involved in this."

She stared at me like I had beans for brains. Maybe I did. But I didn't like it when people looked at me as though I was stupid. I dug into the back pocket of my new jeans and pulled out my wallet. Grabbed a credit card without looking and tossed it at her.

"Keep it," I said. "Run it up to the limit, then burn the damn thing. Start your life over, but get out now while you can."

"What—" she began, and glanced down at the card. "Anne Jovi?"

"I think we've got another problem," Grant said, behind us. I had not heard him crossing the room, but he stood by the kitchen counter and had the phone pressed to his ear. Rex was with him, watching me thoughtfully.

"What?" I asked carefully.

"We have messages. From the police. Social services." Grant's jaw tightened, something cold flickering through his eyes. "Byron is gone. And so is Mary."

⊰⊱

TWO days. We had been gone for two days, out of touch, and a man had come asking about the boy.

He had been here before, some of the volunteers told Grant. A tall skinny man, a priest, who spoke with an Italian accent. He claimed he had reason to believe that the boy was being abused, and he wanted to ask some questions. Social services had arrived with him, on a related issue: underage children were not supposed to live in adult homeless shelters.

But Byron had already left the shelter.

I stood in his room. It was located in the private wing of the warehouse complex, which had been set aside for some of the Coop's permanent residents: individuals and families with special needs, who needed a place to call home. Only a handful lived here. It was a special privilege that Grant could not afford to give everyone.

I had been in Byron's room only a handful of times in the past three months. His bed was unmade, surrounded by stacked books and paper. Movie posters hung on the walls: *Lord of the Rings*, *Hellboy*, and *Blade Runner*. Clothes were piled on the floor. He had not taken much with him, if anything.

"The police got involved because Mary attacked Antony," Grant said quietly, standing in the doorway with that gold pendant flashing against his chest. "She tried to claw his eyes out."

I fingered Byron's sweater. "When did that happen?"

"Early this morning. No one's seen them since."

I nodded, chewing the inside of my cheek. Cribari had been in bad shape, but it was possible. And China was only seconds away if you knew someone who could cut space. "Police want to question you?"

"Eventually. But they're not here right now." Grant dangled his car keys over my shoulder. "You drive."

We left the Coop. Scattered sunlight warmed my face. I did not see anyone watching us, and the boys were quiet. I could not relax, though. We were running on borrowed time. Everything, falling apart.

I felt like a moving target as we crossed the parking lot. My car was still somewhere near Pike Place Market, if it hadn't already been towed, but Grant had a Jeep.

We found Killy leaning against its back door, arms folded over her chest. Blood dotted her nostrils. She was too pale to be wearing so much black. Made her look like death warmed over.

"So I was thinking," she said, watching us carefully. "I was thinking about what that . . . thing . . . told me in the bar. That he had my scent. And it occurred to me that getting away from the two of you wouldn't necessarily make me safer."

It was not a question, but she seemed to want an answer I had no interest in giving. I shared a quick look with Grant, found a similar reticence on his face, and turned from the woman to unlock the Jeep's doors. I said nothing when she climbed in behind me. Not *Get lost* or *Run like hell*.

All I did was drive.

John Parr played on the radio. Some acoustic version of "St. Elmo's Fire." I liked the song, but it did little for my nerves. I drove into downtown Seattle, and near the museum found a parking spot outside a narrow brick building faced with a glass display and a delicate door, upon which had been etched the script: SARAI SOARS: ART GALLERY.

The gallery had been closed since its owner's death—or long vacation, depending on whom you spoke to—but I had a key. So did others. I went in, and found myself in another world: bathed in shadows and cool, filtered air, light with the scent of orchids. Paintings hung on the walls. Massive, intricate masterpieces of an incongruous subject: unicorns, lost in scenes of human battles, medieval and modern—covered in blood and sea foam, surrounded by swords and guns. Innocence, in the heart of murder. Purity in death.

There were stairs at the back of the gallery, behind a carved wooden screen. I marched up, footsteps loud, making no effort to hide my approach.

The second-floor landing had only one door, and it stood open, contents spilling into the hall. Books, everywhere. Beyond the door, a maze of them. Piles and stacks, surrounding packed shelves shoved tight against the walls, and tables that overflowed with reams of paper, rocks, and

open crates filled with packing materials and glimpses of
odd artifacts. Lamps burdened with stained-glass shades
perched precariously atop leather-bound encyclopedias—
power cords buried, presumably connecting somewhere,
somehow, to the walls. I saw empty teacups scattered similarly around the room, placed haphazardly along the only
path through the mess: a clear, narrow, and winding trail.

Jack's home. His shadow, still warm over all his belongings.

"Byron," I called softly. "It's me."

I heard rustling. Byron appeared on the other end of the
room, leaning out from behind a bookshelf. He wore jeans,
and a long-sleeved gray shirt. His gaze was piercing; dark
and old, and very tired.

"I'm glad," he said. "I wasn't sure you'd remember I had
a key."

I remembered clearly. Months ago, after Jack's disap-
pearance, I had told Byron to come here if he was ever in
trouble. I had reason to believe he might be one day. Not
just because of his association with me.

If something happened, if I disappeared, or Grant could
not help him—this was a good place. *Come here to the stu-
dio,* I had said. *Come to this apartment.* I had hidden money,
left cans of food. For my own use, too. I had other safe
houses, in other cities. Inherited from my mother.

But this place was no longer safe. No such thing, anymore.

I picked my way through the narrow path, my legs brushing the spines of books. The boys were quiet. Dreaming,
sweetly. Maybe the only calm thing about me. I was holding together, but just barely. Seeing Byron helped. Maybe
this was what being motherly felt like. My own mother
would have called it a weakness. Affection was dangerous
business. People did not last, no matter how much you
wanted them to. People caused trouble, people distracted,
people could not be trusted.

Wrong people, I thought at my mother. Nor was there

any point to saving the world if I felt no love for it—if I was not *in* love with the people in it. Some of them, anyway. I wasn't a hippie, or anything.

The kitchen was not nearly as packed as the rest of the apartment, though the sink was full of dishes, and crumbs covered the counter. Mary sat at the table. I was surprised to see her. Giant daisies had replaced the poodles on her potato-sack dress. The hem barely covered her knobby knees, and the oversized blue sweater swallowing her frame was patched and holey. Her white hair would have made Einstein proud.

Byron stood beside her, pouring hot water into a large mug filled with three tea bags and five old-fashioned cubes of sugar. Mary's hands trembled around the thick white ceramic, and her gaze was fixed on the floor.

"Tea helps keep her calm," said Byron, as though it was perfectly natural for a fifteen-year-old street kid to be taking care of an elderly, somewhat insane and otherworldly drug addict. And for him, maybe it was. He was not a normal boy.

"You did good," I said, as Grant crowded in behind me, awkwardly navigating the narrow trail between books. Killy was with him, frowning, fingers pressed to her brow. Her frown intensified when she saw Mary.

"You okay?" Grant asked Byron.

"Fine," he said, staring past him at Killy. "I saw Mary attack the priest. I found her after she got away. Took her with me."

Very good kid. I ruffled the boy's hair. Mary lifted her gaze, from the floor to her teacup, then Grant. Like watching the sun come up in her face. She beamed when she realized who was standing in front of her; she glowed, and bristled with a smile.

"Grant," she whispered, standing—reaching for him. But her hands stopped just before she touched his shoulders, and hovered instead over the pendant glinting soft and golden in the lamplight. She stared, lips moving, wrinkled skin growing paler, something wild in her eyes that reminded me of Mr. King's creations—while being in every way their opposite.

Mary had drawn that design in ink upon her palm, but it was faded now, almost gone. She laid that hand over the pendant and shuddered, drawing in her breath through clenched teeth. Grant stood frozen, like he was suddenly afraid to be so near her. Byron was tense, as well, but this time his attention was fully on the old woman—and I wondered, briefly, what he had seen to make him want to keep her calm.

"Mary," Grant murmured, saying her name like a song. "Mary. Do you know this? Have you seen it before?"

Killy made a small, pained noise, and closed her eyes. Mary swayed.

"Mary," he said again.

"Antrea," she whispered, and closed her hand around the pendant.

All the color drained from Grant's face. I caught him as his bad leg buckled. His grip on my shoulder was so strong the boys wiggled beneath his hand. "How do you know my mother's name?"

"Your mother," Mary breathed, blinking sharply. "Your mother was beautiful."

Killy cried out, gripping her head between her hands.

"Your mother," Mary said again, louder, her knuckles turning white around the pendant. "I lost your mother."

Killy began to sit down, but there was no chair, nothing to catch her. Byron grabbed her arm, but she yanked away from him as though burned, and fell hard to the floor. She hardly seemed to notice. Pain wrinkled her face.

Mary tugged hard, yanking Grant close. "I had her, like *this*, and she was pulled away."

Killy screamed. Byron stared at me, helpless. I reached down and grabbed the woman under her arms, hauling backward, pulling her away from Mary—who was becoming even more lucid, more wild-eyed.

"Byron," I snapped, and the teen grabbed Killy's legs. We knocked books over, stumbling.

"The Labyrinth took you both," Mary said, but I was no longer looking at her, focused solely on holding the sobbing woman who seemed to be dying in my arms.

"Mary." Grant's voice broke through my concentration. "Mary, calm down."

The old woman's voice quaked. "The others were dead. All of them. The babies—they took the *babies*—and you were the last; you were—"

"Mary."

"—I promised to protect you—"

"Mary."

"—but I *failed* her."

Byron and I managed to get Killy in the hall, but she was still screaming, clutching her head like it was going to explode. Blood trickled from her nostrils.

"Hit her," said the boy grimly. "Knock her out."

I stared at him. Then turned, slamming my fist into Killy's jaw. It was a careful blow, but a good one. Her voice cut off with a choke, and she went slack. Unconscious. Still breathing, heart racing, but safe from the pain she had been suffering. Her sudden silence was deafening.

"Stay with her," I ordered Byron, and ran back into the apartment.

Mary stood nose to nose with Grant. She was not a tall woman, but she was raised up on her toes, and had used the gold pendant to yank the man down until he stared directly into her eyes. Foam flecked a corner of her mouth. She looked at Grant as though he was her lifeline, her reason for breathing. Nothing crazy about it. The old woman was as sane in that moment as I had ever seen her.

"I lost you," she breathed.

Grant grabbed her hand. "You found me. You're safe now."

"No world is safe." Mary turned her head, and looked across the apartment at me—staring into my eyes with clear, striking intensity. "You. One of theirs. I can see it. Blood-spun, grafted. Slave."

"I'm no slave," I said.

"Then they'll kill you," she whispered. "Or try to control you."

"Not me." I strode forward until I stood face-to-face with the old woman. "Not Grant. Not anyone on this world."

Grief ravaged her face. "So we said, when the Aetar first came."

Mary swayed again, placing her palm against her eye. Her grip on the pendant loosened. Grant tried to hold her close, but her knees buckled.

"They're coming," she whispered, and let go of the necklace.

I caught the old woman as she fell, and lowered her gently to the floor. She was still conscious but mumbling nonsense, her eyes distant, farseeing. Mind swimming free again. Just a little crazy. But not *that* crazy, I realized.

Grant knelt awkwardly beside her, utterly stricken. He let go of his cane, and both his hands hovered over the old woman, trembling. Like he was afraid to touch her.

Zee jerked backward against my skin, all the boys swimming with unease.

"Damn," I whispered, trying to process everything she had said. If it was lies, Grant would know. But from the look on his face, everything she had said was true. As true as she knew it to be.

"Maxine," Byron called urgently. I glanced at Grant, but his focus was still on the old woman. I pushed away, moving quickly across the apartment. I did not see Byron until I was in the doorway. He stood at the top of the stairs, hands clenched into fists. Killy was still unconscious.

I joined him, and looked.

A man stood at the bottom of the stairs, leaning against the wall. Shadows so thick I could not see his face. I knew him, though. I would have known him anywhere.

"Old Wolf," I whispered.

"Sweet girl," he rumbled, and slid down the wall to his knees.

CHAPTER 14

M Y mother never spoke about the men in our family. Their existence had the quality of a fable, or myth; no woman in my bloodline discussed the father of her child. Not ever. Not in the journals they kept, not in the lore. Even sex was a taboo subject. I had to learn about it from reading books in the library or snatching glimpses of Cinemax on hotel television late at night while my mother was out hunting zombies.

Made sense, in retrospect. Sex and men led to babies. A baby meant death, murder—a hard good-bye.

My grandfather sat at the bottom of the stairs, legs stretched in front of him. I sat at his side. We held cups of hot tea. I did not drink, but Jack sipped his with great care. A long scratch covered the side of his face. He needed a shave, a shower. His messenger bag was gone. No sign of the shotgun. He trembled every time he took a breath, and I listened to the rattling in his chest with unease.

"I was told you had been captured," I said.

"A lie," Jack replied quietly. "But had he found me, he might have released me, anyway. Torture is a limited

pleasure for my kind. To hurt us, you must find the heart of
what keeps us sane, then take it." A grim smile touched his
mouth. "So I, like a fool, came seeking you."

I leaned against him, ever so slightly. "He's already
done a good job tracking us. At this point, I don't think it
matters where we go or who we're with."

"He plays," Jack murmured. "He tests and toys, and
marvels at what we are, and what we have become. All of
us have changed, my dear. Your bloodline. Me. Grant, too,
is a quality that should not be."

I frowned, wondering what he meant by all that, but
before I could ask, I heard movement at the top of the
stairs. Grant, gazing down at us. His gaze darkened when
he focused on Jack. "Killy is awake."

"We'll be right there," I said, but he did not acknowledge me. Just backed away, still watching the old man with
disquieting thoughtfulness.

Jack didn't seem to notice, but I suspected that was out
of self-preservation. "Is this Killy the young lady you just
dragged screaming from my home?"

"She had an interesting reaction to Mary," I replied,
standing slowly. "How long do you think we have?"

"Moments or hours." Jack rose with me, sighing. "No
longer than that. He never had patience."

"Or a sense of self-preservation. He's reckless."

"Reckless or desperate, or perhaps a little mad."

We started climbing the stairs, leaving our teacups on
the step. I offered him my arm. He took it with a faint smile,
which faded when I said, "I know what he did. Before, to
one of my ancestors. I know he arranged her murder."

Jack stopped climbing, and stared at me—his expression unfathomable. I thought for certain he would ask how
I had discovered that crime, but instead he said, "It was the
final act. It was why I finally arranged his incarceration."

"And the boys? Tracker, helping raise her baby? Oturu?
I would have liked knowing that."

"There is too much history," Jack said heavily, beginning to climb the stairs again. "Too much, my dear. Ten thousand years of stories in your blood. All you can truly know is yourself."

Easier said than done.

Killy was still on the landing, a pillow under her head and a bottle of water on the step above her. Byron sat with her. He tensed when he saw Jack. He had never been able to relax around the old man, nor could Jack look the boy in the eye. Seemed to me that he pretended the teen did not exist as he stared down at the woman, whose eyes fluttered open to stare directly into his face.

"Hell," she said hoarsely. "Another one."

Jack's nostrils flared, and grim amusement passed through his gaunt face. "I could say the same about you."

"He won't hurt you," I said quickly, sensing some alarm in her gaze.

Killy tried to sit up, and Byron reached out to help her—stopping just before he made contact. He could not look at her face, but I thought it was shyness that kept his gaze down. A restrained, quiet, and terrible shyness.

"I should have ditched you folks," she muttered. "Self-preservation, my ass. I'm safer on my own."

Maybe, maybe not. "How's your head?"

She stopped trying to stand and gave me a look that would have been tough—even fearless—had the muscles around her left eye not begun twitching furiously. "It burns," she said slowly. "I don't know if it will ever stop. Where that woman has been, what she has gone through, can't exist."

"You saw it?" Jack asked carefully.

"She projects it. I can feel the edges even now. Like . . . razors are growing in my brain." Killy shuddered, rubbing her arms. "I saw death. I saw her kill. I saw her with a woman and baby, being hunted. She was younger then. That old woman was young like me. I saw other babies—"

Killy stopped, her hand flying over her mouth. She looked down, sucking deep breaths into her lungs, and

Byron hugged his stomach, rocking slightly as he watched her. Jack also looked ill, but for a different reason. I saw memory in his eyes. I recalled Mr. King's words.

Old Jack could tell you about the hunts, if he was here. Chasing the skins of your kind across the Labyrinth. Stealing babies into shackles from their cribs.

I looked into the apartment and found Grant watching the old man. His gaze was cold, hard. Remembering the same thing, no doubt.

"I knew some things about the world," whispered Killy, behind her hand. "I thought I knew enough."

"Jack," said Grant quietly. "We need to talk."

The old man rubbed the back of his neck. "I suppose we do, lad."

Grant turned and limped deeper into the apartment. Jack followed. Killy did not seem to notice, but Byron watched both men, then me, with solemn, knowing eyes.

"I'm sorry," I said to him. "This is not something you should have been involved in. I know . . . everything happening seems strange—"

"I'm not alone," interrupted the boy softly, then hesitated, as if that by itself should be explanation enough; and it was, I understood. "Strange is okay."

It was not okay. He deserved better, but I had nothing to offer. I could not send him away. I knew things about Byron that he did not.

I knew he was not entirely human.

I squeezed his shoulder, gently. "Take care of her, kid. I'll be back in a minute."

I entered the apartment. Found the men in the kitchen. Mary was no longer there—in the bedroom, maybe. I thought I heard a soft humming melody behind the partially closed door.

Grant stood beside the table, one hand gripping the back of a chair. Jack leaned against the counter, arms folded over chest. Both men, watching each other warily.

"I think it's time for some answers," Grant said. "In fact, I insist."

"You insist," Jack murmured, and ran his hand over his mouth, the circles under his eyes deepening as though beneath his skin lived nothing but shadows. *"It will have blood; they say, blood will have blood."*

"Stones have been known to move and trees to speak," I continued, picking up where Jack left off—a recitation from *Macbeth*, which my mother had insisted I study. Part of my education into human nature.

"What is the night?" Grant added, softly. "What is this, Jack?"

"Almost at odds with morning," he whispered. "Almost at odds with everything this world has dreamed. Such words, it dreams. Your Shakespeares and Michelangelos, and your clever Einsteins. And earlier, earlier still, such lovely feats of brilliance that this was and is the golden empire we had dreamed, only its treasures were of the mind, and my kind did not stay long enough to value all it offered."

Jack's shoulders sagged, and when he looked at me, briefly, there was a grief in his eyes that reminded me of every time he had ever said my grandmother's name. "I was a fool. I thought things could go on as they were. I wanted that so badly, to have a chance with you. As normal people do, my dear." He hesitated. "I hoped no one else would notice Grant."

Grant slid his fingers through mine. "So someone has. Why the extreme reaction?"

"Extreme?" Jack smiled bitterly. "Is there anything extreme about eradicating a disease, or protecting life against a natural disaster? You do what you must. You destroy what can hurt you . . . or you harness it."

"Grant is a man," I protested. "He's not a force of nature."

"Isn't he? My kind are victims of their own existence, little more than energy. And you, lad . . . you manipulate energy. You could manipulate *us*. You could *kill* us, with nothing but a whim. And not just us, but any living creature. You have that power." Jack gave the man a chilling look.

"Lightbringer. You, who can force light into any heart. Light *or* darkness."

Grant twitched. "Don't call me that."

"In the priesthood you were called *Father*. What I just named you—*Lightbringer*—is more of the same. It is part of your identity, whether you acknowledge it or not."

I shook my head, frustrated. "You're skirting the essentials. There were others, like Grant. What happened to them?"

Jack hesitated. Grant said, very quietly, "You murdered them."

Sickened me to hear those words said out loud. Horrified me when the old man did not deny it. My grandfather. My grandfather, who only looked human. But worse, I was not surprised. I had already tasted fragments of the truth— out in the dead circus, the forest—and the pieces began falling into place. I watched Jack shudder and swallow hard, as though ill.

"We were desperate," he said. "We had no sense of right and wrong. Morality came later, after watching human-kind, and living in their skins."

Grant stood so still, pale, his knuckles white and strain-ing. Breathing heavier than usual, as though his lungs strained. I was afraid for him. He looked unhealthy. My imagination conjured cold breezes wracking his chest with pneumonia; or blood vessels bursting in his brain from the strain of using such force on Cribari.

Unbonded. Mr. King's voice, hissing a trail of unease into my brain. *Untaught.*

"Jack," Grant said, his gaze searching the old man's face. "How desperate could you have been?"

"More than you can imagine," he said, brokenly. "We needed the bodies. And the Lightbringers . . . would not share their people. Nor could we hide from them in human flesh."

Instinct crept—and memory. "You told me they were the first. First of what?"

Grant gave me a sharp look, but I ignored him, unable to

tear my gaze from Jack. I was watching him die, I thought—in little pieces, each word he spoke cutting him to the bone. He closed his eyes, turning his face from me—and I knew, in that moment—I knew what he was going to say.

"They were the first humans," he whispered. "Found on one world. One distant, now-dead world. All humans, my dear—every human—is descended from them."

"No," Grant said roughly. "Impossible."

"We stole their bodies," Jack told him, relentless, with a growing heat that was desperate—frantic to confess, to unburden. "We bred them, molded their flesh. And when a particular breed of human was conceived, a world was found through the Labyrinth, and seeded with that strain of flesh. Allowed to evolve, and *become*. Time moves differently in the Labyrinth. What took millions, billions, of years, we could have instantly, merely by opening and closing a door."

Jack finally looked at me, his gaze ancient and terrible. "Humans were brought to this planet as nothing but proteins and molecules. Thrown into the hot sea and left to gestate. Part of the lab, the farm. The *grand* experiment. A reservoir for bodies."

My brain felt numb. I thought I might be sick. "You told me your kind brought humans to this world to escape the demons."

"Truth. But there were humans already here, my dear, and those we brought with us were more . . . advanced. They formed an empire in the south, but it was destroyed during the war with the demons. The survivors scattered.

"But *you*," he went on, staring at Grant. "The Lightbringers were long dead before that. Guardians, truth-sayers, judges, warriors. They were all those things, and more. And we killed them. We hunted them. We erased every memory of their civilization, and those we did not murder, we enslaved."

"Old Wolf," I whispered.

He began to reach for me, and stopped. "When the others of my kind discover Grant exists, it will happen again.

If they learn that you, my dear, are a threat to them, it will happen anyway. The Avatars will come to this world and destroy it."

No worse than the demons, I thought. *Fucked six ways to Sunday.*

Dek and Mal stirred against my scalp. I reached up to scratch them, and my little boys eased back into their dreams. I wished I could do the same. I wished this were all just a dream.

I flexed my right hand, finger armor sinking tendrils of heat through tattoo into bone. "Is it too late?"

"We know when our kind die. We feel it, even across the Labyrinth. Ahsen was bad enough. Kill *him*, and others will come."

"He has to die," I said.

"And if I give myself up to him?" Grant asked.

"That's stupid," I told him. "That's so stupid."

"If I give myself up," he said again, flashing me a hard look. "Would that be enough to keep them away from this world?"

I wrenched my hand out of his grip, furious. Jack shook his head. "You mustn't."

"Listen—"

"No," he snapped, eyes feverishly bright. "Not if you're the last. Do you understand? What you are has not existed for *millennia*. But you are here, now, because the Labyrinth hid you, and opened a door to *this* world, and *this* time."

"I won't let people die because of me."

"They'll die if you aren't here," Jack rasped, crashing his fist into the table. "They'll die because of the demons, when the prison veil fails. Or they'll die when my kind come and search this world for more of you. It will be the old days, lad, of gods and monsters, and nothing will be the same when it's over. Sacrificing yourself now won't accomplish anything but to save you some pain. And leave *her* to suffer it."

Grant stiffened. I held out my hand to Jack. "Stop."

"No," he whispered, still staring. "Not until he understands. There is no *win* here."

"Just possibilities," said Grant grimly, slamming the tip of his cane into the floor with such force I felt a shock run through my bones. His eyes were dark with fury. "Are you all such bastards, Jack?"

"No," said the old man wearily. "But there are enough."

I sensed someone watching. Turned, and saw Mary in the bedroom doorway, hair wild, clutching her sweater closed. Her gaze was ferocious, the whites of her eyes brilliant as snow. The hard line of Mary's mouth was thin as a blade.

Jack saw her, and flinched. "Marritine."

"Wolf," she whispered unsteadily, and looked at Grant. "He wants to send me back to the dark place."

For one second Grant's face crumpled, but he pulled it together—sucking in a deep breath, visibly steeling himself. He limped to the old woman, and gathered her close. She looked very small within the curve of his arm, and infinitely fragile.

"No," he whispered, kissing the top of her head. "That won't happen."

No, it would not. I could end this. I could end this now.

I held up my right hand, staring at the delicate armor that encased my hand and trailed like a silver vein to the shimmering cuff around my wrist. Jack looked, as well, and weary resignation filled his face.

"Do you know where he is?" I asked the old man, trying to sound calm, strong. "Where Mr. King is hiding?"

Jack said nothing. His eyes were so grave. Grant turned slowly around to stare at me. I could hardly look back. Hurt too much.

"Maxine," he said roughly. "Maxine, *no.*"

Jack moved. Fast, like a viper, his hand snaking out to grab my shoulder. I dodged him, dancing lightly into the maze of books. He did not follow—simply stood, hunched over, one hand clutching at air. I looked from the old man to Grant, and tried to smile for them. My family. Mine.

"I'll see you when I see you," I whispered, heart in my throat. "Stay alive until then."

Grant grimaced, launching himself toward me. His cane slipped, and he went down sloppily. I grabbed my right hand with my left, and stepped backward. Armor, already burning.

Take me to him, I thought, picturing the fat little man. *Give me what I need.*

Grant shouted my name, but he sounded very far away—and I could not see him, I could see nothing as the abyss sucked me down, stealing my breath. For one long moment I drowned, heart battling like a butterfly trapped in a bone cage. But I saw light, and emerged—breathing hard, faint—not flat on my face, but standing.

In a bathroom.

Checkered tile, three metal stalls, one of which was occupied. The air smelled like marijuana and antiseptic, and the two mirrors above the chipped sink were broken and had been painted over with lipstick kisses.

I turned in a full circle, baffled. Behind me, the stall door rattled. I glanced over my shoulder.

And watched my mother come out.

She froze when she saw me. Both of us, staring. My heart hurt so badly it felt like a fist was squeezing it to death, and there was heat behind my eyeballs, and fire in my gut, and if I had been feeling faint before, I was definitely going to lose it now. I stepped back and bumped into the porcelain sinks. Stayed there, needing the support.

My mother looked young, like me, but with a deeper wrinkle in her forehead. Same jacket, similar jeans, but my mother had preferred high-top sneakers to boots, and hers were scuffed and gray. Just like I remembered. Zee and the others tugged on my skin, aching.

"Well," she said, after clearing her throat, "your grandmother told me this might happen again."

"Again." I could hardly speak, my voice rusty and broken. "The first time was in Mongolia. You were—"

"Only fourteen. But I've seen you twice since then. Your

grandmother was still alive, at the time." My mother lifted her shoulder in a faint shrug, her calm enviable—any emotion she might have felt at seeing me tucked neatly away. "You knew her. She knew you. She liked that. She liked *you*."

I was going to have a nervous breakdown. "I'm not supposed to be here."

"Obviously." My mother leaned against the bathroom stall, each movement carefully controlled. Her behavior was not cold, not exactly, but it was deliberate. As though she was afraid to touch me. "Baby, what do you need?"

I need to find a genocidal Avatar, I thought, staring down at the armor glittering on my right hand. I needed to save the lives of the people I loved. I needed to go and fight. I needed to open myself to the darkness in my heart, and lose my heart.

I needed my mother.

"I have to do something," I told her. "I have to kill someone. But if I do this, I'm afraid of what I'll be afterward. I don't know what I'm becoming."

My mother searched my face, and I held still under her scrutiny—as I had held still many times, waiting for her to find the words that never came easily. I wanted to cry, standing there. I wanted to laugh and stamp my feet, but instead I fell into our routine. I savored our old habit like it was breath and heartbeat, and my life. Like it would save my life.

"I don't know what you're becoming," said my mother, finally. "I don't know what sleeps inside us, but I know what you fear. I can't save you from that. No one can. All you can do is trust yourself."

"I don't," I said. "I can't."

"Then you have nothing," she replied gravely. "Everything we are, everything we become, is born of what we believe ourselves to be. What we *trust* ourselves to be, here, even in moments of doubt." My mother placed her gloved hand over her heart. "So who are you, Maxine Kiss? Who did I raise you to be?"

"A good person," I whispered.

"So be good," she breathed, something bright glittering in her eyes. "Even when the darkness swallows your heart, be good in your heart. Trust that. Trust that your mother did her job right."

I laughed, but it was quiet, and full of tears. "I love you. I don't think I told you that enough."

"You're ten now," she said, smiling faintly. "I'll remember that, the next time you throw a tantrum."

I searched my memory for any night when I was ten that my mother had come home acting strange, as though she had encountered her adult daughter in a grimy bathroom, talking heart to heart across death and time. Nothing came to me. Except the night of her murder. I almost said something about that. I would have. A warning, if nothing else.

Maybe it showed on my face. My mother's mouth tightened, and she pushed away from the stall door. "You need to go now, baby. Time is dangerous. We're not meant to cross those borders."

"I didn't have a choice," I replied.

"You had a choice," she countered wryly. "But you were always stubborn."

"Look who's talking." I held up my right hand, and the armor hugged my skin like quicksilver. "What do I do?"

"Go home," she said quietly, warmth and sadness gathering in her eyes. "Go and save the people you love."

Grant flashed through my mind—Jack, Byron. I wondered how much she knew, but there was no time to ask. No time. She began to fade, as though little more than a ghost. I could see right through her.

At the last moment she took a step, lurching toward me with great urgency and indecision. Her mouth moved. I did not hear her voice, but I read her lips.

You're not alone, she said. *There are others.*

Then, nothing. I still stood in a bathroom, but my mother was gone. So were the lipstick kisses on the mirror, and the stalls were painted black now instead of olive green. The floor was the same, though. Checkered and dirty. Hardly seemed real. The only thing in my mind that remained solid was my mother. Her words echoed. Her face, her presence. Everything.

Behind me the door opened. A woman walked into the bathroom—big, busty, dressed in leather, with dyed blond hair teased and frizzed into pigtails that stood out from the top of her head like basketballs.

"What day and year is it?" I asked her, managing to choke out the words just before she disappeared into the same stall my mother had been in.

She stopped and looked at me like I was nuts. Maybe I was. But she told me. It was the same day and year I had left Grant and the others in. I was not home in space, but I was home in time.

I left the bathroom and entered a dark hall, lit by only a single lightbulb that swung from a long chain in the ceiling—begging to be used as a glass piñata. Metal walls were slick with condensation, and the peeling remains of posters and phone numbers, painted over with graffiti art that was either some very magnificent porn or a pod of humpback whales fighting giant squid.

The hall was narrow, packed with people. I saw more skin than leather, smashed with studs, masks, and whips. My tattooed hands fit in fine. Must have been daylight somewhere, but it felt like the sweaty side of midnight as a deep bass throbbed and ached through the walls. Odd time for a party.

Odd life, period.

I started pushing through the crowd. At the end of the hall I found a cavernous room with fake stone stalactites for a ceiling, and a disco ball glittering red, large enough to crush the bodies crammed, teeming and undulating, beneath it. I saw a bar on the far side of the club, and some platforms with stripper poles being put to liberal use.

The music was loud. High-heeled boots stepped on my toes. Sweat rolled down my back, quickly absorbed. The boys stirred, restless and uneasy.

A young man swayed in front of me. He wore a leather

loincloth and nothing else. I tapped his shoulder, and he leaned backward, smiling when he saw my tattoos. I shouted, "Where is this place? What city?"

The young man didn't even blink. "Toronto, lady!"

Toronto. It sounded mundane. I might have stood on the moon and not known it.

A hand caught mine. A young woman, with a cool grip. She could have been fourteen or forty, and was dressed more conservatively than the others, her curves covered by a flowing black dress that shimmered and clung. A glossy blonde, with Cleopatra eyeliner, and lips that were unevenly plump, like some doctor had been after her with a needle.

"The Erlking is waiting," she said.

"Well," I replied. "Let's do something about that."

CHAPTER 15

W E walked, weaving around men and women who gave us room as the beat pumped harder, dancers melting into the thumping groove. I saw no zombies, which struck me as odd. Demonic parasites liked such places, where there was always some kind of drug use— mind-weakening substances that made a person suscepti-ble to influence and possession.

But, nothing. Just the unending crowd, most of whom seemed to know my guide, and watched her move amongst them with glinting, feral eyes. The young woman ignored them all, walking gracefully, carefully, with a polished el-egance that reminded me of old-time movie starlets—girls of good breeding who glided across soundstages as though they were more than human.

I saw other women like her, standing unnaturally still amongst the dancers: dressed in silk, with perfect hair and bodies. Heads tilted, as though listening to something very distant. No one paid attention to them; but once, briefly, I glimpsed one of the girls leading a man in black clothing, just as I was being led. I tried to see more, but the crowd swallowed them up.

I felt swallowed. Men and women brushed tight against me. Hot air made it hard to breathe, though the hard, thrashing rock music fit my mood as I found my own stalking rhythm, traveling amongst flesh and leather across a stone floor that matched the fake, painted roughness of the immense, sharp ceiling. It took us a long time to cross the room. The path the blonde walked made no sense, not even with the excuse of the crowd. She wound and twisted, without rhyme or reason, curving us from the edge of the walls toward the center, and back again. I got dizzy. My vision blurred.

Someone bit my neck.

A hard bite, through my turtleneck. I heard teeth break, and spun around. Saw nothing but a wall of dancers, none of whom was spitting blood.

Hands grazed my back, followed by a sharp blade, angled between my legs. I felt nothing but the pressure of the blade as it pierced my jeans and underwear, but the disgust that filled me was instantaneous. I slammed my elbow backward, encountering nothing but air—just as fingers tangled in my hair, yanking back my head. Sharp nails raked harmlessly across my throat, and the boys flowed over my face in response, protecting me.

I was let go, abruptly. Stood, heart hammering, and glimpsed sharp teeth shining red under the disco ball—snatches of impossibly long fingers lost amongst moving limbs—cat eyes blinking lazily from the faces of men who wrapped themselves around women whose tattoos suddenly looked like iridescent scales. The dancers never stopped, but they watched me, smiling, covering their mouths as they laughed and whispered in one another's ears.

I tasted blood. I had bitten my tongue. I spat on the floor at their feet, and my blond guide reappeared. Her face was serene. She stepped in my bloody spit, and said, "Come. We're almost there."

I said nothing. Just stared at her until she finally looked away and turned. I hesitated before following her, but I had come too far. I needed to do this.

Again, the dancers made room for us. I kept expecting to be attacked. The anticipation was almost worse than the act. Off to my right, I glimpsed again the man in black who had been led off by one of the female guides. I could not see his face—hardly any part of him was visible—but he stood very still amongst the dancers, and I had a sense he was confused, and afraid.

I glanced at my guide, whose back was turned. Remembered those nails and knives. And then shoved my way through the dancers, toward the man.

I could no longer see him, but I headed in the direction where I thought he might be. The man had not seemed far away, but there were a lot of people in my way. Fingers trailed over my arms and through my hair, mouths breathing against my ear. A woman leaned in to lick my cheek. I pushed her away, and kept going—music battering against me, the beat mirroring my heart. Lights dimmed, the red glow spreading like the air was made of blood. Ahead, faint beneath the pulse of drums, I heard a distressed shout.

I tried to move faster, but a wall of bodies surrounded me, dancers gathered so thick it was like trying to move through a bramble bush made of leather and flesh. I could not breathe. Felt like they were crushing me, and the claustrophobia of that moment was too much—too much like the Wasteland, buried and alone. I was so alone.

A woman stood in front of me, a long braid hanging over her shoulder. I grabbed her hair, kicked sharply at the backs of her legs, and forced her down to her knees. I was too quick, and she was too surprised to fight back. I placed my foot on her shoulder, grabbed the top of another man's head, and stepped up. I snatched at clothing to pull myself along. I grabbed at anything I could, feeling like I was climbing free of a sweaty hole.

Seconds later I teetered on someone's shoulders, arms

pinwheeling—and for one moment I had a clear view of the room. Close in front of me I saw the man in black, being dragged to the floor. Pounced on. Pummeled. I got a good look at his face.

Hands grabbed at my ankles. I jumped away, landing awkwardly on some woman's head. My heel slipped—she stumbled—and I took another clumsy leap, my knee ramming a naked shoulder. I slipped again, but the man being attacked was right in front of me, and I angled my body forward so that I tumbled right in the middle of the action.

I felt nothing when I hit the floor, but the boys were rumbling hard in their dreams and there were stars in my eyes from all the blood rushing to my head. I tried to stand—glimpsed sharp teeth, nails shaped like daggers—and was dragged down. Fingers raked through my clothes to slash my skin, and though I felt nothing, the strength of those hands was immense, drowning.

I stopped holding back. My own nails were like claws, and I drove them into flesh, stabbing and twisting, filleting arms to the bone. Women screamed, voices breaking like glass, but they did not let go, did not stop ripping at me. I felt as though I were being eaten alive without death or pain, slobbered and spat on, covered in blood not my own. The boys drank it up. The boys fought in their dreams. I heard them howling in my mind like baby banshees.

And then, nothing. The attacks stopped. I stood, blinking heavily, staring at the red-lit faces that watched me warily. No one danced anymore. I watched as bodies were dragged away, disappearing into the crowd, which heaved and breathed as the music thundered on.

Someone stepped close: a short, round man, dressed in black. Blood trickled from deep cuts in his brown cheek, and he wiped at them with a hand that shook so badly he ended up rubbing his eyes instead.

"Hunter," he muttered, and swayed unsteadily. I wrapped my arm around his waist, holding him up. My own knees felt like shit.

"Father Lawrence," I said hoarsely. "Good to see you."

❦

NO one touched us after that.

Dancers kept their distance—and from a distance they looked human. I stopped looking too close. The blond woman led Father Lawrence and me onward, swaying along that curving, sinuous path through a room I could have crossed in less than a minute had it been empty of the dancers around us—who continued jamming to music that pulsed through my chest like a second heartbeat.

I tapped the blonde on her shoulder. "What's your name?"

"Name?" She had to think about it. "My name is . . . Nephele."

"Nephele, what is this place?"

She glanced over her shoulder, as though she had never seen anyone quite so stupid. "It is the Hall of the Erlking, my Lady."

Not Mr. King. Not Erl King. But *the* Erlking, as though it was a title.

Father Lawrence frowned. "I know that. From Goethe."

"The poet?"

"Dost see not the Erlking, with crown and with train?" recited the priest, wincing as he dabbed at his bloody cheek with his sleeve. "Erlking. Erlkönig. The *Elf* King. Originally found in Scandinavian folklore, but the creature later ended up in Germanic mythology. Both versions malevolent, petty, and cruel."

Perfect. Although, if Mr. King was the kind of supernatural, feylike creature that legends were built on, then those elves were scary motherfuckers. I rubbed my right hand, fingers sliding over the smooth armor—and glanced sideways at Father Lawrence. Still doing his best to mop up his face, with a concentration that seemed bent more on staying calm than cleaning up the blood.

Get him out of here. Do it now.

I edged closer to the man, but did not touch him. I had a bad feeling about leaving. Had a bad feeling about staying, too, but I was here, with an opportunity to end this. Maybe for nothing. Could be this was a waste.

Survival, though, was a daily process. One more day was all a person needed. Get enough of those, and you might have a lifetime.

"How did you end up here from China?" I asked Father Lawrence, raising my voice to be heard over the music.

He gave me an odd look. "I thought we were still in China."

"I was told Toronto."

Father Lawrence briefly closed his eyes. "Maybe we're both right. I don't know how I arrived. All I know is that I was brought here to die."

He spoke without grief or pity. I tore my gaze from his injured face, searching the crowd—for nothing, anything—until the words clawing up my throat could no longer be swallowed.

"I'm sorry," I said. "This is my fault."

Father Lawrence stumbled. I reached for his arm, but he met me halfway, taking my hand. I was surprised at the strength of his grip, and the intensity of his gaze.

"You're wrong," he said; and then, after brief pause: "You're not what I expected."

"You shouldn't know enough to expect anything," I muttered, thinking about that tattoo on his arm. I rubbed my jaw and the edge of the concealed scar. "Who did you think I would be?"

"Someone colder," he said, searching my face. "Ruthless."

"I'm not exactly Mother Teresa."

"Even Mother Teresa wasn't Mother Teresa. Some legends precede the truth. Like you, Hunter Kiss."

I pulled my hand away, gently. Nephele had turned, watching us, head tilted—and though her eyes were placid and dull, I could not help but think it was a mask hiding a creature just as a feral and sharp as the dancers who continued unabated—as if to stop moving would kill them. Their energy was dizzying, relentless, the rock music so loud my teeth hurt. Zee stirred restlessly, aching to be free.

Too many questions in my head. Not enough time for the answers I wanted. I glanced at Father Lawrence, then stared again at Nephele. "How did you get involved in my life? Pick the short end of the priest stick?"

Father Lawrence examined his hands, which trembled briefly. "I was possessed once."

I looked sharply at him. Nephele swayed toward us, silk gliding over her body, perfect face cool and empty. She stopped, just out of reach.

"You should watch your step," she said.

"Bite me," I replied, still listening to Father Lawrence's words echo in my head.

A faint smile touched her mouth, which suddenly seemed painted in the air, merely floating over skin and bone and muscle. Nephele shimmered like a heat mirage, and another bout of dizziness assailed me. My vision blacked out, streaming with pokes of starlight.

When my eyesight cleared, everything was different.

It was quiet, for one thing. No music. The crowd was gone. Men and women still danced, but in silence: scattered, restrained, bodies tall and pale, cut at odd angles that seemed disjointed—as though legs moved in isolation from hips, and hands from arms. Movements, slow and careful: like watching clockwork dancers in a dark ballet. More silk, less leather. Fabric similar to what the blond woman wore. Each one, in a mask.

Chills rocked me. It was as though we had passed through a looking glass—from Gothic rumble to a Venetian masquerade—where eyes were shadows behind slits of cloth and bone, and bodies labored under glittering jewels and delicate precious metals. Scents of smoke and sandalwood filled the warm air. No disco ball in the ceiling. Just a glow in the shape of a half sun, red as rubies, jutting from stalactites that were no longer plastic or painted, but true stone, long and sharp as daggers. Far away, an impossible distance away, stood massive columns of carved white marble thick around as smokestacks, receding into mist-riddled shadows.

The hall of the Erlking. Or Mount Olympus, Asgard, any temple from legend. This was magic; this was the wild, creepy unknown. And if I had been anyone else, I would have been burdened by awe. I would have twisted like a chime, knotted in wonder.

"Hunter." Father Lawrence touched my elbow, pointing at the stone floor. Faint lines of light snaked and curved; a border, or marked trail, resembling slivers of diamonds and ice. We stood between those lines, which were part of something larger. Franco's tattoo came to mind: the labyrinth of Chartres Cathedral. I was also on that road, a pilgrimage to terrible, violent enlightenment.

"You know this imagery," I said quietly, aware of Nephele listening. "What does it mean to you?"

"What it means to me isn't the same as the truth, and all the truths I thought I knew have become lies." He looked at me, and I found him transformed again—from the gun-toting, swearing man of China—to the quiet, thoughtful priest who had watched me so carefully in the cathedral. "This isn't the first time my order has tried to exterminate your bloodline."

Cut throat. Woman in a grave. Baby, wailing. Visceral memories. I stared at him, and he added, "I'm surprised you weren't aware of this. Aware of *us*, before now."

"Imagine that," I said coldly.

Zee tugged, as did Raw and Aaz. Dek and Mal rolled warm against my scalp and face, and I almost touched my cheeks, remembering suddenly that they still covered me. Father Lawrence had not batted an eye at my changed visage. No one had in this place.

Zee pulled at me again, like a vacuum hose sucking on my skin. I turned. One of the dancers had broken away. Like the others, he wore a mask, but only across his upper face: a simple sheet of pale wood carved with veins of silver; and from its edges spiraled naked ice-tipped branches and bloodred thorns. A crimson cloak covered his body. His skin was snowy white, and his eyes matched the color of the thorns, irises nothing but slits rimmed in amber.

His gaze was hungry, and alien in ways that had nothing to do with color and shape: I recognized those eyes. Everything else might be different, but the way he looked at me remained the same.

Nephele fell on her knees and pressed her brow to the stone. The man ignored both her and Father Lawrence, and smiled only for me, tight-lipped.

"My Lady," he said.

"Mr. King," I replied, unimpressed. I could not look at his new body without seeing, superimposed, a short fat man in a wrinkled suit, stuffing hot dogs and bloody pretzels in his mouth. Far more disturbing than this otherworldly shape, which was too ridiculous, too odd, to be anything but merely curious.

False. Contrived. Costumes and lies. He is nothing but thought and energy. He is nothing.

"Dance with me," he whispered, eyes glinting. "We have words to share."

I flexed my hands, trying to muster the darkness within my heart—wondering, briefly, what it took to get a girl in the mood for murder. Nothing happened. Nothing stirred beneath my ribs. But my gloves were off, and the boys were already dancing death in their dreams.

"Nephele," said Mr. King, still watching me. "Take our other guest for a spin."

"No. I'll wait here," replied Father Lawrence, giving me a warning look. I met his gaze, but nothing else needed to be said. We both knew we were fucked. Him, more than me. He was nothing but a skin in this place.

Mr. King reached for me. I held still, fighting my instincts, but when he touched me for the first time, it was he who flinched. Shuddering, when his fingers wrapped around my right hand. Pain flexed behind his mask, some terrible hunger.

But then his mouth tightened into that cold, thin smile,

and he led me backward into a waltz that floated us amongst the clockwork dancers, who watched behind their masks. *Another game,* I told myself. Part of the old dark game. Only this was not a demon in front of me but something else.

I was not an easy dancer. I had no rhythm. But in this place my feet floated, and I moved as I might fight— without thinking about it. Mr. King did not hold me tightly, but his grip was cool and firm. Not relaxed, but not entirely afraid, either. Cautious, maybe. He had wanted me to come here. Wheels were turning. He had a plan. And I realized that what Jack had said was true: whomever Mr. King held responsible for Ahsen's murder, it was not me.

"So we are here, again," he murmured. "Dancing around each other with death on our minds."

"You're not scared of me," I said. "No matter what I'm thinking."

His smile tightened. "I helped make you. All of us, who were masters of the Divine Organic, had a hand in the creation of your lineage. You were first, my Lady. The oldest of the Wardens. The oldest, and the most trouble. Of course I'm not frightened of you."

But you're frightened of something, I thought, as his eyes ticked down to look at the armor on my right hand. For a moment I thought he might try to bite it off. The sensation was so strong I half imagined my arm disappearing down his throat. I almost hoped he would try. The boys loved cracking teeth.

But Mr. King did not attack me. He licked his lips, jaw flexing as though going through the motions of chewing. Again, I remembered him as that wrinkled little man. Eating, cramming pizza into his face. As though he had gone a thousand years without the pleasure of food and could not get enough of it: that visceral human satisfaction.

I tore my gaze from his mouth and found him studying my face.

"You are like her," he said, softly. "I saw it in your eyes when you killed my other skin. Something in you is the same. Five thousand years dulls nothing for my memories. I remember your ancestor, before she disappeared from this world. Before she fell into the Labyrinth, and she returned with *that*." He looked down again at the armor on my hand. "It would be better if you did not keep it long, my Lady. Objects born from the Labyrinth cannot be controlled by mortal minds. Such things have their *own* minds."

"You're mortal," I said. "I think you're goddamn ready to die, in fact."

"There is sunlight younger than my kind," replied Mr. King, "even if those dark years have been forgotten to save our sanity. I think dying now would be premature."

"Don't bullshit me." I leaned in so close we could have kissed. He smelled like a corpse: a new one, cold and empty. "You're scared. You're scared of Grant, and you're scared of being here when the prison veil comes down. You know what those demons did to Ahsen while she was locked up with them." I smiled coldly. "Afraid of the same abuse? You go weak in the knees thinking about sucking some demon's cock for the next ten thousand years? Or maybe you'll like it. Maybe you *want* it."

I was goading him. I wanted him to lose it. I needed it, because inside me I still felt nothing of that dark entity, not even the tiniest riddle of movement behind my ribs. I had come here with a mission, and so far, I was wasting every second of opportunity.

Mr. King stopped dancing, such raw, naked loathing in his eyes, I almost forgot that he could not hurt me. I wanted to get away from him, desperately. I wanted to *flee*, and the instinct was so strong I stumbled backward. He did not let go. I had never seen such pain.

But it was not for me. He looked *past* me, as though gazing into some terrible memory, and whispered, "If you are not a whore, you are a warrior, and if you are not a warrior, you are a queen—but there is nothing else between within the army of the demon Lords and Kings."

Zee went very still against my skin. All the boys did. As though hearing that rhyme struck them hard, made them dream things they had forgotten. I wanted to rub my arms, but my right hand was still held—and my left rested against Mr. King's stolen arm. His gaze flicked back to me—and in that split second he seemed to remember where he was, whom he was with, and the hate in his eyes subsided into a cold curiosity that I found utterly discomfiting.

"Old Jack," he said slowly, "has done something quite unexpected, with you."

"Really," I replied carefully. "I can't imagine what *you* find unexpected about anything."

He did not smile. "Your blood. He is in your blood. Every Avatar who inhabits a skin marks that skin with a print that is of us, and individual to us. That . . . print . . . is in you. Only one generation removed. I can smell it." Mr. King jerked me against him. "Tampering with your lineage is something even *I* would not do."

"You've tried to kill me."

"Death is safer than the alternative," he whispered. "What you are is inviolate. Which means, my Lady, that you are worth more to me now, *alive.* When the others see you, when they learn what Old Jack has done, he will suffer. He will suffer more than Ahsen."

"You loved her," I said, cold. "That's why you hate him so much."

Mr. King pushed me away, and I stumbled into the dancers. Not one made a sound, and I did not look at them as silk rustled and metal gleamed around my arms and legs. I had eyes only for Mr. King.

"If I cannot possess what I need," he said softly, "I will have to devise a way to take it."

"You're good at that." I gestured at dancers, who swayed, so silent and watchful; unnaturally so, as if they had been made to do nothing more than move along the engraved labyrinth lines. "You've taken so much already."

Mr. King began to turn his back on me. "I took nothing. All of this . . . was offered to me, as in the days of old. This, my temple. And in return, I have given much. Magic.

Lives less ordinary. You would be amazed at how many crave such simple things."

I had seen grown men and women drink blood and avoid sunlight because they thought it would make them vampires. I had observed attempts at witchcraft, or focused meditations in the search of psychic powers. It was the New Age, everywhere; and never mind UFO hunters. Even the idolization of the material and monetary was as much a means of escape as any fantasy of the other-worldly.

So no, I was not amazed. But it frightened me that it had been so easy.

"We fought the war," continued Mr. King, almost to himself. "We built the prison walls. All for this jewel, this sweet island, to save ourselves and the humans who treated us like gods. But they forgot us when we were no longer needed. They tore us down. They built their world with iron. So I take what is mine, as is my right. As is the right of one who *made* them." He flashed me a hard look. "The Labyrinth will not deny me again."

He clapped his hands, and the dancers parted. I saw Father Lawrence, on his knees, clutching his chest. Nephele stood behind him, her palms resting on top of his head. I started to run toward them, and hands caught me. The dancers. Fingers like steel knots.

"Stop," I snapped, heart thundering. "Don't hurt him."

"He is flesh," replied Mr. King. "He is nothing except what I desire. Unless you would unlock the Labyrinth in return for keeping him whole?"

I hesitated, and a faint smile touched his mouth. "I thought not."

Mr. King looked at Father Lawrence, and a charge surged through the air, against my skin. The priest threw back his head and screamed.

Now, I told myself, fighting desperately against the hands that held me. *Goddamn it, now.*

Father Lawrence's voice broke, breath rattling in his throat. His entire body trembled, his head thrown back and held by Nephele. She was smiling at him, gently, but her fingers dug so deeply into his cheeks and brow I saw blood trickling from beneath her nails. Mr. King stepped closer to him, still staring, his hands moving now like a conductor's. The brown skin of Father Lawrence's hands rippled.

I screamed at the Avatar, surging forward, and the boys screamed with me in their dreams. My tattooed flesh grew hot—Raw and Aaz, burning—and the men and women holding me cried out as my clothing began to smoke. I lunged again, and this time no one held me back. Beneath my ribs, inside my heart, the coiled shadow finally stirred.

Mr. King turned to look at me, and I slammed my fist into his jaw, cracking the mask he wore. Only, it was not wood. It was bone. Growing out of his face. He spun, but did not go down, and I snatched his hair with my right hand and grabbed his throat with the other, digging my fingers into his jugular. Hunger rose inside me. Tasted like laughter. His flesh was hard and smooth as marble, and the boys began burning him alive.

He made no sound. No nerves to feel pain. But blood seeped from the corners of his eyes, and though he stared at me first with arrogance, even boredom, that changed in moments. He looked too deeply in my eyes. He looked, without blinking. And the fear that flickered through his gaze, in pieces, was so thick I could have carved it from him.

Hands reached around my body to pull me away, so many hands that clutched and grappled, but nothing could move me. Flesh that touched me burned. And still he stared, and the darkness rustled, rising; and I whispered, "Who ever did you think killed Ahsen?"

Mr. King stopped struggling. I leaned in so close my mouth brushed his cheek, and he recoiled from me as darkness rolled smooth within my bones and blood, slow and easy, as if an ocean brewed inside me: warm, tangled in moonlight. I closed my eyes because I did not need to see. I could feel every breath around me, each heartbeat tingling on my tongue. Those dancers surrounding us, reduced to bone and flesh and blood—life, dripping from them; life, eking through their porous skins as though rivers were contained within. I could taste them. I could touch them, with a thought.

Borders of illusion whispered, too: this stone palace nothing but a figment, a step sideways into a bubble born from Mr. King's mind, which carried a scent small as his soul, rotten and small, so old it was nothing but a crusty knot. Pitiful creature. Nothing and nobody, but what he pretended to be. No one real to call his own.

Except Ahsen. You took that from him.

Small worm of a thought. Pushed away. But not before I remembered her death—and saw Grant in her place.

I tried to open my eyes, but my body refused me. Tried to listen, but heard only the thrumming thunder of shadow-coils rubbing against the underside of my skin. Fought to feel Mr. King, choking in my hands, but sensed nothing but his spirit.

Kill him, I told the creature inside me, recoiling from my own self. *Kill him now.*

It did not. It held back, examining the Avatar. Regarding him with the same cold scrutiny one might give a peculiarly rare species of ant. I could feel its curiosity, which was infinitely alien—alien, and yet, me.

We remember, whispered that soft, sibilant voice, and Mr. King screamed, clutching wildly at his head and my hands, shuddering so violently it was as though tiny axes hacked at him from the inside out.

He was in pain. Brutal, vicious pain. I wondered if he had ever felt pain, but it was in him now, and I felt no joy, no satisfaction. Just horror. I had gotten what I wanted. He was being killed.

Slowly. Tortured.

Something else, too. Memories, scalped from Mr. King. Behind my eyes, images fluttered: thorn-strikes of starlight so dizzying I fell hard to one knee. All I could see was stars, a blanket of stars vast and lonely without end—and others with me, traveling through the nebular night as wolves, in packs, clustered tight as thought—becoming one thought—unity not enough to assuage the crawling, intolerable knowledge that *we feel nothing, we are nothing, even as we scream as one we will never end, we will pass though darkness in desolation and begin as thus again*—

Again and again. I could not escape. I fought, screaming to hear myself past the screams already inside my head—those endless starlit cries of the Avatars, lost in their madness—dimly aware that I was clawing at my own body, fingernails striking sparks on my skin. My voice broke.

Then Zee was inside my head. Zee and the boys, humming a desperate lullaby—and that coiled presence within my heart, the shadows surrounding my heart, broke the connection to Mr. King.

Who, in that moment, fled.

I felt it happen. I tasted Mr. King's spirit—cold, hard knot—as it shot from the flesh of his breaking body like a bullet. Odd, terrible sensation. As though part of my belly button left with him. Nothing I could do. I lay sprawled on the stone floor. I could not move. I could hardly see. My voice was nothing but a hiss and drool.

The creature inside me was quiet. My only weapon against Mr. King—receding, inexplicably so. Every other time it had possessed me, it had killed indiscriminately—and this, the one time I needed it . . .

It had become . . . thoughtful.

Or not.

I managed to roll over. And found myself surrounded by dead people.

CHAPTER 16

I had begun to keep a journal. Not for myself, but for the future. My bloodline. Every Hunter kept a record, meant to inspire and teach from beyond the grave. I felt sorry for the kid who inherited mine.

My grandmother had not been much of a writer. Just one slim volume, meant to describe an entire lifetime. No mention of Avatars or Jack. But as I lay sprawled in the hall and prison of Mr. King, I was reminded of a rough note written on one of the last pages; a scrawled afterthought: *The result of an act is always less damning than the thought that made it.*

I did not agree.

The vast temple had vanished. I was back inside the club—which, I suspected, I had never left—disco ball swinging, music still rocking out with a beat that set my teeth on edge. I was ready to put my fist through the stereo system.

No one was dancing. No one was as dead as I had thought, either. Just unconscious, sprawled in loose-limbed heaps that smelled like leather and sweat. I listened to the quiet rush of breathing—more than a hundred bodies strong—and found the sound comforting, in an odd way. Until I considered what would happen when those men and women woke up.

I struggled to stand, but my knees gave out. My head felt full of holes. For one moment when I fell to the floor, I could not remember who I was.

Until I looked down at the tattoos on my hands. Red eyes stared back at me, glittering amongst obsidian scales and silver veins. I rubbed my hands, gently, and Raw and Aaz rubbed back. I covered my face, breathed deep, and shuddered.

All you can do is trust yourself, whispered my mother's voice. I clung to that memory though it hurt me. I had trusted myself, and failed. Mr. King was alive and gone, and now he knew more about me than was safe. I had lost the element of surprise.

Zee rumbled against my skin. I went still, and beneath the pulsing beat of drums, heard a muffled tapping sound. Felt, more than saw, a presence behind me. Someone reaching for my shoulder. I turned without thinking to grab that outstretched hand—twisting hard—and heard a masculine grunt that was impossibly familiar.

Too late to let go. A large man crashed down beside me, cushioned by an unconscious woman whose breasts had popped free of a skimpy halter top. An oak cane hit my leg. I leaned forward and snatched a fistful of flannel shirt. I used too much force, but fear was running through my veins: fear, shock, and relief.

"What," I rasped hoarsely, "are you doing here?"

"What do you think?" Grant asked roughly, and grabbed the back of my neck—holding me still as he searched my face with startling anger. "Did you really think I'd let you walk away like that?"

"I knew what I was doing."

"Liar," he mumbled. "Jesus, Maxine. You tell *me* to stay alive, then disappear with that look on your face—"

"What look?"

"Like you're marching to the firing squad," he retorted, hauling me into his lap. "Don't play dumb with me."

And then he sank his fingers into my hair and kissed me so hard I stopped breathing. My eyes burned with tears. I held on tight.

He stopped, finally, but his arms belonged to a grizzly bear, and I could not see my way free as he hugged me tight against his chest. His bristled cheek rubbed mine, breath raggedly warming my ear—and we could have been anywhere, anywhere in the world but this place, surrounded by lost men and women, with hard music hammering the air.

"Look at this place," he whispered. "When I saw all the bodies, all the *people* . . ."

"I failed," I whispered.

"You're alive." Grant leaned back to look at me, still holding my face as his thumb brushed over my mouth; and then, again, softly: "You're alive."

I stared into his eyes, grieving. I was alive, but had botched everything. Grant was in more danger now. All of us were.

"How did you—" I began to ask, and sensed movement behind me. I looked, and saw Jack picking his way around the bodies. Shadows bruised his eyes, and his white hair was wildly tufted. His face seemed incredibly gaunt, but I blamed exhaustion for that. And fear.

He gave me a long, steady look, solemn as the grave, and turned away without a word. I could not tear my gaze from him—in my head, trying to reconcile the old man with Mr. King. Both the same. Both so radically different. *Both of them grieving.*

Jack knelt. I glimpsed black cloth beside him. A pudgy brown hand.

I scrabbled to stand, heart lurching up my throat. Grant frowned, looking at me, and I pointed. "Father Lawrence."

The priest was still alive, and lay on his back, unconscious. His breathing was steady, his pulse strong, but both Jack and Grant stared at the man as though he carried some terminal disease that was catching. I got down on my knees beside Father Lawrence and touched his hand. I could still hear his screams.

"Be careful," Jack said.

I wrapped my hand more firmly around his. He looked the same, his face slack in sleep, but I knew that meant nothing. "How deeply was he altered?"

"Enough," Grant said grimly.

My fault. I had stayed for nothing. I squeezed his hand and gazed around the rest of the club. I heard several faint groans, and glimpsed movement. Nephele lay nearby, sprawled on her face.

"Have they all been changed?" I asked the men.

"Most." Jack turned slightly to survey the room, something very quiet and restrained in the way he moved. He was hurting, I realized. Sore. I remembered that he had been sick after transporting me. Grant was a bigger person, and the old man had been running for days, weeks, even months.

I reached up and grabbed his hand, my finger armor glinting against his tanned, wrinkled skin. Jack glanced down at me in surprise—which then shifted into something softer, sadder.

"They're a danger to others," I said. "I don't know what to do."

Grant tore his gaze from Father Lawrence, his eyes narrowing as he looked at the slowly rousing men and women. He reached over his shoulder for the golden flute sheathed in its dark case.

Jack grabbed Grant's arm, stopping him. "You have to choose who's more important, lad. Your resources are not limitless, no matter what you've done in the past."

Grant shook off his arm, but did not reach for his flute again. He looked from me to Father Lawrence, and his expression was guarded. Behind him, Nephele groaned, fingers twitching. More people were moving. I could not stop them all, but I stood slowly.

"Old Wolf," I said. "If they go free, as they are—"

"What they are can't be easily changed," he interrupted, staring into my eyes. "And you can't imprison them. If you kill them—"

"Stop," I said.

"If you kill them," he persisted, "you might save some lives, but you'll be condemning others whose only mistake was believing in the lie of an easy life, the life of one who is . . . special."

I stared at him, torn. Still able to feel those hands at my throat, that knife slipping between my legs. Violent tendencies would not remain inside this club. Nor did it matter that most normal people would be unprepared for any kind of physical violence, regardless of whether their attacker was superenhanced, or not. It was not just innocent lives at stake. Eventually, inevitably, one of those cat-eyed men, or women covered in scales, would end up arrested or in a hospital. The physical differences would not go unnoticed.

I looked at Grant. "What do you think?"

He surveyed the room, leaning hard on his cane: a man as out of place in that club, surrounded by those bodies, as a wolf might be in a cement block. I wished I could see through his eyes. I wished I knew with certainty the truth in the hearts around me.

"I think you have little choice in the matter," he finally said, grim—and gave Jack a hard look. "I think you have to choose your battles."

At any second we would be noticed. The pounding music and wail of synth guitars made me dizzy. I glimpsed spines rocked with hard bone protrusions, and pointed ears tufted with fur. Nearby, a young woman with a sweet face was sitting slowly up. Small iridescent wings, like a dragonfly's, drooped from her shoulder blades. They looked useless, merely cosmetic.

Magic, Mr. King had said. *Lives less ordinary. You would be amazed at how many crave such simple things.*

I missed dealing with demons.

I stooped beside Father Lawrence and grabbed his wrist.

Held up my right hand to Jack. Grant stepped close, his fingers strong on my shoulder.

"You know how to use this thing better than I do," I said to the old man, as his hand closed around mine, his thumb briefly caressing the sliver of armor running from my ring finger to the bracelet cuff.

"But it likes you better," he said.

In moments we were gone.

⚜

WE did not return to Jack's apartment. We slipped free of the abyss and found ourselves inside a dark stairwell made of cracking cement and peeling plaster, the air thick with the scent of exhaust. An open doorway was beside me. I saw a parking garage on the other side—and nearby, Grant's Jeep.

"We've been busy," Grant said, trying to help me as I grabbed Father Lawrence under his arms and dragged him toward the Jeep. Jack moved ahead of us, watching the rest of the garage.

I gave him a brief wry smile. "So much for coming to save me first?"

Grant's jaw tightened. "Jack couldn't find you. Not in the beginning. And the apartment wasn't safe."

"We can be tracked anywhere."

"But it takes time," Jack said, over his shoulder. "And we need time, if only to rest, and plan."

I didn't bother asking why we had traveled here first— why the men had driven to a second location before coming to find me. The mechanics of cutting space were a mystery to me—less science than magic—but I assumed there was something in the act that drew the attention of those looking for it. Like Mr. King.

Grant drove, his cane resting in the passenger seat, beside Jack. I sat in the back with Father Lawrence. His brown skin had an ashen tone, and there were lines around his eyes that had not been present before. I thought about peeling back his lips to look at his teeth but was too afraid of what I would find.

We exited I-5 at Port of Tacoma Road, then swung right on 509 until it turned into Marine View Drive. Grant drove toward the ocean, and I smelled fresh sap and wood chips. Lumberyards were all over the place, along with steel and chemical facilities. Farther along, buildings began drying up, and we passed designated tidelands.

I saw the ocean. A marina.

Grant parked the Jeep at Chinook Landing. Across the waterway, behind expensive sailboats and small yachts, I could see the major cargo terminals and lumbering, fat ships that resembled steel boxes slogging through the sea. There were a lot of boats. Personally, I was no fan. I had issues with fear of drowning.

None of us got out of the car. I peered through the windows, searching for witnesses. No one appeared to be out, but dragging an unconscious man to a boat in broad daylight seemed like an invitation for trouble. It was only the afternoon, though, with hours still until darkness. We could not sit here forever.

"He's drunk, right?" I said, as Jack closed his eyes. "That's the backstory if anyone asks why I'm hauling around a priest."

"I'd be convinced," Grant said dryly.

Jack rubbed his temples and opened his eyes. "No one is here. We should move quickly."

I moved. Ignored the sensation of having a target painted on my back as I dragged Father Lawrence's deadweight from the gravel parking lot, down to the dock. No rain, but the air was cold in my lungs. I was grateful for it. The priest was heavy. I doubted even Grant, with two good legs, could have managed him.

Jack led us to a yacht—some white fiberglass cruiser, almost sixty-five feet long, with a fully enclosed bridge. I could see nothing behind the tinted windows, but sensed someone watching us. Sure enough, Byron slipped outside, the wind blowing dark hair over his eyes. He stared at me and the unconscious priest at my feet.

"Hey," I said awkwardly, unable to imagine what he was thinking. *Don't do this when you grow up,* I wanted to tell him. *Don't be like me.*

Killy appeared behind the boy. I was, once again, surprised to see her. Her black hair was tousled, her clothing rumpled. A deep line had formed between her eyes, which still looked pained. When she saw Father Lawrence, her expression did not improve.

"Shit," she said, and ran for the ladder.

It took all of us to get the priest on board. He began to wake as we pulled him to the deck, and Killy—who had one arm hooked under his—went very pale. I was beside her. No one else noticed, not even Byron—who stood on the dock, pushing up the priest's foot.

"What?" I said quietly to her.

She shot me an uneasy look. "Hurry."

I gritted my teeth, dug my heels into the deck, and hauled backward with all my strength. Father Lawrence slid on board like a greased seal, but I did not stop. I dragged the man toward the main bridge and cabin of the boat. Killy ran ahead of me, and by the time I got to the doorway she held rope in her hands: thick and green, the kind used for crab nets.

I turned him over on his stomach, and without a word she knelt and began knotting his wrists behind his back. He made a small noise as she worked, and Killy tossed me the end of the rope. I tied his ankles, tightening the excess cord. The only way for Father Lawrence to move would be at a swift roll.

Byron appeared in the doorway, as did Jack. Grant was steps behind them, breathing hard. Climbing the ladder, I told myself, but it was more than that. He was too pale. I wondered if he had coughed up blood in the last hour.

Killy made a small, choked sound. I turned. Father Lawrence's eyes were open. His pupils were black, but his irises were bloodred, rimmed in gold. He twisted, staring wildly at all of us, but focusing finally on Killy—who froze, meeting his gaze like he was a semi with his lights in her eyes.

He lunged at her. Not like Father Ross, or the men in the Shanghai bar who had moved as sharks, piranhas, darting and impossibly quick. Something more rough-hewn carried Father Lawrence forward—and crouched behind him, I saw the backs of his hands ripple, and break open with brown fur.

Happened in a split second. I rocked forward, grabbing the back of his collar, but he was too strong and the cloth tore. He catapulted across the bridge as Killy scrabbled backward—crying out his name, just once. All those knots, worth shit in keeping him still.

Just before he reached her, my fingers snared the rope around his ankles. I yanked back with all my strength. Father Lawrence let out a choked snarl, and rolled around to face me, managing to sit up with his round belly hanging over the waist of his pants. Dark fur crawled up the sides of his throat, and his teeth were long and sharp. He snapped at me like a chained wolf, mindless with rage.

I punched him. Father Lawrence's voice broke, and he swayed, shaking his head. I hit him again, this time with a double-handed fist, driving the blow down into the side of his head. He hit the floor and did not move again.

I crouched above him, breathing hard. Staring, as brown, bristly fur slowly receded from Father Lawrence's face, leaving him round-cheeked and human. Killy sat in a small ball, hugging her knees to her chest. Watching the priest, as well. Eyes haunted. Grieved.

Movement, behind me. Byron walked along the edge of the bridge, keeping a wary eye on the transforming man sprawled beneath me. He joined Killy. Stood beside her with impressive stoic calm, and said nothing. When she decided to rise, a moment later, he gave her his hand.

Hands touched me, as well. Grant. I leaned gratefully into his shoulder, but it was like rubbing a live wire. Anger rolled off him. Jack was little better, but in a different way.

He came around to stand beside us, and studied Father Lawrence—but with absolutely no emotion. His expression concerned me. The old man looked at the priest with distant familiarity—in that same way anyone might be familiar with his doctor, or teacher. As though he knew him.

"Well," he said quietly. "Now we have werewolves."

❧

I dragged Father Lawrence below to one of the staterooms. The hall was narrow. I banged my shoulders and elbows. A door creaked open. Mary peered out to watch us pass. Her hair was wild, her eyes sleepy. She looked at the unconscious priest being dragged behind me, and said, "Never trust an old wolf."

She stepped back inside her room and shut the door.

"Good advice," I muttered, and glanced over my shoulder as Grant descended the stairs behind me. He banged his head on the ceiling, and winced.

I pushed open the door at the end of the hall, revealing a small, oddly shaped stateroom with a round bed in the center. Jack had suggested it. He did not claim ownership of the boat, but he had keys to the ignition and was familiar enough with its layout and operation. I could feel the vessel cutting water and hear its engine rumble. We were heading out to sea.

I heaved Father Lawrence onto the bed. A lump was forming on his forehead. I sat beside him. Grant followed me inside and shut the door. He stared at the priest, then me. I leaned forward, resting my elbows on my knees. Trying not to think too hard about everything I had seen.

Grant sat on the bed with a sigh and stretched out his bad leg. His cane went down on the floor. I ran my left hand over his thigh, massaging muscle through his jeans—until his fingers wrapped around mine. His tanned skin was very human against my tattoos.

"Just think," I said quietly. "Six months ago, if you hadn't gone to Pike Place Market, we would never have met, and you wouldn't be in this mess."

"Right. I'd be dead. Possessed by a demon queen. Personally, I think this is the better bargain." Grant kissed my cheek very gently, sighing into my hair—and then leaned back to pull his flute from its case. "Father Lawrence is lucky I'm not going to treat him with the same respect he gave Luke."

"Oh, please. You'd give Lassie a run for her money."

"Woof," he replied, and twisted around to study Father Lawrence. The priest was very still, very unconscious, his breathing deep and steady. Grant reached out with one hand, his fingers waving slightly through the air above the man's leg. A low hum rose from his throat, and power shivered over my skin. Zee rumbled in his dreams. All the boys, shifting.

"He's in there," Grant said finally. "Closer to the surface than Luke was. I suspect that's why he focused on Killy. She was familiar to him. Either way, I can bring out the man."

And then what? His life as he knew it is over. "Mr. King only had moments with Father Lawrence. I'm surprised he was able to do so much."

"Practice makes perfect. Makes you wonder, though, about the world. Jack told me things while you were gone. About fairy tales and myths." He glanced down at the flute, then met my gaze with a faint, sad smile. "I suppose it should make me question my faith, but it doesn't."

I touched his face. "I think you were born believing in something bigger than yourself."

"I don't know. I don't even know where I was born." Grant captured my hand, and cradled it over his heart. "But I know I'm here now. I'm here, in this moment, with you. I'm here, in this moment when I can make a difference. I'm here, alive. And even though I don't understand much of what I've been told about myself—or whether I even believe it—I *do* know there are mysteries that are truth."

I smiled. "No accidents?"

"Not when it came to meeting you." Grant kissed my hand, his gaze full of that same mystery, a truth I could not name, but that I felt, every time I thought of him. "I dreamed you, Maxine Kiss. I dreamed your heart."

He kissed my hand again, then tucked it gently in my lap. I could not speak. I watched him pick up his flute, and his gaze focused, sharpening thoughtfully as he stared at Father Lawrence. Taking measure of the man's soul.

Yet, Grant hesitated. Never had he shown reluctance to help anyone, human or demon, but I saw it then—and I knew it was not because of what had happened to Father Ross.

Father Cribari was the problem. Grant had almost killed him. He had transformed into someone else: murderer, avenger, magic man. A buried side of him, awakening. Like the darkness sleeping inside my own heart.

I knew exactly how frightening that was. I knew how terrifying it could be, to imagine it happening again.

"Grant," I said quietly.

"I know." He lifted the golden flute. "This could take a while."

Grant breathed into the instrument, and a lilting thread of music trilled through the air. Power poured over my skin, which the boys shook off like dogs chasing water from fur—and still, the music sank past them into bone, warm as honey. I had expected fury, the taste of blood and sword, but what flowed over me was a song of a sunlit sea, and it was the sound of Father Lawrence's soul, each note like stardust sparkled from ear to tongue, until it was like being a little girl again—that little me, that dreaming little me—caught tight in wonder, held dear in love.

I looked at Grant, but my vision felt odd, as though he were lost behind a soft lens. I imagined heat rolling off him as he stared at the priest—his gaze unflinching, terrifying in its intensity. Sweat beaded against his brow, and the flute suddenly sounded different; as though the notes were swelling, soaking, growing.

Lightbringer, I thought, remembering all the things Jack had said—realizing, too, that none of it mattered. Whatever Grant had been born to was dead. He could be something new, make his own way with the power given him.

As could I.

The stateroom door opened. Jack stepped in. Something was wrong; I could see it in his eyes. I started to stand—stopping halfway when the old man found Grant, and froze.

I was looking at Jack. I was looking, and so nothing was hidden from me—not the grief, and not the bone-chilling hunger that swept over his face, which was very nearly as visceral and primal as Father Ross's desire to chew up nuns: a killing need, mindless and drowning.

I stared, breathless. Still staring when Jack tore his gaze from Grant and looked at me.

He knew what I had seen—clear as day in his eyes. He knew.

"Old Wolf," I whispered.

Jack flinched and swallowed hard. "You have to stop him. My dear girl, he is not *just* trying to heal that man's soul."

I blinked, startled, and looked back at Grant and Father Lawrence. The priest was breathing more rapidly, body twitching. I watched the skin of his throat ripple like his muscles were contorting, and his eyes moved rapidly beneath his lids. He was becoming something else. Transforming.

Blood trickled from Grant's nose. Blood, at the corner of his mouth, foaming with every breath he poured into his flute.

I moved toward him, but the air suddenly felt like molasses. I was too slow. Too slow when the music stopped abruptly, and Grant swayed. Too slow when the flute tumbled from his fingers. Too slow—too slow to catch him as he slumped backward off the bed.

I fell on my knees beside him. He was so still, his face slack. I checked his pulse.

His heart was not beating.

CHAPTER 17

I died, in that moment. I let myself die for one stopped heartbeat, one lost breath, and the boys roared against my skin.

I roared back.

I found Grant's sternum. His mother's pendant was in the way, and I pushed it aside. Clasped my hands, and began giving him chest compressions. Fast, hard, with all my strength. I broke rhythm only twice to breathe into his mouth—tasted his blood, swallowed it—and began again, pounding on his chest. Cold, hard terror burned through me, leaving my body numb in its wake. I screamed at Grant. I screamed.

Inside me, a flutter, a shadow. My finger armor began to burn.

And then Jack was there, shoving me aside. His face was drawn and pale, his blue eyes brilliant as ice. He laid his hands over Grant's chest and closed his eyes.

A pulse charged through the air—thunder without sound—and everything rose and fell in that room, including me. Grant gasped, arching upward. His eyes flew open.

Jack fell away from him: a scarecrow man, nothing but skin and bone. I pushed my arm under Grant's head. He stared wildly into my eyes and began coughing. Blood spattered my face. I wiped it away with a shaking hand and felt the boys absorb the hot fluid through my fingers.

"You need a hospital," I said, trembling, and looked at Jack—who appeared on the verge of his own heart attack. "You, too."

"I simply need rest," he breathed, leaning heavily against the bed, as though his skull was simply too burdensome to hold up. "Grant will recover, as well. Trust me, my dear."

Bullshit, I almost said, but it was too hard to speak. I gazed down at Grant again, and found him watching my face, eyes slightly unfocused, and bloodshot.

"Wha' happened?" he mumbled.

I had to rock back and forth, counting to ten, before I found words. "You did something stupid."

Grant reached up and touched my face. His hand was clumsy. "Pass out?"

I held his hand against my cheek. "Your heart stopped beating."

He stared at me—and then a cough wracked him. He spat blood into his palm. I held him even closer, bending over his strong, large body—which was suddenly too frail for comfort. Frighteningly so.

I looked at Jack. Found him watching me. I sought my mother in his face; I searched for me. I searched my heart for every ounce of love and affection I felt for the old man and poured it into my eyes, my voice.

"Thank you," I breathed.

Jack nodded solemnly, without a word, something in his eyes warming me—even as those same eyes had chilled me, only minutes before. I clung to the warmth, though. I savored it.

On the bed, Father Lawrence stirred. I peered over the mattress edge and found the priest staring at the stateroom ceiling. I saw little of his face from where I sat, but he was quiet and still except for a slight twitch in his right foot. His head lolled to one side. I met a gaze broken in halves: his left eye was brown and normal, while his right remained crimson, golden—but very human in its confusion. No fur on his face. Nothing but a normal man.

"Hey," he said hoarsely. "I'm tied up."

"Yes," I replied, wishing very much that I didn't have to speak to him at that moment. "Do you know what happened to you?"

Father Lawrence hesitated, and licked his cracked lips. "Bad touching."

Grant made a small sound that could have been laughter. I was not amused.

"You were changed," I said, feeling like crap for the crisp tone in my voice. I had no better way to tell him, though. Sugarcoating the concept of being *turned into a werewolf* was almost as absurd as the actuality of being a werewolf—however one defined such a creature. I couldn't imagine there was a basis for comparison. Not a recent one, anyway.

But when I looked at Father Lawrence to gauge his reaction, he was not paying attention to me at all. He was staring at Jack. With an astonishment that seemed to far outweigh any predicament involving rope, boats, or fur.

"Damn," said the priest, twitching across the mattress; resembling a roly-poly caterpillar more than a fanged manwolf. "Jack. What are you doing here?"

"Whoa," I said.

Grant made another small sound, but it had nothing to do with laughter. He tried to sit up, and I braced my shoulder against his back to support him. He rubbed his chest, wincing—and gave Jack a long look, before anchoring his focus on Father Lawrence.

"Huh," he said.

"Jack," Father Lawrence said, ignoring us, still staring at the old man—who finally, grudgingly, peered over the side of the bed with all the reluctance of a man about to get shot between the eyes, or given a wedgie.

"Hello, Frank," replied Jack mildly. "Small world."

My head was going to explode. "You two know each other? How is that remotely possible?"

Father Lawrence's stare was disconcerting; the uneven color of his eyes lent him a slightly deranged appearance. "Jack Meddle was my professor at Princeton, before I decided to . . . devote my life to God. We stayed in touch." He paused, staring from me to the old man. "How do *you* know each other?"

I had no idea how to respond. Grant leaned into me, shaking his head, and Jack said, very quietly, "Frank, I made a mistake. A rather egregious one."

I heard footsteps outside the stateroom, and the door slammed open. I expected Mary, for some reason—but it was Killy who stared inside, breathless, her gaze floating over Grant, Jack, and me—before settling like a lead weight on Father Lawrence.

She said nothing. She did nothing. Simply looked at him, her eyes dark with terrible heat. Father Lawrence lay in his bonds, frozen beneath her scrutiny. As though she was a sight as unexpected as Jack; and terrifying. I wondered if he remembered attacking her. If Grant had left him any memories at all.

Killy finally looked away, dragging in a deep breath. "Better. You did good by him, song-man."

"It wasn't an easy fix," Grant replied hoarsely, one hand still clutching his chest. I wrapped my arm around him, placing my hand over his. Willing him my strength; anything, everything.

Killy's cheeks flushed, and she nodded silently, staring at her feet. "We've got more trouble. I was coming to tell you. Someone's here."

⌘

AN hour until sunset. Byron and Mary stood inside the bridge, staring out the windows. I saw nothing but cold waters and a cargo ship, too far away to resemble anything but a floating brick. The coast curled behind us in the distance. Overcast skies, but no rain. Not yet.

Cribari waited on the deck. He was alone. Back turned to us, facing the ocean. No mistaking that tall, lean frame, or the angle of his shoulders. He wore simple black: a thick coat that covered most of his body. Zee and the others raged in his presence, tugging so hard it felt like duct tape was being continuously pulled off my body, from scalp to soles.

No one went out to greet him. We remained inside. I stayed close to Grant. He could barely walk. Mary stood near him, as well. She had flinched as though slapped when we walked free of the yacht's belly—and now rubbed her scalp, her cheeks—held her own throat with two hands—never once taking her gaze from Grant as quiet dismay rolled through her face.

"Didn't feel," she whispered. "Didn't hear. Didn't know."

Didn't know you were dead, I finished for her. I had been around Zee and his riddles long enough to understand some of the old woman's vague half sentences. And the fear in her eyes was enough like mine that words were unnecessary.

Grant leaned hard on his cane, a thin sheen of sweat on his brow. The tissue clutched in his left hand was spotted with blood. He watched Cribari as anyone might a loose live cobra: calculating ways to kill. I turned in a circle, staring out the windows. Searching for any other company that Cribari might have brought. All I saw was an old fishing vessel covered in nets and blue tarps; men moving quickly across the deck.

"How did he get here?" I asked, noting how Byron never once took his gaze off the priest.

"Don't know," Killy said, fingers pressed against her temple as she glanced briefly at Mary. "I turned around, and there he was on the deck. Watching the sea. He's ignored us since he arrived."

"And can you . . ." I hesitated, tapping my forehead.

She shook her head, ever so slightly. "He's not open."

"He was in a coma the last time I saw him," said Father Lawrence. His red eye was cold and calculating as he watched Cribari—even as his brown eye remained warm, uncertain. It was like looking at two different men—men still unaware of what had been done to them. I hadn't managed to tell Father Lawrence yet. Nor did I know how far Grant's attempt to heal him had gone.

Too far. Too far when it kills the healer.

"Antony has been altered," Grant said, "but not significantly. If he was in a coma, then what I'm seeing could have been the result of his healing process and nothing else."

"Mr. King turned everyone else into a doll. Why not him?"

"Some men you don't give power," Jack said. "No matter how crazy you might seem." The old man stood beside me, staring out the window at the priest. "I was a fool," he whispered, almost to himself.

"About my grandmother?" I asked him, thinking of Mr. King's words; his mysterious condemnation.

Jack gave me a sharp look. "About everything *but* that."

He began to push past me to the bridge door, but I blocked him. Frustration filled his face. I glimpsed Father Lawrence watching us much too thoughtfully.

"He can't hurt me," I said. "Stay here."

"There are things you don't understand," Jack said, but I had already turned away to grab Byron's collar. He grunted in surprise as I yanked him toward the stairs leading down to the staterooms.

"Go," I told him. "Find a place to hide, and don't come out, no matter what you hear."

"No," he said, fighting me. "It won't do any good."

"Byron—"

"They always find me when I hide," he whispered, and the shadows that battered his dark eyes made me nauseous. I remembered him, months ago, living in a box—and I remembered, too, his bruises, his fear of men. The things he still could not tell me. His voice in my head, speaking of Mr. King.

Sometimes a fight is what turns them on.

This was not his fight. He was just a kid, forced from one dangerous life into another. He could not possibly know what was coming to hurt us, but it was all the same to him. Just one more thing to survive.

I pulled Byron close, staring into his eyes. He did not flinch or blink. Grant touched my shoulder. "We can't keep running," he said.

Just one more time, I thought, as my finger armor began to burn through my tattoos. *One more jump, and then we'll see.*

But Grant's fingers tightened, ever so slightly, and I closed my hand into a fist, willing the armor to quiet. Its hum faded, but only a little: those tendrils of quicksilver that were molded to my skin felt deeper than bone; as though, if the metal were ever peeled back, one would find my muscle had turned to silver, and the rest of my hand to iron bars: parts of me, becoming the thing.

I went outside to speak to Cribari, my right hand still in a fist.

He did not turn to look at me, not even when I stood at his side, and we faced the darkening sky and the gray sea. The boat rocked, as it had since the beginning, but I noticed it more on deck, slammed by the wind, and swayed with my legs spread and knees slightly bent.

"So," I said. "How are we going to do this?"

Cribari smiled faintly. "I expected you to kill me by now."

"He would just send another in your place."

"True." His smile turned colder. "He has many soldiers at his disposal."

I shook my head, aware of Jack standing in the doorway behind me. "You're an idiot. He's no angel. He's no messenger from God. He's as petty as you and I, and as flawed. You're being used."

His cheeks reddened, and muscles twitched around his eye, but he showed no other sign of agitation. Just that cold, fake smile that I wanted to beat off his face with my fists and cut with my knives. "You are made of lies. We should have seen that from the beginning, at our creation, but we were too dazzled by illusions. When the Wardens died, and you were the last—"

Cribari stopped, and finally turned his head just enough to look me in the eye. "We succeeded in killing your kind before, you know. A woman of your bloodline. She trusted our order, and so it was easy to make the kill. She had a child, unfortunately."

Zee yanked so hard against my chest I had to take a step forward. I covered my awkwardness by pretending I wanted to see over the rail, but all the boys were wild on my skin, heaving like little tsunamis.

"I suppose your order was given a divine decree then, too," I said to him, remembering the woman in the grave, and her wailing daughter. "Does murder taste sweeter when you can put all the blame on a higher power?"

His eyes narrowed. "Take care how you speak to me."

"I think not," Jack said, walking gracefully from the enclosed bridge. Father Lawrence was behind him, and Grant. I wanted to tell them to go back, but the men had looks on their faces that were determined and cold. Mary watched from the door, the wind whipping the hem of her loose dress around her knobby knees.

"She is your Lady and Queen," added the old man, and there was a tone in his voice that made me think of lone figures standing on the borders of darkness guarded by flames, firelight, the heat of bodies gathered to hear a storyteller sing of heroes and monsters. "She is the one who will save you."

Cribari turned fully around to face Jack, fury ticking through his gaze. "You are *no one*. How dare you."

Jack stared at the priest with disdain. He rolled back his sleeve—each movement slow and deliberate—until he revealed a tattoo. A tattoo that covered the underside of his upper forearm. A mirror image of the scar below my ear.

Only, the lines of his tattoo were made of a white bone that crested the old man's flesh in slivers and curves. Bone, that was part of his skeleton. Bone, natural grown.

"I dare because I am the Wolf," Jack said quietly. "And you *will* do as I say."

Father Lawrence swayed so badly, Grant had to catch his arm. I felt similarly shocked. Cribari's face turned pale as death, and his knees gave out. He sank to the deck, staring at Jack like he was a monster. "Not you."

"Me," said the old man grimly. "I *made* you."

If Cribari had been holding a gun, he would have put it in his mouth and pulled the trigger. For a moment, I thought he would throw himself into the ocean and try to drown himself. His despair was so profound I could taste it like poison.

"Is she the one?" Cribari whispered. "Does she bear the mark?"

There was only one mark he could be talking about. Jack began to shake his head in denial, but something came over me. I pulled aside my hair, feeling Dek's tattooed body recede from my skin. My finger brushed over the exposed scar. I turned my face to the priest.

Cribari stared, shuddering violently, holding his chest with hands that strained against his black jacket like white claws. Pale, slick with sweat; staring at me with undisguised, speechless loathing. I felt like the boogey-girl, or Jackie the Ripper; or maybe just a rabid dog.

"How much time do we have?" whispered Cribari, his voice harsh and sibilant, and dripping with hate. "How much time until the end?"

I showed nothing. Just looked the priest in the eye, and said, "I have no idea what you mean."

Grant limped to my side, impossibly grim. "No more, Antony. You can't win this. Not in the way you think."

"You're no better," whispered the priest. "Oh, God."

"Enough," Jack said. "You have *my* decree now."

"No." Cribari gave him a hateful look that he transferred immediately to me. "You and I. We are not done, no matter what the Wolf says. We will *never* be done. Even if you kill me, there are others. There will *always* be others."

Behind us, in the cabin, Killy screamed.

I flinched, turning, and Cribari made a stabbing motion at Grant. Grant swung around on his good leg, dodging the flash of metal. A syringe. He opened his mouth to sing, but that one deep breath made him cough, blood instantly dotting his lips. Cribari lunged again.

I moved in front of Grant at the last moment, and the needle snapped against my breast. The priest snarled in frustration, reaching for my throat. His eyes were wild, crazed. I drew back my fist.

Cribari disappeared. Vanished into thin air.

I spun around, searching for him—found Grant doing the same, his hand snaring my wrist. I heard cries from the cabin, snarls. Father Lawrence was gone, and Jack stood perfectly still, his face turned up to the sky, as though listening.

"Jack," I snapped.

"Behind you," he whispered.

I whipped around just as Cribari popped into sight, staggering drunkenly, eyes bloodshot. He grabbed Grant's arm. Grant reared backward, letting go of me as he slammed his cane into Cribari's gut—

—and both of them vanished.

I stared, stricken—the world dropping out from under me in a moment of pure, surreal insanity, in which I felt as though my guts and heart and blood floated in a well of antigravity—and then everything came crashing down and it hurt to breathe, and my body felt leaden and cold and dead. It was agony trying to think past the boys howling against me.

I raised my right hand, finger armor glinting with unearthly light. Ready to kill the motherfucker.

Jack grabbed my wrist. "No."

I snarled, and he yanked me hard against him. "Look," he snapped, and pointed.

That old decrepit fishing vessel I had seen earlier was closer now. Jet Skis were in the ocean, roaring toward us. I saw weapons.

"Cribari was not supposed to take Grant away like that," Jack murmured. "Even modified humans die after a handful of times, manipulating space. He won't be able to control where they end up, not with the burden of an extra person."

I pulled away, and this time he let me. "You killing yourself when you jump places?"

"No," said the old man, eyes glinting. "I make adjustments."

He backed away from me and pointed again, but this time at the enclosed bridge behind me. "Help them. I'll find Grant. You find us."

I hesitated wanting to say more to him—and then ducked as bullets chewed through the deck around my body. I got hit multiple times, but the slugs ricocheted, and the boys swarmed over my face, protecting me as pieces of the hull broke apart and hit my cheek.

When I looked again, Jack was gone.

CHAPTER 18

THE ocean roared with engines. I ran inside the bridge and dodged a man's broken body. His throat had been shredded, and I smelled the piss and shit of voided bladder and bowels. I almost slipped in his blood. I saw another male corpse near the yacht's controls.

Byron shouted, belowdecks.

I flew down the stairs into the narrow hall. Saw an unfamiliar sweatshirt-clad back in front of me and did not think. I slammed my fist into the base of the man's spine, driving forward with all my strength, and broke the bone with a satisfying crunch that I felt all the way up my arm. The man screamed, collapsing—and vanished into thin air.

Cutting space, I thought. *Creating the element of surprise.* Mr. King had waited a long time before pulling that particular trick out of his hat. I wondered why now, why not earlier.

I heard a crash in the master stateroom and slammed open the door. Glimpsed fur and long teeth—a spectral, glowing red eye—then a stranger crashed backward into me, holding his hands over a spectacularly large hole in his throat. I grabbed the back of his collar and shoved him out into the hall, where he fell hard on his knees, gurgling. Boots pounded down the stairs. I glimpsed the muzzle of an automatic rifle

I glanced over my shoulder. Byron and Killy were shoved tight in the bathroom. Mary stood on top of the bed, hair wild and a fierce, crazy smile on her face. Father Lawrence was crouched on the floor. Fur covered his cheeks and hands, and his nails were black and long. His features were human, if hairier—but fangs pushed over his lips, and his right eye glowed. He was covered in blood, and his chest was heaving. So much for Grant's help—though at least Father Lawrence seemed able to determine friend from foe.

"Hey!" shouted a man at the end of the hall, approaching swiftly, rifle aimed at my head. "Hands up. *Now.*"

I balled my hands into fists. I walked into the hall and shut the door behind me. I did not stop moving. More men came down the stairs, piling up—staring at me with uncertainty as the first man shouted. I did not hear a word he said. Blood roared in my ears, and shadows were fluttering in my heart. The boys were howling. All I could see were the whites of that man's eyes.

He shot me. He unloaded his gun into my body, and I felt nothing. Bullets ricocheted off my chest and face, briefly snapping back my head. I did not slow. Other men began shooting at me, aiming around the first man, who ducked low. Bullets rained. Zee stopped raging and began to laugh against my skin. I smiled with him, feeling death in the curve of my mouth.

Guns tried to smash into my face. I blocked them, staggering under the force of the blows. Hands grabbed at me, tearing the remains of my clothes. I used my fists to hammer skulls and break noses. I used my knees and toes. I was relentless, and the hall was narrow. I had the advantage. Men began retreating up the stairs, eyes wild and afraid.

Darkness uncoiled, rising up my throat, and I saw things in those moments—flashes of life—as though my mind could reach into the thoughts of the men around me. I saw wives and children, and girlfriends. I saw fast cars, and football games, and witnessed lines etched into stone. A labyrinth—*the one with the limp must not be harmed*—a cross—*but he'll be ready for transport when you board the boat*—a statue carved from black marble—*there's a boy, an old man; take them alive if you can, but the rest don't matter*—showing a woman in robes, holding a baby—*watch out for the tattooed woman, watch out, watch out*—and I heard a sonorous voice blessing each man—*destroy the boat; blast it*—speaking of sin, and the power of righteousness to overcome fear.

I felt their fear. I ate their fear.

Like a demon would have.

Bodies fell in front of me. I walked over them. I heard footsteps running above my head—away, away—but I locked gazes with one more man, and watched him pull a small round object from inside the pouch hanging from his waist.

He pulled the pin and threw the grenade at me. Ran like hell before it hardly left his fingers. I did not follow. I caught the small bomb out of the air and fell to my knees—curling around it—holding on as tightly as I could.

The explosion knocked me into the wall, splintering wood and crunching steel. I lay stunned, listening to engines roar and fade. Smoke filled the air. Most of my clothes were gone, and the holster holding my knives hung limp off one shoulder.

Grant, I told myself. *Jack. Get up now. Get up.*

I struggled to stand. As I did, something else came to me: a memory, some whisper of warning from the darkness, receding into my heart, leaving in its wake a slow graze of terrible hunger.

Destroy the boat, I had heard in the minds of the men.
Blast it.

I stumbled over the wreckage and bodies in the hall,
and ran. I could almost hear the ticking beat of a count-
down, and the boys rippled over me, straining to be free.
Sunset. Sunset was coming.

I tried to open the master stateroom's door. It was
locked. Bullet holes had pierced the wood. I kicked at it,
screaming names.

Byron opened the door. Pale, eyes huge. He looked at
my half-naked body and flushed crimson. Behind him,
Killy knelt beside Father Lawrence, who was on his hands
and knees, vomiting up chunks of what looked like meat.
Sure as hell wasn't beef; I knew that. The priest was human again—no fur, fingers and teeth normal.

"Up," I snapped, but my voice hardly worked, and I had
to say it a second time, emphasizing my point by grabbing
Killy by the upper arm and hauling her away from the
man. Mary, who had been leaning against the wall with
her eyes closed, glided close and wrapped her arms around
Byron.

"Grant," she said, staring into my eyes.

"Gone," I told her, and grabbed her hand. "Come with
me if you want to find him."

I yanked Father Lawrence to his feet and hooked my
left hand into the waist of his pants. "Byron, Killy, hold on
to me."

The teen did as I asked, but awkwardly, like he didn't
know where it was safe to touch me. Killy wrapped her
fingers around my upper arm and grabbed Father Lawrence's collar with the other hand. Dried tears stained
her cheeks, and a bruise was forming.

"You should have left when you had the chance," I told
her roughly, and squeezed Mary's hand as the old woman
threw back her head and closed her eyes. My armor began
to burn, flaring hot white—

—and an immense roar swept through the room, sweeping back my hair. Explosive heat pummeled our bodies, making the others cry out. I saw fire. I saw the walls flying toward us.

Then, nothing. The abyss folded us away.

I had no destination. I asked for nothing except Grant. And Jack. I asked for their safety, and that was all I could think of inside the void, which seemed this one time to be full of movement—as though, if I touched it just so, I would skim free of the abyss and see the universe in passing.

We tumbled free against rock and grass. I fell hard on my knees, and loosened my iron grip around clothing and hands. I stumbled, running, as fast as I could. I did not look back. I did not listen as my name was called. I was too afraid of being seen. It was night. Time for the boys to wake.

I did not make it far before they exploded from my skin, but I kept running blind through the pain, slipping against loose rock and falling on my hands. I did not stop. I pushed forward as Zee ripped free of my ribs, trailing behind me in a gasp of smoke that solidified into flesh. Raw and Aaz followed him, rising from me like ghosts—and Dek, Mal, my crowns of fire and bone.

I glimpsed Zee racing through the darkness, using every slick patch of night as a gateway into another world, weaving in and out of sight so quickly that he left ripples in the wet air. Raw and Aaz joined him. They chased me like wolves in some forest of swords, and I wanted to let go and never stop.

But I did, finally. I leaned over, hands braced on my thighs, fighting for breath. Heart hammering so hard, I could taste each pulse in the back of my throat. I looked around. Found mountain cliffs rising behind me, towering with snow and sharp edges cut like blades. Some trees, but not many. No snow on the ground, but it was cold enough. I was suddenly freezing. And feeling foolish for being so frightened of witnesses in my transformation. There was little point to hiding the boys from Byron and the others. They had seen too much already. I had probably frightened them more by running away.

Zee and the others crowded close. I gestured to Raw. "Go protect Byron and the others. Bring them jackets, food. Do your best not to be seen, but *keep them safe*."

The little demon nodded, and disappeared into the shadows. Dek and Mal began singing the melody to U2's "I Still Haven't Found What I'm Looking For."

"Grant," I said to Zee, still breathless.

Zee laid his claws against my knee. "Rest, Maxine. We look."

Aaz, however, returned with clothes. Jeans and a lightweight black crewneck. A warm coat. No underwear. I dressed quickly, with impatience, securing the remains of my shoulder holster as best I could. Nearby, I heard the distinct scuff of shoes on stone and thought of Byron. He might have tried to follow. I had abandoned the boy on a mountainside with a crazy woman, a psychic, and a sort-of-kind-of werewolf. Great person I was.

I followed the sound, wondering how I had managed to run so far and fast. Navigating the forested mountainside at a more sedate speed was harrowing enough. I kept losing my footing on rocks and roots.

Minutes later, though, I found the owner of the shoes. It was Mary, crouched in a small clearing, drinking from a trickling vein of water. She was alone. Starlight cast a faint glow on her white hair and limbs, and for one moment she did not look human to me—so far removed, I had to stand still and remind myself that I knew the old woman.

She straightened as I approached, water trickling from her chin. Loose-limbed and graceful, some wild creature of the wood. Even her dress and sweater looked different in the shadows—as though she wore nothing but the night. Her breath puffed silver. She did not seem to notice the cold.

At first I thought she held a knife in her hand, but it was only a stone, sharp on one edge. Shallow cuts lined her sinewy arm. Her gaze was ferocious, the whites of her eyes brilliant as snow. Blood dripped and flowed down her skin to the ground. The hard line of the old woman's mouth was thin as a blade.

"Mary," I said.

"Failed him again," she whispered unsteadily. "A haze I was in. I let it happen, again and again."

"No," I told her firmly. "There was nothing you could have done."

Her face crumpled, and she dug the heel of her palm against her brow—still holding the stone knife, so that the blade came dangerously close to her eye. I took another step, watching despair melt her features, and it made me want to weep—for her, for me.

"Locked in," she breathed. "Can't help him. Can't help him, and he needs me, and this body . . . this body is not what I had. It's *not*"—she cut herself, viciously—"*what*"— she did it again, a shallow strike that glowed red before spilling over with blood—"*I had.*"

I did not let her finish the last blow. I grabbed the hand holding the stone, expecting her to let go—but instead she fought me for its possession. She fought hard. Mary was surprisingly strong—shockingly quick—and she stepped backward and did something with her foot and free hand that sent me to the ground. Dek and Mal squeaked in my ears with surprise.

I lay on my back for one stunned moment—saw the knife flash again toward her arm—and grabbed her ankle, yanking hard. Not enough to make her fall, but a strong enough pull to cause a stumble. I rolled to my feet while she was catching her balance, sensing Zee and the others watching from the shadows. I signaled them to keep away, and tried again to take the stone knife. She kicked at my face with all the agility of a ballerina, joints moving like greased lightning. Her eyes were wild, thick white hair standing off her head—teeth bared in a snarl.

"Mary!" I shouted, grappling with her. "Mary, listen to me!"

Something finally seemed to sink through. She stopped

struggling—but with so much tension left in her body, I didn't dare relax. We stared at each other, caught in a stalemate, and I saw something in the old woman's eyes that was clear and strong, and frighteningly purposeful.

"Grant," she said hoarsely, bleeding all over me. "He's in trouble."

"I know," I said. "We need to find him."

Mary stared up at the sky. Her lips moved in silent conversation, but her body was limp—and a bloody mess. I started to step back, and her hand shot out, grabbing me. I jumped, but Mary did not start fighting again. All she did was stare at the stars, her face filling with startling vitality.

"Can hear his song," she whispered—and then grabbed the back of my neck, her grip strong and sticky with blood. I could not see her eyes—we were too close—but her words were whispered soft inside my ear. "Grant's woman. Lightbringers never stand alone."

"Tell me," I said, hearing the urgency in her voice, sensing there was more I needed to understand. "Tell me what that means."

"One heart burns out," she breathed. "Two hearts live."

I felt those words coil in me like a charm. Dek and Mal, deep in the shadows of my hair, began to hum—and against my legs, Zee brushed close. Mary pulled back, looking at them without fear. She had never been afraid of the boys.

"Found them," Zee rasped, and Mary bared her teeth in a smile or a snarl. I felt like doing the same, and the darkness stirred within my heart: quiet, thoughtful. I should have been terrified—and I was—but not enough to hide from myself. I was ready for a little faith.

I extended my right hand to Zee, but he ignored the armor. His red eyes glowed, and his claws flexed and dug into the ground. "We run. We hunt, sweet Maxine."

"We hunt," I agreed, flexing my hands. "Mary?"

Fierce laughter rolled from the old woman's throat, and she took off: the ghost of a lioness, racing amongst the trees. I followed, and found running easier than walking. I flew.

We moved up the mountain, sprinting along a narrow dirt trail. Mary was a fast woman, and graceful. Years seemed to tumble from her in the starlight, and I had trouble keeping up as Zee bounded ahead of us, Aaz winking in and out of the shadows. I listened to the low drum of heartbeats in my head: deep, wild, like hearing the world breathe and toss while in the throes of some dreamless slumber. Felt old. Old as stone and dirt and blood. Old as thunder.

I lost track of time. When Zee finally slowed, it was at the crest of a knoll in the mountainside. Mary and I crept upon boulders, balanced like goats, and picked our way to the edge to peer down.

I had not stopped to wonder what part of the world we were in—and what I saw below gave me no answer—but in the distance, cradled in the heart of a deep valley, I witnessed lights burning; a town, a small city, maybe. Something undeniably warm in seeing civilization, especially tucked so deep in the mountain wilderness.

But closer—just below us—I glimpsed movement. Two men.

I stood up, and scrabbled down the rocky hill. Mary stayed close behind me, hair wild, her dress flowing in the cold air. We did not try to hide our approach.

Grant saw me first. He sat in the grass, leaning against a large rock. His legs were spread out, his arms folded tightly over his chest. He looked cold and tired, but when he saw me, the warmth of his slow smile was so intimate, and so kind, I wondered how I had ever deluded myself into believing that I could live my life alone, without regret.

Jack sat beside Grant. From a distance, he resembled a scarecrow instead of the big strong man I knew him to be. Close-up was little better. He looked rumpled and exhausted, far too frail for comfort. His hair was a mess. His cheeks were bony and gaunt. But his mouth softened for me, a glint in his eyes that was another kind of smile, and he held his hand up in a short wave.

I stopped, just in front of them. No falling on my knees,

no tears or hugs. I stared into the faces of the two men I loved and forced myself to breathe.

"About time," Grant said, gently wry. "You take a detour to Disneyland?"

"Crossed my mind," I replied. "You're a demanding man."

He held out his hand. I grabbed it, and helped him stand. When he was on his feet, towering over me, he leaned in, and whispered, "But my demands are always manly."

I bit back a quivery smile, hooked my thumb into the waist of his jeans, and stood on my toes to brush my lips over his cheek—too profoundly relieved by his safe presence to do more. What I needed to say required time and silence. Solitude.

Mary hovered nearby: a spectral figure, with stars in her eyes. Grant reached out, and she danced into his embrace on light feet, sagging against him, and not simply from exhaustion.

Zee and the others were scouting the borders of the clearing. Raw was still gone; with Byron, I hoped. I crouched beside Jack, who continued to rest, unmoving. His stillness worried me until he bent one of his legs and rested his arm on his knee: a careless movement, and only a little creaky. Zee loped near—disappeared—and reemerged seconds later with a fleece blanket in his claws. He handed it to me.

"Cribari," I said, tucking the blanket around Jack.

His jaw tightened, hands very pale in the darkness as he pulled the blanket closer. "Down the hill."

I hesitated, trying to read his eyes. Then, slowly, took the old man's hand and pushed back his sleeve. Bone lines caught the starlight, inspiring a primordial, primitive emotion: fear and mystery, and possibility. I ran my fingers over the slight protrusion, which was less a tattoo than a natural growth: like the tusk of an elephant. Only, embedded in his flesh.

I pushed his sleeve even higher. Found other marks, in normal ink: short words, engraved in unintelligible languages against his biceps.

Jack pulled away his arm. I said, "Explain that."

"I remind myself of what is important," he replied gruffly. "I have been alive a great many years, and even my mind can forget the most essential truths."

I touched my face, tracing the web of lines burned into my skin: a gift from the demon Oturu, who had marked me . . . just as he had marked another, five thousand years past. Two women. Two Hunters. Bound. Sharing something in our spirits I did not understand, but that others recognized: Oturu, Jack, Tracker. A demon, an Avatar, and a man—who had known my ancestor while she lived.

"Only one other Hunter ever carried this mark," I said to Jack. "And her memory terrifies you."

"She's dead," replied the old man shortly.

"But what she was lives on," I said grimly. "She almost destroyed the world while she lived. She became . . . something else. And now there's me. Might as well have written 'apocalypse' on my forehead. That's what this scar meant to Father Cribari. And to you, when Oturu first marked me."

Jack pushed down his sleeve, refusing to look at me. "There are some truths that never die, my dear. And some that corrupt."

I grabbed his arm. "Why do I share this mark with her, Jack? Does it have anything to do with this thing that lives inside me?"

"You know it does," he said roughly.

I stood very still, hardly breathing. "What is it, then?"

Jack shook his head, closing his eyes. "I don't know."

"You're lying," Grant said quietly, joining the conversation. He leaned hard on his cane, with his other arm slung over Mary's shoulders.

"No." Jack shot him a look that might have been hateful had there not been so much fear in it, as well. "We were careful when we made her bloodline. We bound *demons* to a human, lad. Demons. And we did it only once, because it was too . . . unpredictable. Maybe this . . . maybe what is happening to her . . . is part of that. *I don't know.*"

"But you're responsible for this," Grant replied. "Antony knew you by that mark on your arm. And you expected him to obey you because of it."

"Old Wolf," I muttered. "What have you done?"

Jack gave me a sharp look. "I tried to keep you safe. All you women, your bloodline. I had good intentions."

"The Catholic Church is trying to *kill* me."

"Just a handful, working in isolation."

Zee spat, making the grass sizzle. "Grim watchers. Bad eggs, Meddling Man. Blood on their hands."

I stood, weary. "Is Cribari dead?"

"No," Grant said.

"But he will be soon," Jack added.

"Yes," I said, sharing a long look with Zee. "That's right."

CHAPTER 19

D OWN the hill. I walked, and Grant came with me. Mary followed at a discreet distance, her transformation evolving, in fragments: she moved like hired muscle, the kind I sometimes saw down at the docks with their Russian Mafia bosses; a sinewy, hard-living woman, quick-draw, with that familiar crazed look in her eye that only enhanced the coiled power of her stride. She looked dangerous. She looked like a woman who had scrubbed blood off her hands.

I did not know what to make of her transformation. I did not know what was happening to her. Such a great distance between the woman I had known and the woman who strode behind me. But it felt, in an odd way, like I was watching someone come home to herself. Odd, strange home.

Grant walked carefully over the uneven ground, and the quiet air seemed to swallow the click of his cane on stone and the soft rasp of his strained breathing. I heard bubbling sounds, sometimes, and his coughs were wet and hacking. I tried not to think about what was coming out of his lungs and craned my neck, staring upward. Stars masked the night, and the ribbon of the Milky Way stretched behind the mountain. I felt very small beneath that vast sky. Everything I was, and could be, nothing but a moment lost in time.

"There's life out there," I said, as Zee and the others prowled through the shadows around our legs—red eyes glinting, claws cutting stone as they whispered to one another in their melodic, indecipherable tongue.

"There's life here." Grant stifled a cough, and pointed to the golden lights of civilization glittering in the distance. "Imagine that."

"If Jack's right—"

He shot me a hard look and wiped his mouth with the back of his hand. "Don't."

I almost pressed the issue. I found the possibilities immensely profound. If Jack had been truthful about the origins of humanity, then all of us were descended from a singular race, of which Grant, and perhaps Mary, were the sole survivors. Worlds, seeded. Worlds, left to gestate. Eons, passing in moments. Grant, tossed through time.

Until here, now. I felt as though there should be a reason for it—for all of this—that there should be a reason, even, for him and me. Because we were impossible. What we were, separately, was impossible. Nothing like us should have existed. Not demons, either, or Avatars; or worlds beyond some hidden labyrinth.

I did not believe in coincidence. But in this case, to *not* believe required belief in something else. And I was not ready for that.

Nor was I prepared to speak about these things with Grant. Because if true—if true—then all I could offer was, ultimately, a discussion about genocide and slavery—as well as how the family Grant had believed in was more or less a lie.

I scanned the hillside in front of us and saw nothing but large boulders and stone shelves jutting sharply from the long, grassy slope. Any farther, and the footing would start getting treacherous for Grant. "What happened after Cribari took you?"

"It's complicated," he said, after a long pause. "You need to see for yourself."

"Grant."

"Just . . ." He stopped, sighing wearily. "Just wait."

I frowned and studied the shadows around us. I saw nothing, not one hint of a man. Grant continued limping down the hill, then cut to the right, toward some boulders. Dek and Mal stopped purring. Zee and Aaz were suddenly nowhere in sight.

Grant took my hand just before we walked around a dip in the jutting round stone. I did not know if it was for his comfort or mine, but my uneasiness spiked, and when I could finally see the other side, I was ready for anything.

Except, nothing was there. No Cribari. Not even a smear of him. Just the boys—even Raw—crouched in front of a craggy rock that was half my height and irregularly shaped, like a squashed pumpkin.

"What?" I said. Zee looked up at me, then shared a long look with the others. Raw and Aaz shrugged.

The boys stepped sideways, away from the boulder.

Which, after a moment, blinked rapidly at me.

I did not blink back. I stood, frozen. Staring at a pair of human eyes encased in stone.

Grant said something, but I heard none of it. Just took one step, then another, until I crouched in front of the boulder and gazed into the remains of Antony Cribari's face.

I could see more than his eyes. Some flesh was visible: part of his cheek and brow, and half his nose—just one nostril, flaring wildly. Stone covered his mouth. A fragment of his ear was visible, so perhaps he could hear. I searched for the rest of his body and found nothing. The priest was too large to be stuffed entirely inside the rock. Part of him, I suspected, was underneath.

His eyes, though. His eyes said everything. He had been weeping. The stone below his eyes was damp, as was the spot beneath his single nostril. I suspected he was having trouble breathing. *I* was having difficulty getting enough air into my lungs. I sat back, faint, heart hammering so hard it made me nauseous.

"Maxine," Grant rumbled.

I started to wave him away, then grabbed his hand, squeezing. I was going to be sick. Antony Cribari in that rock was one of the most horrific things I had ever seen. As affecting as my mother's murder—but in a different way, one that had nothing to do with love, or grief.

I had been buried alive once. Encased in another kind of tomb: unable to speak, unable to breathe—except for the breath the boys had given me. I had stayed like that for a long time. Months, maybe. Years. Time moved differently in the Labyrinth. If I had not freed myself, I would have stayed buried forever.

"I lost consciousness somewhere along the way," Grant said, bending over to peer into my face. "I woke up close by. If I hadn't seen his aura, I would never have known to look for him . . . in that."

"You wish you had never found him," I whispered, and Cribari's gaze met mine, sending a jolt from my heart to my gut that was as painful as a blade, sticking me. I was afraid to look at the priest, fearful of my memories, the things he made me feel.

"I wish a lot of things," Grant replied roughly. "I stayed here until Jack showed up. I think . . . I came very close to ending Antony's life for him."

"Why didn't you?"

He gave me a long, steady look. "According to Jack, there's a promise involved."

I breathed out, slowly. Zee and the others crouched in front of the rock, staring at Cribari. My little wolves, raking trenches through the earth with their claws, spines bristled and quivering, growls rumbling. The priest stared at them, and the weight of his furious helplessness was terrible.

"Sharp man," Zee rasped. "Debt of blood needs to be paid. Your kind cut our old mother dead."

I grabbed Zee's shoulder and forced him to look at me.
"Can you free him? Tear out the stone around his body?"

Raw and Aaz slammed their fists into the rock beside
Cribari's face. Chunks broke loose, and the imprisoned
priest briefly squeezed shut his eyes. The twins giggled.

"Stop," I snapped. "This is not funny."

"Now or later. Dead be dead." Zee glanced over his
shoulder at Cribari. "Stone will break. Stone breaks, he
breaks. Still dead. You promised."

"Then leave Antony to die slowly," Grant said. "Or make
it fast and clean."

I looked at him, startled. Cribari's nose snorted, snot
bubbling from his single nostril—and his bloodshot eyes
filled with hatred. Mary, kneeling a short distance away,
dug her stone blade into the ground. She studied Cribari
with little emotion, though her eyes glittered, and her mouth
twitched suddenly with satisfaction.

"Used man," she whispered. "Gabriel's Hounds have
come."

Grant approached slowly—stopping less than a foot
away, bending close to look into Cribari's eyes. The priest
watched him, eyelids twitching, which suddenly had the
same power as a scream.

"So. Here we are," Grant said quietly. "You have a lot to
answer for, Antony."

Cribari did not blink—with defiance, or fear, I could
not tell. Sweat trickled down his brow, around his eyes.
Grant leaned in closer, and whispered, "It's easier for me if
you're dead. Dead, I won't be able to hurt you. And I want
to, Antony. I'm only a man. I'm weak. You said that, all
those years ago. Born to the devil. You believe that still.
You're afraid of all your secrets that I see."

Grant smiled, and it was chilling because it was sincere;
his smile a weapon, like a wink from the executioner, just
before the ax. "I would like to finish what I started. Remember how that felt, Antony, to have me in your soul?"

Cribari started blinking rapidly. Zee laughed, a hard,
cold sound like broken glass; while Raw and Aaz lounged

in the grass, grinning at Cribari as they idly stabbed themselves with spikes pulled from each other's spines. Dek and Mal hung loosely from my neck, harmonizing Gladys Knight's "Tenderness Is His Way."

I stood on unsteady feet and joined Grant. Unsure what I would find when I touched his hand. His fingers were hot and slid instantly around mine, squeezing hard. Trembling.

He let go of my hand and took one last step toward Cribari. I did not stop him. I did not move, not even when he placed his palm just over the imprisoned priest's head. Both men stared into each other's eyes, and as long as I lived, I would never forget the sensation of cold, hard history that passed between them; or the charge that rode over my skin like the echo of a lightning storm. I held my breath, watching Grant.

Who, moments later, began administering Last Rites.

His voice was so soft I could barely hear him, but his tone was steady and controlled, without anger or joy or pain. He said the words simply, and gently, and Cribari watched him without blinking, until the end. Tears broke, making his cheek shine; but without remorse. Just resignation, and that simmering anger, which seemed to burn through the remains of his pale flesh like a terrible invisible fire.

Grant finished, and after a moment of silence, reached for my hand. He pulled me close until I stood directly in front of Cribari.

"Look at her," he whispered, and this time power flooded his voice. "You look, Antony. She is going to live and have her child. She is going to change this world. Everything you did was in vain."

Cribari stared at him—and then his gaze ticked sideways, settling on me with such weight and darkness my skin recoiled, and my heart pounded with dizzying speed. The boys gathered close, and Grant's fingers tightened, solid and strong.

I'm sorry, I wanted to tell Cribari, as a great swell of pity rose up my throat. But I swallowed the words. I stood still as Zee glided close to the rock and rose on his toes to peer thoughtfully into the priest's face. Cribari's nostril flared, the visible remains of his face contorting in disgust and terror.

"Maxine," Zee rasped.

"Make it fast," I said, and turned, pulling Grant with me. We walked away, and Mary joined us, singing softly under her breath. No one looked back, except for Dek and Mal—sitting high in my hair, quiet as the night.

When Cribari was out of sight, hidden by a curve in the hill and stone, the old woman's voice grew stronger, unintelligible words mixed with a melody so melancholy it was as though she sung a lament, some poem of mourning for the dead.

Grant gave her a strange look. "I know that music."

He tried to join her, his voice sliding over the song like a velvet glove, but within moments he began coughing. He could not stop. He hacked uncontrollably into his hand, doubling over. I stopped breathing until he stopped coughing. Blood covered his palm.

Mary ripped away a piece of her dress and wiped his hand. Grant tried to stop her, but she grabbed his wrist, relentless.

"Never stand alone," she muttered.

The back of my neck prickled. I looked up the hillside, toward the mountain, and saw a lone figure watching us. Starlight made his silver hair glow, but his lean, gaunt frame was little more than a dark slash.

Jack waited for us as we climbed the hill. By the time we reached him, Zee and Aaz had begun prowling through the shadows again. I shared a long look with them, and they nodded once. Raw was nowhere in sight.

"It's done," I said to the old man, suddenly so exhausted all I wanted was to sink into the hill and close my eyes, close my eyes and never see that grisly face again.

"Good," he replied.

"Good," I echoed. "Nothing *good* happened."

Jack's shoulders sagged, but he turned and began striding

up the hill. "The boy came, with the others. They're waiting. We need to decide what to do."

"Jack," Grant called after him, his voice low and dangerous. The old man did not slow, and I sprinted up the hill. He stopped just before I reached him, and looked at me—tense, and wary.

"I want to know how you're involved in all this," I said.

"That's not what you want to know," Jack replied. "What you want is to not feel responsible for any more deaths."

"Like you feel responsible?" I shot back, stung. "Why are you so hard with secrets? Didn't you ever tell your *daughter* the truth?"

Jack flinched. So did I. I had not expected those words to come out of my mouth; too emotional, too intimate. *Your daughter. My mother. My grandfather.*

"Jeannie," he said hoarsely, then stopped, briefly, only to start again, but ever more quietly, his voice broken on words. "Jeannie didn't tell me about your mother. I didn't know I had . . . anyone . . . until Jolene found me. Much later, my dear. Much too late."

"Well," I whispered. "You have me now."

Jack stood so still, until a tremor raced through him, and his face crumpled, ever so briefly that it could have been my imagination. Shadows played tricks like that.

Grant joined us, then Mary. The old man did not look at them, just me, and said, "It started with the Wardens."

I exhaled, slowly. "What did? Cribari's order?"

"*My* order," he said, and started walking up the hill again, carefully. "There were many Wardens in the old days. You cannot imagine their power, or how much they were needed. The prison veil did not hold the entire Reaper army. Many demons were left free, and the Wardens hunted them across the earth. Some humans worshipped them for that."

"Some," I said. "And those *some* became men like Antony Cribari?"

"Don't simplify this," Jack said tersely. "The Wardens predated Christianity by eight thousand years. After they were—after they were gone—all that was left, eventually, was your bloodline. Which had to be protected, at any cost. All I did was harness the preexisting fascination, the mythology created by your existence and the Wardens, to make something that was, for a time, useful."

Jack gave me a serious look. "You are the descendent of women who shook the world, my dear, and who entered the blood of human dreams. Wherever there are dark goddesses, and warrior queens, you will find yourself."

I felt chilled by the idea. "Father Cribari's opinion wasn't quite so uplifting."

"Times changed," he said, grim. "I needed help in those early days and gathered those I trusted, setting them to the task of watching, recording—sometimes giving aid to the women in your family. That first handful of men and women recruited and trained others, and became . . . an order. When it seemed Christianity was going to gain a rather significant foothold in the cultural fabric, they insinuated themselves into various traditions, beginning first in Rome. It was quite convenient. Unfortunately, around the thirteenth century, certain . . . misunderstandings arose. And what I had created was corrupted."

"You mean," I said slowly, "they started to fear my bloodline."

"They always feared it," Jack replied. "In the same way some fear the wrath of an avenging angel. But up until then they had considered your bloodline a force for good."

"What changed?"

Jack did not immediately answer. Grant, who had been carefully silent, slid his hand around mine.

"It must have been the Inquisition," he said quietly. "In the late twelfth century, the Dominicans were given full authority to root out heretics."

The old man did not look at us but instead searched out the stars, as I had done. "Divine fear is something quite different from the fear inspired by torture and condemnation. And while others were being burned alive and broken for crimes as small as praying to a different god, that order was holding a secret that would have . . . changed everything."

The old man paused to take a breath, running a hand over his throat. "Fear led to doubt; doubt led to misgivings. By the time the witch trials began in earnest, the groundwork had been laid to condemn what had once been upheld as the last living force to fight against the Armageddon."

"The falling of the prison veil." I slid my fingers over the scar beneath my ear; so much trouble over such a mundane knot of dead skin. "Cribari wasn't far wrong. There *is* a darkness inside me. You know it, you *believe* in it, or else you wouldn't be wearing that tattoo of my scar. You wouldn't have helped my mother hide so much from me. You wouldn't be afraid that I'm becoming a monster."

Grant made a low sound of protest. Jack finally looked at me. "Never that. Never, my dear."

"I don't believe you," I said. "I remember, Jack. I remember the look in your eyes the first time you ever saw this mark. I remember all your words about hunts and death. You *are* afraid."

Jack's hand shot out, grasping my shoulder. He shook me, ever so slightly, bending to peer into my eyes. "I'm afraid I will fail you. I did that once. I was lax. And your ancestor paid for that."

I stood very still beneath his hand. "I'm not her."

But you could be, came the unbidden thought, mirrored, perhaps, in Jack's eyes. I leaned away from him, and he let me go. I hardly noticed. I did not feel crazy. I felt rooted, my feet on the ground.

I was not a monster, I told myself. Maybe there was a monster inside me—but that was *not* me. Not me.

I thought of Cribari—as well as a fresh-dug grave and a baby sobbing. "What was the name of the Hunter your people murdered?"

He faltered in his steps, but Zee was suddenly there, flowing around my legs. He looked at the old man with grave solemnity, then did the same to me.

"Auicia," he rasped. "Born by the sea."

Jack stared at him, haunted. Ahead, up the hillside, I glimpsed movement. A small figure, standing so much like the old man had, earlier, that at first I thought I was looking at Jack's doppelganger. It was only Byron, though, wrapped in a thick wool coat much too large for his slender frame. It seemed warm, though. Raw had done well.

I found the boys had faded from sight, lost in the shadows. Deadly little ghosts. Dek and Mal, too, twined and receded deeper into my hair, their purrs comfortingly warm against my neck. I squeezed Grant's hand, then let go to sprint ahead up the hill, to the boy.

Byron did not move as I approached. Behind him Killy paced, hands shoved deep inside the pockets of her thick new coat. Her eyes narrowed when she saw me, and her mouth tightened angrily.

"You," she said, "are shit."

"Yes," I replied. "And?"

Killy strode near and shoved me. I held my hands away from her, at my sides.

"Don't," I warned.

Killy swung a hard, fast right at my face. I stepped around the blow and grabbed her wrist, twisting. She went down on one knee, grunting.

"Déjà vu?" I asked her.

"I had a good life," she spat back, her voice thick with rage and grief. "It was good, and it was mine."

"You're still alive, and your life is still yours." I released her and stepped back, light on my feet. "Appreciate that. It might not last."

Killy did not stand—just slumped in the grass, breathing hard. Byron said, "She's mad because you left us. You ran."

"No," she said. "There are other reasons."

"I ran," I agreed, speaking only to the boy. "There was something I didn't want you to see."

"I've seen a lot," he replied, then turned to help Killy stand. A cold, blasting wind stole my breath, but I would have been breathless, anyway. I was suffering a peculiar ache in my chest. Not quite guilt, but something close: a sense that I had been caught in a lie.

I found Father Lawrence nearby, in the grass. He sat awkwardly, round stomach hanging over his pants. I wasn't certain he noticed my presence. He was rubbing his mouth with his hands, rubbing and rubbing, as though that would cleanse him of some violent taste, blood and flesh, maybe. He wore no coat. Like Mary, he did not seem to mind the cold.

I caught Killy watching him—her expression bruised, lost—until she noticed me staring, and her vulnerability hardened into a brittle shell. She rubbed her wrist. "You have a plan?"

I did not answer her, distracted in that moment as Grant, Mary, and Jack caught up. Grant was struggling to breathe without coughing, and his face was pale, drawn, suffering from the cold air and climb—and Cribari. He needed home, warm food, a bed to sleep in, and time to recover. He needed to be safe. We all did.

Killy glanced briefly at Mary and rubbed her brow hard with both hands. I said, "Jack. If Killy and Father Lawrence leave us, will Mr. King be able to track them?"

"He has their scents," Jack replied, his voice rough with exhaustion. "But if they're not with us, he won't be invested in finding them. Not right away."

I met Killy's gaze. "You both should go. Wherever we are, that village down in the valley is only—"

"No," Father Lawrence suddenly croaked, in a voice so torn and battered—so surprising to hear—I flinched. "No, I stay with you."

"Father Frank," Killy protested, but the round little priest shook his head and struggled to stand.

"Holy damn," he muttered. "I hurt."

I offered him a hand, and was not offended when he hesitated, staring at my palm like it might be covered in apocalyptic cooties. It only made it sweeter when he finally did take my help. His grasp was firm and unreserved.

But he swayed, slightly. I dug in my heels, pulling him toward me—just enough to help him firm his footing.

"I made a promise," he said, looking at me with his mismatched eyes—sly and warm, cunning and kind. "Years ago I did this, and it doesn't matter how things have fallen apart. I didn't make that promise to an organization, or an idea. I made it to you and yours."

"Why would you do such a thing?" I breathed, taken aback—even as memory filled me, something he had said in the hall of Mr. King.

Father Lawrence's gaze was unflinching; his single crimson eye glittering like it had been dipped in blood and fire. "A woman saved my soul when I was young. She ripped something dark out of me and killed it before my eyes. I was useless afterward. I had ruined my life. She . . . took care of me."

"My mother," I whispered.

"You look so much like her," he said.

I let go of his hand, but the heat of his palm still burned. "Victims of demonic possessions don't remember what happened to them. Ever."

"I remember," he replied. "Your mother told me to do something useful with that memory."

"I doubt risking your life is what she had in mind."

"I became a priest to serve God against the shadows. When . . . the order . . . began to recruit me, and I discovered their purpose, to watch *her* bloodline . . ." He shrugged, with loose c'est la vie, but that was little more than an act compared to the grim, unflinching determination in his eyes. "Fate, Hunter. God's mystery."

I did not know how to respond. Killy said, "Frank."

Father Lawrence glanced at her, then closed his eyes as though it pained him to see her face. "I'm sorry. I'm so sorry you've been hurt by this. I shouldn't have gotten you involved."

She stared at him, stricken. Grant cleared his throat and looked at Jack. "What about the boy? On his own—"

"No," Byron whispered.

"He would be safe," Jack said, his gaze hooded as he looked from Father Lawrence to the teen. "No one . . . no one can track him. Cribari coming to the shelter was no fluke, but the boy had already made himself an easy target by staying in one place."

"No," Byron said again, growing pale. "No, don't."

"I've done a terrible job protecting you," I told him softly. "Look at the danger you've been in. It's . . . crazy. All of this is crazy."

He seemed to shrink in front of me, swallowed up by his coat until he was little more than a mountain ghost, whose sole connection to this mortal coil rested in his dark, electric eyes.

"I'm safer with you," he whispered. "You don't know what it's like."

"If something happens—"

He shook his head with a wildness that made me shut my mouth. Grant touched my elbow and gave me a long, solemn look that made my heart ache. I glanced again at Byron. We'd had this conversation already.

I'm not alone. Strange is okay.

Better than the alternative. A life so terrible that gunmen and werewolves, and acts of defiance against the laws of physics were preferable.

You would have followed your mother through Hell and back, rather than be on your own.

I was not Byron's mother. But maybe I understood.

Zee, Raw, and Aaz watched us from the shadows, their narrowed eyes mere glints of rubies. Dek and Mal were warm against my shoulders and scalp, singing softly: Jimmy Durante. "Make Someone Happy."

"All right," I said, reaching out to ruffle Byron's hair. He closed his eyes, swaying, and something came over me: I dragged him into my arms, hugging him tight. Byron did not hug back, but sagged against me, slender as a whip beneath his coat. My heart broke again, burning itself into bone, and when the shadow suddenly stirred beneath my ribs, I was not afraid.

I looked over Byron's head at Killy. "You have my credit card. You can go anywhere."

The woman stared—from me to Father Lawrence—and ran her fingers through her short hair, tugging sharply on her scalp. She seemed ready to start laying about her again with her fists.

"Shit," she finally said, looking at the priest. "Fuck you."

He did not seem offended. A faint smile graced his battered mouth, both gentleness and cold scrutiny in his eyes—as well as unease. His hands clutched tight across his stomach, trembling slightly. From nerves, or something else—I could no longer say. Byron, though, was warm in my arms, and Grant was warm beside me. Mary stood nearby, humming tunelessly, twirling the stone knife through her fingers. Jack stared again at the stars.

All of us, together, I thought, heart still aching. Wondering what my mother would say—she, who had lived a life beyond mine, one I was learning about in fragments, and that painted a different picture of the woman I had thought I knew. I could still hear her voice in my head.

Trust yourself.

You're not alone.

There are others.

Dek and Mal growled in my ears. I pushed Byron and Grant from me, snapping around to stare at the hillside. Zee bounded from the shadows. I heard gasps, but paid no mind. It was too late for secrets now. Too late, for so much. Raw and Aaz rolled from the dark places in stone outcroppings, racing for me with all their strength—flying, flying like wolves with wings on their feet.

"Maxine," Zee rasped. "Got bodies coming. Bouncing too fast."

"He's throwing people away," Jack snapped—head tilted, listening. "Using them to cut space too quickly for Zee and the others to track. He's *killing* them for this."

I shoved Byron down on the ground and tried to do the same with Grant—who resisted, reaching for his flute. I said, "Stop—"

An explosion filled the air, and I was slammed backward, off my feet. Pain bloomed through my chest. I glimpsed, as in a dream, Grant's face—staring at me in horror. Blood covered him. So much blood.

I heard more explosions. Screams. I was still falling. I was falling very slowly.

Sharp fingers clasped mine. Small bodies crowded close. My right hand burned, but I hardly noticed. My chest was exploding in fire.

I hit the grass, but only for a moment—the earth swallowed me, then closed.

CHAPTER 20

I lost myself in darkness. I lost myself in dreams, and the boys dreamed with me, sweet on my skin; until I dreamed myself stunned by some river's edge, and in my dream I forced myself to rise and walk, and I walked past trees with trunks older than the first breath of man, and when I stopped walking, I ran.

I ran with memory and dream, like the buds of a spring tree, pushing from the death of winter: nibbles of tender shoots in my mind, delicate and sweet. I remembered forests. I remembered in my hands a fine bow, my hair loose and braided with leaves and moss, my body covered in a slip of linen, and in my focus a white stag, bounding swift on hooves like starry cuffs; hunting animals, hunting men, hunting demons.

I saw demons. I saw strange things. I saw myself, riding atop Zee's back, the boys running large as lions across a rocky desert, through the shambles of a ruined moonlight city—and in front of us, men on horseback, racing for their lives. I saw elephants marching on two feet across snow, bearing armor and swords and small winged women in cages; and a ship powered by sails that glittered like golden spiderwebs beneath a purple sky; and my body, drifting in a world of starlight, my mouth and nose covered by skin—the boys, breathing for me. In space. Above a red planet dashed with clouds.

And then I was in the forest again, but I was blind and heavy, and beneath my hand I touched a long, spiraled horn, cool and familiar as stone.

Unicorn, I thought, and felt a tingle race through me, from my hand, as though small bolts of lightning were knitting flash marks across my skin.

A woman whispered, "Hunter. You should not have come here. Not now."

"I'm dreaming," I whispered.

"You should be." The spiraled horn shifted, sliding in my hand until my knuckles brushed the silken hide of a fine-boned head. "So pretend, Hunter. Pretend this is a dream, and that you do not fall so lightly between the shadows of the Labyrinth. Pretend you are not more than what you seem."

I think I smiled, but the dream was fading, and everything around me felt gossamer, and soft. "I know you. You were human once."

"I was never human," said the woman quietly. "And neither are you."

The horn slipped away, quick as thought—and jabbed me in the chest. Pain exploded, but it was soft and thick, blossoming like the fast-motion revelation of a red, red rose—and the petals that fell were blood, and the blood was sweet on my tongue.

Until, suddenly, the blood was no longer so sweet. The dream broke.

I gasped, choking, and surged upward. I glimpsed a room thick with moving shadows, candle flames flickering—then pain paralyzed me, and I could not breathe. Small, sharp hands pushed me down—followed by larger human ones: quick and warm against my body. My shirt was cut away. I felt soaked, everywhere. I tried opening my eyes, but my lids were too heavy: No amount of willpower could make me see.

"No bullet," Zee rasped, somewhere near. "Taken already."

"Broken bones?" asked a woman, her voice low and tense. "I can't tell from looking."

"Healed. Done and fixed."

"But not the rest of her? Damn fool bitch." Soft cloth was pressed to my chest, just above my right breast. "What was she thinking?"

"Too much blood," Zee murmured. "Couldn't let her blood be scented. Not in the maze."

The woman grumbled something under her breath, but her hands were strong and competent, and even when she poured some burning fluid over my wound, making me scream, I was not afraid of her.

I heard a door slam, and another low voice that was young and soft. A cool cloth touched my brow, and water dribbled into my mouth. Dek and Mal were quiet. After a while, all I could hear was harsh breathing and the thundering skip of my heart.

Then, not even that.

⹸

I did not dream. I entered darkness and abided there, and when it was time, I opened my eyes and was awake.

I hurt. I noticed that first. I could not breathe without pain, and so I breathed carefully, inhaling so very little it felt as though breathing were the same as skipping a stone across still water, light, quick, careful.

I was in a bed, with covers folded up to my waist, and warm, hard stones tucked around my elbows, lower back, and neck. The boys were heavy on my skin, but the heat of the stones soaked through their tattooed bodies, and I was grateful. It felt good.

I was in a simple bedroom, with no windows. Cigarette smoke clung to the air. On my right, wood creaked—and a woman said, "Never the easy way with you, is it?"

I managed to move my head, just a fraction. I glimpsed long legs clad in brown trousers, tucked inside tall, scuffed boots. A white blouse gleamed, obscured by a long scarf and dark braids. Smoke drifted around a tattooed hand. I looked into a face that was mine, only older, lined with the pulse of the wind and sun.

"Maxine, again," whispered my grandmother.

I stared, and she stabbed her cigarette into a porcelain dish that held the brown core of an apple and some bread, as well as the stubby remains of more cigarettes, which had spilled over onto the table. She cleared her throat, then picked up a teacup and held it to my mouth. I needed help to drink. Water dribbled down my chin, but I hardly noticed. I stared into my grandmother's eyes.

"Don't strain yourself," she said, after a minute. "Not like I'm going anywhere."

I did not look away. "*When* are we?"

"Nineteen seventy-four. Been two years since you found us in Mongolia." Jean Kiss gestured sharply at the interior of the bedroom—not looking particularly happy with her surroundings. "Now we're in Paris. Renting a flat from an old soldier I know."

I remembered my brief glimpse of Mongolian grasslands and the blue sky that had burned itself into me as surely as the presence of the woman seated now at my bedside. Three months ago, right before my last battle with Ahsen, I had made the mistake of traveling through time—the first of many, it seemed. The finger armor had brought me to my grandmother then—but I had never thought to see her again.

"Why did you leave Mongolia?" I asked.

"Because I'm not going to be around forever," she said bluntly, "and this world is unkind to ignorant women. Paris has good tutors. Jolene will learn some things."

"I'm sure she hates it."

"I didn't raise a whiner," replied my grandmother, though I could tell she was none too pleased, either, about where they were living.

I did not, however, know what else to say. Maybe she didn't, either. I lay on the bed, aching—watching her watch me. In silence.

Until she said: "Look at us. Talking."

I smiled. "I like it."

"Don't like it too much." My grandmother stood, and pulled an old creased-leather wallet from her back pocket. She unfolded it on the nightstand, revealing thin papers and a tin of loose tobacco leaves. She began rolling a cigarette and glanced at me. "You can make mistakes, but not with time."

"I didn't choose to come here."

"That's right." Jean Kiss struck a match and lit her cigarette. "You were dying, and Zee got you help. Survival comes first. I know that. But this"—and she waved her hand between us—"is dangerous."

"I don't think I'm in any state to change world history."

She smiled grimly. "And what about just ours?"

I stared, unsure how to respond. My grandmother started smoking her cigarette and leaned back in the small wooden chair, stretching out her legs. Still watching me. Watching me so long and hard I felt uneasy.

"Jolene is downstairs," said my grandmother, suddenly. "I made her promise not to speak to you."

"My mother," I said.

"My daughter," she added. "Letting you meet that first time was a mistake. She developed an . . . unhealthy . . . preoccupation with your existence."

"I'm sorry," I said, unsure what that meant. "I didn't mean to cause trouble."

"Trouble," echoed my grandmother, knocking ashes to the floor. "You should have seen the look on her face when you were brought here, bleeding to death. If you had died in front of her, mere *trouble* would have been the least of it."

I could not argue with her about that. I tried to sit up, and managed to do so after a long and careful negotiation with the pain inside my body. Breathing was easier, which was a small consolation. When I looked down at where my wound should have been, all I saw was an unblemished line of tattoos.

My grandmother came to sit beside me. "You'll still have some signs of injury after sunset, but within a day or two even those will be gone. The boys take care of us, when we let them."

"You know this from experience?"

"My mother was hurt once." Jean Kiss picked up my right hand. "You have to go now, Maxine."

I searched her eyes. "Something's happened to you since we last met. I can tell. You weren't this . . . brittle . . . before."

"Brittle," she echoed, and her entire face tightened with pain—just before sliding into the cool, thoughtful mask that had greeted me upon waking. "All of us change. Everyone in this world, from birth to death, becomes someone new. Again and again, we are remade."

"And you lose pieces of yourself along the way?"

"You compensate," she replied, stubbing out the cigarette on her tattooed hand. "You remind yourself of what's important and let that guide you."

"I've heard this before," I said, searching her face. "From my mother ."

My grandmother blinked. "Is that so?"

"And Jack," I added softly.

She blinked again, but this time it was more of a flinch. "I suppose he's still causing trouble?"

"He's *in* trouble," I said, searching for her reaction. "For many things. But also for having a child with you."

"Ah," she breathed, and for the first time, a hint of vulnerability appeared in her eyes. "And you? Are you in trouble for having him as a grandfather?"

"I don't care if I am," I replied sharply. "He's mine."

"Good girl." Jean Kiss closed her eyes and smiled— even as her hand tightened around the armor. "Jolene isn't the only one who thinks of you often."

I think of you, too, I wanted to say—but the world spun around, and the pain in my chest flared white-hot, and nauseating. I could not breathe, I could not speak, and from the bottoms of my feet to the top of my head, a sucking sensation riddled my skin, pulling me in every direction. My right hand burned. Light shimmered behind my eyes, and a dark hand shook me, rattling my heart and bones—throwing me into the abyss like a baseball. I hurtled. I screamed in silence.

Until, abruptly, I could see again.

And found myself surrounded by skins.

CHAPTER 21

I was inside a frozen room, made of ice, polished to dia-
mond sheen. Men and women hung from meat hooks,
embedded in the ceiling. Men and women stood inside the
walls, stored behind plates of clear ice. Men and women
rested upon ice tables, naked and exposed to air so cold my
entire body steamed, and my breath burned white.

I lay very still on an ice-carved floor, trying to make
sense of what I was seeing. I could not. I knew my eyes were
not lying, but in my heart—it was too much. The people
hanging from racks in the ceiling wore clothes: business
suits, jogging outfits, Goth chic leather, jeans and T-shirts.
As though they had all been plucked from their lives and
packed immediately on ice. Fifty in total, maybe, including those on the tables and stored in the walls. Lost lives.

*Cold storage. Mr. King has to keep bodies somewhere,
between experiments.*

My chest hurt. Breathing was hard, but the cold air
helped. I sat up, slowly, hissing in agony as nausea passed
over me. I thought I might vomit and doubled over, breathing hard. Staring at my hands. The finger armor had changed

once again. It had been happening over the last few jumps, but I had stopped looking. Resigned to the inevitability of its growth.

My middle finger was completely encased in metal, and a second silver vein trailed from its base to the cuff around my wrist. I flexed my hand and felt nothing of the armor, which was so much like my flesh it would have been indistinguishable had its appearance not been so different: engraved with coiled roses and knots made of wings.

I rolled over on my hip, struggling against rolling waves of pain, and managed to get my knee under me—then my leg—until I stood on two feet, swaying. My head swam. So did memories of my grandmother. Seemed to me she knew a little too much about time travel and the armor I wore. Seemed, too, that when time-traveling, a person could stand to take a day or two to heal before being shot back to the future—and the time—you wanted.

Like you're some expert. Get a grip.

I turned in a slow circle. The room was perfectly quiet, but the men and women hanging above me were alive. I could see the faintest haze of breath puffing from their nostrils and open mouths. Their eyes were closed, faces slack. The massive hooks they hung from were mostly lost inside their clothing, which gave me some hope that they had not been speared like so many trout.

Zee and the boys were warm on my skin. Even my face was protected in their tattoos: Dek and Mal, coiled in symmetry upon my cheeks. I could feel them, dreaming, as I shuffled painfully around the room, looking for a door.

Aaz tugged sharply on my hand. I followed his lead, but he did not take me to an exit. Instead, I found myself at one of the ice chambers, peering through the cold wall at a slender nude body, and a pale face surrounded by dark hair.

Killy.

I had my nails sunk into the ice before I stopped to think—but I did think—and my hands stilled. If I freed Killy, and she was alive, was it wise of me to take her along?

I was in no shape to protect anyone. I could hardly care for myself right now.

On the other hand, if I left her behind and something happened, if I never found my way back to this room . . .

Damned if you do, and damned if you don't.

I jabbed my hard black nails into the ice, digging into the wall—gritting my teeth as pain raced through my chest. Moments later, Aaz and Raw began heating my palms, and I pressed them flat against the cold surface. Clouds of steam drifted into the air, and water streamed down the wall. I applied pressure, changing angles, running my hands across the ice—sinking deeper, slow and easy—until suddenly I broke through to Killy.

First thing I noticed was that her face had color. Pale, but with a faint rose in her cheeks. Her lips were pink. I had expected blue, some pallor of extreme cold and death. She was breathing, though. She had a pulse. No reaction when I reached through the hole in the ice to touch her.

I ripped away the remains of the ice—stopping once to catch my breath—and pulled Killy free. I hardly had the strength to lower her to the floor and ended up dumping her awkwardly, focused only on protecting her head. I stood, staring at her body, trying to decide what to do for clothes—and then started yanking off mine. I did not feel the cold. I stood naked, except for the shoulder holster holding knives against my ribs.

Not until I began dressing Killy did I realize that the clothes I had been wearing were not mine. Soft pants, a soft shirt, and wool sweater. No boots, just thick socks. My grandmother's clothing. Or maybe my mother's. I pressed the shirt to my nose, inhaling deep. Smelled warm, with some indefinable quality, like spice and sunlight, that hit me deep in the gut. My mother. My mother had worn these clothes.

I was selfish. For one second I regretted dressing Killy—losing that precious scent to another person—and then I pushed those feelings aside and focused on keeping the woman warm. Not once did she stir. I checked her pulse again. It was strong and steady. Stronger, maybe, than mine.

Once I had the woman in my clothes, I knelt and pressed my warm hands between her breasts, then her hands and face. Patted her cheeks—lightly, then harder—suffering a rising panic. Count on me to kill the person I was trying to rescue. Out of desperation, I pressed my right hand on her brow—armored fingers tight against her skin—and thought, *Please.*

My hand tingled, but more: a jolt of electricity that rode down my arm, and that made the boys ripple in response. Killy's eyes flew open, so wildly, with such strength, I flinched.

Nothing else happened, though. She stared past my face at the ceiling, without reaction or acknowledgment. No gasps for breath, no writhing around in discomfort. She showed no reaction. Not even a glimmer. Not even when, quite unexpectedly, she said: "Oh, that's *so* wrong. Not the *chipmunks.*"

I frowned. "Killy?"

"Jesus Christ," she muttered, a crease forming between her eyes. "Who the fuck is in this room with me? Perverts-R-Us?"

"Uh," I said. "Can you hear me?"

"You're the only one not screaming," she said, and touched her brow with a wince. "What did you do to me?"

"Nothing," I replied, wondering if that was a lie. "Can you stand?"

"I could pole-dance Mount Everest if it gets me away from these minds." Killy sat up, moving almost as painfully as me—and then stopped as she looked around the room: at the ice, the men and women hanging, stored, laid out. Her face grew very pale and drawn.

"Oh," she said. "I didn't know."

"You were part of the display," I told her, trying not to make any frightening noises as I struggled to stand. I held out my hand, ready to help Killy to her feet, but she did not move. Just stared at me, too, but with a puzzled frown that was not scandalized—only, it seemed, confused.

I tried not to be embarrassed. Fought a lifetime of rabid self-preservation in less than three seconds. No one but Grant had ever seen me so naked. I would have preferred to keep it that way. I did not know this woman—not one thing about her—except that she was psychic (or a great con artist, in the same vein); she had stayed when she could have run, the boys had not treated her as a threat, and she was in love with a priest.

Actually, that was probably more than I knew about my own grandfather. And grandmother.

"You needed clothes," I said tersely. "I don't feel the cold."

"Thanks," she replied absently, rubbing her forehead. "I can hear your skin humming."

"It does that." I reached down, grabbed her hand, and tried not to black out from the pain as I yanked her up. She practically flew, but her eyes were squeezed shut the entire time, and she held her head with both hands when I let go.

"Everything's turned up," she whispered. "I shouldn't be this strong."

"Do you remember what happened, how you were brought here?"

She shook her head. "No. But they got everyone but the old man and the kid."

Wild hope flared in my heart. I grabbed Killy's elbow and pulled her along. I had noticed the possibility of a door while trying to wake her, and sure enough, there was an alcove between the wall units and the first table. No actual door, just an opening that led from the room into a hall. I glanced down as we passed one of the ice slabs, and saw a teenage girl laid out neatly, unconscious. Many young people, all around me.

Killy pressed her palm over her eye. "Snakes in her popcorn."

I gave her a startled look. "Excuse me?"

"She's dreaming about snakes in her popcorn." Killy's

frown deepened as we passed the girl. "She volunteered for this. For what she thought it would be."

"And?" Ice shelves lined the wall near the door, filled with thin white robes and white sweats and tees. In a small basket were white slippers packaged in plastic. I grabbed a set of everything but the slippers, shrugged off the shoulder holster, and began dressing.

"And nothing," Killy sad quietly, looking at the girl—who seemed serene in sleep, despite her dreams. "She thought it would make her special. Special enough that people would love her."

My chest still hurt like hell, but either I was getting used to the pain, or it just didn't bother me as much. I was able to pull the shirt over my head without breaking into tears. I touched Killy's elbow. "If we do this right, maybe she'll be lucky enough to be proven wrong."

We left the cold-storage room and entered a long ice-carved hall that curved away in both directions. Weird place. Reminded me of photos I had seen of ice mansions; or something from a James Bond film. I thought hard about Grant, sending a silent message to the boys. Raw tugged hard on my left hand—while at the same time Aaz tugged faintly on my right.

Huh. I glanced at Killy, who was beginning to shiver. "What do you hear inside your head?"

She stared at me, rubbing her arms. "Not a lot of people nearby. There are clumps of minds where there isn't much thought at all, not even dreams. Those are scattered. As for the rest . . ."

Killy frowned, closing her eyes—head tilted as though listening. I waited impatiently, twitching backward, wanting to follow Raw's lead—and then stiffened as Killy's face jerked suddenly sideways as though slapped. I reached out, but she shied away with absolute, mind-crushing anguish in her eyes, and started running down the hall—away from me, toward the right. I stared after her, torn—my left hand tugging harder—but I swore silently, dug my bare toes into the icy floor, and chased after her.

She was fast. I was in pain. I tried my best, but she pulled ahead, and I was loath to shout after her. Instead, I practiced throwing rude and unflattering thoughts in her direction. Killy glanced over her shoulder at me, and her pace slowed to a very fast walk. I caught up, wondering how long we could move through this strange ice palace without running into another person.

"Who is it?" I asked.

"Frank," she whispered, and winced. "Oh, God."

I thought of Grant—and Mary—and gritted my teeth. One at a time. Whoever came first. I glanced down at the finger armor, hesitant to use it again to cut space. A faint glow rolled through the metal, and Zee rumbled in his dreams. Raw, sleeping on the same hand as the armor, also fidgeted, sending a faint pulse through my thumb and fingers, which I felt despite the metal surrounding my skin.

My hand flexed, reflexively, as though holding something, and the armor tingled—the boys shifting in response, *again*—until suddenly I felt as though I was eavesdropping on a very peculiar conversation.

Mind of its own, Mr. King had said.

So tell me, I asked the armor silently. *What do you think I need?*

Killy pulled ahead of me, just slightly. I hung back as the armor began shimmering with a liquid light that resembled moonbeams captured in a bottle: brighter, colder, filling me with a thrill I could not fight, which chased my heart into my stomach as I closed my eyes against the brilliant light.

Heat filled my palm. When I looked again, I held a sword.

I knew the weapon. I had summoned it from the armor once before, three months past. Delicate and slender, glowing brighter than the ice with a light that seemed cast from within: the moon's reflection caught in its forging. The engraved silver hilt fit to my hand, and from its pommel ran a chain that bound the sword to the iron armor surrounding my wrist. Runes covered the blade, and I ran my palm hard against the razor edge. Sparks danced. Heat soared through my tattooed fingers as I gripped the hilt. Felt good holding the sword. Natural, an extension of myself: a biting silver needle beneath my skin. The weapon weighed nothing, but holding it made me feel ten feet taller.

I looked up. Killy had stopped, and was staring at the sword.

"What did I just see?" she asked sharply.

"Don't ask me," I said. "I just take what I'm given."

She made a small, ugly noise. "Dangerous people should not be so fucking clueless."

"Aw," I said. "Compliments."

Killy shook her head, looking at me like I was shit— and then turned, sprinting ahead on light feet, leading me to another open doorway. The place seemed to be made of nothing but halls and doors and ice—a polar temple; a cold nightmare. I heard strange sounds inside—hissing, crunching—but peering through the carved archway revealed nothing except a hall. I ran, sword humming in my hand, and felt the boys tug sharply, once.

I smelled blood. Listened to more crunching—bones grinding between teeth—wet, fierce smacks. I knew those sounds.

Killy said, again: "Frank."

I rounded a corner in the hall and found myself inside a cavern that looked hacked from stone and ice; a hollow gray shell filled with jutting edges that resembled ax blades glued together at random angles. A large pit had been dug in the center of the room—an incongruous, unexpected vision—like finding a football field inside a closet. It was at least twenty feet deep; a gladiatorial crater, or medieval prison. Men were in the pit. Hunched figures in black robes, chained to ice walls that could not have held them had they been agitated. Which they were. But not because anyone wanted to escape.

They were eating. Gorging themselves like animals, on all fours. The bottom of the pit was several different shades

of bloodred: old, really old, and brand-new. I saw the remains of an entire cow and several pigs, intestines spilled
in steaming piles, mashed together under knees and feet as
sharp-toothed men snapped at one another, and bent face-
first into the guts and flesh of the dead animals. Humanity,
burned out of their minds. Professionals, students, hus-
bands, fathers—now killers covered in blood. Bile rose up
my throat.

Killy grabbed my arm and pointed. Nearby on our right
were two men, one of whom was being pulled toward the
edge of the pit, hauled along by a second man shrouded head
to toe in black, including a hood that covered his head.

The man being dragged was Father Lawrence. Trussed
in chains, he was spitting and snarling—his single red eye
glowing, face covered in fur.

Killy started running before I could stop her. I pursued,
dimly aware of many eyes zeroing in on us from the bottom of the pit—like frenzied sharks in a pool already red
with chum. My skin crawled. My chest hurt. It was hard to
breathe, but I sucked up the pain and lunged past Killy,
sword swinging. The blade slashed down through the
man's shoulder and chest like his muscles and bones were
made of water. I did not expect so little resistance, and careened into him. He smelled like blood, raw meat—and he
uttered one small grunt just before toppling backward, into
the pit. In two pieces.

"Crap," I said, as his body landed on top of several creatures in the pit, all of whom had stopped eating and were
standing very still, watching us. Silence descended. No
one attacked the corpse, but several of those nearest bent
to sniff carefully at it. Snarls rumbled from them. Howls.
Chains strained against the wall.

I turned quickly. Killy was trying to drag Father Lawrence back to the door, which looked a little like Thum-
belina wrestling with a grizzly bear. He was not fighting
her, but there was a wild look in both eyes that made me
want to warn her off. Instead, I took two long strides and

set the sword tip against Father Lawrence's chains. The links split. He shrugged free and rolled to his feet in one blindingly quick movement.

Below, in the pit, the ice walls cracked.

"Run," I snapped.

Father Lawrence lunged toward Killy—with such aggression that for one moment I thought he might hurt her. Instead, he threw the small woman over his shoulder and ran—hunched over, almost on all fours—her small body flopping awkwardly. No way I could keep pace. I glanced over my shoulder and found dark-robed bodies scrambling up a coiled path that had been carved into the side of the pit. More men than I could count, an overkill of bodies, arms pressed to their sides so that their odd, leaning posture and raging mouths reminded me again of torpedoes and piranhas, or sharks on two feet.

I did not run. I braced myself, digging in my heels, the sword burning with light. *Men with stolen lives,* I told myself. *Have mercy.*

Have mercy and kill them fast, my mother would have said, and I swung the blade like a baseball bat at the first wave of snarling men who rushed me. Bone cracked, blood spraying across my face as the sword sliced straight through flesh with a sweet, humming hiss. Howls vibrated in my ears, sharp teeth flashing. I smelled raw meat.

All I wanted was to give Father Lawrence and Killy time. All I needed was to clean up some of the mess Mr. King had created. There were too many, though—and their momentum was crushing. I staggered, slashing at anything that moved, blind to individual faces and bodies; just mouths, wet and red, and impossibly large. The boys screamed inside my mind. Teeth broke on my neck. I punched and clawed with my free hand, raking flesh to bone under my black nails. Breathing hurt. I could not breathe.

Until, suddenly, a space opened in front of me—and one of the sharp-toothed men barreled sideways into the others, snarling. A shadow clung to his shoulders, an aura like the ghost of a thunderstorm, concentrated into a flickering wisp. It was not alone, either. I saw other shadows appear inside the ice cavern, falling with inexorable promise upon the heads of those raging men. I watched demonic parasites take possession.

And I was glad of it.

Only a handful had come, but that was enough to confuse and push back the others. Bodies slammed, raging, and for a moment it was like watching sharks turn on one another, mouths spilling over with flesh and blood. One of the possessed broke free of the others, striding toward me—standing tall like a man, and not one of those speeding human torpedoes. His aura flickered wildly, and his eyes—I knew those eyes.

"Hunter," he rasped, voice muffled by teeth, low and growling.

"Rex?" I muttered. "Why are you here?"

"Old skinner Jack. He told us about Grant." He spat blood on the ice floor. "So we came to help, enemy of my enemy. Wrap your mind around that."

I could not and backed away, watching as the zombies tore into the remaining men. "These are strong hosts. Who's to say you won't keep the bodies?"

Rex smiled mirthlessly, which looked ghastly given the unending rows of sharp teeth in his mouth. "We gave our word. So go, find Grant. We'll take care of the rest."

"I don't trust you," I snapped. "No matter how much you love Grant."

The zombie's eyes narrowed. "Get out of here."

I did. When I reached the hall outside the room, Father Lawrence and Killy were gone. No sounds or signs of their escape. The ice floor was scratched, but it was like that everywhere, without one definitive track to follow.

Behind me, howls. My right hand tugged sharply.

You're on your own, I told the priest and woman—and raced down the hall, back the way we had come, toward the cold-storage freezer of bodies and beyond, to where the boys were telling me that Grant was being held.

It was hard to move fast. My chest burned. Breathing

was worse. After running for less than minute, I bent over, holding myself, trying not to be sick—struggling instead to imagine those skipping stones on still water: *In, out, breathe.*

I met no one in the hall, though I heard howls, sounds of combat: ice cracking, broken screams. I thought about Father Lawrence and Killy. Mary. Grant. Zee tugged harder against my chest, while the sword in my hand hummed with light. I felt as though I might be traveling in a circle—I passed many open archways cut into ice—but none inspired the right kind of reaction from the boys.

Until the hall ended, abruptly. I found myself inside a cavernous room. And in the heart of the room was a labyrinth.

As in the dance club, the lines had been engraved into the ice floor, embedded with silver. And, too, a woman waited on the ice, dressed in a long silk cloak the color of snow, with a furred white hood that shrouded a young, perfect face.

"He's waiting," said Nephele.

⚜

WE traveled the etched labyrinth, following the path around and around, twisting, and every time I looked up from my feet and the engraved silver lines, I found the room had altered, just slightly. Ice was becoming stone, and a peach glow stained the cold blue walls.

Getting to Mr. King did not need to be so complicated, I realized; but it was homage, a shrine and ritual, in the same way it had been for pilgrims at Chartres. The Avatar might fancy himself a god, but he still prayed, still revered something he found larger than himself.

The Labyrinth.

At the center of the maze, the room shifted one last time—blurring my vision, making me dizzy. When I could see again, I stood in the temple, the hall of Mr. King—the Erlking—with its stone and stalactites, and the vast columns that stood in mist upon an impossible distance. No dancers. No bells. I did not understand this place, how it could exist just beyond reality—how Mr. King could make it exist—and yet not be able to access the Labyrinth.

I saw him immediately. I had expected an army between us—guns and teeth and fire—but Mr. King stood alone. He wore a long crimson robe, loose hood draped just over his head, framing a breathtaking face too perfect to be human—but that was, strikingly so. Black hair, pale skin, blue eyes. A silver circlet rested upon his brow. Black wings arched magnificently behind his back—so vast and lovely, even *my* breath caught. Even *I*, knowing what he was, found myself momentarily lost to awe.

Gabriel. Antony Cribari had never stood a chance.

"My Lady," he rumbled, and his voice filled the cavern like a slow, hot purr. "I felt your arrival. Despite your . . . grievous wounds."

"Mr. King," I greeted him. "You said you wanted me alive."

"I decided that death would be safer. I was right. Somehow, even now, you are destroying all I have made. My soldiers are engaged." His gaze fell upon the armor and sword. "Such trouble for a small thing."

"Sometimes we make our own trouble." I twisted my wrist until the sword blade rested against the back of my arm. "Grant. The others. I want them."

"Or you will kill me." Mr. King's wings stiffened, his eyes narrowing dangerously. "Only the Lightbringers and the demons were ever able to murder my kind. And now you. It was *never* thus with your bloodline. We were so careful when we made you not to cross certain lines." His gaze ticked past me. "*Weren't* we, Jack?"

My heart lurched. I stepped sideways, unwilling to turn my back on Mr. King, and angled my head just enough to see behind me.

Jack stood there. I had not heard him arrive. He was gaunt, pale, but with a fire in his eyes that was unholy and wild. I forgot to breathe, looking at him. Nephele was gone.

"We were careful," said the old man, staring at Mr. King with so much fury I felt very small and young before him, hardly a tick in time. "But nothing stays the same. Not power, not majesty, not dreams. We, of all beings, should know that."

Mr. King's jaw tightened. "You played with her bloodline."

"I loved," Jack said simply. "I did nothing more than that."

"Then how do you explain her?" His mask slipped, just a fraction, and I saw the terrible fear he was hiding, a glittering, visceral terror that was wet and sharp. "It *lives* inside her. I looked into *its* eyes, and was *judged*."

"As we have judged others?" Jack took a step, and another, until he stood beside me, warm and tall. "We have played gods with *worlds*, and yet when faced with our deaths, we cannot swallow the bitterness of our own games?"

"Games of survival," Mr. King whispered. "You remember what it was like to be lost in ourselves, without flesh to anchor our minds. You remember your insanity. You can feel it now, as I do, always waiting for us. None of us are safe. So *if* we have played at being gods, then so be it. I am sick of your judgments. You are no longer a High Lord of the Divine Organic. You gave up that right when you anchored yourself to this spit of mud and these skins. You gave up *everything*, and yet you punished Ahsen. You punished me, and others. For nothing more than staying sane."

"Sanity is no excuse for cruelty."

"Cruelty is a construct. It means nothing." Mr. King looked at me. "You might understand that one day."

"She has a heart," said Jack coldly. "More than I can say for you."

"Old Merlin Jack. Still defending your knights. Even the ones who will destroy you." He stepped sideways, sweeping aside his robe with careful grace. The tips of his enormous black wings dragged across the stone floor. "You want the Lightbringer, yes? And the old woman? Two of the same kind. But you knew that."

"The Labyrinth brought them here," Jack said, a note of urgency entering his voice. "You speak of judgment, and there is your proof. They are of the First People. Even *you* can see that. The Labyrinth *saved* them."

"For us," said Mr. King sharply. "We need their blood to help us survive when the demons break free. No other weapon is left to us."

"And nothing will be left when you're done with them. You cannot clone a soul," Jack snapped in disgust. "You won't breed anything but what we already have."

I grabbed his arm. "Enough talking. Where are they?"

Mr. King looked at my hand on the old man's arm and a tangled snarl altered his perfect face into something ghastly. "If I give the Lightbringer to you, what then? You want satisfaction. You are a wolf, and wolves care for nothing else. In the company of wolves, all that can be expected is blood. And Hunter, you *dream* of blood."

I must have moved. I must have. Later, I could not remember. Only, the distance between us suddenly did not exist, and when I blinked, the sword was pressed against Mr. King's throat, and my left hand twisted his right ear. Fear filled his eyes, but when he spoke, there was only a slight tremor in his voice.

"I will have them killed," he said.

I made no reply. Simply tilted the sword so that it angled up, in front of his eyes. He took a good long look. He could not help himself. He stared, from the blade to the armor, and the desire in his eyes was as strong as a body gone years without touch, like he might stop breathing if he looked away.

"You are cruel," he whispered, and leaned against the blade, closing his eyes as the steel bit into his flesh and made him bleed. A tremor raced through him, and he let out a sigh that was less pain than pleasure. I pulled the blade back, just enough to break contact, and he tried to follow—desperation haunting his face.

"No," murmured Mr. King, shivering. "No, bring it back."

"You want this," I said, studying the terrible hunger burning through his eyes; and the aching loneliness, the despair, that twisted his beautiful stolen face.

"I want freedom," he breathed. "I want you to free me from this prison."

"You are free. Free as any of us."

"Free to die." Mr. King squeezed shut his eyes. "The Labyrinth has denied me. I have been turned back, again and again, though the doors once opened at a thought."

"None of us can walk the old roads as we once did," Jack said, behind me. "What you want—"

"—what I will *have*," rasped Mr. King, grabbing the blade with his hand; squeezing until he bled. "What I will have is my dignity, and respect. I will be as I was, and not this . . . thing . . . trapped on a world already dead."

He turned his gaze on me, and it was bright and glittering with hunger and disgust. "Give me what I want, Hunter. If for nothing else, then for mercy's sake. I do not want to die here. I do not want to die at the hands of the demons, when they are loosed upon this world."

"And Grant? Mary?" I trembled, the armor and sword growing hot in my hand. "Don't bullshit me. Maybe you'll promise to leave them here. Maybe you'll tell me you won't ever come back. But you said it yourself: You *need* them. Your kind *needs* them. You'll destroy this world for them, just as you've put a dent into it with your games of flesh." Each word made me angrier; each word felt like a hammer on my tongue. And the hunger that suddenly bloomed inside me was so tangled with my own rage I could not tell if the shadow stirred inside my heart. But I thought it did. I thought it stretched beneath my skin, coiling softly.

"I won't do anything for you," I whispered.

Desperation filled Mr. King's face, and his wings flared wildly, with such strength that he managed to push me away. The moment I stopped touching him, he vanished.

Jack grabbed my right wrist, and without a word we fell

into the abyss—spat out, moments later, in another stone room much like the one we had left. Small, dark space, cold as ice. I did not see Grant, but Mary sat on the floor, naked and sinewy, her wrists caught in chains bolted into the floor. Too short a leash to stand, and her knees were raw and bloody. Half her face was swollen purple, but there was a crazed clarity in her eyes that burned bright when she saw me.

A tattoo covered her chest. I had never seen the old woman naked, never wondered what she might have been hiding under her clothes. But over her sternum was a coiled circle of knotted lines that I recognized—golden and glittering as the pendant that suddenly swung from Mr. King's pale hand.

"Look what I found," whispered Mr. King, staring at Jack. "On the Lightbringer himself, I found this. On the old woman, growing from her bones. You know what that makes her, Wolf. You know what she is. And if she came with the Lightbringer, then you know what *he* is."

Jack stared at the pendant, then at Mary. A shudder raced through him. "It does not matter."

"It *matters*," hissed Mr. King, wings flaring. "It matters for all the lives that family took, and for the army they led. It matters because you were the one sent to exterminate their bloodline. And you said you did."

Jack's jaw tightened. "It was enough."

Mr. King snarled, fingers tightening around the pendant. Mary's chains rattled violently. I found her straining toward the Avatar, pulling so hard her wrists bled beneath the restraints.

"Grant's woman!" Mary cried at me, her voice cutting straight to my heart. Her eyes glittered; and the golden tattoo shone between her wrinkled, sagging breasts like another kind of armor. The sword in my hands burned hot. Zee yanked on my body.

I ran to Mary. Mr. King shouted, but he was too late to stop me as I swung the blade and cut the chains binding the old woman. She threw back her head, baring her teeth in a snarl, and grabbed my arm. Behind her, Mr. King stretched out his hand, returning her stare. Eyes glowing. Jack shouted a single sharp word.

"Silent, in shadows," Mary hissed. "Find his voice."

I clutched the sword to my chest, staring into her wild eyes, and all the boys trembled in their dreams. *Grant,* I thought, burning up with his name. *Grant.*

I half expected to fall backward into the abyss, but the world remained. My vision blurred, though, and I saw inside my head a place of darkness, a cold tomb; and within, as though sleeping inside a coffin made of ice, a man. My man.

He felt close. Close, in the same way a person might feel sunlight warm on skin. Everywhere, all around me. I sank into that sensation. I turned in a slow circle, trying to feel its source, and on my left, I felt a tug, a disturbance and ripple, a tickle from the boys. Behind Mr. King.

I saw only stone, featureless and smooth like the inner wall of a mountain cave. I did not trust my eyes. Mr. King stared at us, rigid and trembling, his hand still outstretched. Jack watched him, and a low, rumbling growl, quiet as thunder, rolled straight from his chest, a sound like that of a wolf. It cut to the primal part of me that was human. He stared at the Erlking with so much hate, I feared for him. I had never seen the man who lived in Jack's eyes, but I imagined him swelling, straining the confines of skin.

"Jack," I whispered.

"I see it," he said tightly. "A fold in space, like the one that hides this place."

Mr. King narrowed his eyes. "You will not take him from me. I will change both the Lightbringer and his assassin before you do that. I will alter them so far beyond your reckoning, they will be monsters to you."

"You lie," Jack whispered, but Mr. King ignored him, staring into my eyes with pure, hard resolve. Bluffing or not, the fear that cut me was real enough. No matter how fast I moved, I had seen what he could do to Father Lawrence, in just moments. Grant would be an easy mark. So would Mary.

But that did not stop the old woman from lunging at Mr. King. She moved incredibly fast, swinging the ends of chains still attached to the ends of her wrists. Steel whistled through the air like short whips, and the edges of the broken links snapped hard against Mr. King's eyes. He showed no pain—no nerves in his body to feel a thing— but he flinched. A small distraction. Jack said something sharp in a language I did not understand, and Mr. King jerked forward, clutching his stomach. His eyes widened in surprise.

Jack made a tearing motion with his right hand, and a shadow lifted against the wall, like a curtain. A stone platform appeared, covered in a slab of ice.

Mr. King groaned, wings arching backward. Sparks tumbled from his shoulders, followed by a single bright cloud of light—like the aura of a demon, only golden and pale. It hovered, straining, struggling against some bond I could not see. Jack's hands remained outstretched, fingers arched like claws. Heat rose from his frail body, and his blue eyes were so bright they seemed to glow, as though moonstruck.

"I can't hold him long," hissed Jack, sweat beading against his brow. "Free Grant. He's the only one who can kill him outside his flesh."

I had already begun to move. His words chased me across the room as I sprinted past Mr. King toward the ice coffin, the boys surging against my skin. Mary was already there, beating at the ice with the ends of her chains.

My hands burned red-hot, and the sword vanished in a flash of light, back into the armor. I reached the slab in moments, and Mary stepped back as I slammed my palms down on the ice, with such force it cracked. Steam blinded me, but I raked my nails deep, clawing away massive chunks of ice. Mary reached in, as well, ripping and tearing with her bare hands, grunting with pain as her own nails tore.

We finally broke through. Grant lay very still, his eyes closed. I touched his face, but he did not stir. Like Killy's, his sleep was too deep.

Jack went down on his knees, gasping. Mr. King's aura shuddered. The armor on my hand flared white-hot—and I could see, in that moment, the future spread before me. I saw Mr. King free. I saw Jack dead, *truly* dead. And I saw Grant enslaved, skin grown over his mouth so that he could never make another sound.

I saw it so clearly, so fiercely, I knew it was true—and I lost myself in that moment. I shed my heart, and the shadow inside me exploded from sleep, twisting so violently beneath my skin, I thought my body would transform. Electricity raced over me, and the boys began howling in my mind.

Lightbringers never stand alone, I heard Mary whisper. *Two hearts live.*

I understood. I glimpsed in my head visions brief as heartbeats: men and women, voices tumbling with power, standing under a golden sky and ankle deep in mud and blood; and with them others, silent companions brandishing weapons: whips glittering like diamonds, and humming swords translucent as crystal. For every singer, a warrior, and between them, bonds of power, rivers of power.

I saw Mary. Mary, as a young woman: blond and sinewy, and dark from the sun. Perched on the edge of a rocky outcropping with the stillness and grace of a hawk. She wore little, a patchwork of leather and steel that formed a flexible armor across her torso and legs. A piece had been cut away above her breastbone, revealing the embedded metallic tattoo.

Beside her stood a young, brown-haired woman—carrying a baby in a sling. She had solemn, grief-stricken eyes, and her long, cream-colored robes were filthy with blood and mud. One hand covered her baby's head. A pendant hung between her breasts.

Marritine, whispered the young woman, as she reached

into the air and made a ripping motion with her hand. *Mar-ritine, promise he will live.*

He will live, rasped Mary, glancing over her shoulder as screams filled the air somewhere distant behind them. *I swear it.*

I swear it.

I closed my eyes, burning up with those words—with darkness—burning with the light of the armor, tempering the darkness—and slammed my hand against Grant's chest, above his heart, pouring my strength into his body: a stream of dark light, from my heart to his. His eyes flew open, breath rattling, but I did not stop. I could not.

I swear it.

"Maxine," he rasped.

Jack cried out again. Mary ran toward the old man, but I did not watch her go. I reached more deeply into the ice coffin, cradling Grant's head with my left hand. My right stayed on his chest, all the hearts of the boys beating against my palm, in time with my heart. In time with Grant's.

"Hey," I whispered. "Time to sing."

Grant frowned, but only for a moment. I felt the curious sensation of something brushing against my mind, sliding around the dark spirit inhabiting my heart. Memories smoldered. Grant closed his eyes, sucking in his breath. Pain creased his brow.

But when he opened his mouth again, the sound that poured up his throat was not human. Not anything born of thunder, but older, primal, as though some visceral *om* was clawing its way from his lungs or from the heart of a star. Heat poured off his skin, bleeding through the boys into my soul, and I closed my eyes and watched inside my mind as Grant's body broke apart in light, becoming light, his voice reaching around the Avatar spark to hold it in a vise.

I felt Mr. King squirm—only, he was not Mr. King, but countless names and skins—and I saw again the vastness of space, suffered the insurmountable pressure of endless time—until, suddenly, the pressure broke—and I witnessed the Avatar's first memory of flesh, the sensation of a simple touch so much a miracle, so grounding, that what had been madness settled into hunger, and desire. I felt desire. I felt greed. I felt hate and power. Not mine, but Mr. King's.

I felt his loneliness.

I felt his fear of the vastness of space—and of the vastness within himself.

I felt his desire to *be*.

I felt his terror of Grant and me.

And in the last moment, I heard him whisper, *Our kind are done, we are done, all that we were and created, our worlds and myths, are done, and we are done.*

Labyrinth, take me.

The finger armor flared white-hot. Grant's voice twisted.

And the essence of Mr. King—his immortality—dissolved into nothing but air.

As, moments later, did we.

CHAPTER 22

⟡

I woke in darkness, but I was not alone. A heart beat next to mine, light against my shadow, a steady pulse bound to mine, same as mine, linked forever to mine.

Grant, I said, weary.

I'm here, he whispered. *Rest, Maxine.*

Rest, mumbled Zee.

Rest, breathed my mother.

And so I did.

⟡

THE next time I opened my eyes, it was night, and the boys were awake. I was tucked deep under soft flannel blankets, curled against a soft, sagging mattress. The pillow under my head smelled like Grant. Zee cuddled close under the covers, while Raw and Aaz were heavy lumps on top of the bed, behind my knees and against my stomach. All of them, sucking their claws and holding teddy bears and small baseball bats. Popcorn bags and hot-dog cartons littered the bottom of the bed. Dek and Mal hummed the melody to Madonna's "Live to Tell."

I lay very still, savoring the sensation of being alive and home. Home, in Seattle. Home, in the loft. For the first time, more at home here than in my car or a hotel room. I could hear the television in the other room, and low voices; the clank of plates and the creak of hardwood floors. Homey sounds, but alien, too. I felt displaced within the darkness of the room where I lay, cocooned inside an entirely different world.

Just like my heart. I searched inward, for the darkness, that hungry, raging spirit that was of me and separate—and that had judged Mr. King, terrifying him. I found that dangerous presence as easily as breathing—sleeping within me like a fragment of the abyss. Tucked beside it, a new companion: a small golden rose, coiled and burning. Pulsing in time to my heartbeat.

Grant, I thought, and heard movement behind me. The mattress sank, and a strong warm hand touched my face.

"My dear sweet girl," Jack murmured.

"Old Wolf," I whispered, turning to look at him—soaking in the sight of his pale face and glittering eyes, and the faint curve of his smile.

"So," he said. "We live again."

I searched my memories, but all I could recall was Mr. King's voice inside my mind and the echo of his death.

"How did we get here?" I asked, my voice breaking. Zee withdrew a water bottle from under the covers—a bottle I was certain had not been there before—and Jack took it from him, unscrewing the lid and holding it to my lips. Tasted good. Water trickled from the corner of my mouth into the pillow.

"Slowly," Jack said quietly. "I brought us home one at a time. We were in Sweden, inside a rich man's eccentric dream. A private home modeled after some famous hotel made of ice. I believe its owner was killed. I found photographs. He was a fat short man who wore glasses, and had bad taste in suits. I suppose that might sound familiar?"

It did. "What about . . . that other place? The temple?"

"A twist in space," Jack said quietly. "His former prison,

where I put him. He could still access it, as he wished. After so many years, I suppose it felt a little like home."

A swift pang of regret filled me, then faded. "I'm surprised you're not sick from transporting so many people."

The old man shifted uncomfortably. "Grant . . . gave me energy to feed on."

"Ah," I breathed, remembering the terrible hunger I had seen in his eyes. "You've craved that."

Jack looked away from me, down at his hands. "There are many shameful things I have not told you. And I know it has been a frustration . . . what you call my riddles. But I love you, if it helps." He closed his eyes. "I loved your mother."

I love you, I told him silently, unable to say the words out loud, afraid of the words, as much as I ached for them. I forced myself to breathe. "Did you do something to my mother that she passed down to me? Did you change us?"

"I don't know," Jack whispered, meeting my gaze with haunted eyes. "But what your grandmother and I shared . . . what Jeannie and I did . . ."

He stopped. "I regret nothing. I regret *nothing.*"

"But you're saying that you should."

"There are rules. Like a teacher violating some trust with a student. That is what I did."

"My grandmother was no Lolita."

"She was a firestorm," he murmured. "Jeannie."

It was the way Jack said it. Part of me was embarrassed to hear the intimacy in his voice when he spoke my grandmother's name, but I was hungry for it, too. Hungry to know someone had cared for her. Hungry to know my mother had been the recipient of such affection, even from a distance.

And me. I wanted that love, too. I wanted a grandfather.

My fingers grazed Jack's shoulder. He reached back and covered my hand with his. Human hand; pale, dry skin. Nothing alien about him.

Nothing but the heart, my mother had once said, when

I was very young. *Bodies break when the heart breaks.*
Even a dog will die from grief.

So be strong, she had finished. *Don't grieve for me.*

If she had been alive, I would have called that bullshit
to her face. *Do not grieve.* As if that were weakness. She
had probably grieved for her mother as much as I still
grieved for her. Only she had never talked about it.

But Jack grieved. I thought, perhaps, he might grieve
her for as long as he lived.

"Why are you so different?" I asked him, remembering
Mr. King in his stolen bodies: angel and human, divine
and disgusting; in all those incarnations, rotting on the inside, without compassion or mercy.

The old man held up his wrinkled hands. "See how
transient is the flesh? How it passes from life to death? I
have been reborn again and again. I have fallen into the
wombs of human mothers, thousands and thousands of
mothers—good mothers, bad mothers—from poverty to
royalty to divinity—and I have done so without my memories. I have done this with all that I am, hidden from me.
Because, if you are going to live as human, then you must
live. Surrender yourself to the experience, unconditionally,
so that you exist as you were meant to—in the moment,
purely yourself, shaped and molded by experiences that
are raw as mortality allows. So that when you do remember who you are, you remember humility, as well. Humility and compassion . . . and love."

He closed his hands into fists, and shook his head. "He
who called himself Mr. King, my brother, never understood that. Never understood that to be a true master of the
Divine Organic was to become what we create, in every
way. Not simply to ape it, like ghosts within puppets, but
instead to learn, and become *more.*" Bitterness twisted his
mouth. "Many still believe as he did. Simply to take and
take, and nothing more."

And they'll be coming here next, I thought grimly—
though that was all I had time to consider. I heard a distinctive clicking sound outside the bedroom. Heat spread

through my heart—my tugging, aching heart—and I struggled to sit up as the door pushed open, and golden lamp-light spilled inside.

Grant limped into the bedroom, pausing briefly on the threshold to stare at me. He was pale, but not packed-on-ice pale, with a healthy look in his eyes that had been missing for days. He leaned hard on his cane, but the rest of him was straight and strong, and even from the bed, I could smell my shampoo on his damp hair. He wore loose black sweats and a dark green sweatshirt. Around his neck hung his mother's golden pendant.

He stared, and a rushing warmth moved through me—between us—so strong, so real, I found myself touching the air in front of me, imagining I might find something solid linking our bodies. Grant smiled faintly, and a pulse flowed through my chest—the echo of his heartbeat.

"Hey," he said, limping close. "Get back under the covers."

A shadow appeared behind him. Mary. White hair wild, and dressed in another kooky dress covered in giant orange cats. Only this time, she wore a wide leather belt, the kind used to support someone's back while lifting heavy machinery. It looked old-fashioned, perhaps found amongst the machinery in the basement, but it emphasized her slenderness; and the long white cardigan draped over her slender frame like a cloak. It should have been a ridiculous outfit, but on her, it was perfect. She looked like a fighter. I could not explain the difference; it was her posture, maybe, or her eyes: glittering wildly, as though actual lights danced through her pupils. It lent her a crazed intensity that seemed unpredictable as lightning.

"Bonded now," she whispered, staring at me. "Rivers golden as the sun."

"Bonded," I echoed, pressing my hand over my heart.

"Between us," Grant said, sitting on the edge of the bed. He laid down his cane and leaned in to tug the covers up to my shoulders. Zee peered over the flannel edge, red eyes glowing, while Raw and Aaz tumbled into the man's lap, dragging their teddy bears behind them as they rubbed their heads against his arm like lethal, razor-armored cats. Dek and Mal chirped a low greeting, which slid into a harmonizing arrangement of Heart's "Tall, Dark Handsome Stranger."

"Golden light," he went on, searching my gaze as he scratched small necks and chins. "You made a link between us."

"It had to be done," I said, unable to tell if he was displeased, but the moment I spoke, he leaned forward and grabbed the back of my neck—dragging me close, hard against his shoulder and chest. A jolt rode over my skin, and static sparks flashed between us in the darkness. I leaned against him, held so tightly I could hardly breathe. Letting him say everything words could not.

"You should have died a long time ago, lad," Jack said quietly. "But you're strong. You have good instincts. I thought you might not need. . . . someone else. Not for the small things you were using your gift for."

"You play too many games," Grant said. "You should have told me."

"What do you mean, he should have died?" I asked Jack—though I knew the answer. I had seen it already. I had felt it, in my gut.

"Two hearts, stronger than one," Mary whispered, closing her eyes and placing her hands over her sternum. "Antrea should have told him, too."

Grant flinched, touching the pendant hanging from his neck—and I saw in my head that young, brown-haired woman, standing with an equally young, strong Mary.

His mother. Filthy and covered in blood. Concerned only with his safety.

Remembering that vision was little easier than recalling a fading dream. I wanted to tell Grant, but I did not know how. Not here. Not yet.

Jack did not look particularly pleased. "Energy is not available simply when one needs it. If already present, it can be manipulated, altered—but to effect greater changes requires something stronger. And Lightbringers draw from themselves to use their gifts. Draw too much, and they die. So they make bonds," he said, studying Grant and me. "To draw from others the strength they need."

"Can you break the link?" Grant asked. "Jack. Will this hurt her?"

"You need me," I protested.

"I don't know," said the old man. "There is no precedent for your bond, no way to know how it will affect you both. Lightbringers always attached themselves to humans. And Maxine . . . is not normal."

I pinched Grant's side. "Maxine is right here."

Mary made a slow choking sound, carefully pushing back her sleeves to stare at the fresh scars on her arms. "Not normal. Right here." She closed her eyes, and whispered, "I remember death. I was sharp. Sharpest of my sisters. We protected. We killed."

Assassin, I thought, remembering what Mr. King had called her. Recalling, with perfect clarity, all he had said. About Jack, too.

I did not look at the old man. I felt the pendant between Grant and me and stared into his eyes. Found him staring back. He carefully brushed a strand of hair from my face and leaned in to kiss my mouth.

And then he turned, ever so slightly, and gave Jack a warning look. "Is there more you haven't told us?"

"Yes," replied the old man, but he sounded distracted as he stared at Mary, an edge of melancholy in his voice, and something deeper: real grief, and uneasiness. I did not think it had anything to do with us—not in that moment. Instead, it felt as though some notion had just occurred to him, a memory, something terrible. I studied him, seated so still in the shadows on the edge of the bed: my grandfather, afraid to move, lost in thought.

"Old Wolf," I whispered. "What is it?"

"I hated him," Jack said quietly, with both wonderment and grief in his voice. "He who was Mr. King, and my brother. But he was one of us, and I knew him as long as I have known myself. We have no other children. We cannot make children in our true forms. When one of us dies, there is nothing left. And we feel it, in ourselves. We feel it as though we are missing pieces, and the ache will never leave us. It will dull, but never die." A grim, bitter smile touched his mouth; ghastly, more like a grimace. "I suppose absence becomes another kind of immortality."

"I thought you wanted him dead," Grant said.

"I did," Jack replied. "But there's always a price."

"Others will come," Zee rasped, peering over the covers. Raw and Aaz sat up, as well, rubbing their eyes. "Meddling Man. Even now they feel what you feel."

I pulled the pillow over my head. "Rock and a hard place. If we hadn't gotten rid of Mr. King, he would have destroyed us."

"And now that we've destroyed him," Grant said, "all we've done is buy ourselves time."

Time. Time for the prison veil. Time for Avatars. Time to live, time to fight, time to die.

Zee grabbed my hand, peering into my eyes. "We are strong," he whispered, as Dek and Mal rumbled with purrs. "Sweet Maxine. We are strong."

Strong as our hearts will let us be, my mother had once said. Grant took my other hand, pressing his lips to my palm, but it was less a kiss than a benediction.

"Again, we are remade," Jack murmured.

I heard footsteps approaching the bedroom, and Zee ducked under the covers. Raw and Aaz vanished. Byron appeared, just outside the door. Backlit by the golden light of the living room, slender and silent, he seemed more like a ghost made of shadows than a boy. But his eyes glittered, and he looked at me and no one else, and when I smiled there was no smile given in return, but his gaze was solemn and old, and unflinching.

"You're okay," he said softly; and then: "There's something you need to see."

It was not as difficult to move as I had thought it would be. I was not weak, merely tired, and Grant tugged on my hand as I scooted out from under the covers. I wore sweats and a tank top. My arms were pale and bare, and my right hand glittered. I took a moment, staring. The armor had grown again. A third vein of quicksilver curled from the wrist cuff to my ring finger, but tendrils of it seemed to lace out like roots, ending halfway across the back of my hand.

I glanced at Jack and Grant, and found both men staring at the armor. Neither said a word, but the old man seemed especially thoughtful. I closed my hand into a tight fist.

"Oh, what the hell," I muttered, and got out of bed.

There was a small crowd in the living room. Killy and Father Lawrence sat on the couch. He and the woman were not touching, but they were sitting close together and looked exhausted. Rex leaned against the arm of the couch—in his human body, red knit cap askew. His aura flickered when he saw me, but except for a brief, knowing nod, he said nothing, and went back to watching the television.

I had little time to feel relief that everyone was together, in one piece. The late-evening news was on, and the newscaster cut to a fuzzy video that seemed to have been captured on a cell-phone camera. Hard to see details, but the picture was clear enough to show that it had been taken from inside a vehicle. People were screaming as a skinny man in black repeatedly charged at the car, crashing into the door and window with such strength the glass cracked. His mouth was full of teeth. His eyes were crazed.

He gave up after several seconds and ran away, in silence, with incredible speed.

I stared, breathless, hardly hearing the newscaster as he laughed weakly, and called the creature a vampire. Police, he said, were on the alert for someone playing a prank. And then he laughed again, clearly creeped out.

I did not laugh. It was not a prank.

Killy closed her eyes. "Change the channel."

Father Lawrence grabbed the remote, hitting the buttons until he found a rerun of *Cheers*. Norm was sitting at the bar, and Sam was making googly eyes at some blond chick. Mundane, normal, and everything I wished life could be. My brain felt dirty from seeing the news clip and all those sharp teeth.

"We killed all of them we found," Rex said, giving me a hard, careful look. "None escaped."

"He would have set some loose. Other creatures, too. Just because." I looked from Jack to Grant. "What about those who were imprisoned in the ice?"

"I made some calls," Father Lawrence said quietly, his single red eye burning crimson and sharp. "They'll be cared for. With Cribari dead, there won't be any trouble. Not for a little while." He looked from me to Jack and frowned with such uneasiness my skin crawled.

Killy twisted around, staring at the priest, who was no longer as round or bumbling as I remembered; his stomach tauter, his cheeks not as soft. Her eyes narrowed with displeasure. "And you? What kind of trouble will you be in? You can't go back there, not to the Church."

Father Lawrence hesitated, again tearing his gaze from her face to glance from Jack to Grant—and then to me. He started to speak, and Killy made a small, exasperated sound, shaking her head. "No, that's stupid."

The priest sighed. "Stay out of my thoughts, please."

"Stay out of mine," she snapped, though her ire crumpled into pain. "Jesus, my head."

Father Lawrence stared helplessly. He began to reach for her—stopped, staring at his hands—and pulled back. Or tried to. Killy grabbed his wrist—just for a moment—and then let go as though burned. Both of them, burned. Byron, standing beside me, watched the young woman with his dark, quiet eyes. I ruffled his hair, and he tore his gaze from Killy to look at me.

"It's only just starting, isn't it?" asked Byron softly, and my hand fell from the boy's head to his shoulder—my right hand, covered in armor—my heart filling with both grief and resolve. I started to tell him it would be okay, and stopped, swallowing hard. I fought for words—anything, anything to give him. Until Byron, gently, reached up to touch my hand. As if he was the one who needed to reassure me.

"You're not alone, either," he said.

My breath caught. Byron pulled away from me and walked to the couch. He plopped down between Killy and Father Lawrence, and the young woman, after a moment, patted his hand with a sigh. *Cheers* played on.

I needed some distance. I went into the kitchen, leaned on the counter—staring into the living room at all these people in my life. My nomad life, setting down roots.

Grant joined me. Mary stayed behind, watching him—and Jack watched her, in turn. Her, and the others, his fist pressed against his stomach, as though he hurt. He looked very old and alone, and it broke my heart. Pained me even more to think of my grandmother with that same look on her face—sitting in a bedroom in Paris. Time, I realized, was a thin veil—the thinnest of them all—but it did no good to know that. My grandmother and Jack would never see each other again. He would live on, as he had lived after her death, and his daughter's. And mine, when it was time.

Grant brushed close, and gave me a faintly bitter smile. "Think maybe we'll live to see morning?"

I kissed his shoulder. "The odds are good. But I'll be gone by then."

Grant flinched, and his heart shuddered inside mine, as though our pulses merged, momentarily, to beat twice as strong. The sensation made me sway, but only because of the consternation that followed it. Not mine. His.

I grabbed the front of his sweatshirt, leaning in with the same urgency I had felt, clawing him from ice. Such a surreal thing to think of now. Ice and men with wings, and death. Like a dream.

"I meant," I whispered roughly, staring into his eyes, "that I needed to go hunt that creature. I'll be back. I'm not leaving you. You're stuck with me."

"I know," he said, slightly hoarse, his thumb caressing the corner of my mouth. "But I wasn't certain how you felt about that. What's between us now is different, Maxine."

"Is it?" I asked him simply. "I don't think so."

Grant closed his eyes and pressed his brow against mine. I heard the television behind us, and soft voices, but it might as well have been another world. Me and my man, inside our own labyrinth.

"I still don't know what I am," he whispered. "I don't want to hurt you."

"Don't steal my lines," I replied softly, and kissed his mouth. "Don't be afraid."

Grant's arm tightened, and he leaned us both against the counter, taking the weight off his bad leg so that he could put his cane aside and use his other arm to hold me. His fingers wound through my hair. Dek and Mal purred.

"I never had a plan," he told me, so quietly I could hardly hear him. "I had power, and I used it. I took it for granted. I pretended it was harmless."

He stopped, staring into my eyes. "It's the same thing, isn't it, what was done to Father Ross? What I do to demons, how I alter them and others against their wills? There's no difference."

"You're wrong," I said. "Not in a million years could you compare the two."

"But if I were a million years old?" Grant smiled bitterly. "Older, even? What would I be like with this gift, Maxine, if I lived too long? As long as an Avatar? Would I become like Mr. King? Is that what the power to change people does?"

Is that why the women in my family live such short lives? I wondered, briefly. *Because we are corruptible, and the boys are ruled by our hearts? Because power needs to be given and lost, and not hoarded?*

I looked down and saw Zee peering around the kitchen counter. Raw and Aaz were with him, baseball hats tugged low, their teddy bears still dragging behind them. My boys. Sweet and deadly.

Zee gave me a toothy smile, and I laughed, clutching a fistful of Grant's sweatshirt and dragging him even closer. I stood on my toes, and stared into his eyes, savoring the heat between us, the light in my heart that curled around the darkness.

"You're a good man," I told him fiercely. "You're going to die a good man, a long time from now." I reached out and brushed my fingers over his cheek. "Maybe in a bed, in my arms. You old, ancient man."

Grant's gaze never wavered. "I could live for that."

And so could I.

Also Available from *New York Times*
Bestselling Author

Marjorie M. Liu

THE IRON HUNT

"The boundlessness of Liu never
ceases to amaze."
—*Booklist*

Demon hunter Maxine Kiss wears her armor as
tattoos, which unwind from her body to take on
forms of their own at night. They stand between
her and her enemies, just as Maxine stands between humanity and the demons breaking out
from behind the prison veil. It is a life lacking in
love, reveling in death, until one moment—and
one man—changes everything.

penguin.com

M425T0309

Don't Miss the #1 *New York Times*
Bestselling Series from

PATRICIA BRIGGS

||||||||||||||||||||||||||||||||||||||||||||||||||||||||||||||||||||||||||||||||||||||

THE
MERCY
THOMPSON
SERIES

||||||||||||||||||||||||||||||||||||||||||||||||||||||||||||||||||||||||||||||||||||||

"The best new urban fantasy series I've read in years."

—KELLEY ARMSTRONG, *New York Times* bestselling author

"I love these books."

—CHARLAINE HARRIS, #1 *New York Times* bestselling author

"Top-notch paranormal mystery...a tense, nimble, crowd-
pleasing page-turner."   —*PUBLISHERS WEEKLY*

MOON CALLED
BLOOD BOUND
IRON KISSED
BONE CROSSED
SILVER BORNE

penguin.com